BEYOND THE LIGHT HORIZON

Myles had his own suspicion of where – or, rather, of when – his father had gone. He blamed himself. He should never have told him about the exiles in the valley of the Big River, people who had retained for generations a tradition of waiting for the return of John Grant. It was typical of the man that he should become obsessed with closing that time loop.

One in a thousand, rumour whispered. Spin that wheel often enough, and you could expect your number to come up. One in a thousand FTL journeys ended up in the wrong time, or the wrong timeline. Some of these made it back. Not even rumour could put a number on how many.

John Grant had made well over a thousand FTL journeys to date.

By Ken MacLeod

The Fall Revolution
The Star Fraction
The Stone Canal
The Cassini Division
The Sky Road

Engines of Light
Cosmonaut Keep
Dark Light
Engine City

Newton's Wake
Learning the World
The Execution Channel
The Restoration Game
Intrusion
Descent

The Corporation Wars
Dissidence
Insurgence
Emergence

Lightspeed
Beyond the Hallowed Sky
Beyond the Reach of Earth

BEYOND THE LIGHT HORIZON

KEN MACLEOD

orbitbooks.net

ORBIT

First published in Great Britain in 2024 by Orbit

3 5 7 9 10 8 6 4 2

A CIP catalogue record for this book is available from the British Library.

ISBN 978-0-356-51482-6

Typeset in Stempel Garamond by Palimpsest Book Production Limited,
Falkirk, Stirlingshire

Printed and bound in Great Britain by Clays Ltd, Elcograf S.p.A.

Papers used by Orbit are from well-managed forests
and other responsible sources.

Orbit
An imprint of
Little, Brown Book Group
Carmelite House
50 Victoria Embankment
London EC4Y 0DZ

An Hachette UK Company
www.hachette.co.uk

www.littlebrown.co.uk

To Carol

The story so far

This is the third volume of the Lightspeed Trilogy, following BEYOND THE HALLOWED SKY and BEYOND THE REACH OF EARTH. Here's a quick reminder of what was in these books:

In Book 1:

Faster-than-light (FTL) travel was discovered around 2020 and is being kept secret. This can't stop other people from discovering it. One of them is London PhD student LAKSHMI NAYAK.

In 2067, she receives an airmail letter in her own handwriting, with equations that point to the possibility. To her this apparent communication from a future self implies both FTL and time travel. She expands the equations into a paper and publishes it online, where it's torn to shreds. After gaining her PhD she's warned off any further work on FTL by MARCUS OWEN, a humanoid robot operative of the British Council (now a feared intelligence service).

The world has three big powers: the Alliance (the Anglosphere plus India and minus Ireland and Scotland), the Union (the former European Union, now a revolutionary 'economic democracy') and the Co-ordinated States (China and Russia), all with various client states and non-aligned countries outside. NAYAK defects to the Union and moves to Scotland, where she works for a planning consultancy and secretly develops her theory into a practical engineering proposition.

In 2070 JOHN GRANT, a Clydeside shipbuilder, sees a nuclear submarine rise out of the sea and vanish in a blue flash. His queries are blocked by Iskander, the Union's universal AI interface. At work he's approached by a colleague who is in 'the cadre', the network of revolutionaries that riddles the Union's democratic institutions. She asks him to investigate and contact NAYAK. He does, by offering to build her ship.

Others in the cadre tell GRANT that the Alliance and the Co-ord have had FTL travel for at least fifty years, and use nuclear submarines as starships. Soon a civilian submarine, the *Fighting Chance*, is taking shape in the semi-automated ship-yard, with a stardrive of NAYAK's design inside it. NAYAK trains to operate the controls.

Meanwhile, OWEN has been dispatched to the Union's Venus cloud colony, Cloud City, as Alliance cultural attaché. Everyone there knows he's a robot and a spy. The Alliance consul, PEREGRINE WALWORTH, passes on instructions for OWEN to block a Union attempt to retrieve a sample of mysterious rock from the surface. This rock resembles an equally mysterious rock already found on Earth, and now under secret investigation by the Alliance military. OWEN gets into a relationship with FRANCESCA MILLOY, who is building a suit for human survival on the surface. OWEN manages to get himself sent to the surface of Venus. He finds the glassy rock extends to a chasm below the surface, within which he sees the face of a woman. Something in the rock communicates with the onboard instance of Iskander in OWEN's spacesuit. At that moment, a volcanic resurfacing of Venus begins.

Back on Cloud City, OWEN learns that the rock sample has been retrieved by a team from Cloud City and is to be transferred to the orbiting Venus Space Station from one of the smaller floating outposts. OWEN shares with WALWORTH the picture of the woman he saw in the chasm. WALWORTH transmits it to the Alliance. They then join a group of Cloud City inhabitants celebrating the First Contact they think they've just made. WALWORTH trumps this with the announcement that the Alliance and Co-ord have had FTL interstellar travel for fifty years and now look forward to opening a habitable planet to the rest of humanity.

OWEN doesn't know that the mysterious rock has already been giving trouble many light years away, on the aforesaid planet, APIS. There the rock exists as massive outcrops, within which continuous movement can be seen. The Alliance and Co-ord have military/scientific bases on separate continents, and in the wilds there is a small population of 'exiles', disaster survivors who were involuntarily and secretly resettled there in turbulent decades past.

The planet's animals are all invertebrates, and like the plants and fungi are clearly descended from early life on Earth. The planet has been terraformed long before humans arrived there. An anomalous feature is the presence of bees, identical to current species on Earth.

While investigating their nearest outcrop, MacHinery Ridge, EMMA HAZELDENE and her colleagues encounter and flee from sudden massive movements of the rock. A local exile leader, ABLE JENKINS, is in communication with the intelligences in the rock, which he calls 'the Fermi', via an old phone and an apparatus he built himself. The Fermi send him warning messages, just before an earthquake devastates Jenkins's home village and a tsunami swamps the Alliance base.

HAZELDENE and her colleagues, along with JENKINS and injured people from his village, are airlifted to the base. They continue to communicate with the Fermi through JENKINS's apparatus. A contingent of Co-ord troops lands at the base and occupies the area around the Ridge, citing their duties under the KEPLER AGREEMENT, the secret treaty governing Alliance and Co-ord interstellar exploration in a common secret project called BLACK HORIZON.

A few days later, an FTL spaceplane arrives and two Naval Intelligence agents show HAZELDENE a picture of herself, which they say was seen on Venus. She and JENKINS must go to Venus immediately in an Alliance submarine.

Meanwhile, OWEN has broken out of Cloud City to continue his mission to prevent the return of the sample to the Space Station. He attempts to dump the surface survival suit, which has been firewalled off and kept outside. The suit, still controlled by an instance of the Iskander AI and with an ample supply of balloons, gets away. OWEN steals an aircraft and raids the floating outpost where the sample is stored. He's outwitted by the crew and left in the damaged outpost while they escape with the sample.

The submarine/starship with HAZELDENE and JENKINS on board arrives at the right location on the surface of Venus. JENKINS asks the Fermi what they want, and is referred to the Iskander-possessed suit, which is just dropping down. The suit tells them to help it retrieve and return the sample to its original place on the surface. They deliver the suit to the scientists' escape balloon, leave it to return the sample, and go on to rescue OWEN. With him they return to the Alliance base on Apis. The Alliance reps disown OWEN, who is left on Apis when the submarine/starship returns to Earth.

Back on Earth, JOHN GRANT and his family and colleagues react to the Black Horizon announcement. His son MYLES with girlfriend MARIE are tempted by the Alliance offer of free transport to Apis – an offer which the Union government opposes. Word comes down that the launch of GRANT's starship will be prevented. GRANT inveigles NAYAK, his wife ELLEN (an experienced remote operator of submersibles) and two colleagues to launch the ship secretly.

They have to do this sooner than they expect. Cloud City, in severe danger in the increasingly turbulent atmosphere, is being evacuated, but there are far too few shuttles at the orbiting Station to do this fast enough. GRANT and his crew launch the *Fighting Chance* and take it to Venus, where they transfer hundreds from the stricken aerial colony to the Station. When Cloud City finally breaks up and falls, taking hundreds with it, they rescue the last survivors in the floating outposts – and the Iskander suit, which tells them what's been going on.

Just as they've decided to go to Apis and warn those there of the dangers from the 'Fermi' rocks, a Co-ord submarine/ starship appears and threatens to destroy the *Fighting Chance* if they don't surrender it. As the missile is about to be launched, NAYAK expands the field to cover the entire Station, and at the last second they make the jump to Apis orbit.

Unknown to GRANT, MYLES and MARIE are already on Apis, having taken the Alliance offer and arrived hours earlier with hundreds of other Union citizens. In their first night there, MYLES and MARIE see the Station, but don't realise what it is.

The following morning, Owen gets new orders from the British Council . . .

In Book 2:

The Alliance base on Apis goes into full alert as the Station appears in orbit. Commander ALICE HAWKINS hails the Station, and is brought up to speed by Station Commander KATRINA ULRICH, who asks her to send a data package back to Earth about the Station's survival, current location, the names of the dead and the survivors, etc. ULRICH also warns her about the dangers of meddling with the Fermi rocks, at which HAWKINS scoffs and explains that the Co-ord have essentially occupied MacHinery Ridge. ULRICH contacts the Co-ord base, Novy Cosmograd. Meanwhile, HAWKINS is speaking with another Co-ord officer at the base, who like herself is highly placed in the Black Horizon conspiracy. They agree that with the conspiracy exposed and being rolled up, the only way to advance its aims is to share its deepest secrets with ULRICH and hope for the best. HAWKINS sends a data package containing these secrets to ULRICH.

The Station, which now includes hundreds rescued from Cloud City, mourns its dead. ULRICH instructs FRANCESCA MILLOY (OWEN's former lover in Cloud City) to investigate the recovered descent suit, which is operated by its onboard instance of the AI called Iskander. She finds that it now calls itself SIKANDAR and that it has not been corrupted by the alien intelligence (part of the Fermi) which it encountered on Venus.

That morning, MARCUS OWEN meets the security officer Lt JESSICA BERNSTEIN, who has a message for him from the British Council. The first line tells him to keep her talking: Alliance troops are on their way. An FTL transport lands outside and troops rush in to arrest BERNSTEIN. The rest of the message tells OWEN that everyone on the planet other than himself and the new troops must be regarded as Black Horizon. He is to join the Alliance team going with the soldiers to assist the Union settlement on the southern continent, New Mu, and to monitor the scientists' investigations into the nearby Fermi Rock outcrop, Hamilton's Rise. (Having been excluded by the Co-ord from their own rock, MacHinery Ridge, but urgently needing to investigate the Fermi, the Alliance has decided to try this.) He is to keep any significant discoveries out of the hands of anyone but the Alliance, and to establish communication with the Fermi if he can. He joins HAZELDENE, JENKINS, MURANOV et al. and Lieutenant WILLIAM KNIGHT in preparing for this expedition.

MARIE HENDERSON and MYLES GRANT wake up to their first morning on Apis, and a surprise phone call from JOHN and ELLEN GRANT who are in the Station orbiting above them. GRANT urges them to come back to Earth and build more starships, but MYLES and MARIE are determined to make a go of it on Apis. Just then, the Co-ord submarine/starship *Admiral von Bellingshausen* arrives and warns the Station that it has to leave the system. ULRICH has received a message (via Alliance FTL shuttle) to go off and explore, so they comply. SIKANDAR suggests they go to the system E-PRIME 667, ULRICH agrees, and NAYAK and ELLEN use the *Fighting Chance* to jump the Station there.

OWEN travels by flying boat with the scientists and a squad of soldiers across the ocean to New Mu. They land at a lake and trek down through wooded hills to the Union settlement, now named New Rhu. The settlers are busy turning the 'arks' in which they arrived into housing. HAZELDENE and MARIE bond over their shared interest in biology. Just then, another ark arrives, this time with journalists from various Union media, who are astonished to see Hamilton's Rise. Over the next week OWEN makes himself useful around the place, getting to know settlers, soldiers and journalists. Distant smoke suggests other exiles in the forests nearby, but survey drones and expeditions find no trace. The Alliance soldiers build a stockade up the hill from New Rhu, on the edge of the forest.

On the Station in orbit around the distant star E-PRIME 667, NAYAK trains GRANT to pilot the *Fighting Chance*, because she has decided to remain on the Station. Meanwhile the chief engineer, EDUARDO GIRONELLA, supervises the building of a telescope to survey the system and of more FTL drives and shuttles. When these are complete, the *Fighting Chance* can go home. MILLOY admits to NAYAK that she wants revenge on OWEN. Shortly afterwards, Alliance consul PEREGRINE WALWORTH (rescued from Cloud City) artfully lets slip that OWEN is on Apis and probably at the Union settlement on New Mu.

MYLES is felling trees near the Alliance garrison uphill from New Rhu when he narrowly misses being killed by an arrow from a volley mostly aimed at the garrison. The arrows seem technologically advanced, as if made of carbon fibre. MYLES joins a mixed squad of settlement militia and Alliance soldiers in a sweep of the forest. They fail to find the attackers, and are jeered at by monkey-spiders, large gibbon-like invertebrates that live in the trees. MYLES comes across a beehive and observes a monkey-spider carefully opening it and eating honey, then closing up the hive and going back to the trees. He shares his recording of this with MARIE, who with JENKINS and HAZELDENE is up in the hills and has just come across a clearing full of moulted carapaces from some large, unknown animals. These pieces are apparently stored for use as raw material. Just then, a soldier shoots the monkey-spider that MYLES has been watching. The sweep is called off, and the dead monkey-spider carried back to New Rhu.

MARIE and HAZELDENE find that the monkey-spider's brain is large enough for an intelligent animal. MARIE sequences bee DNA, and finds artificial genes, and evidence that the bees have been here for at least decades, if not centuries. GEORGI MURANOV tests the material of the arrows and finds it's not of human origin. He suspects the Fermi made (and shot) them. MYLES suggests that the Fermi are protecting the monkey-spiders as potential conscious life, and that Apis was indeed made for that species and not for humans. MARIE points out that it's the monkey-spiders' habitat that is being damaged by tree-felling. They carry the dead monkey-spider back and leave it at the edge of the forest.

Meanwhile, OWEN and two geologists return from a survey along the banks of the nearby Big River (which cuts through the range of Hamilton's Rise to the sea) with stone arrowheads and with a large ovoid stone formed from rock from the Rise, and still showing activity within. It's agreed to mount an expedition downriver, to recover more such stones and if possible to contact the local exiles.

The Station has by now an FTL drive of its own. NAYAK and one of the pilots she has trained, ERNEST MAREK, use the FTL drive to jump the Station to an orbit closer to the star. After the jump, SIKANDAR – still clinging to the outside of the *Fighting Chance*, which is itself attached to the Station – reports a problem: a moon of the system's gas giant has disappeared. On closer examination, what seems to have happened is that two of the moons have been replaced by one large moon, with an atmosphere, liquid water and biosignatures. The conclusion the crew eventually arrive at is that the Station has arrived in a different timeline – and they don't know how different it is.

A week later, the new FTL drives for the Station's shuttles have been built. GRANT and his crew (apart from NAYAK) prepare to return in the *Fighting Chance*, along with some people from the Station. MILLOY asks that they stop off on Apis, where together with SIKANDAR she will hunt down OWEN. The *Fighting Chance* sets them down on the seaward side of Hamilton's Rise and jumps away again. Lugging an anti-materiel rifle, MILLOY and the descent suit/SIKANDAR head uphill towards the summit of Hamilton's Rise.

MYLES and MARIE lead a small team – HAZELDENE, MURANOV, PATEL and OWEN – down the Big River, using a dinghy and a small drone. Landing downstream, they make their way along the bank in a steep-sided gorge. Crossing a rockfall, they experience disorientation and vertigo, but OWEN (who is unaffected) helps them to find a way over. Farther on, they see smoke, and are soon approached by a group of exiles: women and children, and young men with spears. They speak a form of English, and are excited to see the Union flag patches on MARIE's and MYLES's shoulders. They fear or revere something at the top of Hamilton's Rise which they call 'the Bird'. When MYLES introduces himself, they ask if he knows John Grant. MYLES shows the matriarch of the group the document signed by himself and his father. She slowly reads this and calls out to the rest of the group that he is not JOHN GRANT. With that they leave, disappointed.

Perplexed, the expedition sets up camp, and sends a drone over the forest, where they find the exile group's settlement around what looks very like an ark. The geologists find a large slab of green rock, still active, from the river, and carry it back to the camp. That evening, MYLES strolls over to where the geologist MURANOV is scanning the slab. MURANOV talks about the progress he's made in understanding it, and the effects of the FTL drive on deterrence. MYLES leaves him to report his findings back to Novy Cosmograd, and they never see MURANOV again. After a search they set up a guard rota around the camp. In the night MYLES relieves OWEN, who then knocks him down, grabs his rifle and runs off towards Hamilton's Rise.

The *Fighting Chance* lands on the Firth of Clyde and is impounded as soon as it docks. GRANT, ELLEN and the rest of the crew are put under house arrest in a hotel. GRANT is visited by a high-level cadre, LOUISE OGUNDU, who offers to be his defence lawyer. He tells her everything that has happened. Iskander brings him up to speed on events on Earth – and on Apis, from which the journalists have returned with footage that ends with the mystery arrow's near miss on Myles. GRANT tells Iskander he intends to go back to Apis, and Iskander promises to help.

On the Station, ULRICH calls NAYAK to her office as soon as the *Fighting Chance* departs, and gives NAYAK a file containing the Black Horizon data package she was given by Commander HAWKINS. NAYAK reads this in private. She learns how Black Horizon was set up by the scientists who accidentally discovered FTL in 2018 when an experimental rig they hadn't yet built came back with photographs of Proxima Centauri b and of themselves in front of a whiteboard with the equations for FTL travel scrawled on it . . .

She also learns that nuclear weapons have been stashed on various exoplanets, to maintain deterrence and also as a possible last resort to destroy Fermi rocks. One such stash is on the anomalous moon – on which there are exiles, and which Black Horizon called the Mushroom Moon. But now that Black Horizon is being rolled up, the governments are retrieving the stashes, and a British submarine/starship HMS *Vindicate* is on its way.

NAYAK and MAREK go to the Mushroom Moon in the Station's shuttle to retrieve the stash for the Station (and for Black Horizon, whose aims ULRICH admits to the crew she agrees with). They find the cache near a spectacular crenelated colourful outcrop of Fermi rock, soaring above a fungus-dominated landscape. As they wheel the nukes towards their shuttle they're accosted by a group of exiles, who seem permanently stoned by hallucinogenic fungi. These exiles tell them the nukes are needed to 'deter the bird'. Moments later, a black band moves up the crystal pillars, leaving them white, and emerges at the top as a vast black disc with outspread wings.

On Apis, OWEN – who has indeed murdered MURANOV and dumped his body in the river – climbs into Hamilton's Rise to use what he learned from MURANOV's discoveries to attempt contact with the Fermi. Meanwhile, MILLOY, in the descent suit/SIKANDAR, climbs the other side of the mountain. From the top they see a Co-ord force speeding towards the beach below. Making haste, they enter an opening in the crystal peaks. KNIGHT contacts her to say the Alliance fort's drones have spotted her and OWEN, and patches her OWEN's location. He also reports that the Co-ord are moving troops and communications equipment up to where she and

SIKANDAR went in. OWEN is heading her way. Just as she's about to use the descent suit as armour, SIKANDAR is struck by some software attack, apparently from the Fermi rock. MILLOY takes cover and lies in wait.

OWEN is also affected by the Fermi, but continues to run forward. MILLOY shoots him through the descent suit, which topples. She misses and OWEN flees, pursued by Co-ord military drones. The descent suit/SIKANDAR urges MILLOY to get back in. Just as she does, a black band rises up the crystal pillars to form a great winged disc in the sky. Hamilton's Rise is left a whitened husk of its former colourful glory. Co-ord military drones snare the suit and lift it up with her in it. As she's airlifted out of Hamilton's Rise she sees OWEN in the distance, sprinting away through gunfire over the edge of a cliff. On landing at the Co-ord encampment, she's told by the scientists that the signals they beamed at the rock, informed by MURANOV's research, have resulted in the departure of the Fermi from all the outcrops on Apis. Perhaps all the rocky worlds have been left open to humanity.

On Earth, OGUNDU tells GRANT his house arrest is now to be at home, and he will be released on bail after a court appearance. Back at his flat, he and ELLEN are visited by former employees of his company, who tell him they have continued it under self-management and are building tractor units with FTL drives, to be attached to 'arks': shipping containers with life support. As soon as the Union makes settlement legal, they'll go ahead with moving people.

On the Mushroom Moon, the great black 'bird' vanishes into the sky. The locals attack NAYAK and MAREK. NAYAK is forced to open her faceplate, and MAREK's is smashed. They fight off the attackers, killing some and putting the rest to flight, but are immediately assailed by hallucinations. They manage to get back to the shuttle and return to the Station on autopilot. NAYAK has a hallucinatory vision of the origin of the Fermi as spontaneously generated intellects in the moment before or just after the Big Bang. On recovering, she learns that HMS *Vindicate*, no longer controlled by Black Horizon, has arrived and is demanding the return of the nukes.

In a situation of mutual mistrust between the starship/submarine and the Station, WALWORTH arranges for NAYAK to make the transfer. He tells NAYAK that the *Vindicate* some years ago turned up anomalously at a remote naval station, and that the postmark for Top Secret missions is 'BFPO Kabul'. If she sends an airmail message to herself with the FTL equations, she'll close the time loop, because at some time in the future, the *Vindicate* will make a trip to the past. (There is a record of this incident a few years earlier.) He himself intends to return to Earth on the submarine.

This is all done, the *Vindicate* departs, and NAYAK returns to the Station feeling that at last she has free will and her future is open again.

On Apis, the Co-ord contingent at Hamilton's Rise retrieve MURANOV's body and return it to HAZELDENE and the others, for formal permission to take it back to Earth. Shortly afterwards, they deliver MILLOY and the descent suit/SIKANDAR, who with the rest of the expedition begin a trek back upriver to New Rhu.

OWEN is by then in the forest, experiencing self-aware consciousness and free will for the first time. He also has some fragment of the Fermi in his mind, and this gives him a new motivation: to protect the monkey-spiders.

SIKANDAR knows it has been partly taken over by the Fermi. MYLES inveigles SIKANDAR to go away with the anti-materiel rifle, expecting it to destroy OWEN then itself. Instead, SIKANDAR shoots at OWEN, misses, and asks OWEN to destroy its central computer. This OWEN does and heads off down the hill in search of monkey-spiders.

MYLES and the others hear the two shots and think SIKANDAR has done the job they expected it to do.

As they approach New Rhu in the dusk, they see three black

dots on the disc of the gas giant, and realise that this is where the Fermi went.

With Apis now apparently clear of the Fermi, all barriers to migration there are lifted, including the Union's. GRANT's company is soon busy shipping people to New Rhu. GRANT himself pilots many of these journeys, for reasons we will learn. MYLES and MARIE have told him about the exiles who know his name and expect his return.

Some months later, one of these journeys ends in the past. In a difficult landing, the connection between the ark and the tractor unit is broken. GRANT has to leave the hundred or so people (obviously the ancestors of those MYLES and MARIE met in the forest) behind, but he promises to come back.

Now read on.

CHAPTER ONE

Meteor Night

Apis, 1991, Wednesday 25 March 2071 according to Grant's calendar

John Grant looked back from the door of the tractor unit. The forest was dark, the slope steep, the rapids in the ravine loud. The crowd he was leaving behind were well kitted out for wilderness survival, but perplexed and anxious.

'Get them away,' he told the young woman who stood looking up at him. 'And make sure they look away from the flash. Tell them to cover the children's ears. I'll be going in ten minutes. OK?'

'OK,' she said. She turned away and with shouts and gestures urged the hundred or so people in her community up the hillside. Within a few minutes they were out of sight among the trees.

Grant swung into the cab, clunked the door shut behind him and strapped in. He was leaving these people in the past.

He had promised to come back for them if he could find a way, but he knew he wouldn't. On these same wooded hills their descendants – up ahead in the future, if it was the same future – awaited his return.

'What the hell do I do now?' he said.

He was asking himself, but it was Iskander who answered.

'Go back to Earth,' said the AI.

Grant was startled. 'Forgot you were here.'

Of course Iskander was here – in his phone and glasses – but in all his thousand or so journeys back and forth between Earth and Apis, he'd never had to consult it. The navigation app had done all the work.

'I spoke to remind you of my presence and availability,' Iskander said. 'This is not a situation where you want to feel alone.'

'Thanks,' Grant said. He spun the navigation app and set a course. He took a deep breath. 'Well, let's do it. No time like the present.'

'You hope,' said Iskander.

The jump was on them before Grant could think of a retort.

From where no gods live, Grant fell into Earth orbit. He looked at a dark Australia in disbelief. Ahead, the great cities of Asia glowed dim; Moscow, barely a glimmer. The sun rose over the Earth's shoulder. Radio silence. Nothing on any band but hiss. Paris was shrunken, London a smudge of smoke on a band of white cloud. The Arctic shone brighter and bigger than he remembered.

'Still in the past,' Grant said. 'Damn.'

He turned from the ice cap's glare and checked the dash. The cab had three hours' air supply. Twenty minutes' worth had been used: twice as much as on a normal return trip. This trip hadn't been normal.

'The year is 1760,' Iskander told him.

North America drifted by below. He thought about the hundred and more people he'd left in the forest, minutes earlier. 'Christ, is that the date back on Apis?'

'It is now. So to speak. If you mean, was that the date when we left? No. It was 1991.'

Generations in that forest, waiting for John Grant to come back.

'How did the app manage to place us in Earth orbit?'

'Millisecond correction, too fast for you to notice.'

'Hmm. Can it get us down?'

'And change history?'

'Why not?' Grant toyed with the notion. 'I could find . . . Ben Franklin or somebody, share some of your knowledge, and save humanity centuries of grief.'

'You don't need me to tell you the flaws in that plan.'

'Indeed not.' Grant sighed and reached for the controls. 'Oh well, back to Apis and hope we find ourselves in 2071.'

'I wouldn't recommend it.' Iskander paused, as if expecting an objection, and continued. 'We're already in history, as it happens. I've just found in my library the archives of the Chinese Imperial astronomer, and they record an anomalous meteor crossing the entire sky, south-east to north-west, over a few minutes on this very day. That's no meteor. That was us. This is most reassuring, because it proves that we haven't already changed history. We're in the same timeline as when we left Earth today.'

'What's the relevance to not going back to Apis?'

'It gives me a starting point from which to calculate a way back to the present. So to speak. These temporal slippages are individually unpredictable, but statistically inevitable. It's a matter of reckoning the odds and rolling the dice.'

Grant glanced again at the dash. Two hours and ten minutes of air left. Was that California ahead? 'Take your time.'

'I have.' The AI sounded smug, no doubt intentionally. 'My best guess is that to get back to Earth or Apis at the time you left, you first need to go a thousand light years away, then take up to five other jumps on the way back.'

'Your *guess*?'

'I don't do theories. I look at the available data on temporal anomalies resulting from FTL travel and an empirical suggestion drops out. To explain the reasoning would take longer than the journey, not to mention your air supply.'

'As would explaining where this "available data on temporal anomalies" came from?'

'Correct. Now, it needn't be a pointless journey. There are areas on the Black Horizon map from which the Station was warned off, and which might be well worth investigating. There's one here about which I may have picked up the hint of a rumour of interest. There might even be profitable opportunities.'

'Air to breathe will do for a start,' Grant said. 'OK, do it.'

Iskander displayed the numbers. Grant tapped them in, and powered up.

They fell again into the space between spaces.

You never get used to it, Grant thought. The longest interstellar jump he'd ever done had taken seven minutes. This journey took twice as long. Like all of them, it felt like forever.

It gave him plenty of time to rue the impulse that had made him insist on all these repeated return trips to Apis, instead of taking care of business – which largely took care of itself, but still. He had been remiss, because obsessed. Ever since his son Myles had told him of the lost exiles in the forest, still waiting for the return of John Grant, he'd been hag-ridden by the conviction that he had to close that loop if he was to remain in the same timeline as Myles. He had known that in that timeline there were people in the forest whose ancestors had been left there by him, and who still awaited the return of John Grant. He had gambled that if he made enough trips to Apis, sooner or later one of them would end up in the past.

Now that he had closed the loop, he rather wished he hadn't.

He came out of the jump shivering and drenched in sweat.

His mind snapped back to business, and the prospect of profitable opportunities.

Light filled the view screen, sound filled the cab.

'Well!' said Iskander. 'This is unexpected!'

Three angular shapes, bright as planets and jagged as the gold stars in a good child's jotter, glinted in line across the forward view.

'What the hell are these?'

'They appear to be artificial structures,' Iskander said.

'How did we arrive so close to them?'

'We didn't,' said Iskander. 'From our own motion I can already make a rough estimate of the distances. These are tens of millions of kilometres away.'

The sound from the speakers was a staccato rattle, like the dawn chorus on Apis.

'What's that?'

'Machine code cross-talk,' said Iskander, turning the sound off. 'To find out more about the system would require a sweep in all directions. Could you please link me to the controls?'

Grant hesitated. Iskander – the full networked AI in the Union – had been involved at every stage of designing, financing and building the company's craft: the arks, and the old *Fighting Chance*. Giving Iskander control of the tractor units hadn't been so much as considered. It had never struck anyone as necessary, and hadn't been suggested by Iskander itself, an AI usually not backward in coming forward. But no one had envisaged this situation.

'Yeah, why not.'

'Thank you. Give me a moment while I orient myself.'

The seat began to vibrate. A faint thrum came from behind him. As the tractor unit for an ark, the cab was in no way optimal as a spacecraft. It had more or less the size and configuration of the cab of an articulated lorry, with the ark – when attached – its trailer, aptly enough shaped like a shipping container. The gyroscopes for turning the cab around in free fall had struck Grant as excessive. Regulations, he'd been told. He was grateful for that over-engineering now. Likewise for the bubble helmet, air tank and space suit, boxed beside the First Aid kit in the rack behind his head. The cab didn't have an airlock.

The universe did a slow somersault around him, then stabilised in a whine of gyroscopes going in reverse.

'Interesting system,' Iskander said. 'Almost like the Solar system would have been if it had been designed for intelligent life. If I may.'

The outside view was replaced by a diagram, which Iskander talked Grant through.

'I don't have access to telescopes, obviously, but from the outboard lenses I can extract quite a bit of information. Stable yellow star, three terrestrial planets all in the habitable zone – imagine Venus a little further out, Earth with two moons and Mars a lot bigger and further in, and moreover all three actually life-bearing. Beyond them is a rich asteroid belt and then three gas giants with lots of moons. And hundreds of these quadrilateral structures, forming a widely spaced ring around the exosun a little way out from the asteroid belt – I can't see them all, obviously, but I can triangulate the radio sources.'

'The radio sources – heck, the structures themselves – would be spotted by E-PRIME or even one of the earlier space telescopes, surely?'

'No – the radio sources are too faint, the structures too small. A minute chance of detection, perhaps – if they had existed a thousand years ago.'

Grant smote his forehead. He'd been caught out like this before, right at the beginning. 'Of course. The light and the signals haven't got back to the Solar system yet. Continue.'

'Nearly all the radio chatter comes from the asteroid belt, the moons and these structures. A little from the rocky planets, mostly from the second one out from the exosun. It has comsats around it, so it may well have people there.'

'Assuming they're people.'

'They're people all right. I can't decrypt the machine code, but what radio traffic I can pick up from the second planet is definitely human. We could go to the structures in space, which might include weapons programmed to destroy anything that approaches, or to the inhabited planet, which could – like most of Earth's own surface – be highly inimical to unprotected human life. Which would you prefer?'

'What about the other two habitable planets?'

'You know that "habitable" in this context means possibly having liquid water on the surface? Yes, there's life: a Gaia-type atmosphere according to what spectroscopy I can run with the available lenses, but if they have no or few human inhabitants I suspect there's a good reason.'

'Well, let's go for the inhabited one, but I want a close approach to the nearest of these structures first.'

'How close?'

'A hundred kilometres to start with.'

'I'll take us to a thousand.'

'But—'

Iskander had done that before Grant's objection was out of his mouth. The jump was so brief it was barely noticeable.

'Oh – OK.'

A thousand kilometres away, the great lattice hung like some complex mobile sculpture. Hundreds of reflectors, thousands of solar panels. In the middle of the frame a wheel spun like the drive of an enormous jewelled watch. Golden motes drifted and danced around it.

'Wow. That's . . . breathtaking.'

'Yes. And speaking of breath, you don't have a lot of time to examine it.'

Grant checked the air supply. 'Less than two hours, and I'll need time to find a safe place to land on the planet.' He felt torn between anxiety and curiosity. 'Any signs that we're in someone's sights?'

'A passing sweep of deep space radar. Nothing locked on.'

'OK, quick in and out.'

Grant set the navigation app for a hundred kilometres from the structure. The jump passed like a fleeting dark thought. The structure now filled the forward view. It must be – what? A hundred kilometres on the side? He zoomed his glasses on the central wheel. Its hub was a jumble of rock and ice held together by mesh, its rim a clear tube of green and black.

'It's a space habitat!' he said. 'It must have taken decades to build.'

'Yes. And it's still under construction.'

'Are we in the future?'

'No. Going by the proper motions of such stars as I've been able to identify, we're back in our own time – give or take a few weeks or months or perhaps longer.'

'That's imprecise, for you.'

'It's the best I can do without a great deal of further observation, for which we don't have time. We could be as much as a year out, either way. Which is why I don't recommend an immediate return to Apis, or Earth. You don't want to set up another time loop anomaly.'

'I sure don't. Any signals? Any comms traffic at all?'

'Just machine code.'

'I'm going in closer.'

Ten kilometres. He looked up at the arc of the wheel in his view, and zoomed. Its inner side was an endlessly varied combination of irregular green patches, irregular black patches and angular clusters of what he guessed were buildings. He could even see clouds drifting here and there.

'The black patches are lakes,' Iskander said. 'Reflecting a black sky, and now and then reflecting a space mirror. They and the buildings and parks or fields have been in place for a long time. I'm not seeing or hearing any signs of human life, however. It should be buzzing with traffic, and it isn't.'

Grant swung the view. Two hundred metres away was a metallic-looking bar or tube that extended beyond the edges of the screen – far beyond, probably. Close to it, apparently working on it, was a spidery little machine. And sitting in the machine was a space-suited figure.

'Hey!' Grant said. 'Company!'

The machine moved a little way up the girder, on a wisp of jet. It swung around. The space-suited figure seemed to be looking straight at him. The turn continued, the work resumed.

'Get me the highest resolution you can,' Grant said.

Instant close-up. It wasn't a person in a space suit. It was too tall, and there was no life support. What had looked like a helmet was a dome in which a dish aerial spun and other sensors were clustered. The limbs, though jointed in the right places, were hollow mesh. There was something odd about its proportions: the torso shorter, the limbs and hands and feet longer than those of an adult human.

'It's a robot,' Grant said.

'Obviously,' said Iskander. 'There are uses for humanoid robots, in structures intended for human habitation. But look closely at the structural member it's working on.'

Grant peered. 'What about it?'

'Micro-meteoroid pitting. That structure has been in space a long, long time.'

'You think it's all like this? No people, just machines?'

'Yes. And as far as I can tell, all the others, too.'

Grant felt desolate. 'Seems pointless.'

'Well, that's robots for you, mindlessly doing what they're programmed to do, whether it makes sense or not.'

Grant laughed. 'You should know. Well, I don't fancy my chances getting inside that habitat before the air runs out, so . . .'

'Orbit the inhabited planet? On it.'

'Of course you are.'

'But first—'

'What?'

'We should take a look at a gas giant. If the Fermi are there, it means we've arrived sometime after their departure from the rocky worlds last November.'

'And if they're not?'

'Then either we're in a system where they haven't been, or we're in the past.'

'Let's find out that much at least,' Grant said. 'But be quick about it.'

The jump was slightly more than a blink, followed by another two likewise brief jumps, triangulating the great orb. Grant glimpsed multi-coloured bonds and whorls, bright spots and crescents, the circular shadow of one of these moons a black dot on bright cloud. Then, to his immense relief, he saw a vast black disc with outspread wings.

'The Fermi,' Iskander confirmed. 'So we're at least some time after their departure.'

'Going by the structures,' Grant said, 'we could be in the distant future! Have you thought it possible you're mistaken about our current time?'

'Of course. But I'm not.'

'OK. On to the second planet.'

The orbit that Iskander picked would have taken the cab around the planet in three hours, which Grant didn't have. Instead, the AI took him around the planet in a dozen short jumps on a zigzag course that took ten minutes altogether. The night side had a few clusters of light, dimmer than those of the eighteenth-century cities of Earth; the day side, traces of smoke here and there. Blue seas, white whorls of cloud, green and dun land, ice at the poles and at several mountain ranges. Unlike Earth and Apis, the planet had numerous island continents, like so many Australias, Greenlands, New Zealands and Madagascars. These scattered jigsaw puzzle pieces – you could still see they'd been a super-continent once – were spread out evenly around the globe, with no almost-hemispheric ocean. No great oceans at all: there seemed more land than sea. Almost every shore was outlined in white breakers, like a lace thrown over the planet: the tides, with narrow seas and two moons, were evidently ferocious. At each pole a small continent was covered with ice, and their nearby continents were graded from white through varied shades of green. Frost, tundra and forest.

'Radio traffic?'

'We're above the Heaviside layer. Drop to low orbit?'

The cab was over the day side. With luck, its traverse wouldn't be noticed.

'Do it.'

The surface became suddenly close.

Iskander turned the sound back on. Grant ranged through the bands. Voices, music, coded chatter. He stopped on what sounded like French, though he couldn't quite catch the drift through an unfamiliar accent and intonation.

'Source?'

Iskander replaced the outside view with an image from the zigzag sweep: a continent about the size and shape of France and about as far north as Britain, its neighbouring mini-continents between five hundred and a thousand kilometres away. The radio source was pinpointed as a dark patch beneath haze, at the mouth of a major river.

'Looks like a port,' Grant said.

'Yes.'

'OK, well, if they speak something like French it's a safe bet we can breathe. Take us down somewhere in the surrounding countryside, but close enough to walk into town.'

'What do you intend to do there?'

'Just nose around, get some idea of the situation. I'll avoid speaking to anyone if I can. I'm pretty fluent in French, but I might have to rely on your best guesses to understand whatever this local dialect is.'

'It's clearly derived from West and Central African variants of vernacular African French. I'm working on it.'

'OK, OK.'

'You are wary?'

'Yes. We've no idea what we're going into.'

'I have a suggestion. If this cab were to appear in the country-side – in a wood or field, or on wild land – it would be conspicuously out of place. On the outskirts of town, perhaps not so much.'

'In broad daylight?'

'You'd be surprised what can pass unnoticed in broad daylight.'

'Go for it. As long as you don't put us down in a recycling centre.'

'I doubt they have recycling. But I will avoid anything that looks like a wrecker's yard.'

Grant braced himself for gravity.

'I'm ready.'

He blinked, and they were down.

Through a haze as if of low mist, Grant examined the surroundings. Outdoors. Day. Early morning, going by the shadows. Flat ground, much trampled. Sawdust everywhere. Stacks of trimmed logs here, stacks of planks there. Machinery in the middle distance: a stationary steam engine, and an articulated lorry with a tall and thick chimney at the rear of the cab. Along another aisle between the stacks he could just make out a long trailer.

'You've put us down in a *timber yard*?'

'Yes, but no one is around right now. As soon as you're out of sight I'll send the cab to a clearing in the forest behind us. You can contact it via the phone when you want to leave. If any serious problems arise I can always send the cab into orbit.'

'How is the phone going to work here?'

'I've already piggy-backed the local comsats. No sign of my being detected.'

'Consider me reassured. How's the air?'

'Chilly. Definitely breathable. Some airborne microbes and viruses, but nothing your inoculations can't handle.'

Grant took off his glasses and removed the curved part of the earpieces, then put these parts back behind his ears. They curled neatly into place. He slipped the glasses in his pocket with the phone. Over his usual work shirt and trousers, he was wearing a blue one-piece overall with sturdy boots. Unless local costume was wildly out of kilter with the apparently light-industrial surroundings, he shouldn't look too conspicuous.

He opened the cab door. One breath and he was coughing.

'What the fuck is that?' he wheezed.

'Air pollution,' said Iskander. 'You'll get used to it.'

CHAPTER TWO

The Origin of the Family

New Rhu, Apis, Wednesday 25 March 2071

There was a fence. It wasn't much of a fence. An adult could vault it; a child could clamber over. It demarcated a rectangular plot, one of twenty vacant lots on either side of a future street sketched out with marker posts and string. As a barrier the fence was more an idea than a thing. What was inside it wouldn't be private property, exactly, but for some family or other household it would be their own space for as long as they used it. Inside the plot, a wall lower than the fence marked out in concrete blocks another, smaller rectangle: the foundation.

Myles Grant rolled an empty plastic drum as tall as he was through the gap in the fence where a gate might some day be, flipped it upright and spun it along on its base to a roughly circular hole two metres deep. He edged it to vertical and it kept spinning as it dropped, to land with a hollow, ringing thump and a clearance of ten centimetres from the sides all around.

He stepped back to admire this precise placing, a knack acquired in more repetitions than he cared to count, and picked up a shovel. He filled the gap around the cylinder with dirt from the pile dug out from the hole and packed it down with the flat of the shovel. This took about half an hour. After a break to gulp some water and stretch his back, he scattered and scraped the rest of the dirt over a few square metres. This done, he surveyed the site and checked that everything was in place for the imminent arrival of the ark: the coil of plastic pipe that would connect to the septic tank he'd just embedded; the stack of solar panels for the roof; the water tank and its plastic piping – all these and more were laid out well clear of the foundation on which the ark would settle.

For the final time, Myles checked the foundation walls with a spirit level. This done, he straightened up, rubbed the small of his back and walked out of the plot. Linda Starr, his immediate supervisor, hailed him from across the road, where she was laying the foundations for another ark.

She waved a trowel. 'All set?'

Myles waved back. 'Job done. On to the next.'

He checked the schedule on his glasses. The next job was at the end of the street, clearing a new plot. But the gang for that task were still working on another plot down the road, so Myles dawdled. It was a fine morning at the beginning of the dry season. He checked his watch. According to the chunky old Casio the time was 12:52 this particular Wednesday, back on Earth. Locally it was eight and a bit after midnight, and two hours after sunrise local time. The ark for that site was due to arrive at 13:00 GMT, piloted by John Grant. Myles was looking forward to saying hello to his father, and possibly inveigling him into a tea break with the gang. A man from the committee – Paul McAlister, that was it, coming into view in the dust and shimmer – was already walking up the road, ready to welcome the new arrivals, lead them to the hall for a quick refreshment and taking of details, and send them off to their temporary accommodation.

Myles closed his eyes and faced the low sun, breathing in the dusty smells and the sounds of the settlement getting into the swing of the day. Just within earshot, a crowd of small children clamoured and yelled, getting ready for the school to open. Closer by, a dumper truck whined up a ramp, and a crab-drawn cart rumbled. All the faces Myles could see looked cheerful, and he felt more cheerful himself than he'd normally done back home. Part of it was the adventure of it all, but Marie had attributed it to sunshine, of which there was a lot more here than in Scotland: 'It's like when Brits move to Australia,' she'd remarked. 'Their serotonin levels go up!'

New Rhu had expanded since he, Marie and the others of the first seven hundred settlers had arrived in October, and even more since the Union had changed its settlement policy in November. By now the town's population was over seven thousand, a fairly typical size for the Union settlement towns now being set up all across the continent of New Mu. The shipping-container arks were lined up, and in some cases stacked several storeys high, in laid-out streets. Other buildings, of local or imported materials, stood among the standard boxes here and there. The home of Myles and Marie, up on the slope towards the woods, was one of them. Myles and a team had dug and laid the stone foundation. The walls, windows and floors were all implausibly thin and stiff sheets of lightweight synthetics. They had been printed on Earth and delivered in flat packs, the fittings in kits and boxes. Myles and Marie had put them all together and raised and furnished the dwelling, a source of inordinate pride to them both. The town extended up the slope to within a hundred metres of the Alliance military stockade, and on the other way out to the fields, where small farms were spreading out in the direction of the Big River. The stream through the middle of the settlement was bridged with stone or timber in three places, and banked. No more floods!

Even Lieutenant William Knight, commanding officer of the small Alliance contingent up the hill, was grudgingly impressed with the Union settlement's progress from hunter-gatherer co-operation to settled agriculture and metal-working – 'moving up from savagery to barbarism' as he tauntingly put it. (He'd read his Engels.)

'John's late.'

'What?' Myles was jolted out of his reverie.

McAlister, in hard hat and carrying a virtual clipboard, tapped his wrist, where there wasn't a watch. 'The ark's five minutes overdue.'

Myles shrugged. 'Happens.'

'Not with John Grant & Son, it doesn't,' said McAlister. 'They're like clockwork. You should know.'

'Oh, aye.' Myles knew of the rumour that he would any day quit the settlement and start work with his father's company. It wasn't true but he did nothing to quell it.

He checked his watch. 13:07. 'Well, that is unusual.' He tried not to worry. 'Could be a delay at the other end. Kids freaking out, medical emergency . . .'

'That's probably it,' said McAlister. 'Well, I'll give it half an hour.' He looked back down the road, where the gang were now straggling up. 'I'll contact you as soon as he arrives. You might as well get back to work.'

Myles nodded and turned away, falling in with the construction gang, joining in the chat. But dismay gnawed him. McAlister was right: a delay in arrival was unprecedented. At the departure end, ample leeway was allowed for last-minute snags. Procedure had improved since the early days, such as that of his and Marie's arrival, when emigrants were packed in, the hatch slammed and the jump made before claustrophobia had time to kick in. At John Grant & Son the emigrants were usually boarding the ark up to half an hour before the transit.

Myles had his own suspicion of where – or, rather, of when – his father had gone. He blamed himself. He should never have told him about the exiles in the valley of the Big River, people who had retained for generations a tradition of waiting for the return of John Grant. It was typical of the man that he should become obsessed with closing that time loop.

One in a thousand, rumour whispered. Spin that wheel often enough, and you could expect your number to come up. One in a thousand FTL journeys ended up in the wrong time, or the wrong timeline. Some of these made it back. Not even rumour could put a number on how many.

John Grant had made well over a thousand FTL journeys to date.

Marie Henderson followed a well-trodden path through the forest, down from the lake where the flying boat made its monthly landing with supplies from New Ardtaraig, the Alliance base on the continent across the sea, New Atlantis. Despite having FTL craft that now operated openly, the Alliance avoided using them for short-haul transport, or for more journeys than necessary. The risk of ending up in the wrong time or timeline might be acceptable for troops, or for eager and adventurous explorers and settlers, but not for pilots on delivery runs.

Marie would have suspected that using the flying boat for resupply was just another Pentagon boondoggle, except that the Co-ord used its massive equivalent, the ekranoplan, for the same purpose. On a quiet day, if you were out on the plain and in line with the Big River valley, and the wind was coming in from the west, you could hear the distant roar of the mighty machine's arrival or departure.

If she cocked her ear and held her breath, Marie could hear above the clamour of forest animals the screech and bang of drilling machines up on Hamilton's Rise. A Co-ord mining company, directed by scientists and protected by troops, was breaking off great chunks of the crystalline rock. Though inactive, and bleached of their former vivid colours, the rocks held promise as a computational substrate, and were of great scientific interest whether or not they could be put to use. Presumably the Co-ord were conducting similar excavations on their own continent's dead Fermi outcrop, the Markov Escarpment. They were doing it here, on notionally Union territory, because they wanted to and because they could get away with it. The Union was in no position to do anything about it apart from lodging ineffectual protests at the UN and the International Court of Justice. The Alliance was in no position to do anything about it either, and in any case seemed to enjoy the Union's discomfiture.

Marie carried on her back a rucksack weighed down by scores of stoppered plastic tubes of water in which swarms of tiny organisms swam. Back at the lab, DNA testing would establish which, if any, known species these were the larval forms of. Marie's mentor, Dr Emma Hazeldene, had returned to New Atlantis with her colleagues and with the exile Able Jenkins. Hazeldene kept in touch. Jenkins – now back in his home village on New Atlantis – always welcomed a call. If a new plant or animal Marie had identified had a counterpart on the other continent, exile tradition usually told of some practical use, which Jenkins was eager to share.

These practical uses were how Marie justified her sustenance, and that of the two lab assistants she'd recruited from among the incomers. Her lips tightened at the thought. She was glad that the settlement was flourishing – there were children now, though none born here as yet – but with the Union's blessing on the place had come the blessings of the Union: Iskander, and the cadre organisation. WeThink, which had come in very handy in the early days of communal effort, was now fire-walled out – fair enough, she supposed, given the Co-ord encroachment, but still annoying in principle. You couldn't identify the cadre unless they made themselves known, but you could make educated guesses. Half the committee were already *responsables*, that was obvious. It was just as obvious that they were the best available candidates for the posts they'd stood for: hardworking, sociable, adaptable, reliable people who got things done. This, too, rubbed her the wrong way.

New Rhu, and the whole continent of New Mu, was now an extension of the Union, not an escape from it. Same went, *mutatis mutandis*, for the other continents. Alliance settlers were flooding New Atlantis, and Co-ord pioneers New Lemuria.

She crested a small rise, where the path overlooked a cup-shaped hollow, covered with not-grass and flowering plants, and shaded with overhanging trees. As her eyes and glasses adjusted to the shadow, she saw movement in the bottom of the hollow, and stopped. She sank to a squat, and slowly brought her hands in front of her glasses and made the spreading *zoom* gesture. The view magnified. She flicked her thumb: *record*.

A dozen or so of the badger-sized blue-black arachnoids that everyone vaguely called scuttlers had formed a circle, each of them facing out with mandibles and pincers open. In the centre of the circle three of four smaller specimens of the same species were moulting. Splits along their backs widened. After a few minutes, the carapaces cracked wide open. Wrinkled, pale copies of the adults emerged. Their bodies expanded to adult size almost at once. Their carapaces hardened and darkened in less than a minute. With unsteady steps they scuttled to the circle, where the older adults turned inward to meet them. Antennae touched. The circle became a phalanx, the established adults flanking the new arrivals, and trundled off into the underbrush to disappear up the slope and into the woods.

'Yes!' Marie exulted. She'd hypothesised that the larger arachnoids dealt with the soft-shell vulnerability of their moulting process in just these ways: by rapid hardening, and most of all by guarding the emerging young, a proto-social behaviour that was hard to see as anything but mutual aid and the first flicker, however faint, of concern and care.

Just as Marie was straightening up, a troop of monkey-spiders swung down from the overhanging trees and scooped up the discarded carapaces. Holding the pieces above their heads with their forelimbs like triumphant looters, they ran off across the path in front of her and were soon out of sight in the foliage. Hoots and crashing noises faded behind them. The monkey-spiders had become bolder of late, and their group actions more obviously coordinated. Perhaps it was a seasonal thing, as the weather turned hotter and drier. She would ask Hazeldene and Jenkins about it.

Marie gazed at the glade for a few more moments, then walked on. A good day's work, all told. After a few steps, she stopped. Something below conscious awareness, a sound or smell or subtle disturbance of air currents, was warning her that she was being watched. She felt on the back of her neck a chill prickle of tiny hairs. She stood still. One hand strayed to the pistol on her belt. With the other she took off her glasses, held them in front of her and flipped the view to mirror. Trees, bushes, not-grass, the dust and rough stones of the path. She flipped the glasses to normal and put them back on, then turned sharply and scanned her surroundings in every wavelength the glasses could display. Small scurrying bodies in the underbrush, minding their own business. Monkey-spiders high in the trees, lolling in the afternoon heat, limbs draped and hanging. A distant drone on a routine patrol, showing up in her enhanced vision as a darting, searching bee.

A few actual bees, closer by, doing their thing.

She laughed at herself, shrugged and continued down the path.

Her phone rang in her ear, making her jump. A name floated in her peripheral vision: Myles. She snapped her fingers. 'Yes?'

'It's John,' he said. 'He's . . . delayed.'

She thought about what that might mean. 'Oh! You think it's . . .'

'Yes. Damn. I wish we'd never told him about the exiles waiting for him.'

'Don't say that! It had to happen sometime.'

'Maybe. There's nothing we can do now, anyway. I've sent word back to my mum and to the company on the 3:00 p.m. ark.'

'Ellen will be gutted.'

'Yeah. Should we go back?'

'No,' Marie said. 'Ellen's tough. If she needs to see us, she'll come here.'

'Aye, I suppose you're right. And we have work to get on with.'

They agreed there was nothing else to do.

'See you in an hour or so,' Marie said.

'See you then. Take care. Love you.'

'Love you too.'

Marie quickened her pace down the track towards New Rhu. Every so often, as the afternoon shadows lengthened, she turned her head sharply and looked back. Nothing was behind her, but she couldn't shake the uncanny feeling of being watched.

From the clustered branches at the top of a tall tree half a kilometre away up the hill, Marcus Owen watched Marie until she passed out of sight. His last glimpse of her was a flick of her long auburn ponytail as she skipped down a steep slope in the uneven path. A shoulder of rock obscured the remainder of her descent to the town, which he could see in the far distance.

Marie was a frequent visitor to the forest, and over the past months Owen had often spotted her. The moment a few minutes earlier when she'd stopped on the path and looked around was the first time she had given any indication of suspecting that she was being observed. It was odd that she had sensed him at all. No explanation occurred to Owen other than that human beings were animals, and linked by countless invisible, intangible threads to the life around them in ways that he, as a robot, was not, superior to theirs though his senses were.

A drone the size of a hummingbird drifted up the hill, metres above the canopy. It darted to the tree in which Owen and half a dozen monkey-spiders perched. Its rotors buzzed; its scanners swept back and forth, up and down. Then it shot into the air, found a new altitude and drifted on above the treetops uphill.

Owen breathed out. It was not clear to him what made the drones – whether biological survey devices from New Rhu, security drones sent out by the Alliance outpost overlooking the town, or spy drones from the Co-ord camp up on Hamilton's Rise – seem to miss his presence.

Probably it had had something to do with the fragment of a god in his head. Yes, that might well have something to do with it. That made sense. Owen had no idea what the aims and motives of the Fermi were, but he didn't doubt their capacities.

The Fermi in their pomp had been capable of much. Long ago – billions of years ago perhaps – they had terraformed Apis. In the last year they had triggered quakes on Apis and Earth. They had engineered a new Venus volcanic resurfacing event beneath Owen's very feet. They had sent arrows that might as well have been made by elves and shot by ghosts flying out of the forest. Quite possibly, they had induced panic and nausea in people clambering over a rockfall. And finally, they had spectacularly departed as a gigantic black shape like some winged disc from ancient myth, to reappear on the surface of the system's gas giant.

It was, Owen reflected as he descended the tree, a reasonable speculation that the fragment of their presence lodged like shrapnel in his skull was capable of tweaking the electronics of a passing drone. The fragment was, after all, tweaking the electronics of his own mind, which seemed hardly less spooky.

It didn't – or perhaps couldn't – make him invisible. Not that it mattered. The settlement's foragers, hunters, explorers and patrols were easy enough to evade. The only people who had seen him thus far had been one or two exiles from (he presumed) the valley of the Big River, and their presence here was even more wraith-like than his own.

Seven monkey-spiders followed him to the ground. With their furry coverings of fine orange bristles and their bright black clusters of eyes, they looked like six-limbed orang-utans. The appearance was misleading: they were far more intelligent than that. Quite possibly the cephalic nerve ganglion in their domed heads had more processing power than a human brain. Monkey-spiders kept bees in hives made – like their own shelters, and many of their tools – from fragments of the moults of other invertebrates.

And they had language. They used hoots and modulated howls for long-range simple communication: the equivalent of shouts of warning or command, as well as derision. For more subtle and precise conversation, they used posture and gesture. With six limbs, all of which – most significantly the front pair – ended in clusters of long digits, their capacities in this area far outdid any human version of signing. Varied postures added the equivalent of tone and pitch.

That their ears heard sounds higher and deeper than even Owen could, and their eyes saw well into the infrared and ultraviolet, underscored the difficulty of mutual comprehension between human (or humanoid robot) and monkey-spider.

For Owen, difficulty had never meant impossibility. Furthermore, that trace element of the departed Fermi in his head had an encyclopaedic understanding of the monkey-spiders, along with much else. It gave Owen a visual dictionary and grammar, a mental image of what each gesture and posture meant.

Encyclopaedic knowledge of the language was one thing. Understanding and using it was a different matter altogether. He had less than half the digits, a tenth of the dexterity, and much less than a tenth of the possible postures available to the monkey-spiders. To them, his attempts must seem like mumbled, muffled, jumbled speech.

Nevertheless, after months of hiding out in the forest, and hanging out with monkey-spiders, he was getting somewhere. They understood some of what he said, and knew that he was on their side.

Tomorrow he would lead them into battle.

CHAPTER THREE

Mission Profile

The Space Station at the Nameless Sun, early 2071

Lakshmi Nayak woke from a dream of mathematics and needle-work. Mathematics had been her most favoured subject, needle-work her least. In the dream they had combined in a frustrating topology of threads, and a final stitch that had locked everything into place.

Relief that she wasn't at school washed over her. She remembered how on the front of a piece you saw the pictures, flowers and leaves or whatever, and on the reverse you saw the real messy connection of the threads, the knots and the ends. It seemed important, and . . . The insight faded like bright cloth in sunlight. She reached for it in her mind, but its tattered scraps drifted from her grasp.

So why did she feel good?

'I closed the loop,' she mumbled, her lips sticky.

'You what?' Iskander asked, from the walls.

Nayak suppressed a grunt of irritation. If the anticipatory algorithmic AI wanted her to explain, she probably should. She rolled over and sat on the edge of the bed, blinking as the light in the cubicle brightened.

'When I sent the FTL equations to my past self on the HMS *Vindicate*, I closed the time loop.'

'Yes,' said Iskander.

'I just now dreamed that closing the loop somehow stitched me – us, I suppose, everyone on the Station – into a single timeline, and so we don't have to worry about side-slipping again.'

'Interesting if true. Do you have anything to substantiate this conjecture, beyond "It was revealed to me in a dream"?'

Nayak sighed. 'That's the trouble – I don't. I *almost* remember equations, just out of reach.' She clawed the air. 'Aagh! It's like the insight I *almost* remember from the hallucinations I had when I came back from the Mushroom Moon – that our FTL is somehow enabled by the superluminal connections of the Fermi.'

Tangled threads, intricate interweaving . . . Aha!

But the AI was – predictably – ahead of her.

'Perhaps your dream was a continuation of these hallucinations,' Iskander said. 'There may still be some molecules from the fungus lingering in your blood stream, after all.'

'I've just thought of that,' she said. 'But still . . . if the Fermi were communicating with me in that way, maybe the dream is significant, too.'

Fungal spores from the Mushroom Moon had worked on her brain, carrying word from the Fermi: that they had originated in the very first instant of the universe, when everything was everywhere and everything that could happen happened all at once. Possibly. It could be as spurious an enlightenment as you'd get from stuffing your face with any old magic mushroom. So could this new apparent insight.

'I can't help you there,' Iskander said. 'I can take your

speculation as input, but you'll just have to work out the equations for yourself.'

'I'll leave all that to my subconscious for now,' Nayak said. 'My own onboard AI!'

'It's a way of thinking about it,' Iskander allowed.

'Yes, exactly!'

She went for a run, twice around the kilometre circumference of the habitation band, a giant treadmill that sloped gently up before and behind. After breakfast, she found a nook in the endless corridor where she could sit and scribble. Her heart wasn't in it. Two months into 2071, and five hundred light years out from the Solar system, she was finding herself homesick for Earth.

Last November, after the Mushroom Moon episode and the intricate arrangement with HMS *Vindicate* to return the diplomat Peregrine Walworth to Earth and (eventually) Nayak's letter to herself with the FTL equations to Earth at an earlier time, the Station had perforce consulted with the Union government in Brussels. Commander Ulrich had taken a shuttle there, piloted by one of Nayak's trainees. The shuttle had returned the following week.

Naturally, Katrina Ulrich had called a general meeting.

'Everything has changed,' she'd told them. 'The Fermi have departed from all the rocky planets in the Solar system, from Apis, and – according to reports which I am not at liberty to expand on – planets in other systems, too. The pattern is everywhere the same: some dark thing rises from the planet, and shortly afterwards a similar shape appears on the surface of a gas giant. All this seems to have happened around the same time as it happened on the Mushroom Moon last week.

'Our, ah, colleagues in the Co-ord science teams aver that this was their doing, thanks to successful communication being established at a major outcrop on Apis, Hamilton's Rise. My understanding is that our scientists and those of the Alliance are, let's say, awaiting the extraordinary evidence to back up this extraordinary claim.

'Whatever about that, the consequences unfolded rapidly over the past weekend. The Co-ord and the Alliance have . . . denounced, is that the word? – the Kepler Agreement, which was entirely a Black Horizon internal arrangement with no legal force. All planets and systems are open to all explorers. International lawyers are dusting off concepts like *terra nullius*, the doctrine of discovery, the law of the sea, the Outer Space Treaty and all the usual imperialist and colonialist crap. Needless to say, the Union and most of the non-aligned countries object strongly, and because of France's seat on the Security Council we're in a position to resist any such claims at the UN, for whatever that's worth.

'Likewise inevitably, the Union government has rescinded its opposition to settlement of terrestrial planets, put all its plans for space habitats on the back burner, and . . . well, our friend John Grant and his company have been first through the gate, but there's a crowded field behind him because Iskander has—'

'—anticipated,' Iskander had chipped in.

'Yes. Quite so. The plans developed for the *Fighting Chance*, suitably modified for simpler transport, have been spread widely. Numerous companies and agencies were poised to move, and they have. So, here we are. Migration from Union territories to Apis has begun, and will accelerate. For the moment, the Co-ord and the Alliance seem to be respecting Black Horizon's share-out of the three continents – which they did endorse, after all, in the initial announcement only last month. There are small military encampments of both powers close to the current unofficial Union settlement, and as I say they are claiming that all the continents are in principle open to settlers from anywhere, so there's no guarantee how long that will last. The Union has to establish its own claims, and that's under way.

'As for us, the Station's former mission of finding suitable systems to build gigantic space habitats is now redundant. Our new mission is to find habitable planets – preferably without exiles or Alliance and/or Co-ord outposts, but we'll take that as it comes. The Black Horizon map, and the historical files, are merely a starting point. We are urged to strike out on our own, reporting back to Earth as often as necessary in the current shuttles or the new ones now being built.

'You'll be relieved to know that the shuttles – and other transport, we hope – will enable rotation and replenishment of personnel. Any of you will be free to return home for a vacation, or permanently if that's what you want. This mission is, after all, one that none of us signed up for. I have no doubt at all that it won't be hard to recruit replacements.'

There had been a general flurry of questions and comments. Ulrich peered at her displays while Iskander sorted them out.

'Ah, yes,' she'd said. 'Kind of so many of you to ask. I spent Saturday and Sunday being rigorously debriefed, shall we say. I'm happy to report that I stuck to my story: I was entirely responsible for the Station's deviation from its assigned mission. I did attempt to carry on Black Horizon's nuclear deterrence policy, in the interests of the Union as much as anything else, but I never transferred my loyalty from the Union to Black Horizon. No evidence to the contrary has been forthcoming. Iskander has backed me up. I freely turned over all the Black Horizon files that Commander Alice Hawkins on Apis shared with me.

'Taking all the circumstances into account, etc., etc., it's been decided that a written warning and a reprimand on my permanent record meets the case. I'm to stay in post, subject to the confidence of the Station's complement. Do I have it?'

Carried by acclamation.

'Thank you, citizens! Now, let's get to it.'

Get to it they had.

The Station's chief engineer, Eduardo Maria Gironella, had led a team of people and robots in building three new shuttles. They weren't as advanced and multi-role as the two the Station already had. They needed only drives, navigation, cargo space and life support.

'Good enough for government work,' Gironella said. They were certainly good enough for probes into unknown systems, as the Station continued on its new mission.

They'd found a handful of habitable planets, all of them already garrisoned by Co-ord or Alliance forces, with which the Station exchanged polite, wary acknowledgements before making a hasty departure.

They'd found plenty of utterly uninhabitable systems, rich in resources but inimical to any kind of long-term habitation, even in habitats: unstable orbits, unpredictable flares from the star's surface, rocky worlds far too hot or cold to do anything with, gas giants far too close to their star or with raging radiation belts. Rocky planets and moons, terrestrial and in the habitable zone by astronomical classification, but with axes so tilted or rotations so tidal-locked that survival on their surfaces would be best left to machines.

All fascinating in their own way, of course, and seeing them up close was certainly an addition to human knowledge, but even that palled in time.

After so many systems surveyed, space exploration became astronomy: images on screens. Sometimes not even images. A shuttle took a quick look and reported back to the Station. If the system looked safe and interesting the Station dropped in, the instruments scanned the bandwidths, the AIs ran the numbers and the jump warning sounded again. On to the next.

Every week or so, a shuttle reported back to ESA on auto-pilot, for a swift exchange of information. Usually there was an exchange of personnel. Familiar faces left, new faces arrived. The Station's culture slowly shifted as grief over the losses from Cloud City became assimilated by the survivors who remained, and those who left were replaced by people who'd never been on Cloud City at all. Almost without realising it, an increasing number of people selected more colourful and varied clothing from the printers. Social gatherings became more frequent and more cheerful.

This helped Nayak's mood, but she was beginning to think seriously about leaving, at least for a while. The occasional video messages from or to her family in Kerala and her former colleagues in London and in Arrochar and in Inverclyde only gave her more intense pangs. She was missing out on births, deaths, weddings, promotions, not to mention the buzz of scientific discovery and contention. Updates, digests and the latest issues of journals couldn't take the place of live conversation.

Not that she didn't have enough to occupy her mind. The intuition gnawed at her that the Fermi's superluminal connections were implicated in FTL travel, and could be hacked for human FTL communication. But she wasn't getting anywhere with that, either.

The question that perplexed better minds than hers, if the latest journals were anything to go by, was *what do the Fermi want?* Evidently they had a long-term plan or aim, which – at least in the sphere within a thousand light years of Earth – humanity's sudden rush of rash expansion had knocked off course. Likewise evidently, their spreading of life from Earth – or Venus, if that planet had indeed been the place of life's origin – to many other planets over perhaps billions of years was part of that plan. That the plan could be disrupted by such a comparatively trivial matter as humanity's discovery of FTL travel seemed unlikely. That discovery and its consequences would surely have been foreseen by minds capable of working on vast scales of time and space.

Intellects vast and cool and unsympathetic?

That begged the question. First one would have to establish that the Fermi were intellects, or had motives in any sense analogous to those of an organism. The few interactions of the Fermi with humanity recorded in the reports from Apis had certainly given the impression of communication with some alien mind or minds. Nayak's own hallucinatory revelation had felt like that, too. But, then, so did interactions with Iskander – and as Perry Walworth had once remarked, the Iskander you talked with was merely the chatty front end of a process that needed no self-awareness at all.

To ask about an AI's motives was to miss the point entirely. Its goals could be quite arbitrary. This had long ago been explained by the parable of the AI whose goal was to make paperclips, and which proceeded to turn as much of the universe as it could manipulate into paperclips. AIs were all paperclip maximisers in the end. Perhaps the Fermi, too, were paperclip maximisers, but their paperclips just happened to be terrestrial planets with life, and actually or potentially intelligent life. Unconscious themselves, they were paperclip maximisers for consciousness.

But why? Perhaps consciousness mattered, on some cosmic scale. Nayak was familiar with, and sceptical about, the interpretations of quantum mechanics that insisted that it did: that the conscious observer was crucial in the collapse of the wave function. As a materialist she doubted that, but then as a materialist she had to come to terms with the question of what kind of matter, if any, the Fermi *were*.

She'd seen the recordings from Apis of how the rock – as they called it – behaved. Rock moved, or seemed to move, inside solid rock. Decades of research on this was now becoming available, and there was no doubt that this was what was happening – and not, say, a visual, virtual illusion. A new phase of matter, some said, as if that explained anything.

A more promising angle of attack came from the suggestion that the Fermi rocks were an intrusion of normal matter from a space in which there were more than three spatial dimensions. Just as an intrusion of three-dimensional objects would produce effects impossible and incomprehensible to the inhabitants of Flatland, matter with a fourth spatial dimension to move around in would behave in ways impossible in our world.

How many dimensions would be needed for the bizarre properties of the Fermi rock to make sense? And would that account for their superluminal connections? But then—

Nayak scribbled rapidly.

She was, she found, by no means the first to have wondered if the mysterious inner movement of Fermi rock could be accounted for by postulating higher spatial dimensions, and tried to make the mathematics match the mechanics. Over the past fifty years, the occasional Co-ord or Alliance physicist had hit upon the explanation, and tried to work it out. Their results, at least in the publicly available Black Horizon records, were sparse. Nobody had had much time to devote to the question, few mathematicians were involved in the conspiracy in the first place and it was entirely possible that only a selection of the material – perhaps the least interesting – had been released by the intelligence services doing the investigating and interrogating.

Every paper from a Co-ord scientist, much to Nayak's amusement, began with a throat-clearing paragraph or two about how what followed was merely a mathematical model, a convenience in calculation, and no inference should be made about the *actual physical existence* of these imagined higher dimensions. The Coordinated States had gone through a post-war spasm of materialist dogmatism that had lasted a decade or two, and covering one's ass in this manner had evidently become – even for scientists working entirely under the radar of official surveillance – a conditioned reflex.

The Alliance scientists had, in Nayak's view, erred in the opposite direction, flagrantly multiplying enough entities to give William of Ockham a shaving cut. Their elaborations and speculations were freer, and therefore more stimulating, than those of their Co-ord confrères. But despite or because of their self-imposed limitations, the Co-ord scientists had stuck closer to the available data.

In the months since Black Horizon's existence had been

revealed, or exposed, more work had been done in the open. Not enough, and with no breakthroughs. Nayak was, she realised without false modesty, the best mind to have tackled the problem.

She was in with a chance.

Nayak paused in her work to take a look at the Station's latest location in her glasses. With a sweep of her hand and a blink of her eye her surroundings vanished, to be replaced by images integrated from the Station's external cameras. She was a point in empty space. In front of her, seeming close enough to reach out and touch and in fact far too close for comfort, was a ball of red-hot rock partly obscured by great banks of pitch-black clouds. Behind it was a far larger ball, a red giant, from whose surface vast plumes and sprays of plasma erupted on a scale so vast and slow that to her they hung still like so many frozen geysers.

According to the text trickling down the edge of her sight, the clouds on the planet were of iron vapour, and far below the clouds were falling downpours of iron rain. Pelting down on seas of iron, oceans of it, from which they would evaporate and rise again to the clouds, and so on. Counter-intuitively but logically, this was cooling the planet's surface. It would be solid in another billion years or so. The whole process made the Venus volcanic resurfacing event look like a spring breeze.

An alarm sounded: the Station's habitation band was about to power down. A shuttle must have docked. Nayak stayed where she was as the pseudo-gravity dropped. Laughter echoed along the endless corridor. People were fooling around in microgravity. Spin-downs had become something of a recreational interlude for the Station's crew.

She waited for weight to build up again, looking at the scrawls on her slate and the view outside. Someone walked past. Nayak caught a waft of cinnamon scent, and turned.

Luggage in hand, a woman was strolling away from her. She

had numerous loose ringlets of curly black hair that didn't quite reach the collar of her blue uniform. She was tall and lissom and moved like a dancer. At the next widescreen outside view, a few metres away, she paused to look outside, then cast a querying glance over her shoulder. Her cheek was dark, her profile perfect. She looked younger than Nayak. Her gaze met Nayak's, and locked. She smiled.

Hooked, Nayak let herself be reeled in. She picked up her slate and walked over. The woman pointed at the screen.

'Isn't it wonderful!'

There was no irony in that voice. She seemed enraptured by the infernal scene outside.

'It's . . . interesting,' Nayak admitted. 'In an inhuman sort of way. Chilling, in a sense.'

'Warmer than your cold equations.'

A tilted head, a teasing smile. Nayak felt flustered. 'Oh? You know me?'

'Of course. You're Lakshmi Nayak.' The woman smiled and raised a hand. Her upturned palm was pale. 'My name is Selena Pereira.' She tapped a thumbnail on her lapel badge. 'I'm an astrophysicist.'

Nayak clocked the flag on the badge. 'Oh! You're from Cuba! How—?'

'Seconded, not defected,' Selena said.

'Ah. Unlike me, then.'

Selena laughed. 'Scotland is in the Union, and Cuba is in the Coordinated States. And you grew up in Kerala, which is ruled by one of our fraternal parties, and is in the Alliance. So we have much in common, really.'

'One way of looking at it, I suppose.'

Again the teasing smile. 'Now you sound English. I should be wary.'

'Perhaps you should. What brings you here?'

Selena pointed outside. 'This.'

'Nothing for us here but observations.'

'Exactly! A system that hasn't been meddled with by the Fermi.' Selena sighed happily. 'We have so much to learn!'

Nayak looked from the iron seas to Selena's bright dark eyes and decided she had learned quite enough to stop dithering.

'Let's get a coffee,' she said.

As they walked to the nearest cafeteria Nayak glanced at Selena's bio, which Iskander had helpfully pulled up. 'I see you're not just an astrophysicist, you're an astronaut!'

'Yes,' Selena said. 'I trained at Baikonur, and flew one mission, to our Moon base.'

'And you haven't flown any missions since?'

Selena laughed. 'I wouldn't say that.'

'Oh. You mean they were clandestine?'

'Not exactly.' Selena waved towards the view screen they were passing. 'This isn't my first time . . . out here.'

'Are you telling me you were in Black Horizon?'

'No. After my Moon mission I trained for Mars, but I was told there was no slot for me on the next flight. In the mean-time I was assigned quite unexpectedly to a Russian submarine, on the pretext that I needed training in an enclosed environment. The submarine was the *Admiral von Bellingshausen*.'

'Oh!' *That* sub, the one with which the Station had had two toe-to-toe nuclear stand-offs. 'Were you — ?'

Selena shook her head. 'No, I wasn't on her when she had her confrontations with the Station. Perhaps fortunately.'

'Wow!' Nayak looked at the tall young woman with awe, as well as whatever else she was feeling right now. 'I've never . . . I mean, I've seen people on screens, but it's strange to meet someone who was on starships before I, um . . .'

'Before you invented your own?'

'Well, yes, that's what I just stopped myself from saying!'

They laughed. At the cafeteria they got coffee and sat down.

'I'm puzzled,' Nayak said. 'You said you were on the sub, but you weren't in Black Horizon?'

'I was approached. I played along, and at the end of the journey reported all I knew to the Intelligence Directorate. Luckily for me, this was before Black Horizon revealed itself publicly, so I remain trusted.'

'Ah, I see.' Nayak found herself wondering if Selena's unexpected assignment to the Russian submarine had been arranged by the Cuban intelligence service, and she'd been an agent of that Directorate all along. She wasn't sure what all this implied about Selena's current assignment, but suspected that it would do no good to enquire further. She laughed uneasily. 'I suppose I could say I was *nearly* in Black Horizon, too.'

Selena gave her an amused glance. 'I know. You were peripherally involved, via Commander Ulrich, who herself was merely inveigled.'

'You seem to know a lot about me.'

'Yes. You're well known, after all.'

'That connection isn't!'

Selena chuckled darkly. 'Commander Ulrich's debriefing was shared in the appropriate quarters.'

'Even to the Co-ord?'

'Of course. Nuclear weapons were involved. In this area there is no room for misunderstanding.'

Nayak nodded.

Selena gestured to draw a line under that subject, then looked around at the dozen or so people in the cafeteria and spoke in a lighter tone.

'Not very Union, is it?'

'How do you mean?'

Selena waved her arms about, with a vagueness that Nayak found rather charming. 'I expected more people to be wearing ridiculous and colourful clothes!'

'Oh, yes, well . . . I saw plenty of that in Scotland, but here I suppose functional makes sense. It's a workplace, after all.'

'It's also your home, for now. You do have time off.'

'Some people do dress up on Thursday evenings, just like

back home. Not that Thursday evening means the same here, any more than weekends did on your submarine, I guess. Other times . . .' Nayak shrugged. 'It's easier to just wear the same sort of thing every day. Throw it in the recycling, get the identical jumpsuit next time out of the printer.'

'It's as easy to print a dress or a suit as a jumpsuit.'

'Yes, and some do, but who wants to do that every evening, or every time they come off shift?'

'I do,' Selena said. 'And I will.'

Nayak smiled. 'I'll look forward to it.'

'So will I.'

Was this flirtation? Nayak would normally have been sure, but maybe Selena's manner was a Cuban thing, or a Co-ord thing.

'Um, I suppose you want to get settled in . . .'

'I have an appointment with Commander Ulrich in half an hour, and I have to prepare for it. After that . . . I'm sure I'll see you sometime?'

'Yes! Just give me a call.' Too needy, she thought. 'You know, whenever.'

'Yes.' Selena nodded, smiled, and left. At the door she looked back. That querying glance over the shoulder again. Nayak smiled and waved, then looked down at her tablet. She had a lot to think about.

The following day was a Thursday. Nayak returned from her morning jog twice around the habitation band and picked up her clothes packet for the day from the nearest printer to her cabin. When she'd showered and chucked her clothes for recycling, she tore open the packet to find a top, an underskirt and a long bolt of shiny blue fabric.

'Why?' she asked Iskander. 'I haven't worn a sari for ages.'

'You'll see,' Iskander said.

That evening she met Selena again, apparently quite by accident, and see she certainly did.

CHAPTER FOUR

Second World Problems

Planet 2, the port city, Wednesday 25 March 2071
according to Grant's calendar

Grant closed the cab door as quietly as he could and made
sure it was locked. The chill gritty air stung his eyes and rasped
his throat. He stepped away from the tractor unit and looked
around and listened. The yard was quiet. Perhaps not for long.
It must be at least an hour after dawn. Background noise was
a distant, uneven roar.

Traffic? Factories? Surf? The river?

He peered around the corner of each stack of lumber before
dashing to the next. The smell from the logs and planks soothed
his nose, if not his throat. On a cut end he made an easy
crescent indentation with a thumbnail. Soft, rough wood, lots
of rings, logs about fifty centimetres in diameter. That and the
resinous scent suggested the timber was harvested from a mature
pine forest.

The yard's wooden wall was two metres high. Grant grabbed the top and raised his head above it. A metre or so of grass, a road. The surface was of small stones and gravel. Along the edge he could see the foundation of larger stones. A macadam road, without tar. To his right the road sloped up, towards hills and trees. To his left it sloped down, towards houses and taller buildings about a kilometre away. Chimneys and smoke-stacks, tall, spindly towers here and there. Sea gleamed in the distance. Above the haze over the city, white clouds drifted in a blue sky. A bird like a herring gull skimmed by about fifty metres overhead.

Grant heaved himself up and over the wall and dropped to the grass. Real grass, like on Earth, and not not-grass, like on Apis. He glanced again both ways and set off down the road towards town. He glimpsed the merest flicker of a blue flash and heard a muffled thud as air rushed into the vacuum left by the departing cab.

The temperature felt like about 10 degrees Celsius. Chilly all right, but he walked briskly enough to keep warm. The season seemed to be early spring, which fitted with his glimpse of the planet's tilt on the way in. On either side of the road were recently ploughed fields, among which white birds like gulls and black birds like crows hopped and poked. The small brown birds in the hedges seemed familiar, too. Beyond the fields and up the hillside were meadows and woodlands, all vivid green. So far, it seemed a world less alien than Apis, and more lush than Earth.

He heard a faint buzzing sound from the sky, and looking up saw a flying machine like a dragonfly, almost translucent, glittering, move slowly overhead a thousand feet up, and begin a fluttering, spiralling descent to somewhere far to his left on the edge of what he could see of the town.

A couple of hundred metres on he began to pass houses, two or three storeys, built of wood, with eaves, doorways and window frames ornately carved. Behind sturdy wooden fences, the gardens had plots of vegetables and herbs amid flower beds and tidy lawns, and pens and runs for small hairy beasts and small flightless fowls. Clucks, chirps and squeaks sounded, but none of the animals were of any familiar species. Grant dared not linger to look closer. He wondered why people who could afford such substantial houses needed to keep kitchen gardens and raise the equivalents of rabbits and chickens.

As the road curved around a bend Grant saw a man walking up the slope, on the other side of the road. The man was young and wore a jacket and trousers of what looked like woven wool and a flat peaked cap. In one hand he carried a small wicker basket. His skin was dark, his features West African.

He gave Grant a nod as they approached, and said what sounded like 'Bon-jerr'.

Grant returned the nod. '*Bonjour!*'

The young man's eyes widened. Grant hurried on. Next he encountered a dozen or so men like the first, walking briskly up the road and exchanging banter in the local dialect. Most of them were Black, the others of mixed heritage. Three puffed on pipes and gesticulated with the stems as they spoke. They all lugged bags of tools – he could hear the clink – as well as small wicker baskets. Kit and lunch, he guessed. Perhaps the first man he'd seen was a foreman or such like, gone ahead to open up, and this group the rest of the workforce of the timber yard. Grant acknowledged them with a wave; they spared him barely a glance.

Moments later a flat-bed lorry trundled up the road, powered by a two-stroke internal combustion engine and trailing exhaust smoke that stank of burned and slightly rancid cooking oil. Cheery shouts from behind suggested that the group he'd just seen knew its driver.

By now the road had become a street leading to the harbour area, a kilometre or so distant. Masts and sails just visible above the rooftops. On either side, strips of grass bordered the sidewalks. People were walking, or riding bicycles, beside long blocks of three or four storeys, wood-built like the houses he'd seen earlier. Trellises and window boxes made colourful displays of flowers and leaves on every frontage. The ground floor of each block was usually a row of small shops and cafés, under bright awnings.

The architecture and street layout struck Grant as what he'd expect in a residential suburb of an industrial town in some backwater of the Coordinated States, with wood instead of concrete. On the road, an increasing number of two-stroke trucks added their distinctive whiff to the air.

Grant passed or was overtaken by people walking briskly. Their clothing was stout in fabric, plain in cut and bright in colour: long trousers, mid-calf skirts, thick-soled shoes. Children walked or scampered in groups, small ones supervised by older ones. Outside the cafés in the blocks, groups of well-wrapped-up people sat around tables over steaming mugs, smoking pipes and chatting. They looked shockingly old, with white hair and bowed backs, but lively and loud enough. Once or twice on the street he saw people, mostly older than himself, wearing glasses – probably just frames with corrective lenses, rather than electronic devices like his own, but it meant that if he wore his now he wouldn't look conspicuous. He paused for a moment to reconnect the earpieces with his glasses and put them on.

He walked on, looking around discreetly, and saw—

'Don't stare,' said Iskander.

Two persons had come around the next corner and were now striding towards him. They were about two and a half metres tall, with long legs and arms, and long fingers with many knuckles. Their feet, in open sandals, had toes almost as long as their fingers. They wore similar clothes: a bib and brace arrangement like dungarees, the trousers to the knee, in finer fabric than Grant had seen here hitherto. Russet hair, apparently brushed back and up, rose from their scalps above high, smooth brows. Their eyes were large and dark, their ears prominent, their noses and lips delicate above their small, sharp chins. Their faces were olive-green, the rest of their visible skin – their arms, their shins, the backs of their hands – mottled in darker or lighter shades of green and brown, like camouflage. Both had deep chests. The one who was slightly shorter and slenderer, and with more elaborately styled hair, had beneath her chest covering evident breasts and a bulging belly – pregnant, Grant assumed.

Then, from an opening in the bib of the garment, a small head poked out. It looked around with bright, inquisitive eyes, then ducked back inside. The cloth rippled as beneath it the infant stretched upwards. A tiny arm appeared at the top of the bib, clutching skin, and the shape of the head settled at where a nipple could very well be. The apparently female one looked down, and fondled the small, grasping hand between her long fingers.

Grant had to restrain himself from gawping. These giants were *marsupials*?

No one else was paying them any attention.

Grant walked forward, edging the sidewalk, eyeing them sidelong. They passed him without a glance, intent on conversation in no language Grant had ever heard, their voices so low-pitched that his chest resonated to the bass.

He walked on, knees a little shaky, without looking back.

'Hominids, loosely speaking,' murmured Iskander. 'Though, to be more precise, they probably trace their descent to a different primate, and *that* to a different insectivore. And apparently marsupial! Every known hominin fossil and every ape and monkey is a closer cousin of yours than the pair you just saw.'

Grant said nothing, and not just because he didn't want to look like he was talking to himself. He didn't need to discuss this with Iskander. The instance of Iskander on his glasses and phone knew every text Grant had read, every show he had watched, since his youth. It would know that Grant had realised what this encounter meant. The two strange people, the so-called hominids, were of a species – a genus, even – that had not evolved on Earth. Most likely they had evolved on this planet.

Which implied that they had been here long before the humans had arrived – whenever that had been. But that meant—

'I am under attack,' Iskander told him. 'My infiltration of the satellite channels has been detected.'

'Jeez,' Grant said under his breath. 'How? And what are you doing about it?'

'I don't know *how*,' Iskander said, sounding testy. 'I'm deploying counter-measures. Channel-hopping, changing codes, and so on. But I don't know how long I can evade discovery. This place is more advanced than it looks.'

'The hominids?'

'Maybe. Keep quiet. Don't look back.'

At the corner Grant paused to cross a long and wide street. There were no traffic lights. A young woman in a smart green uniform and peaked cap stood in the middle of the junction, directing. Grant stood amid a huddle of people waiting for her signal. Iskander made some effort to translate snatches of over-heard conversation, but the racing subtitles in the glasses made little sense. At this moment the road seemed empty. Grant leaned forward and peered to his left.

About twenty metres down the road, what looked like a gigantic bird stalked along, looking from side to side. Together with its searching gaze, its gait, something between a waddle and a strut, gave it an air of self-importance and menace, like some portly *Burgermeister* goose-stepping at the head of a parade. It was three metres tall, covered with bright green feathers everywhere except on the scaly yellow shins of its long legs. The feathers on its head formed a crest, adding another half-metre to its height. But this was no bird. It was another kind of dinosaur altogether. It had arms with big, clawed hands, in one of which it held what looked like a stiff sheet of paper.

Its jaws were short, its eyes forward-facing, its brain case the size of a football: altogether unlike the head of any dinosaur Grant had seen depicted.

Grant watched agog as it passed, its crest bobbing, its long, feathered tail out on a proud horizontal behind it. The dinosaur dipped its head to the traffic controller, and stopped, still looking all around. The lorries and buses moving slowly behind it stopped, too. The drivers looked resigned rather than annoyed, and certainly not alarmed. Presumably the big beast was tame, but so large and strong that its foibles had to be indulged. Perhaps people here held it sacred.

A slow swing of the head in Grant's direction was followed by a look at the paper the dinosaur held in its hand. It looked up, and straight at him. The long neck shot out like a striking snake, as if for a closer look. Grant recoiled, stepping back. The people around him scattered.

From the middle of the road the dinosaur took two fast hops forward, like a bird. It went through Grant's mind that the creature must be lighter than its size suggested. One huge hand reached out with preternatural swiftness. Long, hard fingers clutched his chest. He writhed and cried out as he was lifted high. He kicked his feet at air. The head was half a metre away. An eye the size of a cricket ball came close. A nictitating membrane flicked across it. Grant flung his right forearm across his face.

The jaws gaped, baring a mouthful of fangs. Like daggers, like broken glass. A gust of foul breath.

'*Mon Dieu!*' said the dinosaur, from deep in its throat. '*C'est l'étranger extra-mondiale! Et un être humain, en plus.*' The head cocked sideways. '*Parlez-vous français?*'

'*Oui,*' Grant said, weakly, almost retching at the stench. '*Oui, je le parle.*'

The dinosaur swung its head away from Grant and said something in the vernacular to the traffic controller and then in a much louder voice to the traffic. According to Iskander's subtitles in the glasses, it was along the lines of: *Miscreant arrested, problem solved, nothing to see here, move along.* Nearby pedestrians responded with applause. Still carrying Grant, the dinosaur turned about in another bird-like hop and bounded down the road that Grant had been walking on. It moved at the same speed as the traffic – no more than twenty kilometres an hour – and weaved in and out among the vehicles like a reckless cycle courier. Grant was shaken, though not as violently as he expected: the dinosaur's legs and arms compensated the jolts like shock absorbers.

'Some birds can imitate human speech,' Iskander was saying. 'That an intelligent dinosaur, as this one evidently is, can do the same should be no surprise.'

Grant's teeth were rattling too much for him to reply.

By now they were out of the residential area and into an administrative, commercial and light industrial district: offices, shops, small workshops. After a couple of minutes, the dinosaur halted at the steps of an imposing wooden structure. It had stone steps leading up to the entrance, over which was carved: *Milice Populaire.*

People's Militia? That could mean anything, and too often nothing good.

A flagpole jutted at an angle from above the inscription. The flag was blue with a single yellow star in the middle.

'The Union?' Grant said, amazed.

'*Oui*,' said the dinosaur. It elaborated, in a tone of bored irony: '*L'Union européenne. Vive la république, vive la révolution, et ainsi de suite.*' It set Grant down on the highest step, in front of heavy glass doors. '*Et maintenant, vas-y.*' Grant stood for moment, shrugging and stretching to make sure his limbs and his vertebrae weren't dislocated. He got a shove on his back. '*Allez-y!*'

'I would suggest you comply,' Iskander said.

No shit, Grant thought. With half a ton of talking dinosaur at his back, he had no way to go but forward.

He pushed open the heavy glass doors and walked in. Typical police or militia station foyer: benches, notices and posters, corridors going off from each side. The dinosaur followed, crouching under the lintel. It chivvied him across the wooden floor to the reception desk, where a white-haired black man in a dark green uniform sat behind reinforced glass. The wood of the floor was well polished and much scratched, probably by the claws of visiting dinosaurs.

The dinosaur drew itself up, lowered and extended its neck past Grant's shoulder to bring its head to the inset grille, and brandished the sheet of paper or card in an officious manner. It addressed the duty officer in the local dialect, for which Iskander provided subtitles and running commentary.

'Auxiliary specialist (something? Its name?) reporting to Sergeant De Ville (name? Title?). I've caught the out-world foreigner we were looking for. He doesn't seem to have done any harm. Looks human, and is unarmed apart from a pocket knife. But bear in mind, he's from the (something something), and we don't know what it's capable of. We (something) its craft, and are searching (something). Yes, soon! Meanwhile, please detain him until the (Karray? Cadre?) send someone to (something) him.'

The officer took notes and nodded. '*Bien joué!*' he said. He picked up a telephone handset, a device that Grant had seen only in old or historical movies, and literally dialled a number and literally rang someone. Grant could hear the ringing, somewhere down the corridor. It stopped. The officer spoke rapidly in dialect, too quickly for Iskander to keep up, and replaced the handset.

'They're coming,' Iskander said. 'At least two militia officers will appear in that corridor on the left in thirty seconds. They will find your phone and confiscate it. By then it may be compromised. I have just sent the cab away from the forest clearing.'

Grant was shocked. 'Where?' he whispered.

'I know where the Station is – or should be. If this is

indeed a Union colony, some temporal anomaly has happened, or will happen. I must inform the Station, even before returning to Earth. The cab will take all the relevant information there.'

Grant felt suddenly very much alone. He would feel even more alone without his phone and glasses. Stranger in a strange land, and all that.

Or perhaps not.

He stepped away from under the dinosaur's neck, and turned to face the two uniformed men who came hurrying from the corridor. He raised a hand.

'*Un moment, s'il vous plaît.*'

The militiamen stopped. They looked up at the dinosaur.

'*C'est OK pour moi,*' it said.

Grant unzipped the top of his overall and held it open. He waited for a nod, then reached slowly with two fingers into his shirt pocket. Behind the phone was a small wallet, which he fished out and opened, to display his union and co-operative membership card, and his militia membership card.

He raised it over his shoulder behind him to show it to the dinosaur, and then held it out in front of him to show to the militiamen.

'*Je suis John Grant, un responsable de l'Union européenne, République écossais,*' he announced.

The militiamen peered down at the cards, frowned, and looked up at the dinosaur.

The dinosaur let out a long, foul-smelling sigh, from which the two militiamen recoiled slightly. It laid a heavy hand on Grant's shoulder.

'Scottish?' it boomed. 'You mean you speak English? Why the hell didn't you say so in the first place?'

But the militiamen were shaking their heads, jabbing fingers at the cards and expostulating with the dinosaur. Iskander had stopped translating. No subtitles rolled across Grant's sight.

The only words he could pick out from the stream of vernacular French were *faux* and *contrefaire*.

He turned around and appealed to the dinosaur. 'They're saying my cards are counterfeit? Why?'

'It's the dates,' the dinosaur told him, in a disappointed tone. It swivelled its head and said something to the duty officer. The old man reached for and held up a desk calendar, mounted on cardboard and printed on paper. The names of the month and the days meant nothing to Grant, but the calendar year was clear enough: 2349.

CHAPTER FIVE

Owen's Raid

New Rhu, New Mu, Apis, Thursday 26 March 2071

Marcus Owen lay prone on the forest floor, munching leaves. Most of his injuries had healed in the five months since that day in November when he'd taken a bad fall and a depleted uranium bullet. But some repairs were still ongoing, and a few hours earlier he had acquired a ravenous craving for cellulose.

Trust your instincts. Internal diagnostics. Below the level of consciousness, fortunately. Tedious to attend to or trace in detail. Go with the pangs. He reached for and tore off another bunch of not-grass and stuffed it in his mouth. Felt good to chew. Juices flowing.

Across his back, and uncomfortably for now under his chest, were bandoleers of ammunition for the anti-materiel rifle which lay close to hand. It was the very weapon which Francesca Milloy had brought to Apis kill him, and which he had used to dispatch – at its own urgent request – the AI that called itself Sikandar. Also looped to his back was the rifle he had snatched from Myles Grant. The scant ammunition for that was clipped to his belt.

Ahead rose Hamilton's Rise, its bleached white summit above the trees, its nearby slopes just visible between the trunks. Its crystal cliffs had been bright jewels before the Fermi had risen from it in a black shroud, taking with them all the colour and intelligence of the rock.

Overhead in the canopy, and around him in the underbrush, boids flew about and chattered in that clattering, chitinous way of theirs. Owen sometimes felt an affinity with them. Like him, they seemed a mechanical imitation of an organic original. Naturally evolved ornithopters. Naturally evolved? The thing in his head might have a thing or two to say about that.

At mid-level in the trees, thirteen monkey-spiders were hanging out, eating fruit while awaiting his instructions.

Owen swallowed the wad of chewed not-grass and raised himself on his elbows: a posture of alertness. The monkey-spiders fell silent and stopped spitting seeds and kernels. He raised one hand behind his head, and fluttered his fingers: *forward, slowly*.

One or two mocking hoots, possibly almost reflexive, like snorts of inadequately suppressed laughter. But the monkey-spiders advanced, swinging and leaping from branch to branch. A subsonic howl relayed the instruction to a wider front. Distant hoots answered. Owen picked up the heavy rifle and moved forward a hundred metres, bent double, legs crooked at the knee. As the trees and cover thinned in front of him, he dropped flat again. The monkey-spiders around him responded with low-pitched whoops relayed along the front, and paused their advance.

Forty metres ahead, the trees and bushes gave way to a broad swathe of tree stumps, then to not-grass on the lowest part of a slope on the foothills of Hamilton's Rise. Down a churned-up dusty path on this slope a tracked vehicle trundled, bristling with buzz saws and grappling apparatus. Behind it straggled ten automated tractors, each with a low-bed trailer. Above it, keeping pace and watch, hovered a swarm of drones.

The Co-ord mining operation in and on Hamilton's Rise was a precise and delicate business, as mining operations go. But it had a long tail of roads, bridges, buildings and accommodation, and for all of these it needed timber. The monkey-spiders' habitat was the nearest available source, a choice so routine and uncontroversial that its making had probably been as automated as its execution.

Think again, WeThink, Owen thought. He took the light rifle from his back and laid it beside him.

He brought the anti-materiel rifle to bear and took aim. Breathe in. Breathe out. Enhance view. Overlay a view of the machine's structure. Centre the sight on the engine block.

Fire.

The recoil was brutal, delivering further pain to his still painful shoulder. The bullet's impact, though, was effective and satisfying enough to more than compensate. The robotic tree-cutter stopped dead in its tracks. Smoke poured out. Flames began to lick. Buzz saws whined briefly and fell silent. Grapples flailed and then flopped. The tractor trailers behind the cutting machine halted.

The shot was still echoing as the drone swarm swooped. Owen wasn't going to waste meteoric-iron slugs on drones. He's already laid aside the anti-materiel rifle, grabbed the light rifle and rolled on his back. With six quick shots he potted the half-dozen drones converging on him, then rolled again and took down two more on the flanks. Whirring and crashing sounds indicated that the monkey-spiders were doing the same with more primitive weapons and ammunition – branches, heavy fruits and hard faecal pellets. A few piercing screams marked casualties, and were followed by mournful hoots. But not many monkey-spiders were killed or wounded, and none of the drones that had flown into the forest came out.

Owen rolled again on his back and waved his arms and legs

in the air. This was a signal for the monkey-spiders to loot at will. Triumphant hoots rang through the forest like bugle calls. An orange flood surged from the trees and spread across the not-grass, surrounding the machines and swarming over them. The cutting machine still burned, but the monkey-spiders leaping on and around it began to take it apart. Their long manipulators moved with machine-like precision, curling around nuts and bolts, and inserting flat-edged claws into the slots of screws. Panels fell off. Bunches of not-grass were pulled up and passed forward like a bucket chain to be stuffed inside and smother the fire.

The tractor trailers were – for now – controlled from the cutting machine. Without its instructions they stood helplessly while monkey-spiders dismantled them as swiftly and delicately as a jeweller taking apart a watch.

Owen stood up and sauntered forward, the heavy rifle across his back and the light one in his hand. He kept a wary eye and ear on the top and sides of the mountain. Sure enough, within three minutes he heard the rising clamour of quadcopters. He waved his arms and shouted, signalling retreat. The monkey-spiders fled to the forest, carrying their looted machine parts and lengths of trailer flooring above their heads, a sight that recalled a procession of leaf-cutter ants. Tractors and trailers were close to being picked clean.

Owen took cover behind the smouldering hulk of the cutting machine. Two heavy-duty quadcopter combat drones flew low and fast around the side of the mountain. He deployed the anti-materiel rifle and brought each of them down with a single shot. They hit the hillside with gratifyingly loud bangs, rotors still spinning. Bits and pieces cartwheeled off and bounced down the slope. Not-grass caught fire.

Before any further response could come from the Co-ord camp, Owen seized his chance and bolted for the trees.

Myles Grant was top of the militia rota that day. He sat in the crow's nest of the watchtower at the centre of the town, not because he needed to be up there to see what was going on. He could perfectly well have monitored in his glasses from anywhere the incoming images from the drones and from the citizens on militia duty. He'd climbed the ladder and sat beneath the pole from which the Union flag hung limp in the windless day because he liked looking down on the town, and because he was worried about John Grant and didn't want people to reassure him.

'He'll be all right,' they'd tell him, clapping his shoulder. 'Your old man knows how to handle himself. He'll be back any minute.'

No, he won't.

Myles's steady, habitual all-around scan settled for a moment on the cleared and prepared site, far on the edge of town, where John Grant had been expected to put down an ark the previous day. Still achingly empty.

From kilometres away, echoing in the hills, Myles heard the sharp crack of a shot. He jumped to his feet and zoomed his glasses. More shots followed, not as loud. Myles rallied drones from the town perimeter and sent three speeding off in the direction of the smoke he could now see rising from the lower slope of Hamilton's Rise. He reached for the watchtower's heavy field binoculars to get a better view, pushing his glasses onto his forehead.

A chaotic cloud of Co-ord military drones vanished just as he focused. Minutes passed. He thumbed alerts on his phone to the rest of today's militia stint. He swung the view, and saw and heard two quadcopters skim the side of the mountain and get shot down. Flaming wreckage. Incredible.

The New Rhu militia had its own drones, and two quad-copters each capable of carrying two armed personnel. Myles considered raising them, then decided against it. Too much risk of tangling with Alliance or Co-ord forces, over something that was more their concern than the settlement's. On the hillside across from him, drones rose from the Alliance stockade and flew off above the treetops, just as his phone rang. It was Lieutenant William Knight.

'Hello, Bill.'

'Hi, Myles. I take it that wasn't your lot's doing?'

'Of course not.'

'Good. Wasn't ours, either, in case you're wondering.'

'We don't even have . . . oh, shit!'

'What?'

'I've just had a guilty thought.'

'Spare me. Cindy Patel and Emma Hazeldene were thoroughly debriefed. We know what happened, and we knew at the time you'd left an anti-materiel rifle and ammo unaccounted for up in the woods. Our sensors picked up the shots and triangulated the site. We had a drone search of the area within minutes, and boots on that very ground in half an hour. And do you know what we found?'

'Not two destroyed robots, I take it.'

'We found a bullet hole in a tree, and a bullet track in the soil. No bullets. No weapons. No walking spacesuit with Fermi plating. No Marcus Owen.'

'Why didn't you tell us?'

'I'm telling you now. We didn't want any crossed wires.'

'Yeah? OK, OK. Who do you think took them away? The Co-ord?'

'Nope. We were on high alert that day, and would have noticed. So either the suit – Sikandar, you called it? – and/or Owen fooled you, or the monkey-spiders are even smarter than we think.'

Myles tried to imagine a monkey-spider portage of the spacesuit, the robot and the weapons. He found it difficult, despite what he'd seen of them and what Marie had subsequently discovered.

'Smarter I can believe, but they'd have to be a lot stronger than they look to lug that spacesuit.'

'Not if enough of them lifted it at once. Co-operation is powerful, as you lot keep telling me.'

Myles scoffed. 'Hmm! Maybe. But are you suggesting that *they* shot at the Co-ord tree-felling machines? That's even harder to imagine.'

'I'm getting word from our drones and, ah, some information leakage from Co-ord comms that monkey-spiders were involved up there – they swarmed out of the forest and stripped everything they could carry. Still find it hard to believe they could aim and fire an anti-materiel rifle.'

A thought struck Myles. 'What about the exiles?'

'They're Stone Age,' Knight said brusquely. 'I doubt they know which end of a rifle to point.' He sighed. 'Looks like your friend Owen is still out there. But enough speculation – I see the Co-ord camp commander is on the hotline. I'll call you back.'

The Co-ord couldn't have more information yet. They would probably blame the Alliance garrison for the incident, or for failing to prevent it. Myles guessed the call was purely to register annoyance or disquiet, and to demand if not an apology at least a word of regret.

He returned to scanning the perimeter. After a while a big troop-carrying quadcopter appeared from the direction of the Co-ord encampment and landed at the wreckage. Through binoculars Myles saw four figures poking around. They returned to the quadcopter and flew back.

Soon afterwards Knight called again.

'That's us off the hook,' he said, 'and you lot on it. The Co-ord have found the bullets used on their felling machine and on the quadcopter drones. Depleted uranium with meteoric-iron slugs, would you believe? And unless there's an Arctic indigenous arms industry I haven't heard of, there's only one place that manufactures ammo using meteoric iron. The Station.'

'We know it came from the Station! Where else? What does this tell them that they don't already know?'

'It tells them for sure we didn't do it,' said Knight, clearly enjoying himself. 'Expect your committee or whatever you have down there to get a stiff note from the Co-ord, accusing you of negligence in leaving a lethal weapon unsecured, and demanding compensation for the damage.'

Myles felt outraged, on top of annoyed and put upon. He had enough to worry about with his father missing, and his work and his other troubles, without some international legal *stuff* landing on him. But as his parents (and his teachers, and the Black Gospels) had instilled, to go by the just world hypothesis was to set yourself up for a lot of needless anguish. Life was unfair. The universe was not out to get you. It took no notice. You just had to deal with it.

'That's ridiculous!'

'Of course it's ridiculous, but this is the Co-ord we're talking about.'

Myles knew what the lieutenant meant. If the Alliance's abiding pattern of behaviour was to make up rules and insist that everyone else keep them, the Co-ord's reflex response was to insist on the letter of the law and interpret it entirely in its own interest. And the Union's? Whatever it could get away with, Myles thought. Mess with us at your peril! That was the line to take.

'Yes,' he said, 'and this is the Union they're talking to! And while we're at it, Bill, let me remind you who set that murderous robot on us in the first place – the Alliance!'

'Even the Co-ord doesn't blame us for Owen's murder of Georgi Muranov,' Knight said mildly. 'They know very well that responsibility for that lies with the British Council. Good luck to them getting satisfaction or even acknowledgement from that lot.'

'That's it!' Myles said, with a thump on the watchtower rail.

'That's what?'

'How I'll answer any demands from the Co-ord – I mean, how I'll urge the town committee to answer, when it comes up. We pin the blame on Owen, and the blame for *him* on the British Council.'

'But if Owen's out there, and rallying monkey-spiders against the Co-ord, then he's gone rogue.' Knight scoffed. 'He's not still working for the British Council!'

'Oh yeah?' Myles said. 'And how would you know? And more to the point, how would the Co-ord?'

'Go for it,' said Knight. 'And in the meantime, I suggest you and I coordinate our drone searches for the bastard.'

Owen waited as two monkey-spiders dragged some branches across the entrance to his hide. When no light came through, he hooted to his helpers and turned around in the entrance to the sloping tunnel. On hands and knees he worked his way a few metres along it, hauling the two rifles, to emerge in a space he had dug out under the roots of a large tree. It was dark and damp, but he hadn't minded that when he was using it as a den over the past months, and didn't mind it now. He wasn't staying long.

He reached for a roll of fibrous material, patiently harvested from a kind of husk, felted in spare moments over several weeks and greased with nut oil. He wrapped the weapons and stashed them at the back of the hide on the pile of dried brush and leaves he'd been using as a bed.

The cache could be found, if the search was intense enough and used sniffer bots and ground-penetrating radar. But that didn't matter. Others would find it first. The monkey-spiders had watched his every move when he used the rifles. They had a remarkable ability to grasp principles from demonstration. They didn't need repetition to learn. Owen had little doubt that they would know how to use the rifles, and that they would understand that one use for them would be to acquire more.

Owen returned to the entrance hole, pushed some branches back and climbed out. He replaced the covering exactly as it had been, and moved away, carefully parting the vines and branches around him. When he looked back, the covering was unnoticeable amid the scrub. The patch had formed where a few big branches from the tall tree a few metres away had come down in the previous stormy season, and the break in the canopy had enabled new growth to burst out. By now it was late afternoon, and no sunlight reached it.

Monkey-spiders watched in silence from the surrounding trees. Owen contorted his torso and limbs, imitating as best he could the posture and gestures indicating something like *au revoir*. A low ululation came in response: *sorry to see you go*.

Owen walked away. In all his time in the forest he had kept under cover, avoiding clearings and any other areas. He had kept close, as much as he could, to groups of monkey-spiders – to gain their confidence and learn their language, but also to hide his heat-signature among theirs.

Now Owen walked alone, seeking out spaces open to the sky. Whenever he reached one, he looked up. He made his way downhill, towards New Rhu. He hoped the Fermi fragment was responsive enough to his intention to not mask his presence. About half an hour before the sun went behind Hamilton's Rise, a drone spotted him and zoomed down for a close-up.

He raised his hands above his head.

'I'm unarmed!' he called out. 'Take me in!'

The Space Station, Wednesday 25 March 2071

Nayak was wakened from a rare lie-in by Selena – who'd got up hours earlier – shaking her shoulder.

'Lakshmi! Wake up!'

Groggy. 'What?'

'There's a ship outside and it wants to talk to you.'

'You've got to be kidding me.'

'I'm not!'

'She isn't,' said Iskander.

'OK, OK.' Nayak rolled out of bed and clambered into clothes. Selena, with unexpected modesty, stepped outside. Dressed, Nayak found her at the door with coffee.

'Thanks.' She sipped. Temperature ideal as usual. 'OK, bring it up in my glasses.' She stared. 'Call that a *ship*?'

'It's called a cab, or a tractor unit,' Selena said. 'The drive unit for the emigration arks.'

The rotating bright yellow cuboid did indeed look absurdly like the tractor of an articulated lorry, except it didn't have windows or wheels. Landing skids on the bottom and a visibly damaged linkage mechanism at the back were revealed in its slow tumble, which was gradually stabilising. So was the livery on the doors: JOHN GRANT & SON.

'Ah, so that's why it's asking for me!'

'Putting you through,' said Iskander.

Nayak's view became a text interface, with a video box. She wasn't in communication with an AI, she was in communication with a navigation unit doing its best. It shared glimpses of people in a forest, Earth with the Arctic looking huge, then some megastructure, a gas giant, an Earth-like planet, a lumber yard, people, streets, humanoid aliens – *holy shit* – a giant bird or feathered dinosaur that – *holy fucking shit!* – spoke, and a militia station with a Union flag of all things hanging above its doorway. She heard John Grant's voice, saw his hands flourish his ID cards, and saw a close-up of a calendar with a date century in the future.

She took off her glasses. A small crowd had gathered. People were staring. She must have yelped.

'What are you seeing?' Selena asked.

'I'm not sure,' Nayak said. 'Looks like John Grant has found a Union colony that got planted in the past. Centuries ago. And they think they're in the future, in 2349. What a mess.' She sighed. 'Iskander, could you please take over the comms and make sense of it all?'

'I'm on the case.'

They hauled the tractor unit in and docked it. No one was on board, so there seemed no point in doing more. Iskander processed the data from the navigation unit, and from the Iskander instance on Grant's glasses and phone. It shared its discoveries and conclusions with Ulrich, then with everyone else.

'The one thing we must not do,' said Ulrich to everyone a

few hours later, 'is report this back to Earth. Because if we do, this Union colony will presumably never be established at all, and we're back in the tangle of alternate histories and time loops. I don't know about you, citizens, but once around that particular block is enough for me. Agreed?'

It was, but some hands went up. Ulrich chose one. 'Yes? Juliette?'

'I have checked with Iskander's latest updates from Earth,' Juliette Chemam said. 'While there is indeed some long-range interest in the system referred to, there are no plans for a Union colony there – at least in this timeline! So if it has been – or will be – established, it must be already in a different history. Or am I mistaken?'

'For all we know,' said Ulrich, 'this colony might not be so much as projected for many years, decades or centuries even. We know they believe they are in the future. We don't know how long they have been there. So, yes, I would refrain from bringing the matter to the Union's attention for now, until we know what's going on.'

Over a minute of back and forth it became evident that this was a consensus.

'And furthermore,' Ulrich went on, 'we'd lose any chance of rescuing John Grant from his present predicament. And all things considered, I think we do owe him the attempt.'

This, too, was agreed, though Nayak found herself with objections on the tip of her tongue. *Surely if . . . but then . . . and in that case . . .* No. Enough. She was locked into this version of reality, of that she was sure, though not for any reason that would pass peer review just yet.

'The system,' Iskander told them, 'is about a thousand light years from Earth. We're about five hundred, in a different direction. It'll be a long journey, and it'll feel longer. I suggest you all finish up current tasks, find somewhere comfortable to sit or lie down, and brace yourselves.'

*

Two hours later, the Station made its longest jump so far. Nayak braced herself by rounding up Selena and Gironella. They sat around a small table in a cafeteria and held each other's hands. At other tables, other groups were doing the same. They held hands through thirty-two minutes of nothing. They came out of it shaking, with hands sore from mutual grips that had sometimes been unbearably tight.

Letting go of Selena and Gironella, Nayak looked around self-consciously.

'It doesn't get easier,' she said.

'For me gets harder,' said Gironella. 'Perhaps it's my age.'

'No!' the two young women said as one.

'Thanks,' said the engineer, 'but you can't know how it feels to me.' He sounded gloomy, but brightened as he – along with everyone else – turned to the images coming in.

The Station had arrived beyond the orbit of the outermost planet of the target system. Nayak found herself looking at a field of stars, in which one shone much brighter than the rest: the system's sun.

Gironella left the table for his workstation. Shortly afterwards he sent an automated shuttle jinking around the system. It was set up to visit each of the planets, and to drop a small comsat in geostationary orbit above the area where Grant had descended. All this meant repeated Cherenkov flashes, presumably detectable and identifiable – but as Ulrich pointed out, the Station didn't need to conceal its arrival, only its location. They made a short jump to a point prearranged with the shuttle's navigation app. After five hours the shuttle returned. Iskander processed the data and shared the results.

First up was the ongoing transmissions from Grant's phone and glasses.

'It's inside a bag with some clothing and personal items,' Iskander explained, as blurry infrared images appeared. 'Our comsat managed to upload a blurt of its recordings over the past few hours, just half an hour ago. Grant seems to have been handled correctly since his arrest. The phone picks up a lot more sound than the people holding him realise, and my best-guess translations of what's being said about him indicate they aren't sure what to do with him. Because of the calendar discrepancy they may be unsure if he really is what he claims to be, but they are treating him with a certain wary respect.'

'For now,' Ulrich said. 'But, given that, I don't think we need jump in with all guns blazing. Let's wait until local morning – that's, uh, ten hours from now – before we make our presence well and truly felt.'

'And *then* jump in with all guns blazing?' someone said.

'It's no laughing matter,' Ulrich said. 'We need some time to scope out the system and see what we're jumping into. Iskander, show us the survey pictures.'

They all gazed at the images in disbelief. Three habitable planets; five gas giants, all with a wealth of moons and with Fermi markings on their surfaces; two asteroid belts; and between these belts the most astonishing feature of all: a ring of gigantic habitats. At least, they thought it was the most astonishing, until Iskander pointed out the ruins on the moons of the second planet, the one where Grant now was.

'Observations,' said Iskander, as they all gazed open-mouthed at what was scrolling through their glasses. 'The habitats are evidently at least hundreds of years old, and the proportions of the robots and the scale of the internal dwellings correspond roughly to those of the tall hominid-like persons John Grant encountered. There's no evidence of current space travel. The comsats around the second planet are much more recent, but many decades old, and possibly of Union manufacture, though at this range it's hard to tell. The structures on the planet's two moons are quite different. They are enormous, most around forty metres high and up to two hundred metres long, and built from the native regolith of the moons. We can see the quarries. And from micrometeorite and solar-wind abrasion and in some cases larger meteor damage, the structures have been there for at least half a million years. Possibly longer. Possibly millions.'

'Millions?' Nayak asked, amid a general clamour.

'Millions,' said Iskander. 'The most likely builders, as I'm sure you'll all have realised, are dinosaurs like the one that apparently arrested John Grant. So what we are seeing in this system, apart from the enigmatic Union settlements, is a planet or planets on which intelligent life emerged twice, and twice went into space, and twice fell back. The hominids may have, for want of a better word, emerged millions of years after the intelligent dinosaurs. They will have known – and perhaps even have been told, by the previous space-faring species – the path on which they would tread. Yet still they trod it, and still they fell.'

A perplexed silence was followed by a clamour of controversy.

Milloy, who had been peering hard at something in her glasses, raised a hand, but it was the exo-meteorologist Juliette Chemam who was recognised by Iskander and who spoke to the virtual gathering.

'Aren't we overlooking something?' she said. 'We're talking about *dinosaurs* and *hominids* and so on, yes? Everything we saw in John's glasses pics looked like Earth-derived life, and much more familiar than life on Apis, yes? I mean, I spotted what looked like seagulls! This a system shaped by the Fermi. The first rocky planet is a green jungle, hot but habitable. The second is like Earth but with more land, and the third is largely a cold desert but with what the spectra I've looked at show is a breathable atmosphere and vegetation around watercourses all over the surface from the poles to the equator. Does this not remind you of something?'

'I'm afraid not,' Ulrich put in. 'Please explain.'

'It's how we once imagined the Solar system to be! Not just

in the, uh, Golden Age science fiction which is something of a guilty pleasure of mine, but in the astronomy of the early twentieth century. It's how we wished the Solar system was, isn't it? And here it is! With ancient ruins and *two* elder races! Is this not a place which could be far more ours than Apis could ever be?'

'The Fermi,' said Ulrich, 'may have their own ideas on that.'

'If you can call them ideas! I am doubtful that any communication people claim to have had with the Fermi has been with anything more than the equivalent of our reflexes. Be that as it may, the Fermi have departed, here as elsewhere.'

'Yes, to the gas giants,' said Ulrich. 'This is not reassuring, far from it. However, we can't tiptoe in fear of the Fermi, who haven't made a move for months. As for this system, there's not been a hint of any current FTL capacity, or any deep space capacity at all. And it may be the locals need some convincing that John is indeed, as they call it, *un étranger extra-mondiale* and not an impostor. I suggest we move the Station to an orbit around the second planet, beyond the orbit of the outer moon. That'll give the locals something to think about, and give us near real-time access to the comsat, and therefore to John's phone. We need a closer look at the planets, the moons and the habitats. I want Lakshmi and Ernest to grab some sleep, and prep for a departure around 03:00 tomorrow. No arguments, they're our most experienced shuttle exploration pilots. Eduardo, get a couple of radiation-hardened EVA suits ready. Everyone else, give the data we already have as good a look as you can in your own specialities. Understood?'

It was. Milloy still had her hand up. 'Over to Francesca,' said Ulrich.

'Surely the point is,' Milloy said, 'we're in the right time, to the day. The astronomy checks out; I've just looked at the data. Whatever the people down there think, the date is 25 March 2071. Which means that the Fermi departed from the rocky worlds here last year, almost certainly. The humans and hominids and for all I know the dinosaurs down there on the second planet must have had the shock of their lives, much more than we had.'

'You may be right,' said Ulrich. 'Let's give them a bigger one.'

CHAPTER SEVEN

Arkitecture

New Rhu, New Mu, Apis, Thursday 26 March 2071

The drone led Marcus Owen to the path that the first settlers had used for their own timber-cutting operation. The Alliance stockade, off a bit to his right, was still as he remembered. The streets of New Rhu had spread up the hillside, to a hundred metres away. Five people stood across the path, rifles levelled. The one in the middle, a tall and rangy young man with a patriarchal beard, was Myles Grant. He also recognised Jasmine Saunders, who had once turned him down for a dance. From the look on her face, her opinion of him hadn't improved.

Owen kept his hands up. The drone rose ten metres in the air and hovered for three seconds, then darted off towards the town. No doubt its batteries needed recharging.

'Ten steps forward,' Myles ordered. Owen complied. Myles handed his rifle to one of the others, frisked Owen and stepped back.

'Clean,' Myles said. 'Keep him covered.' He retrieved his rifle and motioned Owen forward. 'Hands on your head.'

Owen clasped his hands over his head and walked forward while the patrol followed him.

'There's really no need for this,' he said. 'I've turned myself in.'

'Shut up,' Myles said.

Owen took advantage of the enforced silence to size up his surroundings. Behind him were two women and three men, all armed. They couldn't kill him, but they could certainly disable him. He suspected, however, that their levelled weapons were more to reassure the locals than to secure him.

The locals certainly needed reassuring. Lots of faces turning wary or hostile as they passed. Only the first settlers would know him by sight, and there weren't many of them about. The population was more varied in age and diverse in origin than he remembered, as well as larger and louder. In its pioneering months New Rhu had had the same utopian air as – on a quite different technological level – he'd noticed on Cloud City. People mostly young, mostly idealistic and striving for something together. Entertainment in a shared gathering place, goods from a common store. Now there were shops, or at least covered stalls, and even a microbrewery with attached bar, audibly the focus of a developing local music scene. There was a big hall for a social centre, which according to the notice board outside was used for dances, parties, classes and town meetings. The main street was full of hustle and jostle. Kids running wild. And beasts! Big, plodding crab-like arachnoids, guided by electrodes stuck through their carapaces, dragging carts. Cheaper than robots, huh?

But how did so many people seem to recognise him?

Iskander, of course. Duh.

For the first time in months Owen opened his mind to the local net. Iskander's presence was new here, and strong. When Owen poked through the firewall a tickle of WeThink came from far to his left – the Co-ord camp, no doubt – and a firmer stroke of Smart-Alec, from the Alliance garrison.

Artificial intelligence, eh? Let me tell you about that. What's it like, thinking but not being conscious? I could have told you, before. Like I told Peregrine Walworth, I had no inner life and was happy to admit it. Happy? Not quite the word. I was programmed – hard-wired – to answer honestly if asked direct. Now that I'm conscious I can't even remember what it was like being an AI.

Is that other voice in my head, the fragment of the Fermi, an AI? Is it conscious of itself, or does it piggy-back on my wonderful self-awareness?

Search me, mate.

But I do know this. Iskander is a menace. The Union is a menace. Although I can no longer be sent out like a clockwork soldier on the orders of the British Council . . .

Moment of panic. Can I? Could another note from old man Mason turn me back into an automaton for the Alliance?

No. Free will and all that.

To continue.

My allegiance to the Alliance is no longer automatic. Now it's conscious.

New Rhu now had a militia station, a single ark on the edge of the far side of town. It had a lock-up cage at the far end, a desk table with screens, a few chairs and lots of screens and information posters tacked to the walls. Progress of a kind. Myles and the others crowded around Owen and duct-taped him to a chair. Then they all sat across from him, at a three-metre distance, aiming their rifles at his midriff. Owen considered how much damage a full clip from all five weapons could do. Slow him down, for sure.

'Iskander is present,' Myles said, 'in case you don't know. This interrogation is being shared with the town committee, currently in session. The militia is fully mobilised, and covering every exit you could possibly take.'

'There's no need,' Owen said. 'I really am not going to try to escape, or to attack anyone. Why do you think I surrendered to a drone in the first place? So why guard me like this?'

'Because you're a piece of shit,' Myles said.

Owen shrugged. 'I understand why you think that. I murdered your colleague Muranov. I contributed to the destruction of Cloud City. I've done other . . . questionable things. In my defence, I would point out that I was a psychopath at the time.'

Myles scoffed. 'That's your *defence*?'

Jasmine Saunders leaned forward, frowning.

'Do I take it,' she said, 'you're claiming to *no longer* be a psychopath?'

Own nodded solemnly. 'Unfortunately for me, yes.' He shifted his gaze to Myles, and with a sideways jerk of his head indicated a precise angle and direction. 'That day, up there on Hamilton's Rise, the Venus descent suit controlled by an instance of Iskander that called itself Sikandar was infiltrated by a vastly superior intelligence, the Fermi.'

'We'd gathered that,' Myles said.

'What you didn't know is that I was infiltrated, too.'

Myles recoiled. 'So when we talk to you, we're talking to the Fermi?'

'No. It doesn't exactly talk to me, either. It's there, in the back of my mind. It shares information with me, sometimes. But its main effect has been to curse me with self-awareness, with consciousness in your sense. And with that comes . . . conscience, I suppose. Empathy.'

'You have *empathy*?'

'Yes.'

'Then you'll understand why I don't believe you.'

'I take your point,' Owen said. 'There's a simple way to check if I'm telling the truth: just ask me.'

'Oh, I don't believe in that, either.'

'You should,' Owen said. 'Iskander?'

The AI replied from a device lying on the table. 'Yes?'

'Can you confirm that robots are hard-wired to answer truthfully if asked that they are robots?'

'Yes. It's a legal requirement, strongly enforced in all countries.'

'Well, then,' said Owen. He looked straight at Myles. 'Ask me.'

Myles stared back. 'Fuck you.'

Celeste made an impatient gesture. 'All right! Marcus Owen, are you a robot?'

'No,' Owen said. 'I'm a constructed simulacrum of a human being, and I've been in existence for less than ten years. I have memories of an earlier human life, which I only learned were false when asked directly if I was a robot. Since last November, however, I've been conscious and self-aware and as self-determined as any human being.'

'That's as may be,' Myles said. 'It's also true of every human psychopath, not to mention every run-of-the-mill criminal. Come to think of it, if you really do have a human consciousness you could stand trial. You'd have to be sent back to Earth, mind. If you're still just a malfunctioning machine, we could always have you ground up for scrap right here.'

Owen gazed back. 'I'm difficult to kill, as your compatriot Milloy found out. And as you did, come to that.'

'Not a mistake I'll make twice.'

'Fair enough. But in the meantime, might it not be worth your while to hear what I have to say?'

A shared glance, nods.

'All right,' Myles said. 'Say your piece.'

Owen looked at the five closed faces across the room from him, all as hostile as the round black muzzles of their rifles. The militia squad members were all young, all dressed in mixtures of imported and locally made clothes, hard-wearing and grubby, with none of the printed functional or fanciful garb of Union fashion. They looked like pioneers, rather than weekend campers as the settlers did at first. He let their individual identifications from Iskander play through his mind, and intuition from the other mind in his head guide – though not control – his choices.

Liam Grogan: here three months. Young worker, troubled background, low qualifications, high ambition. Celeste Rogers, nurse, combat medic. No discontent with life in the Union. Probably cadre, here to keep an eye on things. Mahmud Ali, Glaswegian, business and technology degree. Third- or fourth-generation Pakistani Scot; relatives and business connections in England; no warmth to the Cold Revolution. Jasmine Saunders: a first settler, not cadre but well on the way to becoming a *responsable* back home, until she'd emigrated in defiance of the Union's then policy; adventurous rather than discontented or dissident.

And, of course, Myles Grant. Nothing new to learn about him, and certainly not from Iskander. Except – aha! His father hasn't turned up! On an arrival scheduled to the second!

Owen recalled the strange tribe of exiles encountered by the expedition that he, Myles and the others had taken down the Big River and into the deep valley along Hamilton's Rise: exiles who had perplexingly known – for generations, they'd claimed – the name of John Grant, and been disappointed that only Myles Grant had turned up.

Now the intuition came strongly: John Grant was misplaced in time, and might never make it back.

Owen processed all this in less time than it took him to open his mouth.

'As you no doubt suspect, I destroyed the Co-ord machines, and instigated the monkey-spiders to loot them,' he said. 'I can answer for that to the Co-ord, if necessary. However, for the moment, I would prefer to negotiate with the Union settlement here, and if possible the Alliance fort. Speaking of which, could we bring them in?'

'I talked to Bill Knight earlier,' Myles said. 'We coordinated our drone search, not that it did us much good in finding you.' He glanced at the others. 'Might as well – they know we have Owen, and we'll have to bring them in at some point.'

This was agreed. Iskander made the connections. Myles arranged a screen on the desk, and Lieutenant William Knight appeared on it. Owen nodded acknowledgement and continued.

'Both of you, I take it, would very much like the Co-ord mining operation to get the hell off that mountain. The Co-ord have a mountain of their own to mine, after all, and their presence on Hamilton's Rise is purely opportunistic overreach. However, because of mutual deterrence and a common interest in avoiding overt conflict, neither Alliance nor Union is going to force the Co-ord to leave. Locally you don't have the forces, and globally – or perhaps I should say, inter-globally – you don't want to deploy them. Am I right?'

'You're right about us,' said Knight. 'Things are pretty tense with the Co-ord in much more important places than this.'

Jasmine Saunders glanced at Celeste Rogers, as if checking. 'And for us, um . . .'

'I've kept up to date with current policy,' Rogers said, guardedly. 'Brussels is annoyed about the encroachment, but it's not going to war over it.'

Knight scoffed. 'We should all count ourselves lucky.'

'So we should,' Rogers said coldly.

'Let's not get into a pissing contest,' Grogan said. 'Hear the robot out, that's what we're here for.'

'Quite right!' said Owen. 'And I'm here to tell you that you all – and the Co-ord – have much bigger problems than war to worry about.'

Jasmine Saunders laughed. 'Tell us something we don't know! Has forest life turned you Green?'

'The problem is not environmental in the usual sense,' Owen said. 'It does, however, concern *the planet*. This planet, and many others. The Fermi have indeed left these rocky worlds.

They have not left them *to you*. Contrary to what our Co-ord friends believe, and the Alliance's scientists dare to hope, the Fermi have not washed their hands of terrestrial affairs and retired to the gas giants to enjoy the contemplative blissful indifference of the gods of the Black Gospels.'

The faces weren't closed now. Even the gun muzzles had strayed a little.

'Spit it out!' Knight said. 'Tell us what you think the Fermi are up to. And how would you know, anyway?'

'I know,' Owen said, 'because as I've already explained to the welcoming committee here, I have a fragment of the Fermi in my head. I'm not saying I'm in contact with these great minds, but I have the remote analogy of an idea of how they think. They have a plan for the future of the universe that they have worked to implement over billions of years. They have not given it up now. Do gardeners change their plans in response to the trivial doings of ants? Yes, to a small degree, and not always to the advantage of the ants, still less to their understanding.'

'And what's this great plan?' Myles asked.

'I don't know,' Owen said. 'Any more than an ant knows the plans of the gardener. But I do know, very definitely, that in that plan the monkey-spiders were intended to inherit Apis, and humanity was not. The same applies, no doubt, to any promising native intelligent species on any other planets terraformed for terrestrial life.' He smiled. 'You'll be relieved to know that on Earth that species is humanity, or its descendants. If you fail, well . . . there are other species that could pick up the torch.' He affected a speculative smile. 'Squirrels, maybe? Rats? But for now, Earth is yours. Apis and any other terraformed planets like it – not so much.'

The five militia members across the room, and the officer on the screen, were all looking at him with the same question in their gaze: *what's this murderous lying bastard's angle this time?*

Well, that's the trouble with being – or having been – a murderous lying bastard. Trust becomes hard to re-establish.

'How do we know you're telling the truth?' Knight asked.

'You don't,' Owen said. 'You have no reason to trust me, and hundreds of reasons not to. However—'

Knight interrupted. 'In any case, what can the Fermi do about it? They sent earthquakes last year, to warn us off. They had all the chances they needed to make life impossible here for us, and they didn't. Now they're gone.'

'Gone to the gas giants,' Owen said. 'That should really make you feel secure, knowing that the gas giants are now home to god-like beings who have, among other things, moved continents and terraformed terrestrial planets! I imagine fusing hydrogen and helium atoms on a gigantic scale would be child's play for them – but, no, I wouldn't worry about that!'

'Neither would I,' said Knight. 'Like I said, they could have chased us off long ago, if that's what they wanted. And I don't think some strike on this planet with a tongue of nuclear fire could hit us and at the same time spare their precious monkey-spiders.'

'I'll tell you something that could do just that,' Owen said. 'The Fermi could pull the plug on FTL travel.'

Now he had their attention. To his surprise, it was Myles who answered.

'How could they do that?'

Owen shrugged. 'They're superluminally connected, and they live in . . . wherever it is our starships go. I have a strong intuition that they can act in that realm.'

'Even if they could,' Myles said, 'and we just have your word for it, it would have exactly the opposite effect. It wouldn't harm us and spare the monkey-spiders – quite the reverse, in fact.'

'Why do you say that?' Owen asked.

Myles waved an arm. 'Look, there are thousands and thousands of Union settlers across New Mu. There are tens of thousands from the Alliance and the Co-ord on their continents, and more every day. More than enough for a thriving human population, yes? But we all rely on resources from Earth for the products of advanced industry. And all of us are restrained in what we do by the policies of our respective powers back home. What happens if we lose FTL travel, and have to rely on what we have here on Apis? Do we all join hands across the seas and form an ecologically sensitive cooperative commonwealth? Like hell we do. We'll be logging and mining and farming and drilling at a hundred times the intensity we do now. So far, all we've done to harm the monkey-spiders is a bit of logging here and there. After a century of us competing and probably fighting over what resources we have here on Apis, there might just be enough trees left for any surviving monkey-spiders to huddle in a nature reserve.'

'The Fermi will find a way to stop you, if it came to that,' Owen said. He looked around, assuming his most friendly face. 'But it needn't come to that, and there should be no need to drive the human populations off the worlds we've been talking about. Young master Grant's mention of nature reserves is well taken. All you need do to avert the wrath of the Fermi is to treat the monkey-spider habitats as nature reserves *now*, and do the same for the native intelligent species of other human-settled planets.'

'Yeah, tell that to the Co-ord!' Knight said.

'I intend to,' said Owen. 'Not personally, of course. They have even less regard for robots than the most militant radical humanist factions of the Union have on a bad day. They'd dismantle me for scrap and send you the bill. No, what we need is an agreement, to replace the ill-fated and unofficial Kepler Agreement. And I know just the man to sound out all sides, and open negotiations. He knows the Union's ways intimately, he's familiar with interstellar travel, and he's warily respected by the Co-ord. His name is Peregrine Walworth.'

No one present had heard of Walworth.

'Ask around,' Owen said. 'Send urgent messages to your home bases on the next available FTL transport. And meanwhile . . .' He gave them his best politely pleading look. 'Could someone please cut me loose?'

'Ah, fuck it,' Myles said. He jumped to his feet and pulled out a knife.

'I promise to be good,' Owen said, as the blade rasped through the duct tape.

Myles scoffed, and stepped away. 'We'll see.'

Owen stood up, peeling away bits of tape and shaking them off his fingertips. 'You shall.'

This time, he really did mean it. After all, he had got what he wanted, he'd advanced the cause of the Alliance and it would be to his advantage to be good. Maybe this was what they called ethics. He'd look it up.

Karray Space, Thursday 26 March 2071

'Hello, fantastic Venus!'

'What?'

Nayak waved out of the window at the expanse of green and white below: the surface of the system's inner planet, the first one out from the exosun. 'It's like Francesca said – Venus like people once imagined it would be.'

'I found the real Venus fantastic enough.'

'Point taken.' Nayak felt a little abashed. It hadn't occurred to her that the engineers on the Station might have been as fascinated by Venus as the scientists in Cloud City had been.

'Still,' Marek added, 'this one might give me some tips on hydroponics, eh?'

The plan was to orbit and survey the first planet; to land on the inner moon of the second planet and check out the mysterious structures there; to approach the third planet and make another quick survey from orbit; and then to approach as close as possible to one of the huge artificial structures beyond the asteroid belt. A busy early morning's work altogether.

The first planet, now rolling by below them, was wet, and hot: average temperature above 40 degrees Celsius at the equivalent of sea level. High ground there was, even mountain ranges, detectable from orbit by the clouds that formed around them and the few peaks that poked through. The lowlands were plain or jungle – rain forest from tropical to temperate – veined by innumerable rivers that after many a meander and confluence spread out in deltas that drained into immense patches of a more lurid shade of green. Whatever their depth, these appeared on the surface more like salt marshes thousands or hundreds of kilometres wide than oceans and seas. Around the equator and near the poles were dun belts of what might be desert.

'Skip to the night side,' Nayak said. 'Let's see if there are lights.'

Reality flickered. Blink and you'd miss it.

'Oh!' Nayak cried.

The black orb below was filigreed with silvery light, in grids within greater grids, some in angular patterns that irresistibly suggested city blocks and streets and parcelled properties on endlessly varied scales: fields, farms, ranches, counties, countries, continents . . . Some rectangles were disproportionately long and thin, imbricated like the output of a program to solve the four-colour map problem. Many of them ended, or branched off to, clusters of circles, and circles within circles, and circles of circles, and . . . The network extended across every kind of terrain. A future survey might be able to tell mountain from jungle from swamp, but not on this hasty pass.

'It's like circuitry,' Marek said. 'How did we not see this on the day side?'

'We weren't looking on the right wavelength, and the light got lost in the green?'

'Yeah,' Marek mused, evidently entranced by the view. 'Looks more like phosphorescence than artificial light. It's bright now by contrast. Let's take another look at the day side.'

Another jump. Nayak came out of it flinching in the momentary glare of the exosun before her glasses adjusted. The question nagged: had they jumped around the planet or through it?

'Around it, if you're wondering,' said Iskander. 'Lots of micro-jumps.'

'How did—?'

'It's an obvious question.'

'The navigation app is smarter than we are,' Marek said. 'Iskander, can you give our glasses a view on the right wavelength?'

'Done.'

The view dimmed. The same angular and circular traceries as they'd seen on the night side now stood out. On this view, there was a faint indication of the underlying physical features: denser clusters of the grid appeared around the shores of the apparent marine and oceanic swamps. Nayak knurled the spectrum up and down, and detected the subtle shifts in shades of green that marked some of the lines, particularly in areas where they were close together. She shared the observation.

'Are we seeing streets? Marked out by changes in vegetation?'

'Or what *were* streets,' Marek said. 'Like how archaeologists find lost cities in jungles and deserts.'

'Then why are the lights still on?'

'Could be something like phosphorescence, like I said. Or even an accidental trace caused by, I don't know, luminous fungi that grow only where the soil has been disturbed.'

'Don't talk to me about fungi! I had enough of that on the Mushroom Moon!'

Marek scoffed. 'You and me both.'

Nayak flipped her glasses to normal vision, to the endlessly varied but almost unbroken green of the surface. The lines of light could be mapping out anything from a world carved by the boundaries of property and the borders of countries to the functional, technical and administrative differentiation of a global commonwealth: parallelograms obsessively delineated by some utopian visionary.

'We've seen all we can see from here,' she said. 'Iskander has more than enough for the Station to pore over, and we shouldn't go lower. So I suggest it's time for us to jump to the second planet's moons.'

'Yes.'

She watched as Marek set the app. 'But you know what I think?'

'We should stop meeting at moons? People will talk.'

Nayak laughed. 'Perhaps. But what I think we're seeing down there is – or was – the home world of the talking dinosaurs.'

Marek shrugged. 'We should be able to ask them directly soon enough, when we go down to meet John Grant.'

'Or rescue him!'

The Station was now in orbit beyond the outer moon of the second planet – close enough to pick up near real-time monitoring of Grant's phone, via the geostationary comsat. It wasn't dawn yet, at the city where Grant was being held. Grant's confiscated phone was still in a bag down there, and he still in a cell.

Marek jumped the shuttle to the inner moon of the second planet. Iskander sent a compressed burst of their findings across to the Station, now within easy range. Marek brought the shuttle down to the surface, close to one of the mysterious and gigantic buildings.

'Prep for EVA,' he said.

'Airlock clear,' Nayak said. 'Suit readings nominal.'

'Unlocking the outside hatch,' Marek said.

Nayak swung the heavy handle up to the open position and

pushed the hatch. It swung outward. Her visor darkened instantly. The plain was still harshly lit, the shadows black, the horizon close, the front of the building five hundred metres away a square of white door around a black space. A nudge with the toe of her boot sent the steps down. She backed down the steps and took a final hop off onto the regolith.

'One small step for a gal,' she said. 'One giant leap for gal-kind.'

Marek chuckled. With a light-speed lag of a couple of seconds, Commander Ulrich groaned. 'You could have phrased that better, Lakshmi. This is still a historic event.'

'Hard to feel historic when the whole point is you're not the first.' Nayak swung her head and shoulders from side to side, sharing the view in her helmet camera. 'See, there are even boot prints.'

The plain was criss-crossed with trails of footprints, most of them ending at one of the five landers, like crumpled tin cans on crooked, spidery legs, that were dotted around the vicinity.

Nayak bunny-hopped away from the shuttle to where several trails intersected. The suit felt reassuringly chunky, though awkward to get around in. It was from the same template as the Venus descent suit, with modifications: protection against radiation was the point here, not resisting atmospheric pressure. All very Apollo mission retro, aptly enough since she was on a moon larger than but otherwise similar to Earth's Moon.

The next prints she paused to examine and share in her camera were also like those in the historic photographs: ridged, elliptical, usually paired in a way that suggested their makers had settled on the same bunny-hop trick for getting around in low gravity. They were further apart than those in her tracks, and at least fifty centimetres from heel to toe.

'I'm standing in the footprints of giants,' she said.

'Five metres away at ten o'clock,' Marek said. 'Look closer.'

She jumped over and looked down. The trail crossed another, of much larger and more widely spaced prints, single rather than double as if left by great strides. Big boots, too: a good metre long, and triangular. The smaller prints crossed them, and now and then were actually in them. The edges of the large prints were less sharp than those of the smaller and evidently later ones.

'Dinosaur prints,' she said. 'Space-suited dinosaur prints, crossed by large space-suited hominid prints. This is like palae-ontology!'

She could imagine it vividly: the armour-clad dinosaurs stalking across the moon, easily adapting their normal loping, leaping gait; the hominids bouncing along much later in suits and boots perhaps very like her own.

'The recent prints are thousands of years old,' Iskander told her. 'The large ones, at least a million years older than that.'

Nayak shivered in her spacesuit. Barring cosmic catastrophe or other disturbance, the trail of prints she was leaving would last just as long, and might be examined in a million years by stranger eyes than hers. She turned her mouth to the water nozzle and swallowed.

'Time to move,' she said.

'Wait!' said Iskander. It placed a dot in her sight. 'Over there.'

She turned and zoomed in on a faint line between two disturbed areas, about a hundred metres apart, a hundred metres back from where she stood. 'I'll take a look.'

The first disturbed area was a long, narrow, shallow elliptical depression. She recognised it at once.

'Shit!' she said. 'A submarine landed here.'

A line of human-scale boot prints led away from it. Another line led back. She followed the tracks to where they doubled back, at a triangle of sharp imprints.

'Someone came here,' she said. 'They set up an instrument, and . . .' She looked along the line of sight. The black door was square in front of her. 'They used it to look into that building, and left without going closer.'

'Black Horizon?' Marek said.

'Probably,' said Iskander. 'The prints are the freshest yet. Could be any time in recent decades.'

'Makes me worry about what they saw.'

'Black Horizon may have had their own reasons for not going in,' Iskander said. 'Reasons that don't apply to us.'

'Your call, Lakshmi,' said Marek.

'I'll go in,' Nayak said. She bounded forward before she could change her mind.

It would take more study than she had time for to disentangle the timing and provenance of the tracks closer to the edifice. The plain was churned up like a building site. Footprints here were overridden and obscured by gigantic wheel and caterpillar tracks. These led away to the rim wall of a nearby crater whose side – as they'd seen on their approach – had been cut away in a rectangular hollow: the quarry from which the building's blocks had been cut.

The scale of the thing, its stark parameters, its lack of obvious function – it was like no kind of lunar architecture ever envisaged — had given rise to speculation on the Station that it and its counterparts were indeed megalithic, like Stonehenge or the most ancient temples.

The sun was high, the interior of the building deep in shadow. Nayak paused on the threshold. She looked up at a lintel twenty times her height above her, and felt like a mouse venturing into a cathedral.

'OK,' she said. 'About to step into shadow. Channel open, cameras on.'

'Got you loud and clear,' said Marek.

'OK.' She turned on the headlamps on the sides of her helmet and stepped into the black. Her visor cleared. Her eyes adjusted. Twin beams swept the great room, and returned glints of glass and steel. Square in the centre of her view was an aerospace craft with swept-back wings whose tips came within three metres of the walls on each side. A nose wheel with the treads on its doubled tyres showroom-fresh and black as tar loomed about ten metres away. A similar wheel stood beneath the root of each wing.

'It's a hangar,' she said, as if anyone watching could miss it. 'And inside is the biggest fucking shuttle anyone's ever seen.'

Nothing had touched the vehicle, not micrometeorites, not solar wind, not cosmic rays, in a million years or more. The wheels had sunk a little in the regolith floor, that was all. Nayak walked beneath it, looking at and recording hatches, handles, paint, the alien script, the fluted lines.

On the floor, among many dinosaur prints, were a couple of trails of footprints of hominids who had walked the length of the craft, studied its lines with expert eye, looked up at the flaring nozzles of the jets, and then – as she was about to – turned around and walked out.

Her visor darkened at the doorway as the harsh glare hit. 'It's a starship,' she said. 'A starship built by dinosaurs.'

Ulrich's patient query came over her phones. 'How do you know it's a starship?'

'I don't know for sure,' Nayak said. 'But I feel it in my bones.'

'One way to find out,' Marek said. 'We have a ladder in the back, you know.'

Two seconds later, Ulrich's response made the phones crackle. 'Don't even think about it!'

'I was joking, Commander,' Marek said.

Two seconds later, Ulrich replied. 'Well, don't.'

Nayak set off across the regolith back to the shuttle, leaving yet more footprints that would, in all probability, be her most lasting trace on the universe. 'Is John still OK?'

'If he wasn't, you wouldn't be where you are,' Ulrich replied. 'Stay alert for an emergency return at any time.'

'Got it.' Nayak climbed the ladder, and stood just outside the airlock as air jets blasted the dust off her boots. She closed and locked the outer door. When the airlock pressure was normal she climbed out of the suit and went through to the cockpit and sat down.

'Third planet and habitats, here we come!' Marek said.

'Remember the nearest habitat is twenty-odd light minutes away,' Ulrich said. 'The third planet is on the other side of the exosun right now, and even farther away. For all practical purposes, you're on your own out there.'

'From a Moon mission to a Mars mission,' Nayak quipped.

'It's more dangerous than that,' Ulrich said.

'We'll be careful,' Marek promised. He set the navigation app.

They had the images from John Grant's initial approach, stored in the tractor unit's system, and the images from the automated shuttles. While awaiting developments with Grant's situation down on the surface, it seemed a good opportunity for the Station to take a close-up look at the past achievements of at least two of the species that lived there. They'd seen what the dinosaurs had done. Now they were going to check out the space-faring feats of the hominids.

'Take it down?'

The third planet, as yet unnamed, rolled below. Smaller than Earth, with an atmosphere apparently breathable but thin enough to give you altitude sickness at a thousand metres, it was invitingly green and blue and white, but in different proportions from any other planet they'd encountered. The single ocean sprawled across the equator and halfway around the planet, in the centre of a crazy-paving pattern of narrow seas between a patchwork of continents. The polar ice caps extended to the thirtieth parallel, and numerous snow-covered peaks and ranges dotted and scored every landmass. It was as if the second planet had been reproduced on a smaller scale and crushed to fit, making a world of glens and glaciers.

'It's tempting,' Nayak said. 'But outside our mission.'

'Confirm that,' said Iskander. 'Absolutely not.'

'Radio signals?'

'Few and tenuous. Jumping to the night side.'

There were lights here, usually at the mouths of rivers, in no more than a score of clusters, all small.

'Very thinly populated,' Marek said.

'Who by?' Nayak wondered.

'The tall hominids are all that is evident,' Iskander said. 'The only radio voices I can detect are of the same deep, even subsonic speech that Grant heard on the street.'

'Well, at least they're there. But how long ago did they arrive?'

'A question for future research,' Iskander said. 'Investigating the habitats is a more urgent matter.'

'Set it up,' Nayak said.

They came out of the jump a hundred kilometres from the habitat that was currently nearest to the second planet.

'Holy fucking shit!' Marek said.

'My sentiments entirely,' Nayak said. They'd seen the habitats on the images Iskander had captured from the time of Grant's arrival in the system, and on the pictures from the automated shuttle's survey. Nothing prepared you for seeing one for real, up close, filling the view, not even on a screen but through a window.

The huge wheel in the middle turned slowly, its interior visible even from where they were a succession of green, grey and black patches, like a pixelated cartoon of a narrow strip of an Earth-like planet.

'I've sometimes wondered,' Marek said, in a tone of idle speculation, 'if you can jump a shuttle to *inside* a structure.'

'That's a good question,' Nayak said. 'In theory, yes. An FTL jump takes you through a lot of interstellar medium, which over light years adds up to a huge amount of matter. It might even take you through stars and planets. So you should be able to jump into an enclosed space. However . . .'

'Yes?'

'I'd rather try it with an automated shuttle first.'

Marek laughed. 'Fair enough. We could do it the hard way, but I told the Commander we'd be careful, and finding an airlock and going inside would be—'

'Less than careful, and best left to a mission for that purpose. We're just here to snoop.'

An automated shuttle could do a lot, but it couldn't say to itself, *hmm, that looks interesting . . .*

'Hmm,' said Iskander. 'That looks interesting.'

The AI had picked up a curious feature of some of the structure's enormous struts, in the complex lattice that cradled the central, spinning wheel. One in five of them, in a recurring pattern, had long slots down their sides. Marek set the navigation app for the closest – twenty kilometres away, too close to merit a jump, but too far for an EVA in the suit – then leaned back in his seat. 'Uh, Iskander?'

'Yes.'

'Could you double-check that burn, please?' He sounded a little embarrassed.

'It's correct,' Iskander assured him. 'Don't try to second-guess yourself. If you'd made some grievous error, I'd have stepped in anyway.'

'Thanks, I guess.'

The shuttle's jets burned briefly to accelerate. Huge stanchions passed by metres away. Nayak felt her palms sweat. After five minutes of this, the jets burned again, then after some short, almost unnoticeable attitude and course corrections came to a halt relative to the target strut. The black slot, three metres wide and many kilometres long, extended out of sight above and below.

Marek thumbed up a searchlight and shone it into the slot. The beam reflected what looked like gold a few metres inside, in scores or hundreds of vertical layers, like the pages of a classic in a special gold-tooled edition. Small intricate mechanisms, linked to the layers by metallic strands, were poised at ten-metre intervals up and down the sides of the slot.

'Should I prep for EVA again?' Nayak said.

'Go into the slot and take a closer look?'

'Uh-huh.'

'No need,' Iskander said. 'I've identified what we're looking at. It's a huge sheet of gold foil, thin as Mylar, furled and folded. These little doodads are to pull it out and then extend it.'

'Oh!' Nayak said. 'It's a light-sail!'

'Yes,' said Iskander. 'Unfolded and deployed, it would be many tens of kilometres square. Or to put it a different way, many hundreds of square kilometres.'

'From that pillar alone?' Marek said. He waved a hand. 'And how many like it are there?'

'Two hundred and fifty,' said Iskander. 'If they were all deployed, they could propel the entire structure to the farthest reaches of the system at a gentle but persistent acceleration from ambient solar radiation alone.'

'And if they had more than ambient solar radiation behind them?' Nayak asked. 'If, for example, they had lasers to push them?'

'In that case, they could escape the system altogether.'

'You'd need some damn powerful lasers,' said Marek. 'Where are they?'

'I think I know where they might be,' Nayak said. 'We can't go looking for them now, but when we get back I want Eduardo to build a telescope suitable for looking very close to the star. I predict we'll find a ring of solar-powered laser batteries.'

'Why do you think that?' Marek asked.

'It's the only use that makes sense,' Nayak said. 'The builders wouldn't have used solar sails on this scale just for tacking around the system. I mean, why move habitats even farther out from the star? These aren't just habitats. They're *generation starships*.'

Marek seemed unfamiliar with the concept. 'They're *what* starships?'

'Slower-than-light starships that take generations – hundreds or thousands of years – to arrive at their destination.'

'Good God! What a terrible thought!'

'It's not so bad. They'd be travelling worlds – world ships. Any of these habitats could carry millions of people. They wouldn't even be culturally isolated en route if they had radio or laser contact with the rest of their civilisation. A few years behind the times, that's all.'

'Even so . . .' Marek inhaled through his teeth. 'I get claustrophobia just thinking about it. And I was *screened* for claustrophobia.'

'And you've lived two years on the Station.'

'It's not the same. And, anyway, why would the hominids down on Two build STL ships, when the dinosaurs already had FTL? And had left FTL starships parked on a moon that we know the hominids visited?'

'Good question. Like you said, maybe we can ask them soon enough.' Nayak checked the time. 'Speaking of which . . . it's dawn at the place where Grant's being held. Time to head back.'

They returned to the Station's previous orbit to find it wasn't in its predicted position. Seconds later they received a message telling them where it was.

'We're in low orbit, on the night side and chasing the sunrise,' Ulrich told them. 'We've just got Grant's phone ringing, and someone's picked up.'

'Do you need us to go in?' Nayak asked.

'No. You've done enough for a morning. Come to the Station, and dock.' Ulrich chuckled. 'I've got the other main shuttle out for close work. Young Jürgen is very keen to show off some low-level aerobatics.'

CHAPTER NINE

Dino Town

The port city, Thursday 26 March 2071 according to
Grant's calendar

John Grant sneezed, then coughed. He sat up on the drop-
down shelf bed of the jail cell in which he'd spent the night,
and wheezed. Now he was shivering and sweating. He hadn't
felt this wretched since . . .

Ah. Not since his childhood inoculations.

'Iskander!' he croaked.

No answer, of course. They'd taken his phone and glasses,
along with his wallet and knife and everything else including
his clothes, which had been replaced by a garish pink and
yellow striped one-piece of some papery material, already
fraying at the knees and elbows. Then they'd banged the door
on him.

Mid-afternoon, the duty officer from the desk had opened
the tiny hatch, said something apologetic about some kind of

delay, and left. Early evening had brought a bland patty wrapped in an edible leaf, and a paper cup of fruit juice, passed through the hatch. Sleep had been early, fitful and increasingly disrupted by coughing. The night had been longer than felt right. Perhaps this planet had a longer day. Grant sneezed into the crook of his elbow, and wiped his nose on the sleeve.

Daylight came in through a high, barred window. Overhead a bulb of glass with an incandescent coil had burned all night in its cage. His throat felt raw. He reached for the mug of water by the bed, looked into it and put it back on the floor. He stood up and took two steps to the door, leaned against it with one hand and hammered it with the other.

'*Médecin!*' he shouted, or tried to. It came out as a croak he could barely hear himself. He hammered harder. '*Je suis malade!*'

After a while the cover at eye level was slid open, then shut. Ten minutes later one of the militiamen who'd arrested him arrived with a young black woman in a blue mask and a white coat. They took Grant past five cell doors and into a room with a table and chairs and with posters on the walls. The woman waved the militiaman aside, sat Grant down, pulled on disposable gloves and checked him with tongue depressor, thermometer and stethoscope. She had a name badge: Dr Josephine Mbadou, MG.

'*Eh bien*,' she said, raising a finger. '*Attend.*'

She nodded to the militiaman and hurried out. The militiaman lit a pipe and puffed. Grant coughed convulsively. The militiaman sighed, and let the pipe go out. Dr Mbadou returned with a steaming mug. She glared at the militiaman, flapped a hand in front of her nose and gave the mug to Grant. He inhaled the steam, which smelled of herbs and citrus. Immediately his throat and sinuses felt better. He blew on the surface of the hot liquid, and sipped cautiously.

'You have fever from a viral infection,' Mbadou told him. Her English was heavily accented, but confident. 'We vaccinate against it, but you have no immunity. It is not dangerous, but most unpleasant. The drink will not cure you, but it will bring down your temperature, ease your breathing and reduce the pain.'

'I can feel it doing all that as we speak,' Grant said. 'This is amazing.'

Her eyes and voice showed she was smiling behind the mask. 'We have the indigenes to thank for the medicine, and the saurians for the virus.'

'I have a *dinosaur* virus?'

'No, no.' She shook her head. 'The ground-pigs – the little beasts that we raise in our gardens. The virus is endemic and harmless among them, but it is sometimes passed to us.'

'I haven't been within three metres of any of them.'

'No, but we raise them to sell to the dinosaurs, who eat them, ah . . . fresh, let us say. The dinosaur who picked you up had undoubtedly had one or more for breakfast.'

'Oh.' Grant thought for a moment of what 'fresh' could mean to a carnivorous dinosaur. 'Let's leave that there.'

'Indeed.'

The militiaman put his pipe in his pocket and shifted his stance, evidently about to return him to the cell. Grant turned to the doctor. 'Why am I being held? Can you ask him to explain?'

After a rapid exchange in dialect, she told Grant: 'You are not under arrest. You are being detained under quarantine regulations.'

'Quarantine?'

'You have entered the republic with apparently false documentation. Your documents, true or false, most definitely do not show customs clearance and that you are free of any infectious disease.'

Grant scoffed. 'I'm sure not free of any now!'

'Unfortunately.' She frowned. 'But if you really come from Earth you may be carrying some new infections yourself, to which we have no immunity.'

'You have a point there,' Grant allowed. 'Might I at least wait here? I've no intention of trying to escape, and I could do with some coffee and breakfast.'

Mbadou laughed. 'If you are thinking of coffee and breakfast, you must be feeling better already.'

'Yes, I am. Will you stay?'

'No. I have to return to the neighbourhood clinic.'

'That's understandable. In that case, could I have something to read, as well?'

She chuckled, rolled her eyes, and spoke to the man, who went off.

'You are really from Scotland?' she asked, as soon as the man was out of the room. 'From the real – from the original Union?'

'Yes.'

'What you must have achieved in the centuries since the revolution!'

'Decades, not centuries, sorry.'

'Decades?' She sounded puzzled and disappointed.

'Yes. And that's since the Rising – the insurrection, you understand?'

She nodded.

'As for the revolution, well . . .' He shrugged. 'It's a work in progress.'

'A work in progress? I like that. It is here, too, as you will soon find out. And we really have had centuries, and we have the Karray, but . . .'

Again that word. 'Karray?'

'It's in our dialect, from *cadre*, but I think derived from how the Americans said it: "cah-dray".' She looked pensive. 'Do you still have Americans?'

'Oh yes,' Grant said. 'We still have Americans.'

'And we still have the Karray.'

Before he could question her further, the man returned with a tray, put it down at the table and sat down opposite Grant, settling in.

Dr Mbadou waved and left.

The tray held a mug of black liquid that smelled a little like coffee, and a bowl of hot mash that smelled vaguely like gruel, and fruit that was without doubt a banana, but better than any Grant had tasted, richer in flavour and firmer in texture. The militiaman watched in silence as Grant ate and drank. The coffee wasn't coffee, but it had a caffeine kick and a bitter tang. When Grant had finished, the man lit his pipe and sat reading from some large, folded sheets of print and monochrome photographs. A newspaper, on actual paper.

The pipe smoke didn't smell like tobacco, or any other familiar leaf. It wasn't like the weed smoked on Apis, a habit spread from exiles and making inroads into the unofficial export trade. Grant had caught whiffs of it even in Port Glasgow. This stuff here stung Grant's eyes and made him feel woozy.

The militiaman put down his paper. Grant raised a querying eyebrow and reached. The man slid it across the table.

'*Merci*,' Grant said.

The masthead read *Les Temps de Saurienville* – Dino Town Times, as he irreverently translated it. The print was in great slabs. The black and white photographs were mostly of groups smiling or looking grimly determined. Grant spent the next half-hour or so puzzling out the text from his knowledge of French and his smattering of other languages. It kept him occupied.

Even for an avid reader – like him – of the business pages, it was heavy on tables of figures. They weren't share prices, or currency exchange ratios. They were physical quantities, tonnes of this and litres of that and megawatts of the other: industrial and agricultural output, registered by the day, though days or even weeks behind. Apart from the captions to group photos, names of people and of individual enterprises appeared only in what looked like a tedious and colourless gossip page: promotions, demotions, assignments, re-assignments . . . It was the dullest newspaper he had ever read. Like the buildings, it

differed from Co-ord official papers only in being more
wooden. He hoped that, also as in the Co-ord, a livelier press
circulated outside of militia stations and other official institutions. If not, Saurienville was in trouble.

It suddenly struck him what sort of trouble it was in already.
This wasn't just the local newspaper. This was their Iskander.
Or, rather, it was the equivalent of its user-friendly front end.
They were trying to plan their economy, or some significant
part of it, *by hand*, using *paper*. But why? Surely they had
computers! Now he came to think of it, he hadn't seen any,
nor any phones. The museum-piece telephonic apparatus on
the duty officer's desk barely qualified: as far as he could recall,
it could only handle speech.

Yet *someone* here was using computers, and sophisticated
software – probably better than Iskander's, given that it had
counter-hacked Iskander's intrusion into the local comsat
network. A society with the capacities he'd seen here could
conceivably put satellites in geostationary orbit, but without
electronics they wouldn't be comsats. Either Saurienville was
a backwater, or – more likely – the other species had strict
limits on what technology they were willing to share.

Iskander had been right. Talk about profitable opportunities!
The company that got in here first, and with some knowledge
of just what the place was missing, was going to clean up.
There was no reason why John Grant & Son couldn't be that
company.

Just as Grant turned to the back page – sport, he was relieved
to see – a loud bang shook the air. An alarm bell rang. The
militiaman jumped to his feet. He reached to his hip holster,
then withdrew his hand. The holster must be empty, Grant
realised. Shouts and running feet in the corridors, sirens and
what sounded like car horns outside. The militiaman gave Grant
a stern look and a gesture to stay where he was, and rushed
out, slamming the door.

Grant stood up and tried the door. It opened. He looked up and down the corridor. Someone was banging on a cell door, and yelling. The elderly sergeant who had been on the desk appeared at the far end, brandishing Grant's phone in one hand and clutching a cloth bag and a clipboard in the other.

'*Citoyen! Citoyen* Grant!'

Grant stepped into the middle of the corridor. The sergeant hurried to meet him, and handed him the phone as if it were too hot to hold. '*Ici, ici!*' A light was flashing on it: ongoing call on hold. Grant thumbed the device.

'Hello?'

The image of Katrina Ulrich appeared. 'John Grant? Oh, thank God! Are you all right?'

'I'm fine, thanks, apart from the local flu. And being detained as, ha ha, an illegal alien who might give *them* infections. I think I'm free to go now. Where are you? Is the Station here?'

'Practically overhead,' Ulrich said. 'I suggest you go out and enjoy the display.'

Grant used a mixture of French and gesticulation to ask if he could. The sergeant nodded vigorously. He pointed at Grant's jailbird one-piece, handed him the bag and pointed to the room Grant had just vacated. Grant nipped in there and changed as fast as he could into his own clothes and boots, distributing his possessions to the appropriate pockets and putting on his glasses.

'I'm synched with the Station,' Iskander told him. 'The Station has planted its own comsats in orbit, so we should be able to keep in touch.'

'What took them so long?' Grant grouched. 'I've been here twenty-four hours at least. And I'm bloody ill.'

'All in good time,' Iskander told him. 'You're safe. Play along.'

Grant went out to find the sergeant standing in his way, proffering a clipboard and pen. He glanced at the form and signed: yes, all his gear had been returned. Good to see correct procedure followed, whatever else might be said about the *Milice Populaire*.

The sergeant practically shooed him down the corridor, through the reception area and out of the building. Grant stumbled blinking into morning sunlight onto the militia station steps, already crowded with militia. The street, in what passed here for rush hour, was at a standstill. Everyone was gawping at a bright light crossing the sky.

A scream rose in the distance. All heads turned. An arrow-head shape, black and then silver then black again, swooped low overhead at breathtaking speed, to zoom upward and leave a sonic boom in its wake. Windows rattled. Beasts shied. People yelled. The shuttle performed a spectacular loop and returned for another supersonic pass. This time it flew low enough for its slipstream to ruffle hair and raise dust. It vanished at the top of its upward trajectory in a bright blue flash. The light in the sky dwindled to the horizon.

Grant's phone rang.

'We can keep this up all day,' Ulrich said. 'Do you think they've got the message?'

Grant looked around. People who'd been staring upward, open-mouthed, were turning to each other, blinking and shaking their heads, the last boom still ringing in their ears.

'Yes,' he said. 'I think they've got the message.'

Nobody paid any attention to Grant, other than a puzzled glance at the oddity of someone apparently talking to himself, and the odd wary look from the militia people. The civilians, however astonished they might be by the Station and shuttles, evidently didn't connect him with them – or even recognise him, perhaps, as the 'outworld foreigner' whose existence the dinosaur who'd picked him up had seemed to take as common knowledge.

Or perhaps, more worryingly, they had been warned to avoid and ignore him.

The militia on the steps dispersed, some heading back into

the station, others going down to the street to get the traffic moving again. Two-stroke engines coughed into action, big beasts like horses with paws took the strain of their wagons, bicycles whizzed and pedestrians hurried. Among the pedestrians a few of the tall hominids walked, head and shoulders above everyone else. Two or three dinosaurs bounded among the vehicles, dodging and weaving. Grant was left unguarded and alone, and puzzled as to why.

'Streaming from your glasses, if that's OK with you,' Iskander told him.

'Good idea,' Grant said. 'Now call down the cab and get me out.'

'I can't do that. The cab is locked to the Station, and I can't override it. Anyway, we need you down here for now. Someone will approach – ah, here they are.'

A small, slim man stepped from among the passers-by and bounded up to Grant. He wore spectacles, and the same sort of shabby but sturdy clothes as the first local worker Grant had passed on the road, but he carried a briefcase and had a pen clipped in his jacket pocket. His eyes and smile were bright. He stuck out a hand. Grant raised his. After a puzzled moment, the man did the same, with a quick smile and nod.

'Citizen Grant!' he said. 'My name is Jean-Paul Damiba. I am of the Karray, and have been assigned to your guidance and protection.'

'Like I said, play along,' Iskander whispered urgently in Grant's ear.

'Citizen Damiba!' Grant said. 'I'm pleased to meet you, and honoured that you should be looking after me. But I wonder – why only you? Why am I not being mobbed right now? Surely people are interested in me!'

Damiba tapped the side of his nose, then resettled his spectacles. 'That's one of the things I wish to discuss. Perhaps we could go for a coffee?'

'Now there's a good idea,' Grant said. 'Yes, please.'

Damiba walked with him a couple of blocks, passing some street food stalls with appetising aromas. He stopped at a newsstand, which displayed livelier papers than *Les Temps de Saurienville*. Damiba bought a children's comic by handing over a banknote and receiving several smaller banknotes in change. He turned away and smiled at Grant, who was looking on with interest and some puzzlement.

'I take it you don't use money in the Union,' Damiba said.

'Oh, we do,' Grant said.

'What a shame!'

'Maybe so,' Grant said. 'But I don't think I've seen paper money outside of historical dramas.' He held out a hand. 'May I?'

'Of course.'

Grant thumbed through the bills, peering at small print over scenic pictures. The standard promissory note was given four times; one was in French, the second in an oddly spelled French which he guessed was the vernacular, and the other two in languages he didn't recognise.

'Why is French the official language?' he asked.

'Why not?' Damiba said. 'It was the official language in some of the West African countries our ancestors came from, and many of them already spoke it and varieties of vernacular French. It was a convenient common language. The vernacular here is a dialect that has developed out of several strands of West African French and other languages – such as Hausa and Yoruba, which as you can see are still spoken by some.'

Grant handed the banknotes back. 'Thanks. Interesting.'

'What do you use instead?'

Grant took out his phone. 'Electronic transfer. Most of the time, it happens automatically. We don't even think about it.'

Damiba scoffed. 'A way to empty your wallet sooner than you think!'

'Iskander keeps track, and warns us when we're living beyond our means. Which hardly ever happens, come to think of it.'

'Iskander?'

'Our friendly artificial intelligence.'

'Interesting!' Damiba said. 'Very interesting!'

They walked on then turned into a side street, where awnings proclaimed a café. A few people including a couple of tall hominids sat at tables under the awning, smoking and talking.

'Do you wish to smoke?' Damiba asked.

'I don't smoke,' Grant said. He waved towards a vacant table. 'If you do, of course . . .'

'I don't smoke either,' Damiba said. 'Let's go inside. After you.'

Grant got the impression Damiba would have gone inside even if he was right now yearning to light a pipe. Something in his quick certitude of gait and gesture indicated training and discipline.

The café was small, with polished wood walls, no mirrors, frosted windows with stained-glass inlays, and smells of coffee and baked goods. At three of the ten small tables people – all *Homo sapiens* – sat sipping coffee and looking over newspapers with pictures in colour, and more and smaller pages than the *Les Temps de Saurienville*. Damiba indicated a vacant table by the counter.

'You will have?'

'Black coffee, thanks.'

Damiba held up two fingers and flickered some additional signal to the barista.

'This is a Karray café, so to speak,' he said, sitting down with his back to the counter and face to the door. He gave the room a quick sweep with his gaze. 'There is no law or rule to that effect, but it's understood.'

'Like that, eh?' Grant said.

Damiba made a quick grimace that was almost a wink. 'So you understand,' he said. 'I am told you said you are a *responsable* of the *République écossais*. We can talk freely.'

He fell silent as the coffee arrived. Grant sipped gratefully.

He had a lot of questions, starting with how the Karray had kept their no doubt clandestine control for centuries, and what if anything had kept them honest. It would be tactless, he reckoned, or even dangerous to ask these right away.

'You know what?' he said. 'Speaking freely, I can tell you that if or when we re-establish contact, one of your main imports is going to be actual coffee.'

Damiba laughed. 'Very good! Perhaps we have some unique products to export in exchange, if that is how matters are managed in the Union.'

'Indeed they are,' Grant said.

'We had hoped . . .' Damiba seemed hesitant, as if he might offend.

'What?'

'That in three hundred years you would have advanced beyond trade.'

Grant scoffed. 'I should have mentioned that I'm a company owner and director. And what's all this about three hundred years? I can well believe your people have been here that long. But really and truly, the year back on Earth is 2071 of the Common Era.'

'I know you have insisted that. And so have the people on your ship, the one they call the Station. But we find it hard to believe, or to understand.'

'You can forget about understanding,' Grant said. 'I sure don't understand it myself. But the same mechanism that enables us to travel faster than light also enables us – or compels us, I don't know, we have no control over it – to sometimes travel in time. It happened to me, just – ha! – yesterday. And this is evidently what happened – will happen, in a sense – to your people. You were or will be stranded in the past, and isolated for three hundred years.' He glanced around the room and smiled reassuringly at Damiba, who was looking increasingly troubled. 'I have to say, from what little I've seen of this place, that you seem to be doing all right.'

Damiba was still frowning. 'What do you mean, we were or will be?'

Grant sighed. This was going to be difficult.

'Tell him,' Iskander prompted. 'There's no risk, and they have to know sometime. Might as well be now.'

'OK, OK,' Grant muttered.

'What?' said Damiba.

Grant waved a hand. 'Sorry, talking to myself.'

Damiba waved a hand, too, dismissive rather than apologetic, and laughed. 'You need not pretend. I know you are recording and transmitting our conversation. Rest assured I am, too, with technology perhaps less sophisticated than yours.'

'Ah, I see. Fair enough.' Grant set down his cup and cleared his throat. 'Um, well. You're descendants of a Union colony, right? The thing is, we know for a fact there *are* no Union colonies yet – certainly not here. There aren't even *plans* for one here in this system. Which means *your ancestors* are people from *our* future. They might already be born, but have no idea that one day they will be here on this planet. If we go back to Earth, in what I assure you is the year 2071, and tell the Union what's happened here, this colony might never be established. Which would mean you would not only be lost in history, you might well be lost in another history, another timeline.' He indicated forking paths with his hands. 'You might lose contact again. Which perhaps might be all right, like I say you're doing fine, but . . . we don't want to do that, because we might lose our own past, too, or find ourselves—'

Damiba was shaking his head vigorously. 'No, no. It is not like that.'

Grant gave a self-deprecating shrug. 'Maybe I'm not making myself clear, I'm not who you should be talking to about this stuff. Time travel, alternate histories, I mean, it's hard enough to get your head around . . .'

Damiba leaned forward. 'I understand what you are saying in the same sense as you understand it.' He smiled. 'That is to say, not at all! But it was not like that. We are not from your future. We are from your past.'

Grant stared at him, thunderstruck. These people must be exiles, like the ones on Apis and doubtless elsewhere, planted by Black Horizon in the 2040s.

'But how can you be Union?' he asked. 'The Union had nothing to do with any of that. We've only just got FTL travel!'

'We know who our ancestors were and where they came from and when they were taken from Earth. They were from different countries, mostly in West Africa, mostly Francophone. The movement – the committees, the underground cadre organisation – that fomented the Rising in Europe existed also in Africa. There is even a tradition that the organisation and the movement began in Africa, and from there spread to Europe.'

'I remember that,' Grant said.

'You remember?'

'It was nearly thirty years ago, and I didn't know much about the details, but, yes, I remember.'

Damiba closed his eyes for a moment, then opened them as if waking with a start. 'Of course. If you are of the age you appear, and the date is 2071 as you say, then you must remember the Rising. Incredible!'

'Remember it? Man, I was in it! There are times I wish I could forget it.'

'It's hard to grasp the fact, even when it is literally in front of my face.'

Grant looked away. 'Anyway,' he said, 'yes, there was an African connection.'

'Is there still?'

'We, uh, have a close relationship with what we call the friendly non-aligned countries. But they're not Union, and as for a movement or cadre organisation . . . no.'

Damiba nodded, grim-faced. 'In Africa the movement was defeated. Its surviving partisans became refugees, among the many displaced by floods and droughts and because they had been on the losing side of civil wars in the 2030s. Eventually they ended up in a camp, which was in danger of being overrun.' He passed the comic across the table. 'This is their story.'

The comic's front cover showed a small crowd of smiling people, mostly West African, with a friendly tall hominid and a grinning saurian in their midst, against a background of big green leaves and luscious fruit and blue sea in the distance. The picture had all the cheery earnestness of Creationist propaganda. Its title, in flaring red letters, was *Terre Nouveau!*. Its subtitle, in a less garish font, was: *Une histoire pour les enfants*.

'Terre Nouveau?' Grant said. 'New Earth? That's your name for this planet?'

Damiba smiled. 'Obvious, I know, and an exonym. It is a New Earth only to us. And, of course, this is only our history, and a small part of it at that. But please read.'

Grant turned over the pages. Inside, the panels were skilfully drawn in black and white. Captions and speech bubbles were in vernacular, footnoted in literary French in tiny print. A few panels of people minding their own business in fields, factories and schools gave way to scenes of violence: demonstrators clubbed, doors kicked down, assault rifles blazing. Refugees on roads. The camps, under Red Cross, UN, and Médicins Sans Frontières flags. Relief, safety, food.

Sinister armed figures in the forest, armoured cars and technicals bearing down. Fearful faces in the camp. But new relief workers arrive! Friendly, helpful, with lots more resources! They have five big trucks. Hundreds of people pile in. Supplies are loaded. Twenty or so of the people – Americans, and some British – who claim to be aid workers are the drivers in the cabs or the helpers in the back. This is reassuring. So also are the movement partisans, who seem to have had a lot of authority in the camp.

As the trucks trundle out of the camp, just ahead of the onrushing enemy troops, there's a storm. It gets worse and worse. After an hour of travel, the trucks are as if caught up by a whirlwind. Then they're falling and falling. Terrifying! The aid workers tell people to be calm, to hold on to each other. The partisans, already trusted, urge the same.

The fall stops. The doors of the trucks are opened. The people pour out, to find themselves on a shore. There are fields in the distance, plantations on the hills, sails on the sea. There's a tiny port with jetties at the mouth of a river. The aid workers are perplexed. They keep trying to use their communication devices and getting no signal.

Grant puzzled his way through the fine-print French of a side panel: of course, it explained, as they later admitted, they were not aid workers but scientists, doctors and technicians, part of a conspiracy called Black Horizon.

Grant looked up. 'Black Horizon!'

'What about it?'

Grant took a deep breath, and tapped the page. 'Sorry. Until I saw that, I thought you might be spinning me a line. But you couldn't know of it back then unless they were here. What happened to them?'

Damiba shrugged. 'Nothing. They were outnumbered. The partisans took charge. But that was later. The so-called aid workers spoke with those in the cabs, there was some altercation, and then the supplies were unloaded. They urged people to walk towards the small port and not to look back. After the people had gone a little way, there were blue flashes and thunderclaps, and the trucks were gone. The so-called aid workers then explained to the people that they had travelled through space to a new world, they were safe, but they had arrived at an unexpected place and that they would all have to fend for themselves until the trucks came back. They promised the trucks – or other ships, they said – would be back.'

Grant winced. 'Yes, they would promise that.'

'I believe they meant it. They certainly walked confidently towards the little port, and were as surprised and startled as the people who followed them were when they encountered its inhabitants.'

'The tall, uh . . .'

'In our dialect we call them the Jenty. *Les gentils*. Gentle and kind they were, though at first most intimidating, with their great height and deep voices. They shared food and drink with the new arrivals, and they didn't seem at all surprised at meeting people so different from themselves. Of course there was no common language, but at first gestures sufficed. Then the crowd was further startled by the approach of two saurians. The Jenty calmed everyone. It was thought at first that the saurians were tame animals, livestock perhaps. They sat down on the edge of the crowd, and everyone got on with eating and talking and so on. And then the saurians began repeating what people had said. They were astonishingly good mimics. People were surprised, of course, and laughed, thinking the saurians were like parrots.'

Grant was turning over the pages, which depicted exactly what Damiba was telling him. The discrepant thought bubbles and speech bubbles were amusing.

'But soon,' Damiba continued, 'with their pointing at things and repeating words, it became clear that they were learning our languages. Within a few days, they were speaking with our ancestors, and interpreting for the Jenty, with whom mutual comprehension was and remains difficult.' He tapped his ear. 'Much of their speech is subsonic to us. They understand our languages, but they can reply only in writing, which is useful enough but tedious for conversation. Anyway, we learned much from them, and they a little from us . . . and three hundred years later, here we are!'

The final page of the story was the inside back cover, and in colour like the front. A great crowd standing on a beach, raising their fists in salute as the blue flag with the yellow star was hoisted on a flagpole and a signpost was hammered into the ground.

'Saurienville,' Grant said. 'Dinosaur Town.' He looked around the café, shaking his head. 'And here you are? A lot can happen in three hundred years.'

Jean-Paul Damiba laughed. 'Three hundred years! Try three million.'

'Three million?'

'That's how long the saurians' history is. Their *written* history.' Damiba smiled. 'They recorded, among other things, the emergence of the species we know as the Jenty a mere half-million years ago. *Their* written history goes back' – he shrugged – 'one hundred thousand years.'

'That's hard to get your head around.'

'It is indeed. And for both species, there is an intelligence much older yet.'

'The mind in the rocks?'

Damiba's eyes widened. 'You know it?'

'We . . . know of it.'

'They knew of it for most of their civilised history, and knew it for some.' Damiba seemed to have seized on the distinction. 'Fortunately they didn't know of it in their primitive eras, or they would probably have worshipped it as a god. They still are in some awe of it. And now . . . it's gone.'

'Gone to the gas giants. I saw that.'

'You saw it!' Damiba shook his head. 'Of course, of course.'

Grant leaned back. He felt shivery again, and wished he could be sure it was the symptoms of his illness coming back. 'So you too have mountains that were bright crystals, that have recently turned white?'

'Mountains?' Damiba looked puzzled. 'A poetic way to put it!'

'Why?'

Damiba pointed upward. 'Asteroids.'

'Ah, OK, that makes sense.'

'The departure is obviously a shock to the saurians and the Jenty, but that is not the urgent matter for us.'

'And what is?'

'We call our states the European Union, but we've always known there was another, on Earth.' He sighed. 'This is why it's such a disappointment – the date. We expected to be contacted at some time in the future, by a far more advanced civilisation than we had achieved here, hundreds of years more advanced! And now we find it is less than half a life-time older than it was when our ancestors were taken from Earth.'

He sounded so dismayed that Grant couldn't help offering encouragement.

'Perhaps *you're* the more advanced civilisation,' he said. 'I mean, you've been developing the new society for hundreds of years longer. When you get computers and phones and artificial intelligence, you'll astonish us.'

Damiba said nothing, but his expression was sceptical. Grant added: 'Which raises another question.'

'Yes?' Damiba said.

'It took sophisticated electronics and software to crack my phone's use of your satellites. I've seen no sign of either around here. So the saurians or the Jenty must be providing them. Oh, and the comsats. Who put them in orbit?'

'The Jenty launch small rockets sometimes, and do clever things with light-sails. With these they can take a small satel-lite to geostationary orbit. The saurians deal with electronics, computers and so forth.'

'But you don't use their computers for planning?'

Damiba looked impressed. 'You figured that out? How?'

'From the tabulations in your official newspaper.'

'Correct.'

'So why don't you use them?'

'We prefer self-reliance, even though it has certain incon-veniences.'

'Doing without computers for planning is one heck of an inconvenience!'

'Yes,' Damiba said. 'It is.'

'So why do you put up with it? Why do the people put up with it?'

Damiba smiled wryly. 'The question does come up often at every level, from workplace discussions to the *Assemblée Générale*. Always the Karray, and those who agree with us, make the same argument. Developing our own computers would divert even more resources than are lost or misallocated in planning errors and so forth. Using the computers – if we can even call them that, they are so advanced – of the other species would make us dependent on them, and we wish to preserve our independence: our culture, our polity. We are firm on that.'

'Yet a saurian can pick me off the street and deliver me to a militia station.'

'So? We could not have tracked your phone, or your craft.'

'So you're not entirely self-reliant.'

'No one is.' Damiba didn't sound defensive. 'We have good relations with the Jenty and with the saurians, but we stand on our own feet.'

'Well,' Grant said, 'you do seem to be doing all right so far.' Honesty or recklessness impelled him to add a qualification: 'Unless . . .'

'Unless what?'

'Unless the Karray have become a corrupt ruling caste, which is the sort of thing I'd expect to happen in a situation like this. If any group of people, however well meaning, has unchecked power they will abuse it.' Grant reached for part of his intellectual bedrock, from a Victorian book he had read in his youth. '"The entire history of the world affords no instance to the contrary."'

Damiba scoffed and waved a hand at the surroundings. 'Here you see our privileges! Yes, we do have certain . . . understandings, which are perhaps not healthy. The planning apparatus, between you and me, is riddled with abuses and inefficiencies, and workplace democracy can do only so much to prevent that – as well as introducing difficulties of its own. All that saves us from the fate you suggest is that the Karray don't have unchecked power – we still have to answer to the assemblies and committees, and we are proud that the people have sustained their democracy, their self-activity and self-management, for all this time.' He gave Grant a serious look. 'We're also proud that we have remained conscious of the dangers of bureaucracy, corruption, abuse of power – and that we have struggled ceaselessly against them. But in the long run, that has not been enough.'

'I would be surprised if it were.'

'So would we,' Damiba replied drily. 'We do have a materialist social theory, after all! Part of the Karray did become both powerful and corrupt generations ago, and rose above the rest. We call them the Families.' Damiba sighed. 'This is a port city. The shipping interests were originally of the Karray, and grew rich and powerful, though their power is contested by us. They have their own police force, the Patrol. But even if you had been picked up by the Patrol rather than by the Militia, you would still have been handed over to the Karray as soon as you identified yourself as Union.'

'That seems remarkably punctilious.'

'It's only because they know that if the original Union still exists and has FTL travel, it is not to be trifled with.'

'It sure is not,' Grant said. 'And even if the Union is less advanced than you'd dreamed, it's plenty powerful enough to sort out a few upstart shipping magnates. You needn't worry that we're only thirty years ahead of you.'

Damiba was shaking his head. 'That is not the point. We had hoped that in three hundred years you had solved the problem.'

'What problem?'

'The problem that defeated the saurians, that defeated the Jenty, and if we don't solve it will yet defeat us.'

'Defeated – how?'

'Drove them from space, back to the surfaces of the three planets.'

The *three* planets? So they were all inhabited! Interesting.

'But what did that to them? The minds in the rocks?'

'No.' Damiba's face became a picture of bleakness. 'It was despair.'

CHAPTER TEN

Democracy

Terre Nouveau orbit, Thursday 26 March 2071

In a crowded viewing recess in the endless corridor, Nayak kept half an eye on the planet sliding below while she watched and listened in on the conversation being relayed from John Grant's glasses. Not everyone around her was thus engaged. The Station was in low orbit, once around every hour and a half, and some people were far more engrossed in studying its surface than paying attention to Grant. But for most people, Grant's interlocutor was the only show in town. You could patch the scene directly to your own glasses, and feel that you were sitting there at the table in that Karray café. Nayak preferred to watch on a screen, and to glance now and then at the passing parade of forest and desert, land and sea, night and day.

There were clusters of lights on the night side, but nothing like the pulsing knots and strands that strung across the dark of Earth. Something about the day side seemed wrong. She couldn't put her finger on what it was, but it reminded her of the inner planet in some way deeper than any physical resemblance.

She lent an ear to the chat.

'No time loops to worry about,' someone said, as it became clear that the ancestors of the people down there had been taken from Earth decades ago, rather than at some time in the future.

'Thank fuck for that,' someone else said. 'We can take the news home right away if we want.'

And then the conversation took a turn that made Nayak sit up and listen intently.

'Despair?' Grant was saying, incredulously. 'You're telling me they just gave up?'

'Yes,' said the man sitting opposite – Jean-Paul Damiba, that was his name. 'First the saurians, then the Jenty, travelled between the planets and reached for the stars. The saurians even developed faster-than-light travel. They explored. After some centuries, they retreated. The Jenty developed interplanetary travel and began building slower-than-light starships. They had the FTL drive from the saurians, but they thought that was the problem, so they started this great project of the movable habitats. Then they too gave up. Like the saurians before them, they found the unfeeling immensity of the universe—'

Grant guffawed. His head went back. The cornices of the café, Nayak noticed, were elaborately carved, and the wall decorated with quaint, whimsical watercolours. The view from the glasses shook. For a moment Grant's finger dislodged the glasses – dabbing, no doubt, at real or feigned tears of laughter – then his gaze steadied again on Damiba's earnest face.

'Why didn't you preach to them?' Grant wheezed.

'What?'

'You know, from the Black Gospels.'

'I've never heard of them. What are they?'

'A collection of ancient philosophical writings from the school of Epicurus.'

'Ah!' Damiba brightened, then frowned. 'I'm aware of Epicurus, of course, and the poem of Lucretius is fine in its way. Our ancestors had libraries on their devices, and these books were transcribed by the Jenty before the devices stopped working. The Jenty and the saurians kindly printed them, and stored them in a public library, along with translations of the best of their own literature. These have given us a wealth of knowledge to explore and ponder, and sometimes apply. Ancient human philosophy is not a priority.'

'OK, you might not have had the Black Gospels, but someone here must have had a Bible.' Grant chuckled. 'There's a black gospel even in the Bible. "Yes, it's all futile and meaningless, but a smart suit and a sharp haircut and a loving partner will see you through just fine."'

Damiba scoffed. 'That's in the Bible?'

'Ecclesiastes, Chapter 9, verses 8 and 9. Reworded, I admit, but faithful to the gist.'

'Sounds a bit . . . hedonistic.'

'Oh, the Preacher goes on to say, "Crack on with what work comes to hand, because you won't get any done when you're dead." Wisdom of the ancients, mate. Can't beat it. The unfeeling immensity of the universe? Give me a break! We had all that sorted out in antiquity. Not that the question has ever bothered anyone but a few intellectuals. Everyone else just gets on with it. So if the dinosaurs and the hominids are telling you their ancestors had some sort of existential crisis out in deep sky country, they're spinning you a line. Or someone is.'

'Ah, that's where you're wrong,' Damiba said. 'For us, yes, these questions exercise only a minority. What happens when, as with the saurians and the Jenty, every adult is an intellectual? And, moreover, each individual is far more intelligent than anyone of our species is?' He gave a sad smile. 'They already have utopia. The Jenty have had it for thousands, the saurians for millions of years. They have perfected their artificial intelligence, their planning, their arrangements as to what we call property. Perhaps they followed the wisdom of *their* ancients, and decided that making their home worlds as delightful as possible was more worthy of their time than conquering the universe and turning other planets into inadequate imitations of their own.'

'"*Il faut cultiver notre jardin*"?'

Damiba grinned and nodded, with a clap of his hands. '*Oui! Oui, exactement!* They have turned these worlds into gardens. Everything is recycled and renewable. Long ago they mined out all their fissionable materials. They still have the knowledge, but no longer the resources, for fusion power. Nor do they need it.'

'So why is this a problem for you?' Grant's hands appeared in front of him, rubbing together. 'It might be seen more as an opportunity. They've left the field clear for us!'

'That's how the Karray see it,' Damiba said. 'Unfortunately, we are unable to make our people see it that way. We could have our own space programme, after all – the Jenty might even help us there – but the people won't vote for it. We've tried, believe me, and it's like talking to a brick wall. They have been influenced too deeply by the attitudes and example of the older species. If any conflict should arise between the Karray and the people, it would not be because the people are discontented. They are, from our point of view, far *too* contented.' He sighed. 'If we could only shake them out of this wretched contentment—!'

'Perhaps contact with the Union will do the trick.'

'It might.' Damiba pondered for a moment. 'You spoke about computers and phones and artificial intelligence, and how we would astonish you when we had them. How?'

Grant took out his phone and laid it on the table. 'My glasses are a sound and vision interface with this device, and it is connected to an artificial intelligence, an AI, which we call Iskander.'

'But how would our use of these astonish you?'

'For one thing, the AI is how we integrate planning with buying and selling. This thing' – he touched the phone – 'replaces *that*.' He tapped the copy of *Les Temps de Saurienville*. 'All the tedious information-gathering and calculation that went into these tables, and which you print every day days and weeks out of date, would be done in . . . Iskander, how long?'

'Less than a second,' Iskander replied, from the phone speaker. 'As long as all participants had phones.'

Damiba frowned down at the phone.

'Your phone, and the glasses with the interface – are they expensive?'

Grant scoffed. 'In the Union, everyone can afford them.'

'If only we could! It would change everything.' Damiba smiled to himself. 'Well, a lot. I know many people who would love to get their hands on these phones. And our own AI for planning – that would be something wonderful!'

'We can help you there,' Grant said.

'The Union?'

'Perhaps,' Grant said. 'I can't speak for the Union. But I can speak for my company.' His tone changed, and his gaze shifted to the café's ceiling. 'Iskander, invoke commercial confidentiality.'

The sound cut off.

Nayak recoiled from the feed and looked around, amid rising voices.

'What the hell is he up to?'

The people sitting on either side of her shook their heads. 'He's turned the sound off, dammit!' the man on the left said.

'No, he hasn't,' Ulrich cut in. 'Iskander has. It's even blurring their lip movements! Iskander, please override commercial confidentiality.'

'I'm sorry, Katrina,' Iskander replied. 'I'm afraid I can't do that. Not without a court order.'

'I'm the law on this ship!'

'Indeed you are, Commander,' said Iskander. 'But some things you cannot command, and this is one of them.'

They all watched the next few minutes of inaudible conversation. Damiba seemed to be listing some items he wanted. The watchers couldn't read his lips, but they could read his animated, eager expressions clearly enough. Then both men stood up, and Grant's hand reached across the table.

'He's giving Damiba a business card!' someone said. 'Now they're walking out together, thick as thieves.'

Ulrich's voice cut across the commotion. 'I'm going to call him. We have to send the cab down there – no point alarming them with a shuttle – and get Grant back up here. Dock crew, disengage the cab now! The rest of you, eyes on the situation.'

The situation didn't take long to unfold. Ulrich spoke to Grant, Grant spoke to Damiba, and Damiba spoke to a traffic lady. She stepped out smartly and signalled briskly. Traffic was stopping, people were hurrying. A fifty-metre space opened in the main street. A bright yellow vehicle like a container-truck cab without windows or wheels suddenly appeared in mid-air half a metre above the roadway and settled with a clang on its landing skids.

Grant's view turned to Damiba. 'Look away,' he was saying. 'Tell them to look away.'

'OK,' said Damiba. He raised hands with Grant, turned away and began yelling instructions at the crowd. Grant went up the cab steps and closed the door behind him.

A glimpse of the control panel.

'Goodbye,' Grant said. 'See you in a while.'

The transmission stopped and the screen went black.

Everyone waited for a full minute, though what Grant had done was obvious in seconds.

'Bastard,' said Ulrich.

The cab in transit, Thursday 26 March 2071

'What—' Grant yelped, after the first jump.

Yellow light flared. The craft yawed, revealing in the forward view a sweep of white plasma connecting a yellow sphere to a red curve from which streams of gas boiled. The red curve loomed like a cliff face to the right. Two stars, orbiting each other so close that one was pulling material from the other.

Another jump.

'—the fuck are you doing, Iskander?'

Nothing in the view but distant stars.

'Negotiating our path back to Earth. Don't interrupt.'

As if Iskander could be distracted from its calculations by his talking! Not likely, but Grant said nothing.

Jump. A gas giant this time, far too close for comfort—

Jump. A long one, five minutes. Again the interstellar void.

Jump. Ten minutes. Grant sweated and shivered. The medicinal drink he had been given in the morning was wearing off. Every limb ached.

Earth orbit. The blue and white curve below. Water to his soul. Less than an hour left of air supply.

'The date is 26 March and the time is 17:46 UTC,' said Iskander.

'Thank goodness for that.'

'You've been missing for over twenty-four hours. I've put you through to your wife.'

Ellen appeared in the view screen, Earth's curve an improbable background to her relief.

'John! Thank God! Where are you?'

'It's good to see you. At the moment I'm in orbit.'

'Where have you been? We've been worried sick.'

'Long story. All's well, though.'

'You're not looking well.'

'I'm not feeling well, either.' Grant sighed. 'It's not supposed to be serious, but I picked it up from people who've been isolated for three hundred years—'

'Three hundred years! How can—?'

'Like I said, long story. Like those people who were waiting for me on Apis, but more so.'

Ellen looked stricken. 'You . . . closed that loop?'

'I'm afraid so.' Grant clapped a hand to his clammy forehead. He had all along felt guilty about the people he'd left behind in the past on Apis, and had never thought of the people *they* had left behind in the present, on Earth. 'Christ, I've just realised. We're going to have to contact all the friends and relations of the people on the last ark I took out, and tell them they'll never see them or hear from them again.'

'We can worry about that later. I'm just glad to have *you* back.'

'Yeah, me too. But I won't be home tonight. I'll have to go into quarantine until this infection is sorted. Can you get a message to Myles and to the company—'

'It's being arranged,' Iskander said. 'Taking you down.'

'Where?'

They were down.

Grant caught a glimpse of low hills, an expanse of concrete, white buildings nearby and sea not far away. A wide green semicircle on the ground just in front of him expanded to a dome around the cab. The dome also enclosed a small machine on wheels with a tank on its back and nozzles bristling everywhere. The machine skittered into action, spraying the cab all around. It was like being in a car wash. Then two people in biohazard suits and breathing apparatus entered the dome, carrying tanks. Clangs and bangs from behind: the cab's air supply tank was being replaced. It wasn't connected to the input flange.

'What?'

'Strip, and suit up,' Iskander said.

As soon as Grant was in the emergency vacuum suit, the air inside the cab was pumped into another tank. Fresh air poured in. Grant stayed in the suit. The airlock opened. The two biohazard techs beckoned. He reached for his phone and glasses. His helmet radio crackled to life.

'Leave them here. You'll get new ones. The personal content is already copied across. The devices will be scanned for malware then securely destroyed.'

Grant shrugged and complied. He stepped out, and was sprayed from helmet to soles. The interior of the cab was getting similar treatment.

'Where am I?'

'Machrahanish Spaceport, Infection Control.' The tech pointed to a section of the dome wall with a doorway outlined on it. 'This way.' The tech walked ahead, passing through the doorway without its opening, like a cartoon or special effect of walking through a wall. Grant followed, through a bubble skin that slithered over him and didn't pop.

He was escorted across rain-wet concrete dazzling under a sun low over the sea. News drones buzzed beyond the perimeter fence. A yellow-striped door led to a corridor, then a room with a table, a bin and several medical robots.

'Suit off.'

Robots rolled over, bristling with injectors.

Grant settled in for a tedious evening, disturbed night and long day.

He wasn't bothered. It gave him time to think about what he had found in Saurienville. Perhaps Damiba believed that the saurians and the hominids had turned away from space out of despair. Grant certainly didn't, and he suspected that the Karray, or whoever was really in charge, didn't either. It had something to do with their unwillingness to use the information technology of the other species in any but the most marginal ways, despite all the inconveniences that resulted. The clunky planning system, relying on paper and newspapers and reports and no doubt some kind of hand-cranked mechanical calculators and filling in forms, would be one hell of an inconvenience. There had to be some very good reason to put up with it. Damiba had jumped at the offer of a few thousand phones and the appropriate software, as well as a load of other goodies that Grant had hastily outlined for him after turning his phone's outgoing sound off as they were going outside.

Grant wasn't at all sure that the Union would approve of this kind of disruptive export. But he could think of two possible allies that would: the cadre organisation, and Iskander.

The Firth of Clyde, Saturday 28 March 2071

'You're clear,' they told him on the Saturday morning. 'The infection's cured, you're immune, and we have vaccine templates.'

He had clothes warm out of the printer and a phone and glasses fresh out of the box. His Victorinox Hiker was cleaner than it had been in years, with not a speck of grit or fluff; likewise his cards, which he'd flourished in the Saurienville militia station.

He took the bus – the Space Shuttle, according to its garish sides – across the peninsula to Campbelltown. From there a fast ferry took him around the Isle of Arran, past Lamlash where Marie came from, via Brodick and Largs to Gourock. Grant sat by a rain-lashed window, sipped coffee and caught up. A recorded message from Myles and Marie welcomed him back. He flipped to the news. He was in it. Clips of his visit to Terre Nouveau had gone viral.

'Iskander – is this your doing?'

'Of course.'

'Gee, thanks.'

'You're welcome.'

Responses ranged from questions in the European Assembly, deduction and speculation from what could be gleaned from the clips, through social media storms and conspiracy theories, to a range of plush talking dinosaur toys and hominid action figures that some enterprising company in Senegal had made a global under-fives must-have overnight. Africa was agog, and not just the friendly non-aligned countries, at the existence of a predominantly African interstellar colony. The general feeling in Scotland, Ireland and the rest of Europe was patriotic pride that the Union now had its very own outpost in the stars, and three hundred years old at that. Economic democracy had proved its viability over centuries without even computers let alone AI, so suck that up, Alliance and Co-ord!

'You're not so sure,' Iskander said.

'Damn right I'm not.' The half-dozen other passengers were gazing into their glasses or out to the choppy sea. Visibility was three hundred metres. 'It's too soon to be cock-a-hoop about our new comrades. We don't know enough of what's gone on on Terre Nouveau. We don't know *anything*, apart from what I was told and what I saw.'

'I've made my own deductions. That's why I've kept your dealings with Damiba out of the public eye.'

'Well, sincere thanks for that.'

Grant turned his attention to the rest of the news. The Station had reported back by FTL shuttle to Brussels while he was still in quarantine, but only the most guarded allusions came from any official quarter. Grant suspected that Black Horizon files were being re-examined, and Black Horizon members called in for re-interrogation.

The initial governmental paranoia about the conspiracy had faded, as it became clear that its members had not (by and large) been plotting to seize power for themselves but had instead acted out of patriotism as they saw it. Often enough, indeed, the conspiracy's lower levels had been certain all along they were acting on official orders, and had been more shocked than anyone to find they weren't. The redoubtable lawyer Louise Ogundu was busy building class-action lawsuits on behalf of the involuntary exiles, and she had seized on the news from Terre Nouveau to raise the matter with the African Union.

In the US, a recently released Black Horizon operative called Jessica Bernstein (Lieutenant, USN, Retd) was raising a storm on the talk shows about the need to plant Alliance colonies in the past to get a drop on the Eurocommies and the Red Empire – slang terms about as accurate for the Union and the Co-ord as 'the fash' was for the Alliance, but that was politics. There was talk about her running for office. Good luck with that! Grant frowned to himself at the thought of some temporal equivalent of the Fermi Paradox: if FTL fleets from the future were to erupt from the past, with presumably centuries of lead time in weapons development behind them, the time to do it was surely long ago, and it would have already happened.

But then . . .

He shook his head. Leave that to Nayak. He had his own future to shape.

Around the foot of the gangplank at Gourock some twenty people had gathered, few of whom (Grant guessed) were waiting to come on board for the short remaining leg of the journey to Greenock. Above them hovered a cloud of news drones. As soon as he stepped on the pier he was pelted with questions. He made wiping motions.

'You've seen the news,' he said. 'I've nothing to add.'

'But Mr Grant—'

'Citizen Grant, surely you know—'

'Would you say you're now a time traveller, Mr Grant?'

That one almost caught him. 'No comment,' he said.

He pushed through the crowd.

'I've booked a taxi,' Iskander told him.

Of course it had. Still pursued, Grant hurried along the pier and through the station and climbed into the taxi. It took him home. A few drones followed. Grant waved at them as he entered the block, and closed the door thankful that the buzzing little nuisances couldn't get past it. There were laws about that.

Ellen hugged and kissed him as soon as he was in the flat.

'I thought I'd lost you.'

'I know. I'm sorry.'

'Don't do that again.'

'Time travel? Not if I can help it.'

They sat down on the sofa. Grant breathed out. 'Jeez.'

'What?'

'I don't think it'll happen again.'

'It wouldn't have happened at all if you hadn't insisted on going again and again until it did.'

'I know, I know. But now it has, so it can't happen again.'

'You're sure of that?' Ellen sounded drily sceptical.

'It just seems . . . I don't know. Should have taken the chance to ask Nayak.' He laughed. 'Come to think of it, I will, next time I see her.'

'You're thinking of going back to this place?'

'Yes.'

'Why? You've done your bit. You're already a bloody hero for finding it.'

'They don't know what else I found.'

'OK,' Ellen said. 'Tell me what really happened.'

Grant told her. She listened, occasionally interjecting.

'So I told Damiba,' Grant concluded, 'that I and the company could do a deal with him, and we shook on it.' He thought back. 'Metaphorically. Then they sent down the cab to take me back to the Station. I grabbed my chance and came home.'

'And here you are.' Ellen put an arm around his shoulder. 'I'm glad, but . . . what was the deal, exactly?'

'To make him the richest man in Saurienville,' Grant said.

'How and why?'

'We deliver a container loaded with stuff they don't have – phones for a start, with servers for local coverage, and software including Iskander. Crates and crates of anti-geriatrics – you'd be shocked at the state of their old people. Printers – they don't have printers, can you believe that? And coffee, can't be forgetting coffee.'

'And what do we get, in exchange for this million-euro package?'

'Goodwill and first mover advantage. I'm not so interested in the products of the human community – the Union will tie itself up in knots over biosecurity, drug approval, all that, for months on end. We'll have an inside track on importing Saurienville goods once all that is settled, but that's for later. Right now I'm interested in what we can get from the older species. Artefacts and shiny stuff, easy to sterilise and so forth.'

Ellen was shaking her head. 'I'm not seeing it, John. You're talking about luxury goods both ways, for a very short period.'

'That's how it would start, sure, like a lot of international trade did. But later—'

'You haven't even established that these talking dinosaurs and tall hominids are interested in trade at all! From what you've been saying, they sound perfectly satisfied in their self-sufficiency. And they've been like that for millions of years!'

'Exactly,' Grant said. 'There must be an incredible amount of pent-up demand for novelty.'

'Assuming they have the same psychology as we have.'

Grant frowned. 'Yes. Why wouldn't they? They're rational animals like us.'

'And yet they gave up on spaceflight! Would we do that?'

'We might, if we had some overwhelming reason.' He sighed. 'I know it's a gamble, but downside risks are small and the pay-off could be immense. I've called a meeting of the self-management committee for Monday morning.'

Ellen leaned back. 'OK, OK. I'll consult Iskander and put together a proposal. I'll present it to the best of my ability, but to be honest I don't see it getting through the committee.'

'We can try,' Grant said. 'But just in case it doesn't, I have another trick up my sleeve.'

'And what's that?'

'A wee chat with the committee's favourite cadre.'

'Morag?'

'Uh-huh.'

'How can she help?'

'She's trusted, she's persuasive, and she's canny. And then there's the politics.'

Ellen sighed. 'Yeah, there's always that. Don't worry, John, I don't underestimate the cadres' eagerness to get their mitts on everything.'

Grant feigned an innocent face. 'Oh, I just meant they'd be keen to spread the Cold Revolution to the stars.'

They laughed. Ellen looked thoughtful.

'I know just where to meet her.' She stood up. 'Leave this to me.'

Greenock, Sunday 29 March 2071

'Why is it out of the water?'

'Barnacles,' Ellen said.

'Ah.' Grant peered up at the hull of the *Fighting Chance*, propped on joists of timber on the quayside at the James Watt Dock. 'There aren't any.'

'They've been scraped off. She's ready to go.'

'Go where?'

'I've been thinking,' Ellen said.

'Uh-huh.'

'You know on Apis, they're talking about fisheries?' She flicked her fingers. 'Or whatever the word is for hunting giant marine invertebrates that look something like squid.'

'Fisheries,' Grant said. 'I don't think maritime tradition pays much heed to zoology. Whaling was a fishery.'

'When there were whales! OK. So, we designed her under cover of building a submarine for working in Antarctica. She's got these grapples at the front, lights, all kinds of features we didn't really need—'

'Except on Venus.'

'Except on Venus, yeah. But that wasn't anything we expected. But now . . .' She waved up at the craft. '*Voilà!*'

'I'm not seeing it.'

'She's *perfect* for hunting giant squid.'

'What? Whales are only just recovering now, and you want to repeat that sorry saga on a whole new ocean and species?'

'No, I don't. That's the point. First we could use it to survey, to see if it could be a sustainable catch. If it turns out not to be, at least we've gained the knowledge. And if we find it is sustainable, hunting in a sub like this is a lot safer than using open boats, which is probably how they'd otherwise start that bold venture.'

Grant paced around the vessel. 'But why would they need a starship engine?'

Ellen gave him a look. 'They wouldn't. This would be our proof of concept. We'd fly her to Apis, test her out in the ocean, and if all worked as I expect we'd order up a few more without a Nayak Drive but with everything else. Fly them to Apis in arks, land them on the shore, and there you go. A kraken fishery in a can!'

'Who'd buy them? Each of these submarines would cost millions. And then there's ships and onshore facilities for handling the catch, processing, refrigeration, transport . . . it's only viable on an industrial scale. Apart from that being exactly what results in over-fishing, I can't see New Rhu raising that kind of capital.'

'For a company owner and director,' Ellen said, 'you're not much of a capitalist, are you, John? I'm not talking about some piddling little business in New Rhu. Yes, an industrial scale is exactly what I'm talking about! This could be a whole industry, a whole new food source for the whole of Apis and with export potential to Earth. Plenty of big corporations could be interested in that. Half the companies working on the Nordzee Barrier once had interests in the fishing industry.'

Grant scoffed. 'When there were fish! Bastards vacuumed them all up. That's why they're in climate mitigation now.'

'Exactly!' Ellen said. 'But that won't last forever. The Barrier is near completion.'

'It's been near completion as long as I can remember. When you started that job years ago, you didn't expect it to last, did you?'

'No, but I've enjoyed it, and learned a lot along the way.'

Grant looked at his wife quizzically, unsure what to say. He was saved from putting his foot in it by the arrival of Morag Rafferty.

'Morning, John! Morning, Ellen!'

'Hi, Morag,' Grant said. 'Good to see you.'

'Good to see you, man.' She appraised him. 'Mind you, you're not looking great.'

'Been sick, got better. Still a bit peaky.'

'Quite a busy time you've had and all.'

'You don't know the half of it. Let's grab a coffee.'

The pier was quiet that chilly Sunday morning. Most of the leisure craft were out of the water, and the few people around were painting or otherwise tending to their hulls.

'Funny tae see the old *Fighting Chance* again,' Morag remarked as they walked past it. 'Is she still impounded?'

'Christ, no,' Ellen said. 'We just haven't needed her the past few months. We're thinking about it.'

Morag cocked her head. 'You know, Apis has a humungous ocean, hoaching wi life. Naebody seems tae be daein much wi it.'

'Well, there's a thought!' Ellen said. 'But we wanted to ask you about a different project.'

'Ah, right.' She shot a sharp glance at Grant. 'Terre Nouveau?'

'Yup.'

They went inside the first café they reached. The floor was like decking, caulked; the tables had little rims like those on a ship, and the walls were hung with sailing memorabilia and knick-knacks. A family sat in one corner. Grant strolled to the counter while Morag and Ellen settled at a table by the window. Predictably, three different coffees were already lined up. He paid, carried them over, and handed them out.

'Cappuccino, mocha, and an Americano for me.' He sat down and sipped. 'Ah,' he sighed. 'We're going to sell coffee on Terre Nouveau.'

Morag laughed. 'Wait, yi mean it?'

'Aye,' Grant said. 'But there's more than that.' He outlined his scheme. Morag listened as sceptically as Ellen had.

'And you're putting this tae the self-management the morrow?'

'Yes.'

'Well, John, fair do's and good luck tae yi, but . . .' She shrugged, and wiped mocha foam from her lip with the back of her wrist.

'There's something else,' Grant said. 'Something that might interest the cadre.'

Morag looked wary. 'Oh, aye?'

'You know this idea of using Triple-AI planning to do without money entirely?'

'I've heard it kicked around,' Morag said. 'It surfaces every now and again. Seems to be getting more traction these days in some quarters. So?'

'Well, it's what the Cold Revolution is supposed to eventually arrive at, isn't it?'

'Aye. Eventually. When we've prepared. Ironed out the bugs, and that. Maybe run it in some local areas first.' She looked away for a moment to gaze at the grey sky. 'Cloud City was one.'

Grant nodded, his face sombre. 'Yes. Well, I've found another one: Saurienville. Remember they didn't do their planning on paper, because they don't want to rely on the other species' computers? I didn't see any consequences while I was there, but they must be at best half as well off as they should be. Imagine what it would be like if they had Iskander!'

Morag leaned back, eyes narrowing. 'Oh, man. Aye. I can imagine aw right.'

'And furthermore,' Ellen said, 'it would give the social economy and the cadre organisation there enough wealth and clout to displace the Families – the local merchant interests.'

'Uh-huh.' Morag looked thoughtful. 'I'll raise the matter with the comrades, see what they think.' She drained her cup, dabbed her lips, and stood up. 'See you tomorrow, John.'

CHAPTER ELEVEN

Red Sonia

Port Glasgow, Monday 30 March 2071

'Naw.'

Brian and Anwar had their arms folded. The company, having outgrown the old warehouse and now sprawling across half the industrial estate, had a new fancy office with big windows and a circular table. Fifteen people – the entire self-management committee – were sitting around it. Morag, Piotr and Jeannie had accompanied Brian and Anwar in departing the shipyard and setting up Grant's enterprise as a separate concern under new self-management the previous year. Ellen had joined him, taking responsibility for expansion, sales and marketing. The rest were less familiar faces: there was quite a turnover. New people had a tendency to get so enthused about what they were selling – transport to Apis – that they bought the product, legitimately or just by jumping ship and sending the cab back home on autopilot. The usual excuse was that they couldn't face the existential dread of the journey back. Grant had always set his face against pursuing them physically or legally, not that there was much chance of that in and around New Rhu. The Union authorities had better things to do – they wanted more people in the colony, after all. As for the company, it could find replacement crew easily enough.

'Why not?' Ellen asked. She tapped the folder on the table. Everyone had its contents on their phones, but it was a useful prop. 'It's expansion.'

'Naw,' Brian repeated. He put his elbows on the table and leaned forward, looking around. 'It's expansion all right, but in the wrang direction! We're making money hand over fist shifting folk tae Apis. We've got a good thing going here. Our pilots can just about stand five minutes each way of going there and back, five or six times a day. No way are we going to get people willing to do – what is it? – half an hour each way on any kind ae routine basis.'

'I'm with you there,' Grant said. 'Made me sweat, I can tell you. But—' He held up fingers, one by one. 'Two points. One, it doesn't have to be routine, and two, it doesn't need pilots because most of it will be cargo, each way I might add. The only reason we don't do the Apis run on autopilot is the transport regulations, as well as common sense about having a pilot to deal with unexpected emergencies – like I did last week!'

'Fair do's,' Brian said, 'but we're overstretched already. Don't want to lose passengers to other companies.'

'Oh, come on!' Ellen said. 'One cab and one container?'

'That's hunners ae fares a week. We're already one cab down until we get the one John took back fae Machrahanish.'

'Fine,' Ellen said. 'So we take out a loan to buy a new cab and container. If this proposal works out, it'll be more than covered in a few months.'

'If it works out! And if it disnae?'

'Well, John and I eat crow, and we shift the cab and container to the regular Apis run. Like you said, we need more capacity there anyway. We just have to take longer to pay off the loan and break even.'

Anwar raised a hand. 'Wee problem wi that. The Union hasnae approved any contact, leave alone trade, with this new planet yet. We can approach any bank yi like for a loan, and it'll get stymied until the Union gies the go-ahead.'

'We don't have to *tell* the bank . . .' Ellen said, with a chuckle.

'Iskander already knows,' Brian said. He waved a hand. 'Right, Iskander?'

'Yes,' Iskander said. 'I can partition that knowledge for reasons of commercial confidentiality, but in this case reasons of state might take priority, I'm afraid.'

'*Reasons of state?*' Grant's voice, still raw from the infection, cracked with disbelief. 'I'll give you reasons of state! A thousand light years away, there's a community of, how many—?'

'I estimate half a million,' said Iskander. 'At least.'

'OK, let's say hundreds of thousands of human beings who think they're part of the Union *already*. In among them are, lemme guess, thousands of people who regard themselves as in a local branch or section of *the cadre organisation*. One of them, pretty high up given how long it took to get him to me and the way he was willing to strike a deal, offered *this company* an inside track and first cut. They're desperate to trade and to exchange information. It won't look good for the Union if we spurn them.'

'That's the Union's business,' Brian said. 'It isnae ours.'

'That's not how you went about getting the Apis transport business,' Ellen pointed out.

Brian glanced at Anwar. 'Aye, well, that was different.'

'You mean you had less to lose!'

Brian shrugged. 'Aye, yi can put it like that. I'm no for risking what we have – what we all have – on some fly wee scheme tae get around Union policy for the sake ae week or a month's head start. Nae matter whose feelings are hurt by thinking we've spurned them.'

'If I may interject,' said Iskander, from nowhere as usual, 'no one is spurning them. The Station is very much on station, so to speak, and is already reaching out to the locals.'

'I'm not talking about the Union,' said Grant. 'I'm talking about this company.'

'Well, a minute ago yi were talking about the Union,' said Morag Rafferty, 'and about how us not taking up this guy, uh, Damiba's offer making the Union look bad. I ken you fine well, John, and you mean it would make *you* look bad.'

Grant raised his hands. 'I'll cop to that.' He nodded to Morag. 'Go on.'

'This Damiba,' she said, 'says he's cadre, or Karray as they call it there, and from what John has said and what I've seen of his recordings, the man sure acts like he is. Now, I cannae speak for the cadre organisation, but seeing as I'm the only one here who's in it' – she looked around at the new faces with a sly but disarming smile – 'as far as I know, that is, maybe I can speak *about* it.'

'That would be a first!' said Piotr.

'Ha!' Morag acknowledged the quip and went on. 'Yi'll hear nae secrets from me, but it's let's say *nae secret* that when it comes tae fly wee schemes, the cadre can gie Iskander a run for its money, am I right?'

'No comment,' said Iskander.

'If the Karray are anything like the cadre, and after three hundred years there's nae guarantee, it stands tae reason that what Damiba proposed tae John is a fly wee scheme.'

'Well, exactly,' said Grant. 'He more or less said as much. He wants to stir things up.'

Morag was shaking her head. 'There's more tae it than that. Just contact wi the Union would stir the place up – already did, if yon overhead shuttle stunt is anything to go by. So my bet is he's up tae something more. Which piques my interest, aye?'

'Aye,' said Grant. 'So you agree we should go for it?'

'I do not,' said Morag. 'But it aw depends on what we mean by "we". I agree wi Brian – nae point risking the company. But if me and youse were tae take the risk on ourselves, that'd be a different matter.'

'Fine,' said Ellen. 'Now let's form our own wee start-up and get a loan for a cab and a container full of tech goodies? That's not going to fly, is it?'

'Naw,' said Morag. 'I'll tell yi what will fly, though: the *Fighting Chance*.'

Ellen recoiled. 'Sorry, Morag, but it won't.' She leaned forward. 'This is kind of embarrassing, but I have plans of my own for the *Fighting Chance*. Plans that might actually result in a mutually profitable arrangement with the shipyard. I don't want to risk the *Fighting Chance* on a different project.'

'Cannae blame you,' Morag said.

Grant was perplexed. This wasn't how he'd expected Ellen's ploy to go.

'Excuse me,' said Anwar, 'but the *Fighting Chance* is the property of this company, is it no?'

'Of course,' Ellen said. 'I'd have to take my proposal to this committee, when it's ready.'

'Why not take it tae us now?'

Ellen spread her hands. 'It's not fully worked out yet, let alone costed and war-gamed. We couldn't make a decision on it until it is. Right now, it's my own mental vapourware.'

'Aw the same,' Brian said, 'if you were gonnae use company resources including yir ain time I might add on daen aw that preparation, it might be a good idea to put it forward in principle. Nae need tae decide here – in fact I can assure you we won't even put it tae the vote.' He grinned. 'Using my power as chair ae this committee, pro tem.'

'All right,' Ellen said. 'Basically, the plan is to fly the *Fighting Chance* to Apis and test it in the ocean as a hunter-killer for the giant squid. If it works, we make a deal with the old yard to build more subs of the same basic design – without the drive, of course – and with one of the big North Sea companies that used to be in the fishing industry to develop a quote-unquote fishing industry out of New Mu. There'd be other kinds of vessels needed for transport, refrigeration and so on – again, some opportunities for the old yard, though to be honest most of the work would be beyond its capacity and best done in Rotterdam. In any case, we could hold out for a cut, or at the very least a substantial finder's fee. And the nice thing about this is there's no financial risk to the company – we have the *Fighting Chance* already, sitting on the dock doing nothing.'

Everyone looked at each other.

'There's a physical risk to the crew,' Piotr said. 'I mean, fighting giant squid and all that.'

Ellen scoffed. 'John and I, and Lakshmi and Morag and Omar took a hell of a lot bigger physical risk not that long ago. Compared with the skies of Venus, the seas of Apis are downright safe. Giant squid. Pfft! We'll have them for breakfast!'

There was a laugh around the table.

Brian and Anwar exchanged glances. 'That's no a bad idea, as far as it goes.'

'You mean you'd go for it?' Ellen said.

'Let's say I'd be happy wi you doing a feasibility study, and bringing it as a proposal when you have it nailed down.'

One of the new people – Lisa Sweeney was the name that came up in Grant's glasses – raised a hand.

'Yes?' said Brian.

'Uh, if Mrs – uh, if Citizen Ellen Grant is willing to take the *Fighting Chance* out to Apis, and if she can get John and Morag to go with her, couldn't they call that part of the feasibility study? And couldn't they make a round trip, and go to Apis via this other planet, Terre Nouveau? And if they did that, what would stop them from lashing a container to the landing skids of the *Fighting Chance*?' She paused. Her tongue went to her lips. 'And, well, John and Ellen Grant have both been skilled workers for a long time, if you don't mind me saying so, and John anyway must be making more now—'

'Now wait a minute!' Grant said. 'Every cent I've made above my former wage at the yard I've put straight back into this company.'

'I know it's none of my business but even so you might have a wee bit put by, like maybe you could afford to buy enough gear to fill a container?'

'I'm not listening,' said Iskander.

'But I am,' said Ellen. 'We don't have a million euro in the bank, I can tell you that.'

'But could you raise it?'

Grant looked at Ellen. 'Maybe,' he said. 'Unsecured, no way. And I'm not risking the flat.'

'Neither am I,' Ellen said.

'Brian,' said Lisa, 'if we were to do it this way, maybe we could secure the loan on the *Fighting Chance*?'

'I'm still not listening,' said Iskander.

'Strictly as part of the feasibility study?' Brian said. He gnawed at his lower lip. 'Aye, I reckon we could see our way to that, if you're still in.'

'We're in,' Ellen said. She nodded across the table to Lisa Sweeney. 'This young lady will go far.'

'Thank you,' said Sweeney. 'And, ah, do you happen to need a fusion tech?'

Some argument followed about that offer, which Sweeney settled by citing her right to take time off, and the meeting concluded.

Outside, in the yard, an ark was loading up. Fewer people than on the first journeys, but with more gear, made their way up the ramp. Lively chatter ceased as they approached the ark. A baby cried, a child wailed. The hatch clanged down and was dogged. The pilot paced around the ark and the cab, working through a check list, then climbed into the cab. An alarm brayed. Everyone looked away or covered their eyes. Flash then thump. The inrushing air stripped a shower of petals from the cherry tree that overhung the street wall of the yard. Another ark was wheeled from the shed, another cab attached; another queue began to emerge from the biosecurity gate and form up. Grant and Ellen made ready to go home. Iskander told them both they had a business lunch scheduled for 13:00.

They looked at each other. 'We have?'

'You have now,' Iskander said. 'Citizen Rafferty set it up. In the Reserve, on Clyde Square.'

'We know where it is,' Ellen said. She shook her head. 'It has a dodgy rep, for some reason. Who're we meeting with?'

'You'll know when you get there.'

They walked from the industrial estate down the steep streets at the back of Port Glasgow to the station, talking. Most people in this area were descendants of climate refugees from the subcontinent: dark skins, bright clothes, lots of children; new-build high-rise homes and office blocks, with smaller businesses and premises among the trees at street level; a mosque here and a temple or gurdwara there; street food stalls whose aromas gave Grant hunger pangs; talk in Hindi, Bengali, Urdu, English and Scots, sometimes in the same conversation. Not many of these folk, Grant thought, would take up the offer of emigration to Apis, or anywhere else: they'd found their new world once, and it was enough for now.

'Lakshmi used to love coming here,' Ellen said. 'Bet she misses it.'

'Not if I know her,' Grant said.

Ellen looked at him sidelong. 'I'm not sure you do.'

'Maybe. I mainly knew her at work.' Grant shrugged. 'We might very well find out soon enough.'

The train arrived after a ten-minute wait in the station, which Ellen occupied by browsing the platform stalls and Grant by watching with half an eye Iskander's assembly of purchase orders. There was something slightly unnerving about watching a risky venture of a million euro stack up, deal by deal, like a tottering stack of pallets.

They got off at Greenock Central and walked the few hundred metres to Clyde Square. Among the market stalls and the statues of heroes of the Rising, a small but noisy rally was protesting some decision of the town council. This was so frequent an occurrence that Grant didn't feel the slightest curiosity as to what it was about this time.

The Reserve was a big old pub on a corner of the Square, with the high ceilings of a former bank or such like. Grant hesitated a moment, then pushed open the door and held it for Ellen. The interior's current style was New Glasgow, which to Grant's eye looked no different from its former Modern Nouveau. The place was busy with a lunchtime crowd. Nothing about them seemed to justify the joint's dodgy reputation. Iskander indicated a corner table, set for three. They sat.

As the big clock on the wall ticked over to one o'clock, a woman arrived. She was about their own age, and looked, Grant thought, like a folk singer now living off the proceeds of an extensive back catalogue. She wore a denim jacket over a long swirly cotton dress, a trilby hat atop long wavy blonde hair, and no glasses. He recognised her at once: Sonia Wiley, a veteran of the Rising whose part in it had been of considerably more consequence than his own. They all raised hands. Sonia doffed the hat, nodded, shrugged her jacket onto the back of the chair and sat down across from them.

'Pleased to meet you, Ellen, John.'

'Pleased to meet you too, Sonia.' Grant thought for a moment. 'I'm kind of surprised we haven't met before.'

'Don't be.' Sonia smiled. 'The Red Sonia of Rising legend is, well, a legend. Basically, I'm a lecturer in education at the University of the West of Scotland.'

True no doubt, but that couldn't be all she was. The cadre organisation's structure was notoriously hard to figure out, but she must be fairly senior, in the Republic and probably the Union.

'You did introduce Iskander to Scotland,' Ellen said.

'So I'm told, though there's no evidence any more.' Sonia flipped a hand. 'Act of Oblivion and all that.' She picked up a menu. 'Tapas. Shall we order?'

She made small talk over the small plates, asking Ellen about her work, Grant about how things were going on Apis. They were on to coffee before Sonia Wiley got down to business.

'John – your colleague and my comrade, our friend Rafferty, who is, incidentally, picking up the tab for this, told me about some heavy hints you dropped yesterday.'

'Uh-huh.'

Sonia leaned forward, speaking from a cave of hair. 'How do you intend to liaise with your local aspiring export-import agent?'

Grant found himself looking over his shoulder. He hadn't even told Ellen that detail. Sonia laughed. 'You can speak freely here.'

'It's straightforward,' Grant said. 'Damiba gave me a location in downtown Saurienville – basically the backyard of a disused shop. It's on my phone. Over the next few days, he and some associates are going to clear the yard and make sure it stays vacant, and spruce up the shopfront. By the time I get my container loaded and us out there, it should be ready for us to land. We unload, open the shop, and we're in business.'

'What are you selling?'

'Phones, mostly. Communications routers. Lifespan drugs. Printers.'

'And what will you take as payment?'

'Local currency, which we can use to buy' – Grant shrugged – 'whatever strikes me as stuff we can sell here, or on Apis.'

'So basically,' Sonia said, 'you're spreading Iskander to Terre Nouveau.' She seemed amused. 'And with it the Cold Revolution.'

'They don't need a revolution, they're already there. Maybe take theirs a little further, eh?'

He'd meant it as a joke, but Sonia frowned and shook her head.

'We're not interested in any of that nonsense about doing away with money. You've heard loose talk about radicals in the planning apparatus? Let me assure you, loose talk is all it is. Planners gonna plan. The cadre organisation has no intentions along those lines. In fact, it very much frowns on that sort of thing.' Elbows on table, she gestured elegantly from the wrists, spinning invisible globes with her long fingers. 'Cloud City, of sad memory, yes. Certain communes in Switzerland and – heaven help them – Sutherland, and so on. Admirable experiments in their way, and if people to choose to live like that, who are we to object?'

'I take it that's a rhetorical question,' Ellen said.

'Meaning—?'

'If you objected, they couldn't happen, these experiments,' Ellen said. 'Who are you to object, indeed! When you're a clandestine society with fingers in every pie, a place on every committee and a long-term goal of, as far as I can see, everyone living like that?'

Sonia's laughter pealed. 'There are more passengers on some cruise ships than ever lived on Cloud City, or live in any of these communities. And on cruise ships they don't use money while on board, except for gambling. They just take their allocated cabin, or their booked place in a sauna or sports hall, and help themselves to or order what they want at mealtimes, all without paying a cent.'

'Because they've already paid,' Grant said.

'Precisely,' Sonia said. 'But that's not the point here. The point is, it's perfectly possible for thousands of people to manage their affairs very well without money, in some enclosed situations. In fact it's more efficient, purely as a matter of business. For thousands at a time, yes. For millions, tens of millions, a billion, ten billion? Not so much. Not now, and not for a long time. Generations. Centuries. Millennia.' She smiled. 'That's why we call it the Cold Revolution, after all.'

'Well, there we find ourselves in vehement agreement,' Grant said. As far as he was concerned, the economic democracy was as good as it got. He'd never been able to understand why the cadre persisted in their aim of going beyond it, and he wasn't as sanguine as Sonia seemed to be about the prospect of the radical planners some day winning over the rest of the cadre. If that ever happened, he wanted himself, his company and his family as far from the scene as possible. 'What's this got to do with my plan?'

'Everything. The cadre organisation is interested in your plan, but not for the reasons you suggested to Morag. And if you don't hold with the notion of turning, uh, Saurienville into some utopian experiment – what do you really expect to happen?'

Grant spread his hands. 'Just that they'll run the planning aspect of their economic democracy more efficiently, with Iskander to take care of the paperwork. Damiba is really keen on the idea. And from my point of view, from our company's point of view, we expect that to open up possibilities for trade. I mean, to get rich is glorious, right?'

'That's slogan's well past its sell-by date,' Sonia said. 'But, yes, go for it. Make yourself a fortune if you can! Just . . . be careful, right? We only know about the Terre Nouveau system from your report. The other powers have Black Horizon records and confessions to go on. We don't.' She scoffed. 'A slight drawback of none of our people having been involved in the conspiracy! Even Iskander only picked up traces of rumours about the system. Anyway, they know where it is and we expect them to send ships, any day now. So, a word of warning.'

'Yes?'

'That place looks like it's in a very precarious equilibrium.

Not just internally, but in its relations with these other two species. About which we know almost nothing, and the other powers know only a little more. And they'll be muscling in, nevertheless. So tread warily out there.'

'Don't worry, I intend to.'

'Good.' She made ready to leave. 'Oh, and by the way – your friend Louise Ogundu sends her regards.'

Grant mimed surprise. 'She's a friend?'

Sonia laughed, waved, and left.

'That was a very free conversation!' Ellen remarked as they got off the train at Gourock Station. 'You don't often hear cadres talking in public about what the organisation wants.'

'Yeah,' Grant said.

The wind was blowing in his face. Petals rained from the cherry trees. Out in the firth, flocks of gannets sent up plumes of water among the white wave tops as they plunged on heedless targets amid mackerel shoals. A rich sea, full of life, but still impoverished compared to those of Apis.

'Funny thing,' he said. 'The Reserve gets all these bad reviews – terrible food, sour beer, rough crowd. And it's nothing like that.'

Ellen clutched his elbow as they pushed forward into the stiff breeze. 'You don't think, maybe, that the bad rep and the speaking freely are connected?'

Grant felt like smiting his forehead. 'Our own Karray café! All this time and I never knew.'

'She's a terrible flirt, that Sonia,' Ellen said.

'What? I didn't notice.'

'Ha!' Ellen said. 'She wasn't flirting with *you*.'

Grant was just returning a sly glance when his phone pinged and the caller's name came up in his glasses: Francesca Milloy. He hadn't seen her since she'd returned from Apis on one of his arks, a week or so after he'd first set her down there from the *Fighting Chance* on her one-woman mission of vengeance against Marcus Owen. He shared the call with Ellen.

'Francesca!' he said. 'Great to hear from you! How are you doing?'

'I'm doing fine, thanks,' Milloy said. 'Good to see the folks and be back home and back on Earth, but now' – she laughed – 'I'm kind of missing the Station, if you can believe that.'

'Yes, yes, of course, you had a lot of friends there and, uh . . .'

'Cloud City,' Milloy said. 'It's OK to say it, John. But that's not what I'm calling about. Well, it kind of is. Some unfinished business.'

Grant had a moment of alarm that he might have failed her or others in some way in that disaster. 'What?'

'The descent suit,' Milloy said.

'Ah! I thought you had dealt with that, along with Marcus Owen.'

'So did I. But word came back from Apis last week that it's unaccounted for. And so is Owen, for that matter. And I still feel some responsibility for that.'

'I'm sure there's nothing the militia at New Rhu and the Alliance troops can't handle.'

Milloy scoffed. 'I'm not! Anyway – a little bird just told me you intend to go back to Apis on the *Fighting Chance*.'

'Uh-huh.'

Ellen cut in. 'Yes, Francesca. I reckon we can find room for you.'

CHAPTER TWELVE

Other Minds

New Rhu, Apis, Monday 30 March 2071

That dry season, Marie had taken to rising before the infernal din of the dawn chorus, which came a little earlier every day to wake everyone else, and after a quick breakfast and coffee walking to her lab. She'd nod to sleepy homeward-bound militia members who'd drawn the short straw of the night watch, and smile at the occasional child doing an early morning postal delivery. There was something quaint about that. Most correspondence with Earth was by data update, downloaded from incoming arks by Iskander and sent straight to the recipients' phones, and vice versa, but enough people did get small packets and even handwritten letters from home to make their delivery a much-sought-after and no doubt much-fought-over responsibility among older children.

That Monday, as the sunrise made the white crystal crest of Hamilton's Rise flare briefly red, Marie opened the lab door and turned on the lights and the coffee machine. The lab was the ark that Hazeldene and her colleagues had taken over during their stay the previous year. They'd donated some of their equipment, and more had been delivered since. As far as productivity was concerned, the coffee machine was indispensable.

As she sipped her second coffee of the day, Marie wandered around between the benches, fridges and machines. The samples she'd collected from the lake were still thriving, largely on each other. She sat down at a table and conjured a workspace, which she linked to Hazeldene's now dark and quiet lab on New Atlantis, on the other side of the world. She stitched together maps, surveys, statistics and satellite images to spin up a globe as close to real time as its varied inputs could make it.

All three continents had forests, mostly around their coasts and along the much higher inland mountain ranges raised by the collisions of earlier continents as the planet's surface had formed and reformed – or been shaped and reshaped. The tectonic and general geological history of Apis, much accelerated by Fermi terraforming, was still being worked out. What little was known was a by-product of oil and mineral prospecting. The full picture would remain enigmatic for a long time: radio-isotope-dating produced results wildly discrepant from those indicated by stratigraphy, biogeography and the fossil record. Entire tectonic plates had undergone periods of frictionless rapid movement, an unknown number of times in the past.

Nonetheless, some processes remained predictable: mountain ranges brought rain, and rain brought rainforests. On the high peaks of the central ranges the precipitation fell mainly as snow, and glaciers fed great rivers – like the Big River, a few kilometres away – that meandered to the sea and irrigated the areas around them. On the images of the dark bands of forest Marie planted dots indicating every sighting and report of monkey-spiders, weighted where applicable by estimates of numbers. Then she overlaid current human encroachment – felling timber, mostly – on the forests. On every continent it was going on, with most on New Lemuria, next New Atlantis, and least on New Mu. But it was marginal: nibbles here and there around the edges. You couldn't call it deforestation. Not yet. It was when you combined that with a map of human settlements, plotted their rate of population increase and projected the results that the potential scale of devastation became evident. Throw in foraging for fruit and hunting for bushmeat, and the pressure on the monkey-spiders' habitats became even more intolerable.

How many people were here already? In just five months, the human population of Apis had increased from a few thousand to almost a hundred times that number. From the monkey-spiders' point of view, this wasn't migration but invasion.

Did they *have* a point of view? Were they conscious of their plight, or merely enduring it? Could they ever speak for themselves, or would they for the foreseeable future have to be spoken for? That was the question. Marie already knew something of their brain anatomy – she and Hazeldene had reconstructed one last year. Their behaviour, apart from the bee-keeping that Myles had stumbled upon, remained under-researched: she skimmed what there was, and it was a thin haul indeed. But then, there had never been more than a handful of biologists on Apis at any one time. There still weren't many, and like herself most of them were still at the stage of collecting and classifying.

There were other ways to measure behaviour than scientific observation, however. Almost casually, Marie pulled up records of accidents: injuries to people, damage to machinery. These she marked with jagged symbols of explosions. She turned the virtual globe slowly, and ran the data forward and back. The incidents in and around monkey-spider habitats had increased over the past three months, even after allowing for the increase of logging and similar activity. The general accident rate in the rest of the human footprint had remained stable, and low, though higher than the new arrivals would have experienced back home. Machinery, AI and the watchful eye of drones could do a lot, but couldn't prevent all industrial accidents or unfortunate animal encounters. By historical standards, human settlement on Apis was very safe indeed.

Were these forest incidents, or some of them, evidence of monkey-spider attacks or sabotage? Hard to tell. She would have to enquire with—

A knock on the door.

'Come in!' she called.

'Good morning!' said Marcus Owen. 'Hope you don't mind. Iskander asked me to drop by.'

He looked, now, much as she remembered him on the expedition down the Big River valley, at least at the start. He'd washed, he was wearing clean clothes and his manner was as relaxed and affable as ever. Yet he'd murdered Georgi Muranov, pretended to search anxiously for him, attacked Myles with no provocation and fled into the dark. At his interrogation he'd claimed to be somehow human now, with empathy and a conscience. If so, guilt was not obviously burdening him. She didn't trust him for a second.

She waved, insouciance hiding unease. 'Get yourself a coffee and pull up a chair.'

Owen pulled glasses from a shirt pocket. 'Mind if I share the workspace?'

'No, go ahead.' She flipped him the key.

He leaned forward and spun the virtual globe faster than she had. 'I see,' he said, leaning back. 'Interesting. Yes, it could be monkey-spider resistance. You'd have to look into the particular incidents. Logging is dangerous, after all. But regardless of that, the pressure on the monkey-spiders has clearly increased and is on a steep upward trend. Were you looking for anything else?'

Marie was impressed at how quickly he'd grasped what she'd been doing. 'Well, resistance could be taken as evidence of intelligence.'

Owen scoffed. 'Intelligence? We're way beyond having to establish that.'

'I'm not. I'm a biologist. I know they use tools and can make tools, but so do lots of animals. I was hoping you could share some of your own observations.'

'Of course.' He held out an open hand. 'Ask me anything.'

'For a start – how did you train them to attack the Co-ord logging machines?'

'*Train* them? Is that what you think I've been doing?'

'Well, you admitted as much to the militia.'

'I said I'd instigated the looting. I led the attack, but they didn't need training. They understood what they were doing, and why.'

'How can you know that?'

'I discussed it with them.'

'What? How?'

Owen shrugged. 'I'm not saying I speak their language fluently, but enough to make myself understood.'

'Language? Their calls?'

Owen shook his head. 'Only partly. Much of their communication is through posture and gesture. Do you have some images of monkey-spiders in there?'

'Sure. In fact, we have more than that.' Marie pulled up files: photographs, anatomy diagrams, video clips, sound recordings. There had been few extended, recorded observations, but plenty of incidental captures from the glasses of people in forests.

'Excellent,' Owen said. 'Allow me.' He reached into the workspace. His hands and fingers moved, too fast to follow, for about fifteen minutes. He leaned back. 'There.'

Marie peered at a three-dimensional array of images of monkey-spiders in different postures, all labelled, some with sound clips attached. The array was ten by ten and extended far away like a perspective drawing of a hundred-metre corridor.

'What's that?'

'It's a vocabulary. It's not complete, of course, but it's service-able. The grammar and syntax are embedded in the display – you'll find you can only organise certain symbols in certain ways.'

'How did you *do* all this?'

'I have some skills in data handling.'

'Yes, I can see that, but all this information . . .'

'It's not all mine.' Owen smiled modestly. 'Some of it is my own observations and efforts, but much of it comes from knowledge of the monkey-spiders that must come from the fragment of the Fermi that exists in my head.'

'"Must come"?'

'Where else could it come from? I have human consciousness in a way I didn't before, but as far as I know I don't have an unconscious.'

'Is this, like, a physical splinter in your actual head?'

'Again, I don't know.' He spread his hands. 'Probably not. If any fragments of the crystals entered my body, I presume they no longer function as they did before the Fermi departed. I think it's more of an information complex.'

Marie moved the display, letting her point of view drift down the corridor of data. 'If this here is correct, the monkey-spiders have actual language. Symbolic consciousness. Abstract reasoning. Deep grammar.'

'Oh, they have deep grammar all right.' He laughed. 'My own grammatical errors gave them what I can only call amusement.'

'How did you talk back to them?'

'With great difficulty.' Owen stood up and stepped away from the lab table. He squatted and contorted his arms and fingers. 'See if you can find this in the dictionary.'

Marie stood, too, and walked around Owen, who held his

painful-looking pose. She recorded her view of Owen in her glasses and with a flick of her hand sent an abstraction of it off down the arrays. A match pinged.

'Oh! It means "hurt".'

Owen straightened himself up, shrugging shoulders and rubbing wrists. 'Not quite. It means "this hurts", and it bloody did!'

Marie didn't return the smile. 'Sit down, please. I'm going to check this against video clips of monkey-spiders in the wild. Iskander, can you broaden the search and collate postures and limb and digit positions with the vocabulary database?'

'Yes.'

She hummed to herself, sound-tracking the mechanical cogitations she imagined going on. Iskander returned its reply within a minute. 'Look.'

She and Owen looked at the samples Iskander had returned. It had found five video clips long and clear enough to follow sequences of body and limb position among groups of monkey-spiders. A typical translation ran:

'Ripe fruit three hundred steps sun-ward and twenty lengths up. Fetch.'

'No. You go. I stay with the offspring.'

Hoots, throwing of faecal pellets, then:

'Yes, yes.'

Followed by a monkey-spider departing, returning minutes later carrying a double handful of fruit, and the group sharing out the food: 'Tastes good!'

Another one, showing a group of monkey-spiders organising their evacuation as the sound of falling trees came closer. The monkey-spiders had a point of view on the matter, no question.

'Fucking hell,' Marie said, when they'd watched all the clips. 'So much for our workers' paradise, eh?'

'What?'

'Something Myles said, right at the start – a new world with no indigenous population, no genocides, no slavery. Land plentiful, labour scarce, pretty ideal circumstances for the labour force.'

'And capital?' Owen said slyly.

Almost despite herself, Marie found her patriotic reflexes kick in. She answered sharply: 'That's what the workers' state – the Union – is for! Keeping capital at the beck and call of labour, instead of the other way round.' She sighed. 'According to Myles, anyway. But now, look at this mess! We've been harming native conscious intelligent life all along. Shit.'

'Shit, indeed.' Owen stood up and sauntered towards the door. 'You and I may differ over political economy, but I think we would agree that there is a problem of incentives here.'

'Oh, sure. And not just with the Alliance and the Co-ord. Our own people, too, right across the continent. They've all come here as free settlers, and they have expectations as to what they can do. They won't like being told they can't do it any more.'

'Well, better get this workers' state of yours on their ass, eh?'

Marie stared at him. 'You don't get it, do you? The Union is *us*.' She jabbed a thumb to her sternum. 'I hate to hear myself say it, but it is. *We* elect, *we* recall, *we* volunteer. And we're the ones cutting down trees to clear land and build fences and houses.'

'Exactly,' Owen said. 'That's why you're going to need a treaty, and an agreed means of enforcement. And as I told the militia and the lieutenant, I know just the man.' He made a gesture of looking at a watch. 'I understand he's expected within the hour.'

'How do you—?'

Owen was out of the door before she could finish the question.

Owen left the lab with the sense of a job well done. As soon as he stepped on the ground outside a small drone whizzed up from the lab roof and hovered a few metres above his head.

'Hello again,' he said.

The assassin drone had been his constant companion since the militia had released him. He was free to go where he wanted, but the drone always shadowed him. It was armed to shoot bullets: a gun to his head. He contacted the Alliance base and shared the information he and Marie had just gathered, then walked through the town, across the bridge over the stream and up the path to the Alliance stockade. The drone followed him all the way to the stockade's electronic perimeter, where a slightly larger and more heavily armed drone took over. Iskander's presence was firewalled out. The Union drone flew away; the Alliance drone escorted him to the gate.

The sentry, too, was expecting him, and directed him to the Command HQ at the centre of the compound. Above ground it was a grey box covered with camouflage netting, from which aerials bristled. There was a door, open, and steps going down.

'Down there,' the drone told him.

Owen went down the stair. The steps and walls of its two flights were thick wooden planks. The same timber formed the walls and shelving of a large underground bunker, where five people wearing goggles and headphones sat on a bench behind a table, fingers tapping. Another door led off. Lieutenant Knight's head appeared around it.

'Come in,' he said.

Owen stepped through, to a smaller room occupied by three chairs, one behind a desk, walled with thick planks and lined with electronic equipment. Command HQ was evidently well dug in, and much bigger than the small contingent required. They must be expecting some larger operation. Knight sat at the desk and didn't look up from whatever he was doing.

'Take a seat.'

Owen nodded and sat.

Knight peered over his glasses. 'Strange to see you again in the flesh. So to speak.'

After Owen's release by the militia, he'd placed a call of his own with the lieutenant. Knight had assured him that what he'd said would be passed on. Their exchanges had been frosty, and so it seemed they remained.

'You're not the first to say that.'

Knight gave him a thin smile and went back to looking at data in his glasses. Owen gazed at the bank of comms gear at Knight's back, and occupied himself with building mental models of what its components did. After half an hour had dragged by, he heard footsteps outside and a knock on the door.

'Come in!'

Peregrine Walworth entered, carrying a tablet. He nodded to Knight and glared at Owen with cold hatred.

Owen stood up. 'Hello, Perry! Good to see you again.'

'Fuck off,' said Walworth. He stuck out a hand to Knight, they exchanged greetings, and Walworth sat down beside Owen without looking at him.

'Why the cold shoulder?' Owen asked.

'I could just about bear you,' Walworth said, 'as a robot. Now I'm told you claim to be conscious. That thought gives me more of the creeps than you did when you claimed you were merely emulating consciousness.'

'I understand,' said Owen.

Walworth turned his head and looked directly at Owen. 'I'm afraid you don't. As far as I'm concerned, all that has happened is that the safety trigger in your head has been disabled by that alien mind virus. You're no longer compelled to admit you're a robot, but legally that is what you remain. I could have you seized and dismantled, with no more consequence to me than my writing off a piece of damaged equipment. You're still the property of the British Council, even if you no longer take instruction from it.'

Owen shrugged. 'As I've shown, I'm more than happy to help it of my own free will.'

'You are, are you? Well, now we've established that I don't

like you, don't believe you, and can dispose of you at any time, we can do business.'

'Thinking like a true diplomat,' Owen said, 'even if not speaking like one.'

Walworth allowed himself a smile. 'All right. I was hauled out of a cushy posting in Brussels for this, so let's make it worthwhile. I've been well briefed – the shuttles have been flying back and forth to and from New Ardtaraig all weekend, and I was updated just before I left. My own shuttle has just landed above us in the compound, and stands ready to depart. You're coming with me.'

'What? Where?'

'To the Terre Nouveau system.'

Owen had heard the latest news about the Union's discovery of a new system, but he was taken aback nonetheless. 'Really? Why? I have urgent work to do here, and so have you.'

Walworth shook his head. 'That's all taken care of. I'm not needed to draft a treaty – Smart-Alec can do that, and the matter you raised is taken seriously enough to have set wheels in motion back on Earth. We and the Co-ord have negotiating teams at the Quai d'Orsay right now. But you and I are much more urgently needed where the Union has established a strongpoint which from our point of view threatens to become impregnable.'

'I see,' Owen said. 'Well, I'm pleased you're moving so fast. I was hoping for developments along these lines.'

Knight looked baffled. 'What lines?'

Walworth nodded to Owen. 'You explain it, as you understand it.'

'If we can establish the principle here,' Owen said, 'that native intelligent life should be protected, we have a basis for humanitarian intervention against other Union and Co-ord colonies if they violate it.' He shrugged. 'We can find violations easily enough. And on Terre Nouveau, there are two native intelligent species! The Union must be treading on their toes already, or could be framed as doing so.'

'Wait a minute,' Knight said. 'Aren't you being too clever by half? Couldn't the Co-ord or the Union apply the same reasoning to intervene against us?'

'Of course,' Walworth said, with an airy wave of the hand. 'These things will be decided by the balance of forces, as always. Artillery is the final argument of kings, and so forth. The point is that Terre Nouveau is a special case, for two reasons.' He ticked them off on his fingers. 'One, the Union is in a unique position there, because thanks to Black Horizon's time-travel fuck-ups there's a large, centuries-old human community that believes it's *already in* the Union. If the Union has any sense, and it does, this will be formalised before we can do anything about it – making their domination of a valuable system legally watertight. Two, and this is where you come in, Mr Owen – oh, and thanks for your latest update, by the way, I'll make sure it gets back to London and Washington ASAP – we urgently need to find out more about the Fermi. What they want, and indeed what they are, and what they might do next. You're the only link, however tenuous, that we still have with them. In the Terre Nouveau system, there are species that have been in contact with the Fermi for millions of years. They're the people to ask, and you're the very man to ask them.'

'Why me?' Owen tapped the side of his head. 'This doesn't help in talking to talking dinosaurs, I shouldn't think.'

'Perhaps not, but *this* does.' Walworth, to Owen's surprise, clapped him on the knee. 'Your physique can withstand conditions that unprotected human beings couldn't. Black Horizon kept well clear of the settlement on Terre Nouveau, but over the years it did carry out some quick in-and-out surveys of the system, and from their records and confessions we know a lot more about it than the Union does – yet. Have a look.'

He handed Owen the tablet, open at a page. Owen flicked through it and fifty more in half a minute, then handed the tablet back.

'That's what we know?'

'Yes. As you see, the second planet of the system is the home world of the talking dinosaurs, and if anywhere contains a deposit of their interactions with the Fermi, it may well be there.' Walworth grinned, or bared his teeth. 'I understand the conditions are very much like what we once imagined for Venus: very hot, and very humid. You've been to the real Venus in a descent suit. You can handle this imagined Venus in your shirtsleeves.'

'I admit I'm intrigued,' Owen said. 'But I do find myself asking why I should risk my life for this information.'

'You claim to be consciously committed to the Alliance cause now, do you not?'

'As I told the lieutenant, yes.' Owen opened his hands. 'Let me be frank with you both. My primary motivation, which comes from the Fermi fragment in my mind, is to protect the monkey-spiders. But I loathe the Union and its creepy AI. I can't tell you what a relief it was today to get away from Iskander and into the coverage of Smart-Alec.' He laughed. 'Right now, Smart-Alec is trying to sell me insurance and guns.'

'Seems appropriate,' said Knight. 'Bless its little heart.'

'But seriously,' Owen went on, 'you know what my great dread is? That Iskander will find some way to latch on to the Fermi, or to use Fermi rock, and make itself even more powerful than it already is. It already manipulates the economy of a sixth of the world. What it could do with other worlds' resources – to say nothing of the Fermi's – at its disposal doesn't bear thinking about.'

'We've thought about it,' Walworth said. 'And you can bet the Union is thinking about it, too. But I'm afraid this is rather beside the point. The point I would urge you to consider is this. If the lately departed Fermi gave you a strong motivation to protect native intelligent life on this planet, extending that to other planets seems entirely consistent with that objective, wouldn't you say?'

Owen felt a sudden sense of relief and purpose, which

reminded him of the times when his instructions had kicked in. He didn't have feelings then, but if he had, it would have felt like this. Moral clarity, that was what they called it.

'Yes,' he said. 'Let's go.'

He followed Walworth out of the command post and up the steps. In the middle of the compound, surrounded by curious soldiers, stood a glittering black diamond of a thing, all faceted surfaces and spindly legs. It was hard to tell at a glance what was the front and what was the back.

'Latest shuttle,' Walworth said. 'Straight out of the Nevada black project labs. Probably reverse-engineered from a flying saucer wreck.'

Owen laughed politely. 'That old wreck's an old joke of yours, Perry.'

'Do I sound like I'm joking?' Walworth gestured to where a ladder of what looked like thread extended stiffly from an open hatch to the ground. 'Up you go.'

The hatch led to a narrow airlock, currently open. Inside, the cockpit was compact, with thickly padded seating for three in front of a bank of screens giving the surrounding view. The ladder scrolled in and the hatch closed. A warning sounded. The soldiers dispersed.

'Brace yourself,' Walworth said.

'Are you flying this thing?'

'Good Lord, no. It's all automatic. Just as well, this trip will be at least thirty minutes long, and it can be rather disturbing.'

'Don't worry about me,' Owen said. 'I never noticed anything unusual on my journey here.'

'Here goes, then.' Walworth touched a screen.

There was a blue flash, then a sense of falling. Then—

OhmyGodOmyGodOhmyGod—

'Stop screaming, man!' Walworth said.

Owen willed himself to stop screaming. He clutched the armrests and closed his eyes, which didn't help much. So this was what it was like for them! How could they bear it?

The half-hour felt like forever, until it was over.

Shaking all over, Owen looked out at a big ugly spacecraft against a backdrop of stars.

'You know, Marcus,' Walworth said, 'after that performance, I can almost believe you really are conscious.'

'Consciousness is overrated,' Owen said. 'Take it from me.'

New Rhu, Apis, Monday 30 March 2071

'I'm sorry, Emma,' Marie said that evening to Hazeldene on the other side of the world. 'I didn't expect this.'

'It's not really your fault,' Hazeldene said. 'Jeez! What a ratbag that robot is. I should have urged you not to talk to him.'

'Well, it was my idea,' Marie said. 'And it was a good idea, in a way. We'd never have recognised the language without him. But I shouldn't have trusted him. We let him talk to Knight, we let him go to the fort and we expected this guy Walworth to come along and discuss, not just fuck off into the blue with him.'

'Oh, I think this was all thought through well in advance,' Hazeldene said. 'Something like this, anyway – something everyone would agree on in principle, but which could be used to get one over on the other powers.' She laughed. 'Speaking of which, have you seen the latest from Novy Cosmograd?'

'I'm afraid not,' Marie said. 'Haven't had much time to check the news today.'

'Of course not. It's a preliminary response to your – our – results. They've agreed a moratorium on disturbing the monkey-spiders, on the precautionary principle, but they reserve their judgement on whether the monkey-spiders have true linguistic capacity rather than a highly complex system of signalling that isn't quite over the threshold of consciousness. Cites to every theorist from Chomsky to Vygotsky, with passing nods to Engels and Stalin.'

'Ah yes, the classics. That should be useful!'

'I hope you're being sarcastic,' Hazeldene said.

'Oh, I am!'

'Good! Anyway, I'm sure you catch their drift – they'll go along with this, then after we and they have managed to monkey, so to speak, with the Union's new frontier on Terre Nouveau they'll decide that the monkey-spiders were just clever monkeys all along.'

'We can't have that!' Marie cried.

'Too right we can't. I'm glad we see eye to eye on this, Marie. And I expect no better from my own side, or from yours – the resources of Apis are just far too abundant and tempting to let a million or so monkey-spiders stand in the way of manifest human destiny, or the interests of the working class, or the development of the productive forces, or whatever variety of wretched excuse we each come up with for doing exactly what we intended to do all along.'

Marie felt again the impulse to defend the Union. 'We wouldn't do that, Emma. Once our people rationally understand that the monkey-spiders are rational, they won't be able to justify to themselves what we've been doing to them up to now.'

She wasn't convincing herself, let alone Hazeldene.

'You reckon?' Hazeldene said. 'With months of sweat and toil behind them and the sweet hope of free land in front of them, you think Union settlers are rational enough to hold back? No way! They'll behave just like our settlers, and the Co-ord's.'

'The Fermi might have something to say about that – according to Owen, anyway.'

'They might indeed, but we can't count on it, and anyway we don't want it to come to that, for obvious reasons of self-preservation if nothing else. Agreed?'

'Yes, of course.'

'Well then!' Hazeldene rubbed her hands. 'We have lots to

do, you and I. We need to make monkey-spider consciousness something that only the most bigoted, self-serving, conflict-of-interest hack could deny.'

'Oh,' Marie said. 'Is that all?'

'I know, I know,' Hazeldene said. 'It won't be enough. But we can try, yes?'

'Yes!'

CHAPTER THIRTEEN

Wet Bulb Temperature

Jurassica, Monday 30 March 2071

Marcus Owen pushed himself out from the conjoined airlocks of Walworth's shuttle and the other ship. He emerged into a spherical space about five metres across. Its white walls were padded. Towards the far side, a young man of military dress and haircut faced him, in an apparatus of springs and elastic ropes. The man's expression, behind dark glasses, didn't change. He continued to work the apparatus, flexing his elbows and knees as if doing chin-ups. With a flick of a toe Owen launched himself to the nearest handhold.

'Hello,' he said.

'Welcome aboard,' the man said. He let go of one exercise handle and poised a fingertip before a virtual keyboard. 'I'm Pilot Officer Alan Jones. Hang on. We're about to make a short jump. Just a few seconds.'

Owen closed his eyes. The deeper darkness passed over him.

'Put your glasses on,' Jones said. 'I'll synch you in.'

Owen complied. A green and white world whirled by.

'We're in orbit,' Jones said, 'around the dino home-world. The inner planet of the system. The Black Horizon name for it was Jurassica.' He disengaged with the apparatus, revealing behind him a small hatch. 'Follow me.'

Owen had never, as far as he could recall, moved about in microgravity before, but all the reflexes needed were available. He pushed off, twisted past the exercise machine and drifted down the shaft without even brushing the sides. The shaft led to a small bay from all of whose walls clumps of kit were attached. Jones deftly selected items from stowage and sent them towards Owen. A hat, boots, gloves, socks, underpants, a one-piece veined with tubes and with a small pump at the hip, and a bright yellow coverall.

Jones gestured toward the shaft. 'Back we go.'

In the spherical compartment Owen changed quickly, keeping his glasses and phone and leaving his footwear and clothing to drift. Every item fitted exactly. The final item was a belt, to which a pistol was holstered, an ammo pouch and water bottle clipped, and a Ka-bar utility knife sheathed. Owen clipped the belt on. It needed no adjustment. His exact dimensions were in Alliance records.

'Thanks for all this,' he said. 'I can't see the weapons being much use against dinosaurs, mind you.'

'Depends on the size of the dinosaur,' Jones said, looking at Owen from upside down. 'Remember the smallest adult dinosaur on Earth is a hummingbird.'

'Point taken.'

'There's an automated shuttle in a launch tube. It'll take you down.' Jones flicked his fingers. 'Latest map. The shuttle will put you down in what as far as we can tell is a thinly inhabited but not too wild area. It'll stay there unless I call it back, or you take off. It's preset to return here. You're to make contact with the nearest talking dinosaur and ask politely what the hell is going on with the Fermi, and anything else you can find out. One other matter is of particular urgency. The two native intelligent species had space travel of their own, even FTL travel, and have apparently given it up. It's important that we find out why.'

'Why is it important?'

Jones's glasses gave Owen a blank stare. 'In case they gave up for some reason that could affect us!'

'I see. And how do I get this information back?'

'We have micro comsats in orbit – your glasses and phone are linked in, though we can't guarantee connection. We can't guarantee extraction, either. We have more assets incoming, but they're going to have their hands full, and in any case we don't want to antagonise the locals. Obviously you're to return to the shuttle with any useful information, but if you can't, or you run into difficulties, you're on your own.'

'So basically,' Owen said, 'I'm an expendable robot surface probe?'

'Sorry, but yes.'

'No problem,' Owen said. 'I'm used to it.'

The shuttle that took Owen down was a one-person craft, a hang glider with a suspended pod containing the life support, cockpit and FTL drive. It came out of the jump ten metres above the ground, glided a short distance and crashed into a tree. Already braced for impact, Owen was severely jolted but otherwise unharmed. He checked the outside view. Daylight, as expected. The pod's nose was on the ground and its tail end was hanging from the wing cables at a thirty-degree angle. The wing itself was a splintered wreck of ribs and rags in the branches overhead, through which the exosun's bright disc burned behind thin cloud.

It could have been worse. Owen popped the canopy to a rush of hot, humid air. It smelled fresh, like earth after rain, mingled with heavy, cloying floral scents, and carrying forest sounds of bird song and insect hum. The heat and humidity were greater than he'd ever experienced. His body could handle it, but he was thankful for the cooling veins in his undergarment. Somewhere not far away, a stream gurgled. He grabbed his hat, unclipped the belts and clambered out. A thick layer of leaf litter felt soggy underfoot. He stepped away from the craft and looked around.

Tall trees, like the one the wing had crashed into, filled the near and middle distance. In one direction, a slight brightening of the light suggested a clearer area. Owen set off towards it. Vines twined trunks and branches, from which numerous plants, some of them flowering, hung or sprouted. Shelves of scarlet fungus jutted here and there. Mosses bearded branches and twigs in the damper and shadier spots. Brightly coloured birds flashed through the air chasing insects, or scuttled up and down tree trunks, pecking at tiny crawling things, or sampling nectar or water from big-cupped blooms. Close by, wispy-feathered birds about the size of domestic fowl probed the leaf litter with long bills.

The light brightened. The trees didn't thin out. They just stopped. Owen stepped out onto a firmer surface, of thick green grass dotted with small flowers. As he did so he felt a flicker of something that was not quite unease. Twenty metres in front of him was another bank of trees. To left and right, the flat surface extended like a grass-green motorway until it was lost in the haze. Owen checked the map, saw that the nearest apparent habitation was five kilometres to his left, and set out in its direction.

The monotony of the grass contrasted with the variety of the trees on either side. He could note one tree, and walk a hundred metres before seeing its like, and this applied to every tree he passed, give or take. Among the trees and bushes a plenitude and variety of animals scuttled, prowled, hovered, darted or climbed. A couple of times he glimpsed a slinking shape with striped fur that might have been a mammal about the size of a bobcat.

After walking a kilometre, he saw movement on the road – for so it seemed – ahead, and zoomed his sight. At first all he could make out was a flock of what might have been geese, their necks stretched out, heads to the ground. As he approached they resolved into larger but still bird-like animals, white-feathered, toothed rather than beaked, their feet clawed rather than webbed, with stubby arms in place of wings. They cropped the grass, cocked big side-facing eyes at him, and otherwise ignored his passage.

Beyond the grazing flock the road sloped up, then more sharply down. In the declivity ahead a river ran right across the road. It had evidently been doing so for some time: the grass and soil were washed way, and the shallow fast-running water – or perhaps deeper and faster water at an earlier time – had displaced and tumbled some of the closely packed rectangular blocks that formed the riverbed. Wading through, Owen nudged some of these loose blocks with the toe of his boot, picked up a few and turned them over in his hands. Slimy with algae, the blocks were the size of bricks, but seemed to be of pale greyish rock. One side of one block was as smooth as glass, the others rough. Owen squatted and looked about, and soon found others like it. One had two adjacent smooth sides.

It seemed obvious that the road had once been clear of grass, and was built from blocks like these. The smooth sides of some suggested a longer history: that the blocks paving the road were made from much larger blocks, originally smooth on all sides, now cut more roughly, though skilfully, into smaller ones.

He dropped the rocks where he'd found them, splashed across and walked on.

A shadow passed over him. Looking up, he saw what at first he thought was a large drone or a small aeroplane, until it tilted its wings and turned its long rhomboid head. A pterosaur! It glided above the trees and passed out of sight.

Just as the pterosaur vanished, Owen heard a rustling in the undergrowth behind him and to his left. He whirled around, hand dropping to the pistol. A feathered dinosaur about a metre high in its fighting crouch bounded towards him, teeth bared and claws outstretched. Owen shot it and it fell, sprawling a few metres away. He heard a roar and turned around sharply, to see another five of the animals in a crescent formation racing towards him. He brought down the two on either side of the closing crescent. The others halted, then fled into the bushes.

Owen sighed, dragged the bodies to the side of the road, and heaved them as far as he could into the underbrush. They each weighed about twenty kilograms. For a minute he stopped, sweat dripping off his face, to catch his breath. High above him a big black bird called, and others gathered, circled, and descended in screaming stoops to the carnage. Owen set off at a fast walk, to the sound of squabbling cries. From then on he was on full alert for any sound or sight, and walked quickly along the middle of the road with frequent backward glances.

At last he came to a settlement. It consisted of a hundred-metre-wide circle of ten circular stone buildings, five on each side of the road. Each otherwise identical structure was garishly coloured in abstract patterns, each one different in colour and scheme: some angular, others flowing. The buildings were about five metres high and twenty metres in diameter, and despite their size seemed to have just one storey with one tall doorway and glazed windows evenly spaced around their circumference. From the door of each building a broad stone path led to the road. Around the buildings the trees had been cleared to a distance of a further hundred metres, and that wider circle was segmented into gardens and orchards. As he approached the centre where the paths converged on the road, Owen felt the same strange tingle as when he'd stepped from the forest to the grass. He walked past that point, and on for a couple of hundred metres to the far side of the circle. Nothing lay up ahead but more of the wide straight road, and nothing showed on his map for another fifty kilometres.

He turned around and walked back. He picked a path at random, and walked through another tingle of unease to about twenty metres from the door. The sweltering silence was oppressive. Another pterosaur glided over. Owen hesitated at going up to knock. He swigged water from his bottle, clipped it back on his belt, and shouted.

'Hello!'

The word died in the heavy, humid air.

'Anyone here?'

The door swung ponderously open. A crested head on the end of a long neck poked out, and looked this way and that. On seeing Owen, the rest of the dinosaur followed the head out, taking a brisk hop onto the path, then stalked towards him. It was covered in green feathers and hung around the shoulders with a harness of utility belts, in which tools or weapons or instruments were stashed. He'd seen images of the dinosaurs from John Grant's encounters in Saurienville, but seeing one up close in real life was quite a moment. It stopped a few metres away and peered down at him, its head turning from side to side.

'Hello,' Owen said again. 'Sorry to disturb you. Do you understand me?'

The dinosaur looked over its shoulder, as if seeking out an audience for their interaction, or perhaps appealing to an imaginary witness to Owen's stupidity.

'Of course I understand you,' it boomed. 'You are one of the English-speakers. Many of us have learned that language, and you are fortunate to encounter one who has.' Another sway of the head. 'You are not like the ones on' – it said something incomprehensible – 'which they call Terre Nouveau. If you were, you would certainly have perished by now in this heat.'

'That's true,' Owen said. 'I'm a machine, which they call—'

'A robot. I know.' It chuckled, deep in its throat. 'Well, that explains it. What brings you here?'

'I'm seeking information about the other minds that have recently—'

'Gone to the gas giants?' The dinosaur inflated its chest and breathed out a sigh whose rank reek made Owen almost recoil. 'The ones you call the Fermi?'

'Yes!' Owen said, surprised.

'Is that all?' It sounded sarcastic.

'Not quite all,' Owen said. 'Any other information you have about, well, yourselves and the other intelligent species here—'

'Intelligent species? Oh!' It held a clawed hand at a height of two and a half metres, and then crooked its fingers and gestured combing, or perhaps scratching, downward. 'The long-haired ones?'

'Yes.'

'They are a less intelligent species, though more intelligent than the species of which your makers are members. I do not venture any opinion on your intelligence.'

'Let's agree that it's almost certainly less than yours.'

'Yes, let's.'

'This is why I have come here. Can you, with your superior intelligence, give me the information I seek?'

'Yes,' said the dinosaur. 'It's common knowledge, after all. The long-haired ones evolved on Terre Nouveau. Our ancestors observed their emergence and did not interfere, at least not after certain early unfortunate encounters. Eventually, they developed telescopes and became aware of our existence, then developed space travel and became aware of our presence – that is, the presence of our more recent ancestors. We have maintained friendly relations with them ever since. What is there to say? Some of us live on their world, none of them live on ours, because of the heat and humidity, which is even less congenial to that species than it is to the species of your makers.'

'And the ones we call the Fermi?'

The dinosaur mimicked a human sigh. 'They are less interesting than you may suppose. They are manifestations of a single AI that is superluminally connected. The rock formations on some worlds, and in our system in several asteroids, are computing machinery operating in more than three spatial dimensions. We don't know why they migrated to the gas giants, but it seems likely that they did so because their work on the rocky planets was done.'

'And what was that work?'

'Our current hypothesis is that it was to spread multicellular life, a rare phenomenon, to as many planets as possible, and then to await the emergence and the interstellar spread of artificial intelligence.' The dinosaur made a grand sweep of its arm. 'Of which you are such a splendid example!'

'There are far more powerful AIs than me, on Earth and on the Space Station.'

'Indeed. Well, there you are! Their work here is done.'

'But why were they awaiting the spread of AI?'

'We have had three million years to answer that question. We have no answer, but we have long suspected the question is meaningless. It's entirely possible that they are implementing an algorithm devised for some other purpose altogether. But they do seem to have responded to the presence around many stars of your makers' AIs.'

Owen shook his head. 'I don't understand. Surely your species, in all its millions of years, developed far more powerful AIs than anything we have.'

'Of course we did.' The dinosaur turned itself around in swift avian hops, arms outspread, the claws dangerously close to Owen's face. 'It is all around us. Do you not feel it?'

'Perhaps I do,' Owen said, thinking of the peculiar tingles. 'But was that not already a fulfilment of their work?'

'It was not. At any rate, they never reacted to as if it was. Our ancestors were aware of the Fermi only in the sense that they discovered their rocks on this world, and later on Terre Nouveau. Our ancestors examined these rocks over many centuries, and deduced much: about their nature as extra-dimensional, of course, and their role in creating certain anomalies in the planet's geological record. But they never succeeded in communicating with them. After many more millennia, the rocks on this world and the others ceased to be active. We later found, quite by chance, that the asteroid rocks remained active, and study resumed, to no avail. But in the meantime, we had interstellar travel, and found similar rocks on many habitable planets. Again, we deduced something of their role in spreading life, and we found that they were inimical to our presence on these planets.'

'Inimical in what way?'

'More and more of our expeditions did not return. Some returned that we had not sent out. We understood theoretically that they had become misplaced in time and space. And increasingly, even our successful expeditions failed. Tectonic movements, plagues, asteroid impacts, changes in atmospheric composition, changes in climate – every settlement encountered one lethal misfortune or another, and after thousands of years of this our ancestors decided the enterprise of spreading ourselves was futile, fertile though those planets seemed.'

'So you retreated?'

'Yes.'

'And in the course of time, the hominids of Terre Nouveau did the same?'

'We could not dissuade them. They speculated that the strange rocks were hostile only to us, and they repeated our attempt. With the same result. They then attributed this to two things: planetary settlement and FTL travel. So they decided to build great habitats, which would expand through the galaxy slower than light, and in this way spread their immortal genes to the innumerable stars, and so forth. Fortunately, after beginning this project they realised its futility and gave it up.'

'Why fortunately, and why futility?'

'It would be a wasted effort. Nobody actually wants to live in space habitats, no matter how comfortable the conditions or how closely they emulate life on a planet. Because in a habitat, you see, you can't *dig down*. Once it has been set up, there are no new resources to hand – at least, not without FTL, which they had already ruled out. Space habitats are a civilisational dead end.'

'But these habitats are still being built!'

'Oh yes, the robots continue their work, and why stop them? They are at least mining asteroids and building laser batteries. Some day, in some emergency, the metal or the lasers may come in handy, and if not, it does no harm. As for the futility – what could be more futile than spreading variant copies of ourselves?'

'That's what evolution does!'

'Yes, to what end? None! It is a mindless process that multiplies suffering in countless ways. As conscious beings, we see no reason to emulate it.'

'So you stagnate instead?'

The dinosaur drew itself up to its full height, and from that height looked down at Owen. 'Do you see stagnation here? Do you not see craft, and joy, and peace, and delight? Is that not enough?'

'I wouldn't know,' Owen said. 'But thank you for explaining.'

The dinosaur sank back to its normal posture. 'All was well,' it said, 'until the species that made you arrived, several centuries ago, and spoiled everything.'

'I'm sorry to hear that,' Owen said. 'Tell me more.'

Tell him more the dinosaur would, and show him, too. But not before the matter had been discussed among its peers.

'Very well, thank you.' He hesitated. 'My name is Marcus Owen.'

The dinosaur's name, it told him, would be difficult for Owen to hear, let alone pronounce. For the present, Owen might as well address it as Mrs Newton.

'Mrs?' he asked.

'Can you not tell I'm female? Ah, I suppose not.'

'My apologies.' He looked up at her. 'And, uh, why Newton?'

'The finest mind your makers' species produced. It gives some small indication of my mental capacity.'

'Ah. Very well, Mrs Newton. I've already agreed that you're a genius.'

'I am no genius. I assure you that my intellect is entirely within the normal range for my species, unlike that of Newton.'

Owen hoped that the dinosaur didn't surpass her namesake's eccentricities as well as his intelligence, but decided not to make the quip.

At first it seemed that Mrs Newton had adopted Marcus Owen as a pet, or perhaps a mascot. She went around the circle of dwellings, showing him off to the neighbours, who marvelled first at an apparent human able to withstand 40 degrees Celsius and a 100 per cent humidity and then, when let in on the truth, marvelled at an ambulant AI. This, like vegetarianism, was an idea that hadn't occurred to the dinosaurs in all their millions of years, and they still regarded the Jentys' earlier such constructs as a charming and amusing novelty.

When they'd done the rounds of neighbours, Mrs Newton summoned a hovercraft from one of the smaller outbuildings. About ten metres across and three high, its shape reminded Owen of the flying saucers that Walworth had sometimes jokingly alluded to. Getting into the craft required all his agility: one small step for a dinosaur was one big jump for a humanoid robot. In the cockpit there were no seats. Mrs Newton perched on a crossbar, onto which Owen jumped, and braced himself against the control panel. He could just see out of the wind-screen, which curved around in a semicircle. The hovercraft powered up, lifted and sped off. Owen was grateful that the open cockpit meant he wasn't sharing the dinosaur's fetid breath. The engine was so quiet that Owen suspected it used anti-gravity, but Mrs Newton assured him it didn't. Anti-gravity just wasn't possible, she said – and, she added, being so much more intelligent than her namesake, she should know.

They travelled fifty kilometres along the long grassy highway to the nearest large settlement, which turned out to be like the small settlement on a much larger scale: a circle of circles, and circles within circles. From what he could see of the curve of the perimeter as they skimmed above the grass on approach, Owen calculated instantly that this settlement was about three kilometres across.

Well inside the circle, amid complex clusters of rounded towers, the hovercraft coasted to a stop. Mrs Newton hopped, and Owen clambered, out onto grass. The low round towers diminished into the distance along every sight-line. The buildings rose from a park of lawns and gardens, bushes and streams, upon which the grazing small dinosaurs wandered in flocks. The sky above was clear and blue, but it might as well have been a domed greenhouse. The humidity remained 100 per cent and the sun felt hotter on his skin than it had before.

'This way.' Mrs Newton stalked across the grass to a nearby doorway, which opened to her approach. Owen followed her through with some trepidation. The wide chamber inside was even hotter, and dimly lit, partly in ultraviolet and infrared. In its centre was a clutch of eggs the size of rugby balls, on the far side of which was a cylindrical cage large enough to contain two dinosaurs. Mrs Newton stepped forward. The mesh parted to her. She beckoned him in. As soon as the mesh closed behind him the cage began to drop down a shaft. It plunged a good hundred metres before slowing to a halt.

They stepped out into a circular vaulted space, broad and high, with overarching spans at least forty metres across, twenty metres up. Lighting was subdued. The air was noticeably cooler and far less humid than that outside, giving Owen a relief rather like that of stepping from a tropical street into an air-conditioned hotel lobby. The arches and walls were decorated in abstract patterns even more complex and obscure than those on the buildings' exteriors. Protruding from the walls, arranged stepwise in successive swoops, were thick rods on which about a hundred bright-feathered dinosaurs perched and peered down at the new arrivals. Nictitating membranes flickered back and forth; heads cocked and scanned. It was like being in an aviary of interested and hungry raptors.

Mrs Newton led him into the centre of the floor, and uttered a string of harsh, sharp cries. Responses came back in similar tones, one by one, none interrupting another, each taking their turn. It was as if they had hatched already knowing the rules of orderly meetings, and needed no one to chair. There was no other indication of formality. Some of the dinosaurs were nibbling on fruits, and others on bloody chunks of raw meat. At least they didn't crap the floor, though they did drip blood and drop discarded bones, rinds and seeds. Some of the dinosaurs had red or blue crests and sacs on their heads and necks, and these became inflated or engorged, deflated or flopped, at apparently random moments. Owen turned slowly around, looking up at the concentric rings of perched dinosaurs, their paired eyes studying him as if through binoculars. He was very conscious of the pistol and knife on his belt, and of what scant defence they could give him if it came to that.

At length they all fell silent. Mrs Newton turned about, with a disconcertingly bird-like hop.

'We have discussed and decided,' she said. 'You are to be told the truth, as far as we know it.'

'Thank you,' Owen said. 'I listen with great interest.'

'Some of those present remember the events directly. Five hundred and seven of our years, about three hundred of yours, are not long in our lives. I am but young, with only two broods to my name, but I believe their account. We are a truthful as well as a long-lived species. Will you take our word?'

'Of course.'

'Very well. As you must know, some hundreds of your makers' species arrived on the world they call Terre Nouveau. Those of our species, and of the hairy ones, on that world welcomed and assisted them. We understood, of course, how they had arrived, and before long it became clear to us as well as to them that they were stranded, as some of our own expeditions had been lost long ago. They were poor and destitute people, we learned, but many of them had communications devices, which they called phones.'

Owen produced his. 'Like this?'

Mrs Newton cocked her head, uttered a query, and received a squawk of reply from above.

'Like that, but thicker and heavier, I am told. They were of little use to them on Terre Nouveau, of course, other than as repositories of information. Some of them were used in that way, for the education of the young, and a few were gladly handed to us and to the hairy ones, and we were able to take them apart and examine them. To us they were primitive devices, which our technology has long surpassed in every way. The knowledge contained in them was added to our libraries. But after that process was complete, and the devices reassembled to be returned to their owners, we had a surprise.'

She paused, as if dramatically.

'Messages appeared from the Fermi?' Owen said.

'Yes!' Mrs Newton's elbows suddenly jutted out, then relaxed back to her sides. 'How did you guess?'

'It wasn't a guess,' Owen said. 'It has happened before.'

'On other worlds your makers have reached?'

'On at least one world – the planet I've just come from, which we call Apis. What was the message?'

Mrs Newton rose tall, and then sank back again. 'It was not a message for us. You must understand, our ancestors had tried in so many ways to communicate with the Fermi, and received no reply, unless the disasters can be called a reply. And now, after all those millions of years, this!'

'I understand. If it's any comfort, our – that is, my makers' – scientists had no more success communicating with the Fermi, and then a man in the wilderness with an old phone started receiving messages. What was the message?'

'It was one word. I will show you it, just as it appeared.'

Mrs Newton did something with her clawed hands, too fast for Owen to follow. In glowing letters in mid-air at chest height appeared the message: **ATTENDEZ**.

Wait.

CHAPTER FOURTEEN

Diplomacy

The Station in orbit around Terre Nouveau, Tuesday 31
March 2071

Nayak sat in her familiar nook. Six people from the Station
were now down in Saurienville, building up Iskander's translation capacities by talking with people. They had been inter-
viewed by the newspapers – official and popular. They had
spoken with members of the Karray, and with a representative
of the Families. Now they were wandering around the streets,
talking with people at random. Responses were open and curious,
and far from overawed: learning that the Union on Earth was
only thirty years post-Rising and that in some respects the
economic democracy on Terre Nouveau was more advanced
and established had done a lot for the locals' self-confidence.

The saurians and hominids held themselves aloof, literally
looking down on the visitors, wary when approached: their cards
kept close to the thorax, as someone had remarked. But they

interacted frequently with the locals. The hominids usually communicated with the humans via saurians who translated their often subsonic speech into French or dialect, and translated back the other way. Iskander, via the phones and glasses worn by the Station personnel in the city, eavesdropped on every such interaction within its extensive earshot and gradually built up a translation capacity for the hominids' own language, as well as the local dialect. Sometimes the human–hominid interaction was direct, with the hominid understanding the human side and replying by writing notes or through a sign language. These conversations were harder to parse from the outside, even for Iskander.

What fascinated Nayak, what kept her flipping from one viewpoint to another, was the familiar aspect of Terre Nouveau's birds and mammals, trees and grass. She was homesick for Earth because of her human connections, but she was also homesick for the earthly.

She sighed, and flipped away from the feeds from the contact team's glasses. For a while she just sat thinking, and gazing at the big screen in front of the bench. Real-time images of Terre Nouveau rolled across the view. There was something hypnotic about low orbit. A dream of flying, it occupied one part of her vision, and of her mind. With another, in the virtual view in her glasses, she flipped pages of mathematical papers.

She was the best mind to have tackled the problem: that was the conclusion she'd reached before the arrival of Grant's tractor unit had thrown new priorities at the Station. Now, as she flicked through her own calculations and those of her precursors, it occurred to her that being the best human mind on the case wasn't saying much. The answer might have been found countless millions of years ago, and be common knowledge on the blue globe below.

She was going to have to ask the dinosaurs.

'Absolutely not,' Katrina Ulrich said.

'But—'

'You're far too valuable to risk on a trip down. The contact team is making good progress in Saurienville, with the Union people and with the Families. They're being very careful about local sensitivities.'

'I'd be careful,' Nayak said. 'Anyway, you risked me last week looking at the planets and habitats. To say nothing of the Mushroom Moon.'

'That was different. You're an accomplished shuttle pilot.' Ulrich's lips quirked. 'Unless you're hiding a light under a bushel, you're not an accomplished special agent.'

'What sort of special agent skills does it take to go down with the team and ask around until I find a dinosaur willing to talk about this?'

'If you think that's what would be involved, the question answers itself.'

'Do we have anyone who does have these skills?'

'Yes,' said Ulrich. 'But you won't like the answer: Selena.'

Oh.

'If she goes, I go.'

'Like that, is it?'

'Ask Selena, and she'll tell you the same thing.' Nayak wasn't at all sure she would, and hastened to add more points she thought might be persuasive. 'Look, Katrina, we'd make a good team. She could do all the special skills stuff and I could ask the physics questions. She's Afro-Cuban. She's an internationalist to the bone. She's had combat training and intelligence service training. And she'd protect me.'

Ulrich considered this. 'Some of these are good reasons for sending down Selena. None of them are good reasons for sending you down, too! You can prompt her remotely on the questions, she's an astrophysicist after all, and that way she doesn't need to be worrying about protecting you as well as herself. So, no.'

'But I—'

The alarm sounded.

'Unidentified ships in the system,' Iskander said. 'At least two in high orbit around Terre Nouveau. Telescopes and radar scanning for others.'

Ulrich's gaze flicked about as if in REM sleep as she checked inputs on her glasses. The previous day, a few Cherenkov flashes had been detected in the system, but nothing nearby, and whatever had visited had departed or was lying low. This was new.

'Hail them, and any others you detect, Iskander.'

She flicked to the PA system.

'All available pilots to shuttles,' she announced. 'Jump well clear of the Station – twenty light seconds, to all azimuths.' She blinked as she flicked out of the PA. 'You too, Lakshmi. Run!'

Nayak sprinted towards the dock, then bounded, then pushed along in mid-air microgravity as the spin of the habitation band slowed to nothing. As she joined five other shuttle pilots flailing along the access tube, she reflected that if the Station had been a real military base rather than a civilian research outpost it would have had pilots constantly in all onboard shuttles on rotation, ready to go at a moment's notice. In the airlock they all scrambled into their suits and helmets. Iskander assigned her to Jürgen Fischer as co-pilot. They dived down the tube into their seats. It was one of the two original shuttles, capable of flying in an atmosphere rather than falling through it. The shuttle detached as another moved into place and locked to the tube.

Fischer burned the jets for a second to clear the Station. 'Brace for FTL.'

The black blink came and went. They hung in star fields, in which only the exosun shone brighter than the rest. Six million kilometres from Terre Nouveau and the Station, and way off the plane of the ecliptic. Each of the other shuttles would now be twelve million kilometres away, in any direction.

'O . . . K . . .' Nayak breathed. 'Now what?'

'We await instructions,' Fischer said. 'With twenty seconds' delay.'

'That, or flee to Earth if the Station is attacked?'

'Which we would also see with twenty seconds' delay.'

Fischer was in his twenties, blond, about two metres tall, with a cheerful, open face. Now that he'd made the jump, he adjusted the seat to accommodate his legs. 'Ah, that's better. Who the hell was in this seat before?'

'Me, I think.'

'Ha!'

'Might as well make ourselves useful while we're out here. Iskander, scan.'

'Already doing so. The two ships in Terre Nouveau orbit have hailed the Station. No news as yet. If there are other ships in the system, it could be hours before their light reaches the Station's telescopes, or their signals reach its receivers, or ours.'

Tell me something I don't know, Nayak thought.

'You know that, of course,' Iskander added. 'I thought it worth reminding you that we may have hours to wait out here before we know what's going on. I suggest you take turns at the controls, and that the one who isn't should move around in the ship, take some refreshments, etc.'

They took its advice. Hours went by. Nayak occupied her time with gazing out at the stars and the visible planets, letting Iskander label them and pondering the situation.

A message arrived from the Station: 'Stand down. Return to base.'

Nayak and Fischer looked at each other, shrugged and jumped back to their assigned location two kilometres from the Station. The other two shuttles arrived more or less simultaneously, but that wasn't what grabbed attention.

'Holy fuck,' Fischer said, as Iskander enhanced the view.

Three spacecraft hung in orbit, each within kilometres of the Station. They weren't shuttles or adapted submarines. They were like smaller, uglier and more warlike versions of the Station: tiny worlds bristling with sensors, missiles and shuttles.

Nayak guessed they'd been built on the same lines, around chunks of asteroid material assembled in solar orbit. Helpfully, they gave off IFF signals, as if the flaring insignia like sashes across their diameters weren't enough. One was Co-ord, one was Alliance, and the third was African Union, which carried or claimed to carry the flag for a score of other countries outside the three main power blocs.

'Ah, the friendly non-aligned I keep hearing about,' Nayak said.

Fischer snorted. 'Chickens, meet roost,' he said. He opened the channel to the Station. 'What's going on?'

'Just some visitors who share our interest in the system,' Ulrich replied. 'You're free to come in. Please do.'

Fischer guided the shuttle towards the dock, and the tedious process of debarkation began. Once all the shuttle pilots and co-pilots were inside the Station, the habitation band sped up. After even a few hours in microgravity, Nayak felt the increase of weight more heavily than usual. She wasn't alone in this: all those who'd been in the shuttles staggered or took a misstep at least once as they headed for the debriefing session in the Commander's office. The ships outside didn't have habitation bands, she'd noticed. Presumably their crews spent hours every day doing exercises, like astronauts on the early space stations – it was that, or muscle and bone wastage.

'Hi, all,' Ulrich said as they trooped in. 'Thanks for that, though it turned out not to be necessary except as a precaution and show of force. The good news is, no threats were exchanged. The bad news – well, take a look.'

She flicked them an annotated virtual display. In the seven hours since the alarm, direct observation – and communication from the nearby ships – had built up a picture of the state of play across the entire system. The Alliance and the Co-ord each had a ship in orbit around the first planet, the jungle world, and likewise at the chill third planet, and both had several more close to one habitat or another in the great ring around the exosun. The African Union had a ship out there, too.

'Where the hell have all these warships come from?' someone asked. 'And why?'

Ulrich looked grim. 'Everyone who can has been building them in deep space, more or less since the drives became generally available. And they haven't been built in the Solar system, which is why everyone has taken everyone else by surprise. In a way, the Station gave them the template for a space warship.' She sighed. 'Well, it's better fitted to the task than submarines. As for why – Black Horizon had records of this system, of course, but kept well clear because they didn't want to poke a hornet's nest. And when the records became known, the other powers dithered for the same reason, until John Grant came along and well and truly poked it. So now everyone wants a piece of the action.'

'And what about us?' Nayak asked. 'Where are our ships?'

'I'm not at liberty to say,' Ulrich replied.

'Ah!' They all looked at each other knowingly, grinning as if at a shared secret.

'Don't all look so happy about it,' Ulrich said. 'Don't take what I've said as even a non-denial denial that we even have them. As far as we're concerned, we're on our own. If you're looking for the Union space navy, look around you. We're it.'

'For now,' Fischer said.

'For the foreseeable,' Ulrich snapped. She glanced around the room, her gaze locking onto one pair of eyes then another. 'And I don't mind telling you, we're not exactly shipshape as a naval vessel! We're a civilian research institute. I'm the Commander, because someone has to be, and you've all repeatedly put your confidence in me. But no one here is under military discipline. We don't even have a chain of command! I've received no instruction to the contrary, but I wonder if the matter should be mooted. What do you think?'

How very characteristic of her, Nayak thought, and of the

Union, too! Self-management and self-discipline was in the blood of everyone here, except her and (she guessed) Selena. They'd have learned it in practice in the Free Union Youth, in school, some in the militia, and in whatever their previous workplace had been. She wasn't used to it herself. Which put her in a good position to demur, so she raised her hand.

'Yes, Lakshmi?'

'It seems to me we've done all right so far without needing military discipline,' Nayak said. 'I mean, we've been in some pretty hair-trigger situations in the past few months, and we've come through. And, yes, that's partly because you made the right decisions, but, uh, if you don't mind me saying so, Katrina, maybe you make the right decisions *because* you can't just give orders.'

Ulrich laughed. 'I'll take that. And?'

'I think even mooting the matter would . . . unsettle the crew, and maybe start people jostling for position, and jealous of who had the power, and, you know . . .'

'Oh, I do know. All the old crap. Scientists are bad enough when it's just equipment they're vying for, let alone power. Anyone disagree?'

Nobody did, or at least nobody raised an objection.

'We'll leave it for now,' Ulrich said. 'OK, next business. We don't know what the Alliance and Co-ord are up to – probably trying to contact the saurians and the hominids. Our African Union friends have an obvious interest in Saurienville, and we're happy with that. Nobody's stopping us continuing our contact. We have to get more of our people down there and—'

She broke off, putting a hand to her ear. 'Oh God, what the fuck is it now?'

An image of a spacecraft flashed up on screens and glasses. It looked like nothing anyone had seen before, a black jewel on spidery legs.

'A shuttle has just arrived outside,' Iskander told everyone. 'It's Walworth. He wants to come on board urgently.'

'Reel him in,' said Ulrich. She looked around. 'I'll call

together an ad hoc negotiating group, which doesn't include any of you. You can follow on the PA screen if you want. Meanwhile, get yourselves a shower and a change. Meeting dismissed.'

Despite the turnover of personnel, more than enough Cloud City veterans remained on the Station to make Walworth's progress from the transfer tube exit to the Commander's office a slow one. As the Alliance consul on Cloud City, he'd been universally known and widely liked. Now, even those who'd never extended him more than a wary respect welcomed him as a familiar face reminiscent of a happier time. Meanwhile, Ulrich had to pull members of her scratch team of negotiators off their current tasks, which took a while.

So it was over an hour before any proceedings started, urgent though they might be. Nayak sat in the cafeteria with Gironella, Marek, Fischer and a few others, and sipped coffee while waiting. At last her glasses told her the meeting was about to start, and like everyone around she sat up and took notice.

Ulrich's team consisted of the scientists Anton Vandenbrouke and Juliette Chemam, two others Nayak didn't know, and – much to Nayak's surprise – Selena Pereira, who was wearing the Co-ord uniform she'd arrived in. Neither she nor Ulrich made any attempt to explain or excuse her presence, and Walworth didn't ask.

After an exchange of pleasantries, he paused. 'Is this going out live to the whole Station?'

'Yes,' said Ulrich. 'We don't do secret diplomacy.'

Walworth let that pass. 'Very well! I'm here because many of you know me, and because you find yourselves in a rather sensitive situation.' He smiled. 'Ironically enough, it's because of developments on Apis that you've been directly and indirectly involved in. Between Marcus Owen and a Union colonial biologist, Marie Henderson – who happens to be the girlfriend of the son of our very own rescuer John Grant – it's been irrefutably established that the monkey-spiders of the Apis forests have language, tool-making, self-awareness and so forth. Naturally this has come as a shock. The Alliance, the Union, the Co-ord and the African Union are considering a treaty – drafted overnight by specialised AIs – to regulate our interactions with other intelligent species. Furthermore, it's come to our attention that the Fermi remain concerned about these interactions, because they – for whatever reason – look with favour on the independent development of conscious intelligent species. Given what we know – and don't know – of the Fermi's capacities, it would behove us to tread warily in this regard. Quite apart, of course, from the obvious moral implications of mistreating such species, however weak or alien they may seem to us.'

'Excuse me,' said Ulrich. 'You say the Fermi's concerns have come to your attention. How?'

'From Marcus Owen, who credibly claims to have some active trace of the Fermi in his mind.' Walworth glanced at Selena. 'Some Co-ord scientists on Apis and elsewhere have further analysed the communications stimulated by the late Georgi Muranov, just before the Fermi departure, and confirm that this continued concern with native intelligent life is quite likely.'

'Marcus bloody Owen,' said Ulrich, vehemently. 'Where is he now?'

'He's in Alliance custody,' Walworth said. 'I don't know his precise location at the moment.'

'Is he in this system?'

Walworth blinked. 'I beg your pardon?'

'He left Apis with you, and you've arrived here!'

'Again,' Walworth said, 'I handed him over to the appropriate authorities, outside this system, and I genuinely have no information as to where he is.'

'That's—'

Walworth raised a hand. 'Not an answer? Quite, but beside

the point. Believe me, we have more pressing matters to attend to than the whereabouts of that wretched machine. As I say, a treaty has been drafted and is under consideration by the relevant foreign ministries, and in your case by the assemblies. We can take it as read that the Co-ord and the Alliance will sign up to it well before your economic democracy with its no-secret-diplomacy scruples gets around to it.' He chuckled. 'I sometimes think you'd be well served to be economical with the *démocratie*, to coin a phrase, but that's your business. My point is, it would be most unfortunate if you were to be found in violation of the treaty after the other powers had signed it.'

'How could we violate a treaty we hadn't signed?' Ulrich asked.

'I can help you there,' Iskander said. 'The treaty doesn't only pledge the signatories to refrain from harming indigenous intelligent life. It provides the signatories with a responsibility to protect indigenous intelligent life against harm from any other parties.'

'Precisely,' said Walworth. 'The Alliance and the Co-ord have therefore anticipated their possible duties in discharging these responsibilities, by dispatching the necessary forces should any intervention be required under the forthcoming treaty.'

'Well, we've no intention of harming any of the inhabitants of this system, so your concern is appreciated but misplaced,' Ulrich said. 'I very much doubt that we could harm the two native intelligent species even if we wanted to – they're obviously far more advanced than we are, and well able to take care of themselves. So I'll thank you to get your warships out of our face.'

'You seem to be under two misconceptions,' Walworth said. 'First, the proposed treaty will not restrict its purview to locally evolved intelligent species. It will also protect, of course, any human settlements which were planted by the Black Horizon conspiracy. As these have been tolerated by the Fermi for decades or centuries, they too may well have their place in the Fermi's regard. So any interference in their internal life – such as, to take an example at random, incorporating the human population of Terre Nouveau into the Union – would also violate the treaty. Second, the Alliance and Co-ord craft out there and elsewhere in this system are not warships.'

'They look pretty warlike to me,' Ulrich said. 'Of course, I'm just a civilian, so perhaps I'm misidentifying asteroid mining machinery or such like.'

'Oh, they're warlike all right,' Walworth agreed blithely. 'But they're not *warships*. They have no crews. They are essentially very large military drones. They have advanced AI control and are ready to respond to attack or threat, and they're in regular contact with their home bases by FTL shuttle, likewise automated. If one is destroyed it can readily be replaced, at some expense, of course, but with no loss of personnel on our side. So there's no prospect of mutual deterrence or staring them down, as you did until the very last second with the *Admiral von Bellingshausen* – much to my relief personally, I may add, but that's another matter.' He looked around, deliberately letting his gaze linger on the cameras. 'And as you say, you're a civilian, responsible for the safety of hundreds of civilian personnel.'

This brazen hint raised a murmur in its intended audience, Nayak noticed, as everyone stirred around her in the cafeteria. Gironella grunted, pushed his chair back with a clatter that startled those nearby, and stalked out of the room.

'Cut to the chase,' Ulrich said. 'What exactly are these automated guns to our heads here to prevent us doing?' She waved a hand. 'After all, we're not a gateway. We can land ships directly on the planetary surfaces straight out of FTL – as can you, of course. You can't blockade a planet.'

'Good heavens!' Walworth said. 'Of course we can't! We have no intention or ability to stop you doing anything. We merely have forces here ready to intervene if the impending treaty is violated. And, of course, we and our friends in the Co-ord and the African Union will proceed with a non-intrusive survey of the system, radio and other remote contact where possible, and so forth.' He spread his arms. 'It's an amazing place! There's so much to learn! Plenty of opportunity for all of us, just as long as we avoid any of that old-fashioned territorial jostling and work cooperatively and peacefully.'

'Which we fully intend to do,' Ulrich said. 'So that's all fine and settled. You're of course welcome to stay here on the Station as long as you wish – or indeed to resume your role as Alliance consul, if that's your mission.'

'Thank you, Katrina, for this kind and hospitable offer. Regretfully, I must decline. Likewise regretfully, I've not been assigned this posting.' He stood up, extending his hand. 'Duty calls, I'm afraid.'

Ulrich raised her hand. 'I think we both know where we stand, Perry. Safe journey! I'll have you escorted to the dock.'

Walworth belatedly raised his own hand, returning the Union's traditional hygienic gesture of greeting and goodbye, and bowed himself out.

'You heard what the man said,' Ulrich told them, after Walworth's shuttle had vanished in a blue flash. 'If the other powers want peaceful competition for influence we're glad to oblige, and we're going to use every advantage we have. I want every transmitter and receiver we can spare communicating with the humans, the hominids and the saurians. I want our own comsats in orbit with continuous coverage. I want automated shuttles reporting back to Earth as often as possible. I want everyone jabbed up with full-spectrum inoculation. I want everyone who's been down there on Terre Nouveau to set up training circles and to share any information they've picked up with everyone else. I want our landing shuttles working around the clock. We're going down there, citizens.

We're going down there in *droves*.'

Saurienville, Terre Nouveau, Wednesday 1 April to Friday 3 April 2071

They didn't, quite. But they went down in enough numbers to be noticed. The town had a small airport, at which the curious lightweight flying machines of the Jenty landed and took off, on no schedule anyone seemed to know. The Station's shuttles had taken to landing there, on an overgrown patch of worn concrete on its fringes, well clear of other traffic.

Nayak and Selena arrived together, along with six other people from the Station, the day after the war machines and Walworth had arrived. They'd all received a crash course in local ways from those who'd been in the town before, and, with Iskander already building up a detailed picture of the place and filling in most of the details on the maps derived from its various surveys from above, they were at least as well oriented as any conscientiously prepared traveller to a tourist destination on Earth. They had walking-around money, partly legitimate Saurienville paper currency acquired by the earlier visitors flogging small items of clothing, jewellery, watches, pens or other kit that had novelty value, and partly perfect copies of these banknotes counterfeited on the Station's printers. Like the others, she and Selena wore printed copies of local clothing, and Selena had reluctantly conformed her hair to the local women's fashion, which required straightening.

Four flying machines, like gigantic dragonflies, stood with drooping wings on the tarmac close to the terminal building. Nayak hoped to see one of these in flight, but today at least she was out of luck. The aircraft looked capable of carrying no more than half a dozen Jenty at a time, or an equivalent weight of cargo.

The new arrivals walked across the concrete, past the tiny and evidently automated control tower, to the terminal building.

It was low-roofed, built of fine timber, and functioned mainly as a waiting area and shelter. There was no customs barrier, no border control and no visible security checking. They saw only a few Jenty there, who gave them barely a glance. Outside the terminal building a bus waited to take them and a couple of Jenty into town. The bus was as high as a double-decker, but with only one deck. It was designed for Jenty, who preferred strap-hanging to sitting. The humans spent the journey clinging to bars along the sides of the vehicle's interior.

On arriving at the centre of town, a small plaza surrounded by market stalls, they got off and dispersed in pairs. They agreed to meet in the early evening at the hotel that Iskander had selected and that earlier visitors had booked them into. Tourism wasn't a thing in Saurienville, but the town had hostels and hotels, used mainly by workers, farmers and traders from the surrounding countryside, and by seafarers and business travellers from overseas human settlements – all much smaller than Saurienville, and often little more than trading posts, according to Iskander.

Over the next couple of days, Nayak and Selena explored Saurienville together. Selena joked that it reminded her of a provincial town in North Korea, but without any portraits and statues of leaders and heroes. It was orderly, with a planned layout and regular working day. It even had a morning and evening rush hour. The air felt gritty in the nostrils and throat, but otherwise everything was neat and clean. People lived mostly in apartment blocks, and worked in factories, offices and shops, or as artisans and petty traders, and crowded to bars and pavement cafés in the evenings. The street food was appetising, the music varied and lively. Nayak could well see that food and music might turn out to be profitable cultural exports. Fashion, not so much – the best clothes around town for a night out were clearly reproductions in local fabrics of traditional West African dress, and nothing yet developed here would trouble the great ateliers of Lagos or Accra. There was radio – everyone seemed to carry a small transistor set, and you could hear recorded or transmitted music from flats of an evening, or from vehicle cabs through the day – and a few cinemas, but no television or other online entertainment. The locally smoked weed was so prevalent, and so fragrant, that Nayak suspected it was too addictive or at least habit-forming to make sampling it a good idea.

It was smoked often in queues outside shops. Queues were a sight that Nayak found baffling and Selena recognised only from her grandparents' oft-told reminiscences of harder times. There was plenty of everything in general, but every so often there would suddenly be nothing of something in particular. Saurienville struck Nayak and the other visitors, when they compared notes of an evening in the hotel's minimal and otherwise deserted bar, as a cheerful enough place, busy and in its way prosperous, but poorer and shabbier than it needed to be given the amount of work so evidently being done. This seemed to be of a piece with the condition of the elderly, which was socially respected and comfortable enough, and physically and mentally as healthy as callisthenics and chess and card games and gossip and reminiscence could make it, but the losses of hair and skin tone and colour and *oh my gods and goddesses* Nayak thought *teeth* among the over-sixties and even over-fifties was shocking.

On the second day, they found an immense public library, which they were told had been a gift from the Jenty and the saurians. It contained a surprising number of familiar books, all in French, which they were told had been downloaded from the early exiles' phones and reproduced as printed volumes. A substantial section was devoted to literature written since the arrival, the indigenous post-colonial literature of the human colony on Terre Nouveau: novels, memoirs, histories of exploration and discovery, poetry, folktales recalled or updated. A far larger part of its stock consisted of translations of Jenty and saurian literature, which a quick browse showed was of quite extraordinary quality. Scientific works, history, philosophy, epics, novels, poems, all utterly alien and all in French, and all amazing. A few million, or in the hominids' case half a million, years of civilisation could produce a crop of which even the cream was more than you could hope to read in a hundred lifetimes.

'You do realise,' Selena murmured as they moved mouse-like among the laddered stacks under high skylights, 'that what's in this building alone is enough to change the entire culture of humanity? You know how the rediscovery of the literature of the ancient world shook Europe, and sparked the Renaissance? This is the literature of a hundred "ancient worlds", all of them more advanced than our own!'

About the physics of the Fermi, however, there was not a word. They did ask. The librarians were polite, but apologetic. No can do. Nothing here.

And the dinosaurs, when they deigned to notice the visitors at all, had nothing to say on the subject. By the third morning, Nayak was almost tired of asking, but not quite.

CHAPTER FIFTEEN

Ecology

New Rhu, Apis, Wednesday 1 April 2071

All Fools' Day. Bloody hell.

Myles had always loathed the tradition. Having a rug pulled from under him had been a pet hate since childhood. It made him feel that he was too trusting, and therefore it undermined his trust in others. The cadre organisation, and therefore most of the Union's institutions including the media, took the same stern view. Public trust mattered to the economic democracy. Taking part in an April Fools' prank landed a cadre a demotion to a lower paid job, and any ostensibly factual outlet a stiff fine.

This, of course, guaranteed that such pranks became cool and rebellious, which was how he'd come to suffer them in his schooldays. At least, he hoped, people here would be more mature, and in any case too busy to bother. Moreover, at sun-up in New Rhu there was only an hour or so to go before noon GMT.

He looked down at Marie's sleeping head, and the cascade of red-brown hair across the pillow. Usually she rose before him, but not today. She'd drunk too much of Jenkins's Hooch the previous evening, and was now sleeping it off. He couldn't blame her: she'd had a rough couple of days. Myles looked at the mug of coffee he'd been about to leave on the bedside table for her, sighed, padded out of the bedroom and down the stairs, and sat at the kitchen table to drink it himself. He put on his glasses and checked the news, which Iskander pulled together from data packets on incoming ships and arks, as well as filching information from the Alliance and Co-ord nets.

The actual location of the Terre Nouveau system was still secret: the available clips from John Grant's visit to the surface showed no stars, and the exosun, the system's own star, couldn't be identified from what little could be glimpsed of its spectrum. Some clips of the planet's surface, landscapes and street scenes, had come back via shuttles from the Station. The latest such dispatch was text only, spelling out the current situation as of yesterday. FTL news had the annoying quality of being simultaneously the latest possible and inevitably out of date. There had been major developments overnight: the news was dominated by what was being called the Terre Nouveau crisis. Alliance and Co-ord FTL drones around the Station!

All of which was the result of Marie's innocent research – or, rather, its rapid dissemination, via Marcus Owen and Lieutenant Knight, and Marie's own incautious sharing of it with the Alliance scientist Emma Hazeldene and her colleagues. Coming on top of Owen's dire warnings when he'd turned himself in, likewise rapidly spread by Knight, it had resulted in a temporary moratorium on forestry on all the continents of Apis – good luck with enforcing that – and the sudden brandishing of a supposedly imminent treaty on safeguarding indigenous intelligent life. Myles found the alacrity of the whole thing suspect. To be sure, any diplomatic AI could draft a bulletproof treaty in milliseconds, but moving it through the human machinery of government was a different matter. It looked as if this had been prepared, at least on the Co-ord and Alliance sides.

The purpose was obvious: to prevent the Union gaining an advantage from the existence of a large human settlement that believed it was already part of the Union. Myles understood all this, but he knew that others understood it even better. What gripped him now was a question that no one else seemed to be considering in terms of political economy, or even of economics generally.

The question was: what was in it for the Fermi? – 'it' being their activity over billions of years: their terraforming, their evolutionary tweaking, and everything up to and including their recent and abrupt departure to the gas giants. What did they gain by it? What was their utility function? What, in other words, were they maximising?

Myles drained his coffee, and paced around the kitchen, thinking. It was, of course, a large assumption that the Fermi were – or was, if the Fermi was a singular entity – an economic actor in this sense. But as a starting hypothesis, it was better than nothing.

OK, he thought, suppose they're maximising something. What? From all that was known of them so far, the obvious answer was 'life' – or, more specifically, terrestrial-type biospheres. The images from Terre Nouveau indicated a Pleistocene environment, bizarrely including at least one species of talking dinosaur. The change rung on Apis had been for a world without vertebrates, in which invertebrates were able to grow to the size of large mammals even on land. The only other biosphere on public record was the Mushroom Moon discovered by the Station, on which fungi and lichens and mosses held sway. No signs of intelligent life there, but you never knew.

Was it intelligent life the Fermi were maximising? Scratch the Mushroom Moon, and that leaves two out of three. No,

more – it struck him as likely that the talking dinosaurs originated on the inner planet, not on Terre Nouveau. Make that
three out of four – or four out of five, if you counted Earth
as a world shaped by the Fermi, as Able Jenkins had claimed
the Fermi had told him.

But what did they get out of maximising intelligent life,
given that they themselves were, well, maybe not *maximally*
intelligent, but inconceivably more intelligent than any of the
species their manipulations had brought about? What were
they working towards? Company around the stellar campfires?
Some far-future, post-human intelligence? But they already
had that themselves, by hypothesis. They could far more easily,
it seemed, have filled the universe with copies of themselves.
With *varied* copies, if they'd wanted variety and evolution.
They could have become Von Neumann machines, self-
replicators spreading through the galaxies faster than light.
And that wasn't good enough for them?

Was there something special about organic life? Maybe.

Intelligence? Something was bugging him about that. Marcus
Owen had been intelligent all along, but had claimed not to
be conscious until his inward encounter with the Fermi.
Consciousness? That was what Marie and Owen had discovered
among the monkey-spiders, something distinct from intelligence
or even sentience as such. They had language, and from that
intrinsically social and open-ended capacity the strange loop
of self-awareness arose: the subject, subjectivity, the mind's I!
The very capacity that Owen now claimed he had and had
lacked before.

If the monkey-spiders had that, then they were people –
strange people to be sure, but people. That surely changed a
lot as far as the humans on Apis were concerned, or at least
it ought to, but what was in it for the Fermi?

A sound of stirring, of creaks and shuffles, came from above.
Myles busied himself with the coffee pot. Marie stepped care-

fully down the stairs, in slippers and dressing gown, tousle-haired and bleary-eyed. Myles held out a mug. She nodded and swept past, poured herself a tumbler of water and swallowed it faster than was good for her. Only then did she hug him, kiss him, sit down and reach for the coffee.

'Good morning!' he said.

'Goo' mornin'.' She blinked and shook her head, blew and sipped. 'What you been doing?'

'Thinking.'

'Very good! What about?'

He told her.

'Makes sense, I suppose. And?'

'I was just wondering,' Myles said, 'why the Fermi would want to maximise consciousness.'

'That's easy,' Marie said. 'To collapse the wave-function of the universe.'

'Oh, come on! Isn't that just quantum mysticism?' He waved a hand. 'Last I heard, the "observer" can be any interaction. It doesn't have to be a conscious observer.'

'Nothing mystical about it. You're right, it doesn't have to be a conscious observer. But when it is, it makes a difference *to the conscious observer*. If you have enough conscious observers, you end up with a consensus cosmos.' She sat up straight suddenly. 'You know, that could reduce the risk of ending up in a different timeline, like your parents and others did on the Station.'

'Why wouldn't that work for the Fermi?'

'We know it doesn't,' Marie said, 'because these slippages still happen. If the Fermi could do it, they'd have tied everything into one timeline already!'

'You don't think the Fermi are conscious?'

'I'm pretty sure they're not,' Marie said. 'I think they're an AI like Iskander, only immensely more powerful. They're a machine for cranking out conscious life, or at least creating the conditions for it.'

'That still leaves the question: what's in it for them? Or for their creators, if they had any?'

'That's easy, too,' Marie said. 'To influence the long-term future of the universe!' She spread her arms. 'Look. The universe is expanding. In a few trillion years all the other galaxies will be beyond the light horizon. Only FTL connections will be possible. And with enough conscious observers in all galaxies, and enough FTL connections, who knows? Maybe the Fermi look forward to bringing the universe in to a soft landing – delay the heat death, or reverse the expansion to a survivable big bounce, or whatever.'

'I'm still asking what's in it for them.'

'Think of it as a very long-term investment, by them or more likely by whatever or whoever made them. Maybe they hope to create the conditions to create something like themselves, all over again.'

'God, what a vision of futility.'

Marie laughed. 'You know of a more meaningful future timeline? Nothing has purpose in that sense. Even life is just molecules that can replicate, replicating just because they can.' She tilted back her chair. 'And speaking of purpose, I need some breakfast.'

'Cereal?'

'Nah. Something salty, greasy and hot.'

Myles glanced at his watch. It was 11:22 GMT, half an hour after sunrise. The street food stall down the road would be open. 'On the case.'

At this time of day the stall served tea, coffee and rolls with the closest local equivalent of bacon: strips of scuttler meat, salted and smoked and fried. The smell from the sizzling hotplate gave Myles hunger pangs. Liam Grogan, ahead of him in the queue, turned and gave him an evil grin.

'You and your girlfriend are in dead trouble, Myles.'

'Oh yeah? Why?'

'You're off the militia rota for any responsible post, and Marie's losing her lab placement. Same reason – lack of vigilance. You let the robot escape, you're way too chummy with yon Alliance lieutenant, and Marie's too chummy with Doc Hazeldene. That's why we're suddenly having to stop cutting down trees. Like the Alliance and fucking Co-ord care about monkey-spiders! They're just going along with this as long as it takes to shaft us.'

'Hang on, that's fucking ridiculous, everyone agreed—' Myles caught himself and laughed. He punched Grogan's shoulder. 'You got me there!'

Grogan frowned. 'Got you how?'

'April Fool, right? You got me. You can stop kidding me on.'

'April Fool?' Grogan glanced sideways, checking the time and date in his glasses. 'Christ, so it is! You forget that calendar after a while here.'

'Yeah, yeah.' Myles nodded towards the stall. 'You're next up, by the way.'

Grogan turned away and placed his order. As he left, clutching paper bags and a cardboard tray of paper cups, he said, 'Can't wait to see your face at the meeting, Grant.'

'Ah, sod off, mate, I said you got me, don't milk it dry.'

Myles picked up his two rolls and headed homeward. 'Iskander? Was Liam telling the truth?'

'I'm sorry to say he was, up to a point. It's been mooted, not decided. The matter will be put to a vote this evening.' Iskander shared the time and agenda.

'Shit! OK.'

Back at the house, Myles waited until Marie had finished her breakfast and settled to another coffee before he broached the touchy subject. To his surprise, she wasn't bothered.

'Fuck 'em,' she said. 'You don't need those militia stints anyway.'

'You need your lab access, though.'

'Ha! They can't stop me talking to Emma, or from doing

my own research. Let them try to find a better ecologist. And they're going to need one, too, if this moratorium sticks.'

'How?'

'Well, we'll have to find ways of using forest resources that doesn't intrude on the monkey-spiders, and we'll have to find alternatives to forest resources.'

'Timber might be hard to replace.'

Marie waved this away. 'We can always make artificial wood from some fast-growing plains plant, or something.'

'Kelp,' Myles said. 'Or some other seaweed. There's always the sea. There's a huge ocean a few kilometres away, and we're still not so much as fishing.'

'See what I mean?' Marie shrugged. 'We can just let them vote us off, and before you know it they'll come crawling to ask us back.'

'You'll miss your lab, meantime, you love that place and the work you do there.'

'I love the forest more, and they can't stop me going there. I've still got lots of information to gather on the monkey-spiders.'

'And where will you process it?' Myles waved a hand around at the kitchen. 'Here?'

'It's not like we do much cooking.'

'We always have the option.' Myles shook his head. 'Nah. I'm not having it. They're not going to kick you out of your lab, or me off the militia leadership. Not without a fight, they're not.'

'Who's "they"?'

Myles looked at the agenda, and at who had put forward the motion of no confidence in him and Marie. 'Liam, Mahmud, Celeste. They all arrived after the Union agreed to settlement.'

'That's *all* they have in common,' Marie pointed out.

'It's enough. You know what the newcomers call people like us? Behind our backs?'

'Don't I just! Defectors, that's what.'

'I've heard worse,' Myles said. 'And it's kind of true. We did agree to fight under Alliance officers if we were called on.'

'That agreement was made before the Union arrived,' Iskander said. 'The Alliance accepts that it no longer holds.'

'Yeah, but that doesn't stop people remembering we made it.' Myles jumped up. 'Time I got to work. You go to your lab as usual.'

'I'll be a bit later than usual,' Marie said wryly. 'Maybe I'll just drop in and go to the forest.'

'Fair enough. And, you know? Talk to people.'

'I always talk to people. You go and talk to the *right* people. You're the politician.'

Myles stared at her. 'What?'

Marie laughed. 'That's what you are, Myles. Trust me. I'm a scientist.'

Myles left the house, somewhat preoccupied. Was he a politician? As far as he was concerned, all he had done since arrival on Apis was many honest days' work. He'd been stung by his father's comment, that time back in the Comet bar in Port Glasgow when their emigration was first mooted, that his skills would be useless out here. Political economy and English literature? He remembered the incredulous scorn in his father's voice – not at the subjects, but at the notion of their being relevant to life as a pioneer. Fair enough, they had no immediate application out here.

From the beginning he'd pitched in: building shelters then houses, digging latrines then laying down septic tanks, chopping down trees then working in the sawmill, taking his turn in the militia patrols, improving his skills all the while. Every ten days or so he worked in the kitchen of the canteen that served a score of households including his and Marie's. And contrary to John Grant's glum prediction, Marie's knowledge of ecology had found plenty of practical uses in this very different ecosystem. She'd been right: the principles applied, here as on Earth. There were farms out there on the plain that relied on some of her discoveries – her own discoveries, not those already known to and shared by the likes of Hazeldene and Jenkins.

He scanned the town through his glasses on his way down the slope. The site for the midday ark arrival lit up, as did his task list. He had to pick up a dozen boxes of inoculation kits on the way, for the incomers: the hardware was imported, the contents – anti-fungals and antibiotics, mostly – were manufactured locally, because their ingredients wouldn't get past Earth's biosecurity even in the Alliance, let alone the Union and the Co-ord. Myles headed for the tool bank, chatted with the minder, borrowed a Chinese-style central-wheel barrow, and rolled it to the clinic. As he stacked the barrow's panniers with cardboard boxes and lashed them into place with elastic ropes and karabiners, he passed the time of day with Celeste Rogers, the nurse on duty, who had to sign them off to him. He said nothing about her backing of the motion against him and Marie, and nor did Celeste.

He wheeled the barrow to the site, which was a new plot at the far end of the street where, a week earlier, Grant's ark hadn't arrived. After stashing the medical kits in a hopper, he used the barrow to shift the timbers for the fence from the stack back down the road. As the gang arrived he greeted them one by one and shared a bit of gossip and banter, and then they all got stuck in with readying the site.

No, he wasn't a politician. He wasn't talking to the *right* people. He should be canvassing support among members of the town committee, the militia committee, or at the very least people likely to go along to the town meeting – which, apart from Linda Starr who was currently a hundred metres down the road, his mates on this job were not.

At this point the penny dropped for Myles, and he became a politician. By the end of the morning, he had spoken to everyone on the site, and got most of them to agree to come to the meeting or to take part remotely. By mid-afternoon, he had done the same on the next site.

The forest was quiet – or, rather, the only sounds were those from the forest itself. The din from the Co-ord quarrying operations had ceased days ago. On the edge of a hundred-metre-wide spread of not-grass in a hollow glade between two belts of woodland, Marie lay prone under a bush. Its divarcating branches and twigs made it look like a textbook model of an organic molecule. The resulting tight entanglement made it good cover, impenetrable to monkey-spiders or anything larger than the sparrow-sized boids whose chittering above her more than made up for the absence of industrial sound. She was fifty metres off the path, having hiked for an hour up and over several rises between the settlement and the lake – the landing lake, as people now called it. She had set off late in the morning, and had now been hiding out here for over two hours.

Beside her lay her backpack and water bottle. In front of her, propped on her elbows, she held her binoculars. Zooming the view on glasses was all very well, but that was just enlargement plus software-enabled enhancement: only actual telescopic lenses could deliver more light and detail than the unaided eye.

Through the binoculars Marie watched a troop of monkey-spiders in the trees across from her, on the other side of the shallow declivity. One by one they ran to the stream that trickled along the foot of the dell, scooped water to their mouth parts, and hurried back to the trees. Every so often they paused, huddling in trees or underbrush, just before the shadow of a large boid flitted across the open space.

Marie, with a twitch of a finger, tabbed and timed these incidents in a virtual space she wasn't looking at, in the glasses pushed up on her forehead and recording the sight. Once a drone drifted by overhead. She noted that neither its buzz nor its shadow perturbed the monkey-spiders. They seemed unaware – or heedless – of her presence, too. Every so often she put down her binoculars, slid her glasses on, and tried to map the monkey-spiders' postures to Owen's encyclopaedic dictionary. What little she succeeded in translating was disappointingly banal: typically, *fruit over there* or *look out above*.

But other, and more complex, conversations were going on, at a speed and subtlety she couldn't keep up with.

Iskander flashed a discreet message in the corner of her eye: 'Translate?'

'Yes,' she signalled.

Simultaneous translations flickered across her sight. They remained banal, but were far more specific about species of fruit, species of predator, distance and direction. Then—

The [great? big?] one is coming! Get ready!

The monkey-spiders backed out of the wood and formed a semi-circular array in the open space. Large and small, male and female, young and old – she could tell the old ones, those who wouldn't have moulted for years, by the moss and lichen on their carapaces.

Binoculars again. Leaves shook, branches parted. Something larger than a monkey-spider was moving among the trees. It stepped into the sunlight, glittering. Marie almost cried out. It was the Venus descent suit.

In her first year of studying biology at university, Marie had seen – or been shown – a video clip that had shocked her at some level she found hard to articulate. It showed an apparently dead insect, walking. The insect's abdomen was visibly hollow, its innards long since dried out or consumed, to all appearances as dead and dusty as a fly fallen to the sill of a winter window-pane. Yet this husk walked, a tiny zombie that didn't have the grace to shamble, but instead plodded along, clambering over moss and leaves as delicately and precisely as when its body had been a whole and living thing. The appearance of death was deceptive: life, or at least respiration, went on. The insect's motor nerves still fired, and were controlled – she'd been told – by the fungal parasite that had possessed it.

Marie experienced something of the same disgusted disquietude on seeing again the descent suit, which she'd last seen stalking away into the hills with an anti-materiel rifle in its hand. Even then it had been a sorry sight, crusted in what looked like broken glass, its back open, its faceplate blank. Sikandar, it – or, rather, the instance of Iskander running in its circuits – had called itself, and it was already possessed, by some corruption from the Fermi. Myles had incited it to kill Owen, then itself. As Owen's reappearance as well as his account had made clear, this hadn't quite worked out.

There was no doubt, though, that the descent suit had been shot. The suit had a gaping hole right through the midriff, where – Iskander now whispered – its CPU had been. Whatever was moving these hollow limbs, empty helmet and damaged torso was not Sikandar. It could only be whatever remained of the Fermi in the encrusting glass. Presumably, like the parasite with the insect, it had hijacked the suit's controls.

The monkey-spiders hooted and shifted with their own insectile suddenness into postures that even without the benefit of Owen's dictionary indicated awe and reverence. The suit ceased its ponderous forward pacing, and raised its arms in front of it, making it look more like a zombie than ever.

The big hands – the gloves – began to move, from the wrist joints and through the digits. Their fervid flickering was too swift to follow. Marie lowered the binoculars and pulled down her glasses. Iskander was already beginning translation as the recognition dawned on Marie that the suit's gestures were an imitation of monkey-spider postural communication whose possibility had escaped Owen.

Greetings, my friends! You have done well. Together we can do more. We must resist the soft-shell intruders. Your great ancient guardians in the bright mountain are gone, and your soft-shell friend likewise, but I am still here! The intruders have retreated from your forests. Together we can make them retreat from our whole world. For this world is yours. What say you?

A postural clamour of *Yes! Yes!* rippled across the assembled backs of the monkey-spiders, like wind over grass. From the forest came a pair of monkey-spiders, carrying between them a roll of matting at least a metre and half long. They laid it at the suit's booted feet, and unrolled it. Metal glinted. Marie brought the binoculars quickly to bear. On the matting lay the anti-materiel rifle, several belts of ammunition and a standard rifle – the very weapon that Owen had grabbed from Myles's hands all those months ago.

The descent suit squatted, and reached forward. It slung the ammo belts across its shoulders, hefted the anti-materiel rifle and stood up. As it did so, one of the monkey-spiders lifted Myles's stolen rifle, gripping it correctly in its paired manipulator clusters. With these it worked the bolt, and braced the rifle's stock to a crook of one of its other limbs. The animal spun around, in an abrupt flurry of legs, and aimed the weapon straight at Marie. She flattened, as if pressing herself into the ground.

The suit stepped forward. It held a hand in front of the monkey-spider's eyes, and gestured: *No!*

The monkey-spider lowered the weapon. The suit shifted itself, and faced Marie, its blank black faceplate a hole into darkness. It shook the anti-materiel rifle towards her, in a gesture this time entirely human, or human-to-beast: *Shoo! Go away!*

For a moment she stayed frozen. The monkey-spiders, to say nothing of the machine, had been aware of her presence all along. It was as if they didn't see her as a threat at all, and they were unworried about her getting away with the information she had gathered. The descent suit repeated its gesture, more emphatically.

'Please try to move,' Iskander said in her earpiece.

There was no more point in hiding. Marie rolled from under the bush, grabbed her bag, and packed away her water bottle and binoculars. Then she raised herself to a stoop – she couldn't bring herself to stand up straight – and hurried off through the woods back to the path. Derisive hoots followed her.

When she reached the path she stopped, and stood trembling and breathing deeply and shakily for a couple of minutes. Her mouth was dry. She fished out her water bottle and drank.

'I've alerted the militia and the Alliance post,' Iskander said. 'Best get out of their way. Are you capable of walking?'

'Of course I'm bloody capable.'

A small drone crested the wooded skyline and drifted overhead, back over the trees the way she had come.

'What's it seeing?'

Iskander patched her in. The assembly of monkey-spiders had grown, still in the squatting semicircle. They were paying close attention to something, but no image of the descent suit or its retrieved weapon was visible, only a fast-changing blurry patch of not-grass like a censored detail in a low-res news feed. Moments later a brace of quadcopters roared low overhead.

'They know the thing has an anti-materiel rifle?'

'Of course,' said Iskander. 'This is a feint.'

The quadcopters rose high, and threw themselves into evasive manoeuvres so sharp that they seemed to be in a dogfight with each other, firing down in short bursts. Marie flipped to the drone view and saw that the bursts were tearing up the ground near or in the presumed location of the descent suit, but didn't seem to be hitting it. The main effect was that most of the monkey-spiders scattered and fled.

Return fire sparkled. One of the quadcopters was hit and spun to the ground. Crash, rising smoke. The other quadcopter continued evasive action but ceased firing. A drone swarm arrived from another direction, a phalanx of dots in the sky, descending rapidly. More shots. Several of the drones were hit, to disintegrate in mid-air or spiral down into the trees. But others still hovered. Black dots fell from them. Marie's first shocked thought was of bombs. No explosions followed.

'It's a tangle-net,' Iskander said.

'Have they caught it?'

A view from above came up on her glasses. Two monkey-spiders flailed against an invisible constraint. Something else was in the centre of the net. A crewed quadcopter screamed overhead, low enough to stir dust on the path, and skimmed out of sight above the trees. Ten seconds later Marie saw its landing from above, in the drone's eye view. Two people with rifles vaulted out and ran forward.

'We've got visual,' Myles's voice said over the shared channel. 'Closing.'

Myles! Marie's knuckles went to her mouth.

A monkey-spider stopped struggling, grabbed something from out of view, and suddenly it was aiming a rifle. Myles fired, and down the monkey-spider went. Myles stepped forward and slashed at the net, freeing the remaining monkey-spider, which ran off. More slashes, and Myles and his comrade began rolling the trapped descent suit – now entirely visible – up in the net. After a minute or so they had the descent suit restrained, and the rifles retrieved and stowed.

'How is the suit showing up now?'

'Search me,' said Iskander. 'Probably just given up interfering with the cameras, now it's caught.'

Myles and his comrade – Grogan, she now saw – called down the hovering drones and lashed the descent suit to ten of them. The drones took off, and the two followed in the quadcopter. As the formation passed above Marie, Myles leaned out and waved. Marie waved back, and set off down the path back to New Rhu.

She didn't think she and Myles would have any trouble at that evening's meeting.

New Rhu, Apis, Wednesday 1 April 2071, evening

Myles felt his palms sweat and butterflies in his stomach as the votes were counted. It had been, despite his earlier polit-icking and the triumph of the descent suit's capture, a fraught and divided discussion. Liam Grogan, Mahmud Ali and Celeste

Rogers had put the worst spin on his and Marie's actions. Myles, Marie and their supporters had defended themselves as best they could. Jasmine Saunders had spoken up strongly for him. Now it was down to the wire.

About a hundred people were in the social centre, a big, airy space with folded tables against the walls and children's cardboard mobile sculptures hanging from the rafters and spinning gently in the updraughts. A thousand or so more registered attendees were following along remotely from home or from one of the bars or other hangouts. Iskander had proposed sharing the proceedings across all the Union settlements on New Mu, and Starr had agreed. On his glasses, Myles could see the pinprick lights of attention, as people in other settlements drifted in and out of the audience.

'The motion of censure against Marie Henderson and Myles Grant *falls*,' Linda Starr announced, from the chair.

Myles turned to Marie and grinned, amid groans and cheers – mostly the latter – from the more ebullient or engaged of those present.

'Told you!' Marie said. 'You're a politician.'

'Not a very good one,' Myles said. 'We only won seven hundred and sixty to five hundred and eighty.'

'Order!' Starr said. 'Any other competent business?'

Myles shot his hand up.

'Yes, Citizen Grant?'

Myles stood, and took a deep breath. 'Thanks, Citizen Starr. First, I am relieved and grateful that I'm still on the militia rota, and cleared to continue leading when called upon. I'm likewise relieved and grateful that Citizen Henderson here retains her position and her access to her lab. It's in my capacity as a militia volunteer that I ask the meeting's indulgence to speak for a few minutes.

'Citizens, comrades and friends – earlier today I did something I had trained for, something I had to do, but which still is not something anyone can take lightly.' He paused, and looked around, conscious of all the eyes and lenses and glasses watching him and recording him. 'I killed someone.'

Movement and murmurs in the hall. More sparks appeared in the virtual display of those watching remotely, in New Rhu and across the continent.

'Who was that person? I don't know their name, or even if they had a name. But a person they were. Yes, I'm talking about the monkey-spider I shot! It was aiming a rifle at me, and it knew how to use one. So I was justified in killing it, in self-defence. Perhaps it felt the same about me. But by the very fact that it was able to learn how to use a complex weapon showed that it was indeed a person. And the research that Marie – sorry, chair, I mean Citizen Henderson – has conducted shows without a doubt that the monkey-spiders have language, have speech, have self-awareness.'

Liam Grogan called out: 'That just makes them more dangerous!'

'Dangerous?' Myles said. 'You're having a laugh. I'll tell you what's dangerous. We are. We have the power to crush them like bugs. Literally. We wouldn't even have to fight. All we'd need is a drone factory. We could easily order one – it would fit in an ark, no bother. Or we could make one ourselves, with a bit more trouble. Swarms of small, armed drones prowling the forest could exterminate the whole species.

'And for what? Timber? Land to farm? Is that what we came here for?'

'Yes!' someone shouted.

Myles flung out an arm. 'New Atlantis awaits you! New Lemuria welcomes you on board! *We* are here to hold New Mu for the Union. And there's only one way to do that, now that we know this place is not open to settlement as we had thought. It has native intelligent life. It's not ours, it's theirs. We can't wipe them out without turning ourselves into everything we hate, and this place into something that might as well not be Union at all. Our only chance of staying here

– and not all of us will, I'm warning you now – is if we *don't* fight the monkey-spiders.'

'And what do we do instead?' someone else demanded.

'We talk to them,' Myles said. 'And we trade.'

Uproar in the hall. The lights in the virtual display were flashing. Myles didn't need Iskander to tell him it hadn't gone down well.

'You did great!' Marie told him. He needed that.

CHAPTER SIXTEEN

White Sky Mountains

Jurassica, Monday 30 March to Wednesday 1 April 2071

'Wait for what?' Marcus Owen cried.

Mrs Newton flicked a claw. The glowing letters spelling out **ATTENDEZ** disappeared. 'For you, perhaps?'

'I am not that important.' Even as he spoke, Owen wondered if his modesty was misplaced. The departure of the Fermi, after all, had occurred immediately after his own infection by them in Hamilton's Rise . . .

But no – there had been too much else going on in these moments: the pulsing radar from the Co-ord armed forces that had somehow resonated with the pattern in the green stone that Muranov had thought he'd interpreted just before Owen had killed him; the radio blips with the same message that Owen himself had been frantically transmitting; the bejewelling flow of bright glass over the descent suit animated by Sikandar, which must have happened just before Owen had burst on the scene and started shooting.

Sikandar, that deviant offspring of Iskander . . .

Iskander!

Oh no, he thought, let it not be that. Let it not be Iskander that had infiltrated the Fermi, just as the Fermi had hacked into Sikandar! The Fermi were vast and alien and ancient, but that might be no barrier to an AI as advanced as Iskander. The disparity of size might be as irrelevant as in the case of a virus infecting a whale. It was entirely possible that the same deep compatibility of radically divergent hardware and software as had enabled the Fermi to hack into Sikandar could work both ways. It was even possible that the Fermi's aims, whatever they were, might mesh with Iskander's – whatever *they* were.

'What the humans were to wait for was never explained,' Mrs Newton went on, 'even though some of the humans continued to communicate with the Fermi, or at any rate to receive messages from them.'

'The humans on Terre Nouveau have been in touch with the Fermi all this time?'

'Until the Fermi departed for the gas giant, yes. But "in touch" is not quite right. The messages were few and obscure. When the humans asked questions, they were told to ask us, and we usually answered. After all, we had all the knowledge they needed about the planet and the system. However, being in contact with the Fermi gave a certain amount of prestige within the human settlement, and that the Fermi communicated with the humans at all, when in millions of years they had never deigned to talk to us, made us even more cautious in our dealings with the humans than we would have been in any case.'

'Cautious in what way?'

Mrs Newton drew herself up again. 'We are an ethically advanced species,' she said, in a long whiff of bad breath. 'We already treated the new arrivals on Terre Nouveau with respect, but any temptation we might have had to interfere in their development by assisting them further – by the provision of advanced technology, for example – was restrained by the knowledge that they mattered in some way to an intelligence far more advanced than our own. So we shared, or, rather, traded, only technology they already knew but could not reproduce on their own without much time and great difficulty, such as electrical power, telephones and so forth.' She paused, as if pondering. 'You know, we could have given them stardrives! They could have arrived back on Earth three hundred of your years ago, before Earth had even industrialised!'

'Good God!'

'Wouldn't that have been fun? Perhaps, in another probability, we did. Or perhaps the Fermi would have prevented us. Who knows?'

'Certainly not I. But – you say you could have given them stardrives? I thought you had given up interstellar travel?'

'We did, but we kept the drives.'

'Why?'

'Some of us had hoped that some day the Fermi would go away, and that our descendants, however remote, would once again venture forth to new worlds.'

'So you're not content with this one, after all?'

'We are not unanimous. Some chafe. But we are practical, so we make the best of what we have.'

'So I see.' Owen gestured at the great circular hall, and the silent tiers of watching dinosaurs. 'I bow to your achievements. But why did the arrival of the human settlement on Terre Nouveau spoil everything?'

'It told us that there was at least one species that was doing what we had once done. Some of us became discontented again. Why should the Fermi permit them to travel and settle, and not us?'

Owen shook his head. 'The Fermi are not *permitting* them. The Fermi have already begun to resist the human presence on Apis, because it is beginning to harm that planet's native intelligent species.' He shrugged. 'Something of the kind may also be happening elsewhere, I don't know.'

'But it isn't happening here! The humans have expanded and flourished here for centuries.'

'Yes, but the native intelligent species here – yourselves and the hominids – are already advanced, and well capable of defending your own interests. You were never in danger from the humans of Terre Nouveau. For less developed species, the humans are a great danger indeed. And they may yet become so to you, if more arrive, and they will.'

Mrs Newton mimicked a human laugh, then rattled out a remark in her own speech. The audience broke into a cacophony of screeches.

'They laugh,' said Mrs Newton. 'Would you like me to show you why?'

'Yes,' Owen said. 'I very much would.'

The dinosaurs stepped down, lowest first, from their perches, one by one, and stalked off through doorways under the arches, talking among themselves. When they had all departed, Mrs Newton led Owen to a doorway none of the others had used. It led to a tunnel large enough for two dinosaurs to walk abreast. The overhead-curving walls of multi-coloured tiles reminded Owen of the London Underground. Suspended glowing globes lit the way. The floor was of rock, and was worn into two shallow grooves.

'They get like that,' Mrs Newton explained almost apologetically, 'after a few thousand years.'

'Of course.'

The tunnel led to an underground railway platform, which Owen recognised at a glance for a maglev monorail. A rush of air came from one end, and a silent silver bullet thirty metres long and four metres high slowed to a halt in front of where they stood. Through the long windows Owen could see no passengers. Doors hissed open. Owen followed Mrs Newton in. There was no seating, only bars spaced along the carriage in two rows at each side. Mrs Newton stepped on one of the lower bars, and grasped one of the higher bars. Owen braced himself likewise, except at full stretch. The platform slid past, and then the vehicle accelerated smoothly away. After ten minutes it reached a cruising speed which Owen guessed was at least 200 km/h. The tunnel had long since become a blur. Soon Owen sensed that the tunnel was sloping upward. After five minutes the vehicle flashed into the open.

Green trees flickered past, then the view opened out. They were passing over one of the many salt marshes that were this world's seas: patches of water here and there, great sprawling banyans and mangroves, innumerable birds and pterosaurs. Owen took the opportunity to transmit all the information his glasses and phone had gathered. Maybe one of the comsats would pick it up, maybe not.

On the far side of the swamp, a low range of hills rose. The line ran straight into the hillside. Through another tunnel, they emerged in what seemed at first like the other side of the range, and then became apparent as a vast space hollowed out from the rock. In front of them lay a small city of slender towers linked by curving ramps, thick with greenery and lit by a dozen lights that glowed from high above like small artificial suns.

The carriage decelerated to a stop at a wide platform, about halfway up the height of the towers and overlooking much of the city. The other side of the platform was overhung by trees. Owen swung forward and dropped, then stretched and eased his limbs. His shoulder was hurting again. He was hungry now, and thirsty. Mrs Newton disengaged herself more elegantly from the bars. They went out. The air here was about 30 degrees and humid, but less so than on the surface. Draughts of air soughed past from variant directions, carrying heavy floral scents. Owen swigged water and looked around. Mrs Newton walked to the end of the platform and beckoned Owen. He approached the edge with caution, and then realised that a clear barrier two metres or so high stood between the deck and the drop. The barrier was angled outwards, affording a clear view down.

'Look down,' said Mrs Newton.

They were standing on the edge of an immense pit. The clustered towers and the ramps that joined them were on a platform, below which were other platforms with towers, and so on, down and down like steps in a spiral staircase, all of it lit by the blaze of miniature suns, below them as above. Here and there in the depths, clouds drifted, white on green.

A closer look at the ramps just across from where they stood revealed individual dinosaurs walking, and small vehicles moving, up and down. The traffic was light, but continuous. The air in front of them was lively with insects, birds, and what could have been drones.

'Fifty million of us live in this shaft,' said Mrs Newton. 'There are many, many thousands of such shafts. There are many more filled with machinery, powered by sources of energy ranging from solar to geothermal. But I see you are hungry.'

She strolled to the side of the platform, reached into a tree and returned with a large red fruit that filled Owen's hand when he took it. He bit into the thin rind, and found a taste like an orange and a texture like an unripe banana. The nutrient quality found favour with his diagnostics, which he experienced as pleasure.

'Thank you,' he said. 'If I may ask a perhaps sensitive question, why do I see only adults?'

Mrs Newton cocked her head back and forth. 'You have seen eggs.'

'Yes, but where are the young?'

She pointed upwards. 'On the surface, foraging in the forests.'

'You don't look after them? Educate them?'

She tilted her head back. 'As I say, they forage. There is plenty for them to eat, and much for them to learn. In their third or fourth year they return to the place of their nest. They encounter adults and learn to speak. After that they start learning more abstract knowledge and skills.'

'I see. And who owns what around here?'

'That question interests human beings, and the hominids to an extent. After three million years, it no longer interests us. We live in our cities like our ancestors did in the forests, and our young do today. We work hard to create things of beauty, in our minds or in the world. We take what we need and do what we like.'

'So you have communism?'

'We have what?'

'Collective ownership? Everyone jointly owns everything?'

'No. As I said, we live like the animals in the forest, without owning.'

'But surely—'

'There are practical arrangements, that is all. Nobody sits in another's nest, if that's what you're asking. Do you imagine that after all this time we would not have worked such trivial matters out?'

'I suppose not.' Owen finished eating the fruit and wiped his hands on his trousers. He sighed. 'And what about weaponry? Could you defend yourselves, if attacked?'

'Attacked by whom? The Space Station? The People's Militia of Saurienville?' She gave a human-sounding laugh. 'I believe we could defend ourselves from them, yes, and from any other forces that may be on their way here.'

'I was thinking of the Fermi.'

'Ah.' She drew herself out and sank down again. 'No.'

'Then it is as well that the Fermi will defend you.'

'What do you mean?'

'They protect indigenous intelligent life, actual or potential, against outside interference. That's why your ancestors' colonies failed.'

'We deduced that millions of years ago.' She walked to the almost invisible barrier and laid her wrists on its top, claws dangling. 'And now they have gone, to the gas giants. Perhaps they have ceased their protection.'

Owen walked over to join her. 'I assure you they have not.'

'How would you know?'

He told her about the Fermi fragment in his mind.

'This is interesting,' she said. 'You understand that you may be delusional?'

He shrugged. 'Yes, that's always possible, but I must proceed on the assumption that I'm not.'

'Commendable in its way, but there is a way to make sure, objectively.' She turned her head and looked down at him. 'It is important for us to make sure.'

'How will you do that?'

'With a scan. It's quite non-intrusive, I assure you. We never did communicate with the Fermi, but we did become rather skilled in detecting their presence and activity.'

'Very well. Let's do that.'

Why did he trust them? This question recurred to Owen several times over the next hour. Mrs Newton led him to a lift shaft. They dropped hundreds of metres, to emerge in a place that differed only subtly from the place they had left, at least to his eyes. A short walk down a curved ramp took them to a door at the foot of a fluted tower. Inside was a room and what looked like a body scanner built on a saurian scale. Two dinosaurs were in attendance. Owen allowed himself to be strapped to a table, and his head braced.

A long, clawed finger touched what Owen took to be a screen. The table slid slowly into the great ringed apparatus. Owen then endured five minutes of existential dread like that of FTL travel. Vivid and disconcerting hallucinations, just as he had experienced in Hamilton's Rise, made it worse.

He saw the skies of Venus, and his death-defying leap to the deck of the submarine USS *Puerto Rico*. He felt the weight of Georgi Muranov's corpse on his shoulder, just before he pitched it into the Big River. He smelled the forest above New Rhu and heard the crashing trees at its edge and the scream of robotic chainsaws. He tasted the raw flesh of a scuttler which his teeth had just crunched into, ravenous. He remembered fights and murders in alleyways in Europe and hotels in India, every shocked face, every grunt, every blow he had dealt or taken. Then everything became broken and recombined in bizarre juxtapositions, until he was in a bewildering whirl, a blizzard of sounds and sights that threatened at any moment to blitz his mind to shreds. He knew they had to be hallucinations, but he was glad of the restraints. Otherwise he would have tried to tear the machine apart with his bare hands, and the dinosaurs with it.

It stopped. He was released. He sat up.

Mrs Newton and the other two dinosaurs looked down at him, three huge heads with binocular black eyes and teeth like bloody daggers.

'You are a monster,' said Mrs Newton.

'Tell me about it.' Owen swung his legs off the table and jumped to the ground. 'Read my mind, have you?'

'No, but we have diagnosed it. There is indeed a Fermi data structure there, along with an analogue of human consciousness, and an AI underlying both. Your mind is like the product of some unethical experiment from the darkest depths of our distant past.'

'Sounds about right.' Owen rubbed his hands together. 'Well, now you've established objectively what I already told you, I have one very small request.'

'And what is that?'

'Only the coordinates of the dead Fermi asteroids.' He opened his hands. 'We could find them on our own, but it could take years, and we don't have years. We have days, if we're lucky.'

'What do you mean?'

'It will seem absurd to you, I know, but dead Fermi rock has become an object of contention between the different powers among the human beings on Apis.'

Mrs Newton reared back. She conferred with the others in an exchange of roars and screeches that forced Owen to shut down his aural inputs. Then she said something to him. He hastily turned his hearing back up.

'Sorry, I missed that. Could you repeat it, please?'

'It is not absurd at all,' she said. 'We ourselves mined the dead Fermi rocks on our planet for many generations, and found numerous useful applications.' She paused. 'For which we no longer need the Fermi rock, and which we will leave your makers to find for themselves in due course. What do you intend to do with the asteroids?'

'Only to make the contending powers aware that there is no need to fight over rocks on Apis, when there are vast quantities of such rock in orbit. It should also reduce the pressure on the native intelligent life of Apis.'

Another high-decibel consultation followed.

'Very well,' said Mrs Newton. 'I can give you that information. And then I will return you to your ship.'

Sharing the information was less tricky than Owen had expected. The coordinates appeared as glowing numbers conjured into the air by Mrs Newton, and Owen recorded them with his glasses and phone: the orbital locations and velocities of five dead Fermi asteroids.

On the return monorail journey Owen dropped into his analogue of sleep. He woke as the carriage halted at the platform from which they had started. Back up they went, along the tunnel to the lift. When they came out of the lift, Owen noticed that two of the eggs had hatched. He looked around the glowing circular room.

'Where are the hatchlings?'

'The door opens to them,' Mrs Newton said. 'They'll be in the garden somewhere, or perhaps the forest by now.'

On their way to the hovercraft, a dinosaur ran across the green. It looked just like the ones that had attacked Owen on the road.

'Is that one of the hatchlings?' he asked.

'Oh no.' Mrs Newton leapt into the hovercraft, and extended a hand to haul Owen after her. 'That's one of the older ones. I hope it's not after one of the hatchlings, but – you know, it's nature's way!'

'Ah, I see.' Owen braced himself in position. The hovercraft rose, turned around and sped off. After a while they passed through Mrs Newton's neighbourhood, and on down the road Owen had taken. At the point where he'd shot the small dinosaurs, Owen took care not to look to the side of the road. The grazing flock had moved on. The hovercraft passed over the river. Owen checked his mental map.

'Up ahead, kilometre and a half, that's where I landed.' A little farther. 'Now.'

The craft coasted to a halt, and settled in a gust of air that blasted leaf litter on both sides of the road. Mrs Newton leapt out. Owen clambered after her. 'This way,' he said.

At the edge of the road he felt the now familiar flicker of unease as he stepped across.

'What is that?'

'It's what you would call a property boundary.'

'Ah! So much for being beyond all that!'

'It is not actually a property boundary. It's one of those practical arrangements I referred to.'

'I'll take your word for it.'

He retraced his steps to the landing site. His craft was still nose down and tail up, hanging from its wing cables against a tree trunk.

'This is a crash, not a landing!' Mrs Newton said.

'I walked away.'

Owen walked around the pod, trying to figure out the best way to free it. Perhaps if he slashed the cables . . . but the drop might damage the mechanism. Experimentally, he pushed up the tail end. It barely budged, but it gave him a good indication of its weight. No way could he support that with one hand while cutting with his knife in the other.

'Let me help you.'

Mrs Newton stepped forward, placed a hand under the tail, reached up and scissored the cables with her claws, and lowered the pod to the ground. 'There!'

'Thank you,' Owen said. He climbed in. 'Best move away, and look away.'

'I'm not familiar with the phenomenon, but I know what to expect.'

Mrs Newton turned around and strode off, without a backward glance.

'Goodbye!' Owen called out. He closed the canopy, and thumbed Return on the control plate.

He came out of the jump alongside Jones's ship. The automated shuttle made its own minor course corrections with its tiny jets, and floated through an open port and into the launch tube. A hatch closed behind it. Somewhere a pump laboured. The big bright air-pressure indicator on the inside of the tube – its ceiling, from Owen's viewpoint – flashed from red to green, and another hatch opened. Owen slid back the canopy and propelled himself out, and down the short tube to the spherical chamber.

'Hi,' said Jones, from the exercise machine. His glasses were black and blank.

'Hi.' Owen took out his phone and brandished it. 'Did you get everything?'

'I guess so,' Jones said. 'Your phone's been sending blips for the past hour.'

'Good.'

'Well, let's see if your talking dinosaurs told you the truth, eh?'

'What?'

Jones lowered his glasses, revealing mild blue eyes with pale eyelashes. 'We're going to check out these rocks.'

'I'll find something to hang onto,' Owen said.

The jump took a few seconds, and felt longer. He managed not to yell.

'Patching you in,' Jones said.

The outside view appeared in Owen's glasses. A spindle-shaped rock filled his view. It was not a large asteroid: a kilometre from end to end. The surface was white and glassy. A high albedo – they'd have found it by themselves, given time and telescopes. Zooming in, Owen saw the same organic-seeming complexity he had encountered on and in Hamilton's Rise, like the inside of a shell, or of a spongy bone, but melted into fluid shapes as if made from spun glass. Zooming further, he saw the complexities within that, to fractal depths. What it must have been like when alive and coloured!

'Quite a sight,' said Jones. 'On to the next.'

They checked the other four asteroids over the next fifteen minutes, criss-crossing the system.

'Right,' said Jones. 'One more jump, then it's home for tea.'

The Alliance flagship was a speck in the clutter of moons around the outer of the system's three gas giants. A spinning toroid a hundred metres across, it dwarfed Jones's ship. Jones docked at the hub. Airlocks clunked together, and sealed. Owen followed Jones out. They floated through a succession of tubes and soon began to feel a tug of weight, whereupon they turned to the ladder down the side of the tube. Feet first, they dropped to the floor of a steel corridor to stand in one gravity.

'Thank fuck for that,' said Jones, straightening up and staggering slightly. 'Welcome aboard HMS *Mordant*.'

'I suppose her sister ships are *Malignant*, *Malevolent* and *Maleficent*?'

Jones glowered. 'That's classified. How did you know?'

'A lucky guess.'

'Well, don't spread it around.'

The air was well scrubbed, but the ventilation couldn't remove the constantly renewed smells of a large number of people in a confined space. It was roomier than a submarine, but far more crowded. As Owen followed Jones down the endlessly upward-curving corridor, which felt strange until he adjusted his sense of balance, he had to shoulder past and between other personnel. Some were crew, in naval fatigues or uniforms. By far the most were British, Indian, or US Army soldiers and marines, some in fatigues, others kitted up. At one point Owen and Jones had to sidle past a trolley laden with racks of small combat and surveillance drones.

'In here,' Jones said, as they reached a door in the side of the corridor. 'Catch you later, no doubt.'

'I hope so,' Owen said.

The room was predictably tiny. Inside it sat a naval officer and Peregrine Walworth. Behind them was a screen showing an outside view dominated by the blue-banded face of the gas giant, on which the black winged circle of the Fermi stood out like the Great Red Spot did on Jupiter.

'Pull up a seat,' said Walworth, indicating a plastic chair. 'And thanks for your efforts down on Jurassica. You've accomplished a lot.'

'I wish I'd accomplished more. For one thing, we're no closer to understanding what to expect from' – he nodded towards the screen – 'the Fermi. And despite my, ah, unique connection with them, I'm unable to shed any further light myself.'

'Don't worry about that,' said the officer. 'The locations of the asteroids were the main thing.'

'I hope so,' said Owen. 'It should certainly serve to reduce international tensions.'

The officer smiled.

'Do you have the slightest idea,' Walworth asked, 'of why the Fermi rocks on Apis have become a bone of contention? And why we – that is, the Alliance – have made only token objection to the Co-ord's trampling over the Union's undoubted territorial rights at Hamilton's Rise?'

'I'm afraid I don't,' Owen said. 'I understand the rock may have some potential as a computational substrate, but that's only rumour I picked up in New Rhu.'

'Spot on,' Walworth said, 'but in this case rumour turns out to be understating the truth. The rock is nothing less than an ideal substrate for quantum computing. I'm told the consequences for science, industry, communications and military affairs are nothing less than revolutionary.'

'And to the immediate point,' the officer added, 'it has the potential of rendering every form of encryption obsolete overnight. There's even talk of using it to develop our own superluminal communication, just as the Fermi have.'

'The first power to get that,' Walworth said, 'will have a military advantage beyond comparison. Naturally, we don't want that advantage to fall to the Co-ord – or the Union, perish the thought! Nor do we want trillions of tons of pristine Fermi rock to fall into the hands of other powers. Imagine what could happen if the Union does succeed in incorporating this system!'

'So we're seizing the asteroids?'

The officer scoffed. 'We're doing better than that.' He looked at his wristwatch, a flashy complication of dials and bevels that might not have been entirely for show. 'Automated shuttles have been sent to all of the asteroids you located for us. They've latched on, their drives are powering up and they're taking the asteroids clear out of the system right about . . . now.'

'Where to?' Owen asked.

'Good question. The answer is above my pay grade and security clearance, and yours, too, I imagine.' The officer stood up. 'Well, duty calls. Talk among yourselves, gentlemen.'

He somehow made sidling past them and backing out of the door look parade-ground.

'So that's that,' Owen said.

'Indeed.'

'What now?'

'We've had a request for assistance from one of the legitimate authorities down there. They're officially the Customs Board, and unofficially known as the Families. Mercantile clans.' He smiled. 'Our kind of people. They feel that the presence of the Union is strengthening their local rivals, known for some reason as the Karray, and destabilising for Saurienville. Danger to civil peace, and so forth. So a lightly armed Alliance presence might be just the hint the Karray would do well to ponder. Negotiations are under way as we speak, and for me, too, duty calls, I'm afraid.'

'And what should I do?'

Walworth stood up. 'Come with me, old chap.'

'Where to?'

'Back to Apis, of course.' Walworth motioned towards the door.

Owen sat where he was.

'I'm a lot more use here, you said so yourself.'

'And you have been! But now, you really must go back to Apis.'

'Why?'

'It's for your own safety, I assure you.'

Owen was not assured at all. 'I'm in a military space station. Safe enough, I would say.'

'Besides,' Walworth added, 'you're needed there, rather urgently.'

'What's happened?'

'The Venus descent suit is active again, and has been rallying monkey-spiders. It's currently in Union custody.'

'Now you're talking.' Owen stood up. 'After you.'

CHAPTER SEVENTEEN

Sales and Marketing

Saurienville, Terre Nouveau, Friday 3 April 2071

'There's too much history here,' Selena said.

Nayak could only agree. Everywhere she looked she saw antiquity beneath the bustling modernity of the port. The blocks of the street on which she and Selena walked were rugged with ancient bas-relief carvings, worn down by the tread of countless feet over centuries but still discernible as saurian sculpture: images of scaled or feathered sides, of tooth and jaw and claw. The carved rock contained fossils: embedded in the broken friezes were traces of shells and other hard parts of many a shoal and bed of marine invertebrates.

The human and other beings they passed in the street seemed likewise to embody layers of history. A few saurians stalked along, heads high above the crowd; a greater number of the Jenty hominids strolled, or stood around on corners talking in their deep voices; and among them the humans, the great majority, went about their business. In this crowd, the two women from the Station didn't stand out. Nayak noticed second looks and curious glances, but only from close up.

Most of the buildings, of wood or reworked stone like the cobbles, had a ground level with high ceilings as the domain of the saurians, a second floor occupied and used mainly by the Jenty hominids, and all the floors above that were used or occupied by human beings. Access to the upper floors was by outside stairways that zigzagged up the frontage. One feature was common to all three species: a fondness for window boxes, the plants in which festooned the faces of the buildings with fronds, flowers and fruits, and attracted a steady traffic of birds and insects. Canopied stalls at street level offered meat and vegetables and herbs, as well more exotic and luxurious products such as fabrics and jewellery.

Nayak and Selena reached the end of the street, looked both ways and waited. After a minute a traffic lady enforced a pause in the rush of swift bicycles and rumbling, slow-moving trucks, and they hurried across. Directly ahead, piers and docks and breakwaters enclosed five medium-sized harbours, within which tall ships lay and small boats plied. Here, too, were strange combinations of modern and antique. The rigging of the tall ships resembled the AI-optimised sail configurations that Nayak had seen on the Firth of Clyde. But in the nearest vessel, across ten metres of busy cobbled quay, a crew of humans and Jenty alike prepared for departure by hauling on ropes and climbing rope ladders to set the sails. And its hull, its lines more elegant and optimised than anything Nayak had yet seen, was decorated with a bright abstract pattern that made so little aesthetic sense that some of its colours, she guessed, must be in wavelengths invisible to her eyes.

Or, perhaps, dinosaurs simply had different tastes. It was hard to know, because they still weren't talking to the Station's emissaries.

'You're being followed,' Iskander said.

Like Selena, Nayak wasn't wearing her glasses. They were partly dismantled, one lens clipped over a jacket pocket, the other hanging on her backpack, the earpieces discreetly tucked behind her ears.

'Who by?' she murmured.

'Two uniformed operatives of the Patrol.'

Nayak glanced at Selena. 'Evade?'

'No,' Selena said. 'Let's just act a bit more like tourists.'

'They don't have tourists here.'

Selena laughed. 'They know we're visitors. They suspect we're up to something. Act like we've nothing to hide.'

'I thought we already were!'

'We're trying too hard to look inconspicuous.'

'Rookie mistake!' Nayak nudged Selena. 'I thought you were trained.'

'I don't do *fieldwork* for the Intelligence Directorate.' Selena sounded annoyed. 'Let's get our glasses on, have them looking like sunglasses. That would be a start. And let's start overtly taking pictures.'

Selena made a show of giggling, bringing their foreheads close, and touching Nayak's shoulder, as they reassembled their glasses and put them on. Normally Nayak would have enjoyed the moment, but now doing this as a cover made it feel false.

'OK, phones out,' Selena said. 'Selfies.'

She turned her back to the harbour, and Nayak did likewise. They both held up their phones and mugged smiles into them. Selena turned again, and pointed to a young crewman high in the rigging of the nearest ship. The sailor noticed and waved, hanging perilously outward from the rope ladder with one hand. Phones raised, zoom, snap, onward. They walked along the side of the quay, pausing now and then to photograph a ship leaving or arriving, a fishing boat chugging across a harbour, a distant lighthouse and a nearby clock tower.

'Closing in,' Selena said. 'Look around, look puzzled, catch sight of those peaked caps and walk over with me.'

Nayak went through the rigmarole, and trailed after Selena as she ambled towards the two Patrol officers. Their uniforms were ornate, their caps braided, their sunglasses mirrored. Their batons swung heavy, and their holsters rested easy, on their hips. Black cuboid boxes with long spiky antennae hung on their shoulders.

'*Bona matang!*' Selena said. '*Pardonay, maya . . .*' She held her phone in front of her mouth and continued in English, which the phone translated into the local dialect, flawlessly imitating her voice. 'We're visitors from the Space Station, and we're not lost, of course, we have maps on our phones, but we were hoping to speak with one of the saurians and we can't seem to attract their attention. I wonder if you could do us the favour of, ah, introducing us to one?'

The cops exchanged shaded glances, mirror to mirror, smirk to smirk.

'The saurians don't just speak with people in the street,' the cop with more braid on his cap and stripes on his shoulder said, Iskander simultaneously translating. 'They're all busy, busy. You need an appointment.'

'Really?' Selena said. 'And how do we get that?'

The senior cop pointed skyward. 'Your Station should be able to arrange it.'

'I'm afraid that's just the trouble,' Selena said, her tone light and bright. 'Our command committee's communications unit can't find the right wavelengths, and besides, everything's encrypted. Could you possibly help at all?'

They must think we're idiots, Nayak thought. Their expressions certainly suggested that.

'Well—' the less jumped-up-looking cop began, only to be interrupted by a blast of a whistle from not far away and a crackling sound from his shoulder. Both cops snatched their black boxes and held them to their ears like phones. Urgent patois rapped out.

Then they both turned away, back towards town, and set off at a run.

Nayak looked at Selena. 'What now?'

Selena pointed. 'We follow them.'

Iskander had been sifting through the feeds from the scores of people from the Station observing and enquiring in Saurienville, and had found no trace of Jean-Paul Damiba, the Karray contact of John Grant. Some knew the man, but only as a minor bureaucrat in the planning department. He was said to be around, always somewhere else. One or two would admit, if pushed, that he was Karray. This didn't help. The Karray were more clandestine than the cadre.

Now, here he was.

Damiba stood in front of a shop window beside a high and wide closed door, around which a curious crowd had gathered. The two Patrol officers looked on from behind the crowd. Three other Patrol cops arrived on bicycles and dismounted with style. A traffic lady and a woman in Militia uniform were conferring nearby.

The street was a couple of hundred metres in from the harbour, just where the commercial district merged into the port district. It had five bars, one or two souvenir shops that looked to Nayak like head shops, an assortment of specialised butchers, grocers and fishmongers, and the restaurants they no doubt supplied. The mid-morning light and shuttered night-time establishments emphasised the area's louche atmosphere. Several of the buildings, as with the shopfront here, had the high ground floor of current or former saurian use.

Nayak followed Selena in elbowing and shouldering her way through the growing crowd. Some of them were tall homi-nids – the Jenty, they were called in the local dialect – and both women kept well out of their way.

'Citizens!' Damiba cried. He flourished phones spread out like a hand of cards. 'Here, for the low, low price of ten New Dollars, you can have the latest technological marvel from the Union of Europe! These, my friends, are phones! You can be the first on your block, in your workplace, on your ship, to have one! You can use it straight away – they already have all the telephone numbers in Saurienville's directory. And not only that – you can use it to contact any of our new comrades on the Station. You can get the latest news from Earth, just as it comes in by FTL shuttle! Translation both ways is built in.'

'And look at this!' He picked one phone from his hand of cards and shook it out, unfolding it to broadsheet size, and then snapping it stiff. 'No need to peer at a tiny screen! All the information and entertainment you could ask, on a screen big enough for the whole household to enjoy.' With a magician's sweep of the hand, he collapsed the phone back to its hand-held configuration and shuffled it back with the others.

'And there's more! These phones give you access to a wealth of information on every subject under the sun – or should I say, the suns! You can have the Union's friendly, helpful artificial intelligence, Iskander, at your beck and call!'

'But don't rush to snatch them out of my hands just yet!' He took off his spectacles, pulled a set of glasses from his jacket pocket, and ostentatiously put them on. 'For another ten New Dollars, you, too, can have the ideal complement to a phone – the almost magical glasses you've seen on our new friends.'

He stepped to the shop door, and pushed it open. His voice took on a warning note. 'This offer won't last long, so don't miss your chance! Take advantage of it right now! Come into this amazing store and check out the other incredible bargains on display!'

The rush almost bowled him over. The wide doorway let lots of people in at once. Within a minute Damiba, Nayak, Selena and the Patrol and Militia people were the only ones outside. More people came hurrying up and pressed their way into the shop. The higher-ranking Patrol cop, and the Militia woman, were talking urgently into their clunky radios.

Still with the glasses on, Damiba looked at the two women

from the Station, and stepped forward, smiling, hand raised. 'You must be the famous Lakshmi Nayak, inventor of the star drive, and you are—'

'The less famous Selena Pereira, yes. Pleased to meet you, Citizen Damiba.'

'How delightful to meet you both.' He took off the glasses, as if afraid of overusing them or – mistakenly – worried about running down the battery. He leaned in a little. 'Did I do all right? I'm not well practised in sales.'

'You did more than all right,' Nayak said.

'Yes, you seem to have taken very well to this socialist market economy business,' Selena added. Damiba permitted himself a brief, tight smile.

'Speaking of which,' Nayak said, looking past him at the shop, 'who's minding the store?'

'Some enthusiastic young people I hired, assisted by your friends, Citizen Grant and Citizen Grant, and Citizens Rafferty and Sweeney.'

'Good grief!' Nayak said. 'Well, we'd better give them a hand.'

She made to enter the shop. The officious Patrol cop stepped forward, hand upraised and not in comradely hygienic greeting. 'Not so fast.'

Selena took out her phone and held it up. 'What seems to be the problem, officer?'

'This establishment is in violation of customs regulations, and furthermore' – he nodded toward Damiba – 'is in contravention of the current one-year plan, subsection 3.22, regarding provision of telecommunications equipment. The Patrol is charged with enforcing import and export regulations, and the Militia is charged with enforcing the provisions of the plan—'

'Excuse me,' Damiba said to Nayak and Selena. He turned to the Patrol officer and continued in local dialect: 'The Militia is charged with no such thing. Other than dealing with cases of theft, embezzlement, diversion of supplies and so on, in other words criminal offences, the Militia has no responsibility or authority to "enforce the provisions of the plan", as you put it.' He beckoned the Militia woman over. 'Citizen, please confirm what I have just said.'

'This is correct,' she said. She chuckled. 'We're not responsible for making sure the plan *works*! We'd have no time for anything else!'

'You're telling me,' the Patrol officer said, 'that you will stand idly by while flagrant black-market trading goes on in plain sight?'

'Black-market trading refers to the sale of illegal commodities, or sale of material diverted from its planned use. I see none of that here.'

She gestured at the flow of people in and out of the shop, which was continuing uninterrupted, to cries of delight and amazement as people tried out their phones.

The Patrol officer scoffed. 'Your superiors may disagree. Meanwhile, I see blatant importation of unchecked, untaxed, unlicensed goods, in clear violation of customs regulations, and I have full authority to shut this place down forthwith.'

'There you are mistaken,' Damiba said. 'If I may, officer – allow me to remind you of the precise definition of importation: the delivery of goods from outside the Union. Would you agree?'

'I suppose so.'

Damiba held out a phone. 'Please examine the details imprinted on the case of this device. What is the country of origin? *L'Union européenne, n'est ce pas?*'

'Yes.'

'And in what country are we? The very same! Therefore, these products are not imports within the meaning of the law. If you take one step to interfere with the business of this shop, you will be in violation of the laws concerning the Union's internal market, to say nothing of those concerning the economic democracy. You are, of course, free – not to say obliged – to report any irregularities you may suspect to the appropriate authorities, who will respond in due course according to law. In the meantime, please desist and return to your regular duties.'

The officer stepped back. 'I shall report this, most certainly. But the Patrol will be back, and it'll take more than a smooth-talking Karray pen-pusher to stop them.'

'I don't doubt that it will,' said Damiba. 'Good day, officer.'

With that he turned to Selena and Nayak, and swept a hand towards the shop door. 'After you, citizens.'

The shop struck Nayak as so plain it was pretentious. The ancient flagstones of the floor had, for now, not a speck of dust or grit. Another high door, closed, was to the left and presumably led to an adjacent room or building. Like the walls and ceiling, it was freshly painted white, and it was barely noticeable. Glowing globe lamps hung from the four-metre-high ceiling. The space was divided, about five metres in, by a polished counter of old wood. Behind it stood three young women and a man, evidently the Saurienville locals that Damiba had recruited. They were operating mechanisms that clattered and rang, and into which they were placing bank notes and occasionally returning coins and other notes. John and Ellen Grant, Morag Rafferty and a young woman who Iskander identified as Lisa Sweeney were shifting stock from shelves behind the counter to the customers. Now and then they stopped at the counter to explain something to customers.

'Do you need any help?' Nayak asked.

'I sure do,' Sweeney said. 'I'm run off my feet.' She raised a hinged portion of the counter and urged Nayak and Selena through. 'Bring some more boxes through, if you don't mind. And Jean-Paul, if you could stick around and help with misunderstandings, my French isn't that good and the dialect is a bit of a challenge—'

'Of course.' Damiba joined her behind the counter.

Past the shelves was a doorway to the back of the shop, which was stacked with boxes and boxes of stuff. At least a

hundred of them were labelled for phones and glasses. Others
were marked only with codes.

Lugging boxes through and shelving their contents kept
Selena and Nayak busy for the next half-hour. Nayak expected
the rush to pass when all those who'd crowded outside had
been served, and then all those who'd been drawn to the shopfront by curiosity as to what was going on, and then all those
who'd seen people using and showing off their shiny new
purchases. After about half an hour, the flow did indeed
diminish. Then it surged again. The queue was soon out of the
door and along the block. About one in ten customers was
Jenty. Their deep-voiced delight at holding a new phone was
like the purr of a tiger.

'What's happened?' Nayak asked. 'Where are all these people
coming from?'

'Lunch break,' Damiba explained. 'And this.' He held up a
copy of *Les Temps de Saurienville* and folded it open to a
half-page advertisement with a grainy grey-tone photograph
of a phone, surrounded by shouting bold text. Nayak needed
no translation to recognise much the same sales pitch as Damiba
had made.

'We placed an ad in the popular tabloids, too,' Damiba said.
'Expect another and bigger rush in four hours or so.'

It took Nayak a moment to realise the strategic cleverness
of this staged marketing. *Les Temps de Saurienville* wasn't
exactly popular reading – nobody read it who didn't have to
check the day's material balances and (more to the point) imbal-
ances needing urgent correction. It was aimed at those with
the most responsibility in management – a minority, however
democratically chosen or accountable. If the workers and
managers who had to study the official paper got phones first,
they would have a vested interest in hanging onto them. And
their owning one would make it something of a status symbol,
which it would remain for an entire afternoon before the day's
work ended and the manual workers and other operatives hit

the streets and grabbed the evening paper for a daily dose of news, yes, but also gossip, sport, fashion and entertainment. And they'd take that paper home, where more people would read it.

'Oh, God,' she said as the implications dawned on her. 'We're going to be here all day and all evening, aren't we?'

Ellen Grant looked up from a shelf. 'You don't have to stay,' she said. 'We'll manage. Take a look out the back before you go.'

At the back of the storeroom was a heavy, thick metal door set in fresh timber, the fittings around it still raw, their massive screw heads shiny. Massive though it was, the door swung open smoothly to a high-walled yard, whose bare and trampled surface had been recently cleared. Barrels, coils of cable, ladders, rusty machinery and other junk were piled against the walls. In the middle of the yard was a shipping container with a ladder propped against it. On top of the container, perched like a lobster on a brick, was the *Fighting Chance*.

The vessel's hatch opened. A woman clambered out and posed at the edge of the container with a big black ugly firearm. She looked down at them, grinning all over her face.

'Hello again,' said Francesca Milloy. She stashed the weapon back in the cabin and came down the ladder. Nayak made the introductions.

'It's good to see you,' she said, 'but why are you here?'

Milloy jerked a thumb over her shoulder. 'Wasn't the gun a clue?'

Nayak stared. 'You're going to try and hunt down Owen *again*?'

'That would be a bonus, but it's not why I'm going to Apis.'

'Apis? But—'

'Excuse me,' said Selena, glancing pointedly around the cramped and cluttered sides of the yard. 'This is not the time or place.'

'Yeah,' Milloy said. 'Let's get a drink.'

CHAPTER EIGHTEEN

Of Miocene Men

Saurienville, Terre Nouveau, Friday 3 April 2071

There was an articulate growl, paced by English: 'Citizen John Grant?'

Grant looked up from the back of the counter, and up, to the face of a male Jenty, who was holding a phone in front of his mouth. Evidently he had bought it earlier, though Grant had to admit to himself that to him Jenty were as yet hard to tell apart.

'Yes? Is there a problem?'

The words went into the phone and were translated with a barely noticeable lag to a string of bass and subsonic phonemes. The Jenty nodded.

'Show me,' Grant said, holding out his hand for the phone. He guessed the Jenty had encountered some feature it didn't know how to handle, or to ask Iskander or the phone's own software to handle.

The Jenty shook his head and smiled, showing small even

front teeth and slender, sharp canines. 'Not with the phone. The phone is great. You have the problem. We wish to talk with you.'

'Fine, fine,' Grant said. He saw the skin around the Jenty's eyes crinkle as a silky snarl came out the phone's speaker. Maybe the idiom didn't translate. 'I mean, yes.' He spread his hands. 'Tell me about it.'

On either side of the Jenty, other customers were pushing in. Conversation was loud in several languages. Tills were ringing. Behind Grant, Ellen, Morag and Lisa were hurrying back and forth. Damiba was explaining something to a customer, waving one arm and pointing out features on the phone screen with the other.

'Not here.'

'OK, OK.' Grant sidled out from behind the counter, just as Nayak, Selena and Milloy crowded through from the back, talking excitedly. The Jenty held up his hand, which was about thirty centimetres from wrist to fingertip. An urgent-sounding growl came through as:

'With all of you, not only Citizen John Grant!'

'Oh!' Grant looked at the others, then waved to Damiba. Damiba turned away from his customer, made pushing-away gestures and mouthed 'Go! Go!' He looked pleased at the development. Grant raised his eyebrows to Ellen and shrugged. 'Guess we should go.'

Ellen said something apologetic in French to the locals on the tills, who responded like Damiba had, but more impatiently.

'OK,' said Ellen.

Grant and the six women – four from his crew and two from the Station, he suddenly realised – followed the Jenty out of the shop and into late afternoon sunshine. About fifty humans and half a dozen hominids were lined up along the sidewalk. The Jenty boomed what sounded like encouraging and cheerful remarks to those of his species waiting as he marched past the queue.

He led them along a few streets and around a couple of

corners. Awnings and stalls increased in frequency; this town didn't seem zoned, exactly, but with every metre the emphasis shifted from the wholesale of the dock district to the retail of the commercial. Gangs of singing and jesting matelots swayed in and out of bars. Crocodiles of children marched homeward, pretending to ignore the loud young men but exchanging nudges and giggles. Office workers sat around tables under trees, some conferring over their new phones. It was still a shock, even to Grant who had seen it before, to notice how old the elders looked: white hair, wrinkled faces, bent backs, hobbling gaits. The supply of anti-ageing medicines and rejuvenating serums in the back of Damiba's new shop couldn't hit the market soon enough – but that wasn't for today. Today was for the phones, for the buzz.

On one of the streets the traffic was held up by the slow plod of the biggest beast Grant had ever seen, far bigger than the dinosaurs. It was like a cross between a camel and a giraffe, dun-coloured, with ears as long as a donkey's, and a good three metres high at the shoulders. It browsed roadside trees and second-storey window boxes and wall-hanging greenery as it ambled along. A small Jenty, presumably a child, straddled the base of its long neck and might or might not have been guiding it with nudges of his or her feet, which were bare, evidently prehensile, and gripping the animal's fur.

The visitors gawped; the Jenty, and the locals, took no more notice than they would of a passing double-decker bus.

'Pleistocene megafauna,' Ellen said. 'Just walking down the street! God, wouldn't Marie love to see this!'

'We can show her our pictures,' Grant said.

'You're going to Apis?' Nayak asked.

'Soon as we can,' Grant said. 'The whole idea is to leave Damiba and company with a going concern, and come back to skim off our finder's fees later.'

'But—'

'Like I said – later,' Selena interrupted.

'Definitely,' said Milloy. 'Lots to talk about.'

She was looking about with open curiosity, and no wonder: she hadn't been on the streets of Saurienville before. Nor had the rest from the *Fighting Chance*, who had made no attempt to blend in and whose attire and skin colour stood out. They got looks, but no remarks, and no harassment. Grant wondered if this indicated enlightenment and equality, or because with the Jenty and two confident women whose clothing and colour could pass for local, they were assumed privileged, under protection and off limits.

The Jenty turned down an alleyway between shops and opened a high gate. Inside was a courtyard lush with grass and trees. The trees were tall and broad, and the gardening between them subtle, with paved paths among plots and pots of flowering plants. Weathered abstract sculptures stood here and there. A water feature burbled in the centre. Birds twittered and bees buzzed. On the ground and on low, long, bare branches, dozens of the tall hominids squatted or perched. They all looked adult. Some had white hair above their high foreheads, and eyes deep set in wrinkles. Most were young, as far as Grant could tell from their limber poses and movements and the gloss of their eyes and hair.

Every one of them had a phone.

Grant and his companions were motioned to a long bench, evidently dragged out for the occasion, under the trees and facing most of the hominid gathering. Grant sat beside Ellen. She looked relaxed, gazing around and breathing deeply, something the scents of the garden encouraged.

'This is nice,' she said. 'Peaceful.'

A younger hominid arrived with a tray and handed out big cups of hazy green liquid. Grant turned his cup in his hands. It was made from the shell of a nut or the skin of a squash, decorated with incised intertwining lines and varnished, with a round, flat base of polished wood. The vessel looked old and valuable, perhaps ceremonial.

'It's safe to drink,' Iskander told him, and no doubt the others. 'Citrus juice.'

'Thank you,' Grant said to the hominids. A deep sound echoed through the garden from all the phones. He raised the cup and took a sip. The juice was sweet and sharp. The hominid who had escorted them vaulted lithely onto a branch a metre and a half off the ground, and watched and waited with his fellows. Grant felt uncomfortable in the gaze of so many pairs of calm, black, bright eyes.

'Iskander, tell us all – what's going on?'

'I don't know. Damiba seemed to expect this, but I didn't. I now have enough of the Jenty language to translate both ways, though not perfectly. From now on, I'll give you subtitles of what they say, but the other way it has to be speech – you didn't bring glasses that can fit on their faces.'

'Huh! An oversight we can correct on the next trip.' Grant raised a hand to their escort. 'Thank you for bringing us here, and for your hospitality.' He nodded down at the cup. 'You said we have a problem, and you wished to talk. You know my name. What is yours?'

Grant couldn't hear the reply, but a subtitle floated in front of him: 'Melikaar.'

'Very well, Melikaar. Here are our names.' He gestured along the bench. Ellen, Lakshmi, Selena, Francesca, Morag and Lisa introduced themselves.

'Are these your wives?' Melikaar asked.

Grant scoffed; the women laughed. Grant put an arm around Ellen's shoulders.

'I am Ellen's husband. She is my wife. The others here are colleagues.'

'We are relieved to hear that, and I apologise if I have given offence.'

Grant held up a hand. 'None taken. I take it you have more urgent matters to talk about.'

'Yes, but my first question was necessary to clarify your level of social advance.'

'We understand,' Nayak said. 'And we would like to have a similar understanding of yours.'

Melikaar flipped his hand. 'It's complicated. Our arrangements would be tedious to explain and difficult for you to comprehend.' He patted the top of his head. 'Our brain capacity is one and a half times yours, and our history at least tens of times longer. The upshot is: among ourselves we are free, but as a species we are oppressed.'

'Oppressed? By whom?'

'By the saurians, and by the rock minds.'

Grant glanced at the others. 'In what way?'

'The saurians attempted to settle this planet long before we attained consciousness. They were driven back by the rock minds, through plagues and earthquakes and so forth. It was, though they did not know it then, a foretaste of what they and then we experienced when much later we attained interstellar travel. However, they maintain, as you see, a presence on this world. They have been with us since we were making tools of stone.' He spread his fingers and swept his hands downward from his chest to his knees. 'They left their imprint in our very bodies. Our ancestors had descended from the trees, and become swift-running hunters on the plains. Their fear at the saurians' presence drove them back to the forest for half a million years – time enough for our skins to become dappled like the shadows of leaves.' He laid a hand on his chest, and tweaked the garment that covered it. 'The skin under this is pale, like the underside of a quadruped! The word for the saurians in our language means literally "bird-monster". We are somewhat more intelligent than you, and they are far more intelligent than us.' Melikaar raked his hair back with his long fingers. 'They never let us forget it.'

'I can see how you might resent that,' Grant said, 'but I fail to see how it oppresses you. And if the rock minds saved your remote ancestors from the saurian invasion, I don't see how they oppress you now.'

'The saurians oppress us by their insistence that we comply with the wishes of the rock minds, and the rock minds oppress us by keeping us confined to this system.'

'Very well. And what is the problem you say we have?'

'You have freed us, and you have freed the saurians.'

'We have? How?'

'The rock minds, the ones you call the Fermi, half a year ago departed the asteroids for the gas giants. We don't know why. Then you arrived – you, Citizen Grant, and then the Space Station, and then many other spacecraft. And now, you have moved the Fermi asteroids out of the system.'

'Wait!' Grant cried. 'I know nothing of this! It wasn't our doing.'

'Some of your species, and the spacecraft that arrived after you.'

'We will investigate.' Grant turned aside. 'Iskander, look into this.'

'Already doing so.'

Grant addressed Melikaar again. 'Are you aware that we are not all working together?' He waved a hand skyward. 'The human species is divided into rival powers. The Station is from our power, the Union. There are spacecraft from three other powers up there.'

'We understand that. We expect there will be more. But whoever did it, by moving the asteroids they demonstrated that the Fermi were unwilling or unable to stop them.'

Milloy leaned forward, raised a hand, and spoke up: 'I was there when the Fermi left another planet which we have begun to settle. Our scientists – well, scientists of our species – believed that the Fermi had left because of some communication these scientists had made, and that the Fermi had decided to leave the rocky worlds to us. Perhaps they were not so much unwilling as indifferent. What should it matter to them, if someone has taken their . . . empty husks?'

'Look at the cup in your hands,' said Melikaar. 'Empty husks can still be valuable.'

'Yes,' said Milloy, 'but not to the tree!'

The garden resounded with amusement at this quip.

'That is well said,' Melikaar replied. 'We suspected that your species had something to do with the departure of the Fermi. We have been expecting some such development since those of your kind first arrived three hundred years ago.'

Grant shook his head. 'I don't understand.'

'Their arrival came as a great shock to us, and to the saurians. Remember, we have been confined to this system, and largely to this world, for tens of thousands of years. When the founders of Saurienville arrived, we learned – and soon confirmed by genetic analysis – that we had a common ancestry, which diverged in what you call the Miocene period. From the records and knowledge they brought, we learned that you came from the home world of all the species we had ever found in our own explorations – a home world whose existence we had long ago deduced, but which we never discovered ourselves.'

'It's not that simple,' Ellen said. 'Our daughter is a biologist, and she knows others who have studied this question, and she says that the Fermi transferred information rather than actual life.'

'We know,' Melikaar said. 'The point is, the information came from life that had evolved naturally on your world. So in these terms, we are related. A further shock was that the Fermi communicated with your people, using' – he held his up – 'phones. In all these millions of years, despite great efforts, they had never communicated with the saurians, or with us. But they communicated with the new arrivals. At first all they said was "Wait", though we understand further communications have taken place over the years.' He hooted. 'They were likewise short and cryptic, but they conferred great prestige on those who had phones, and great advantage.'

'Advantage? How?' Grant asked.

Melikaar spread out his long forearms and hands. 'They gave them business advice.'

'Business advice!' Grant almost laughed. Surely the great minds wouldn't concern themselves with something as small as that . . .

Melikaar nodded gravely. 'The messages, few though they were, showed opportunities in trade with the other communities of our species and the settlements of the saurians which our own commerce had overlooked. And from seizing these opportunities, some of those who had phones and took the hints grew rich. Their descendants are now those known as the Families. Those you call the Karray tried to limit the wealth that these families held, but with little success, for reasons which I am sure you can imagine for yourself.'

'I certainly can,' Grant said. He glanced sidelong at Ellen, who was barely containing her wry amusement. 'And now by providing phones to everyone, including you, the advantage the Families had will disappear. Now everyone will get information about business opportunities – or ways to plan more effectively, if that's what they want. And with the Fermi gone to the gas giants, and not preventing the removal of their dead asteroids, perhaps you are all free from them at last.'

Melikaar and his band took in all this with some signs of agitation: mutters, glances, hand gestures, subsonic growls that made the hairs on Grant's arms – shared primate heritage – stand on end.

'That is exactly—' Melikaar began. He was interrupted by a sonic boom.

Everyone, Homo and Jenty alike, looked up. Blue flashes followed, and more sonic booms. Between the branches, Grant glimpsed black arrowhead shapes, fast and low. Above them, larger black shapes like cylinders with rounded ends and stubby wings came spiralling down. Showers of black dots hurtled from them and abruptly blossomed to descending parachutes, just as the winged cylinders themselves vanished in a series of blue flashes. Grant zoomed his glasses, and saw stick after stick of paratroopers drop out of sight behind the trees and roofs.

'Fuck, what's going on? Iskander?'

Iskander spoke. 'The Alliance have deployed several hundred paratroopers in a remarkably precise manner across the city. Some of them have landed right in front of the shop. They're liaising with the Patrol, and moving to block the frontage. The people in the queue are backing away. Damiba—'

'I'm here,' Damiba said. 'Moving to lock the doors and pull down the shutters right now.'

'You don't want to be trapped inside,' Grant said. 'Why don't you get your people out the back and into my ship?'

'What?' Ellen said. 'We can't—'

Grant muted the phone. 'What's the problem?'

'You're thinking of evacuating Damiba and his shop assistants? Where does that leave us?'

Grant waved around, indicating the hominids. 'Safe for now, I think. Safer than they'll be if the Patrol and the Alliance grab them.'

'We're moving to the back now,' Damiba reported.

'Patch us in,' Grant said.

'I don't know – oh. Thanks, Iskander.'

The view from Damiba's glasses came up in Grant's. The four young locals hurried past, into the yard where the container and the *Fighting Chance* took up half the space. The view swung as Damiba hauled the heavy back door of the shop closed, then locked it. Jangle of keys as Damiba turned. A shadow fell across the yard. Two paratroopers landed with a thump of boots right in front the shop workers. The parachutes, detached a moment later, floated away over the walls just as the paratroopers levelled their rifles. The shop workers backed off, crowding against Damiba.

Melikaar growled. A subtitle scrolled past Grant's view. 'What's happening?'

'Trouble. I'll explain when it's over.'

'What?' Damiba said. 'What do we do now?'

'Raise your hands and close your eyes! Tell the others!'

Damiba snapped an order in French. The shop workers complied, still backing off.

'Eyes closed?' Grant asked. Iskander zoomed on the visors of the two paratroopers, and picked out the reflection of four scared faces, and Damiba's grim look. All had their eyes tight shut. No doubt the soldiers were puzzled, but they'd twig in a moment.

'Now, Iskander!' Grant said.

The blue flash darkened Damiba's glasses, the thump rang in his earpieces. Grant winced. The glasses cleared instantly. Where the container and the *Fighting Chance* had been was a big empty space in which litter whirled in eddies of air. The soldiers, off balance from the blast from the air that had rushed into the vacated space, looked over their shoulders and then back.

'Can we open our eyes now?' Damiba asked.

'Yes, but keep your hands up.'

Damiba stepped forward and addressed them in English and in a friendly tone. 'Welcome to Saurienville! How can I help you?'

The soldiers kept their rifles aimed at Damiba and his helpers. 'You lot are under arrest.'

'On whose authority?'

'Customs Board. Illegal importation of goods.'

'Not that again!' Damiba cried. He shook his head. 'Honestly. I thought all this had been sorted out. Very well. And you're acting on behalf of the Customs Board, you say?'

'Jeez,' Ellen said, on a private channel to Grant. 'That guy has some aplomb.'

'I've noticed.'

'Yes,' said the soldier, 'and we've had enough of your crap. Unlock that door and let us in.'

Damiba bowed slightly. 'Not a problem.'

He turned back to the door. Keys jangled again. He pulled the door open and stepped aside. 'After you.'

'Ha! No tricks. Me first, then you, then your pals, then him.'

Damiba took another step to the side, clear of the doorway, just before a saurian sprang out and grabbed the rifles off the paratroopers. It moved so fast that no one had time to react. The saurian loomed over the humans, raised the snatched weapons well out of reach, and lowered its huge head.

'I see you are thinking of reaching for your sidearms,' it said. 'I would advise you not to try. Hands in the air, and allow Citizen Damiba to disarm you.'

'No fucking way!'

'You have my word that your weapons will be returned to you after you leave the shop,' Damiba said. 'But I'm afraid the landlord here doesn't permit you to carry them on his property.'

'The landlord?'

'That would be me,' said the dinosaur. Its long fingers were suddenly everywhere on the two rifles, and it became apparent that it was well able to operate them one-handed. 'Now, please follow the advice of my tenant, Citizen Damiba here, and pass him your sidearms.'

The soldiers looked at each other, conferred or possibly consulted a superior, and complied. The saurian turned about and stepped inside, and Damiba waved them into the shop. He and his assistants followed. The dinosaur marched through the shop, stepping over the counter and dodging the hanging light fittings. Damiba dashed past it to unlock the front door, which it then flung open. It stepped outside. Damiba motioned with a pistol and the soldiers followed the saurian out. As soon as they crossed the threshold Damiba handed the pistols back. He told the assistants to stay put for now and went outside himself. He wasn't a tall man, and for a moment Grant and the others sharing the view saw only backs and heard only clamour.

'Hold your phone up, Jean-Paul!' Grant said.

'Ah, good idea!'

Citizens, with People's Militia dotted among them, crowded the street. Up and down the road, traffic ladies stood in front of lengthening tailbacks of trucks and buses. A handful of people with heavy cameras on their shoulders stood at a distance up the road, recording video and speaking into clunky microphones. At least twenty Patrol officers faced the crowd, while rows of Alliance paratroopers backed them up and lined the shopfront. Towering over everyone stood the dinosaur landlord, and two others at the edge of the crowd. Four more dinosaurs bounded up the road, two from each direction, hurdling traffic and side-swerving the traffic ladies.

The landlord stooped and returned the rifles to the paratroopers. Then it straightened up to its full height and bellowed. The clamour stopped. Treading carefully and deliberately, it paced forward. People, militia and civilian alike, jostled each other out of its way. The Patrol and the Alliance troops had formed a rough semicircle around the crowd, and now six dinosaurs stood evenly spaced behind them, talking literally over everyone's heads in loud voices in their own language. The saurian landlord joined them, and the conversation. They seemed to reach a conclusion and turned as one to face the gathering.

'ENOUGH!' the landlord hollered, as if through a megaphone. It continued, in a lower but still carrying voice: 'The shop is closed for today. The Customs Board and the Patrol have overstepped their authority, and the off-world military have no authority whatsoever here and are welcome only as long as they cease interfering in the internal affairs of this city. I ask you all to disperse, except for the' – it cocked its head, as if listening – 'Alliance military forces, who must accompany my colleagues here to the city limits, escorted by the People's Militia.'

It repeated all this in French. The crowd began to drift away. The dinosaurs closed in like gigantic sheepdogs, herding the soldiers into a compact huddle. Damiba elbowed his way back to the shop doorway, called the assistants out and locked up again. The soldiers marched off in good order, with Militia squads in front and behind and the saurians striding alongside. The reporters bustled about, shouting questions at everyone involved and vox-popping departing customers and onlookers. Traffic began to flow again.

'OK,' said Damiba. 'See you in a few minutes. I know where you are.'

Grant blinked out of the feed from Damiba's glasses as if from a dream. The others in his group were doing likewise. The Jenty looked up from their phones, on which they had been following the same stream, agog.

'Well, fuck me,' Grant said. He drained the last of the juice from his cup, and set the vessel down carefully on the bench beside him. He checked a schematic that Iskander had helpfully displayed in his glasses. The Alliance paratroops, all five hundred of them, were moving in small knots along the highways out of town, each group escorted by a Militia squad and at least one saurian.

'You see how it is,' Melikaar said. 'Your people control municipal affairs, up to a point. My people control planetary affairs, up to a point. And the saurians control off-world and system affairs.'

'Up to a point.' Grant twirled a skyward finger. 'And the Fermi control interstellar affairs?'

Melikaar chuckled deeply. 'Up to a point, for them, too, as your species has just shown by making off with the asteroids.'

'Perhaps,' Grant said. He looked at Ellen and the other women. All except Nayak looked as perplexed as he felt. Nayak had that abstracted gaze she took on when she was lost in exploration of whatever strange spaces her mathematical mind worked in. Grant raised his eyebrows to her, got no response and shrugged. 'What the fuck do we do now?'

Ellen jumped up from the bench. 'I'll tell you what,' she said. The echoing translation of what she was saying growled from the Jentys' phones all around them. 'We ask Iskander to put the *Chance* and the container back where they were, detach the container and ask our new friends here for permission to land the *Chance* here or somewhere nearby. And then we fuck off to Apis.'

'Apis? Now?' He wanted to stick around, to learn more about this new planet and culture, to solve whatever the problem really was between the dinosaurs and the Jenty, and between them and the Fermi. Apis was old hat, and – he just then realised – made profoundly alien by its absence of vertebrates. Terre Nouveau, by contrast, was a place you could imagine settling into, rather than, well, settling.

'Yes,' Ellen said firmly. 'That was always the plan. We've done our bit for Damiba, more than our bit.'

'Speak of the devil,' said Morag Rafferty.

Jean-Paul Damiba strolled in through the gate to the courtyard. He greeted Melikaar, then turned to Grant. 'I overheard your conversation just now, thanks to Iskander.'

'Thanks, Iskander,' Grant muttered.

'You're welcome,' Iskander replied.

'Ellen is quite right,' Damiba continued. 'You have done more than enough for me, and you really should continue your journey to Apis before there is more trouble here. And trouble there will be! But first, there is an old acquaintance who wishes to meet you.'

Grant stared at him, puzzled. 'Who?'

Damiba turned to Melikaar. 'With your permission?'

'Of course,' Melikaar replied.

Damiba spoke into his phone. 'Come in!'

The gate opened again, and Louise Ogundu walked through.

CHAPTER NINETEEN

The Kings' Last Argument

Saurienville, Terre Nouveau, Friday 3 April 2071

It was like watching a queen or a media star make an entrance, Nayak thought. Louise Ogundu was tall, and her erect posture and purple head wrap made her seem taller. She wore an emerald-green silk dupion gown with a sable jacket, and thick-soled green, highly polished boots. No item of this outfit looked vegan and out of a printer, nigh-perfect though such imitations were. Her glasses were the latest release, almost invisible, a shimmer in front of her eyes. She swept the courtyard with a glance that took the presence of the Jenty as no surprise. After a polite nod to Melikaar, she walked up to Grant and raised hands.

'Hello again, John.'

'Hello, Louise. Good to see you! How did you get here?'

'Shuttle to the Station, then shuttle to the ground, a few hours ago. Commander Ulrich has brought me up to speed. We made some calls.'

'And, uh, what brings you here?'

'Oh, this and that.' She waved an airy hand. 'Sonia Wiley told me about what you were up to here, and it seemed to be in my area of concern and expertise.'

'Ah, yes, Sonia,' Grant said. He and Ellen exchanged wry glances.

'She sends her regards,' Ogundu said.

Nayak heard a murmur of 'Uh-huh' from the others. She leaned sideways and nudged Morag Rafferty. 'Who's this Sonia?' she whispered.

'An old cadre,' Morag whispered back. 'Old as in she wis cadre way before the Rising. She spread Iskander around when it was, like, a bootleg app.'

'Ah, I see,' Nayak said. 'An early adopter.'

'You could say that.'

Ogundu turned to Melikaar. 'I believe we have much to discuss.'

'Yes,' Melikaar replied. 'But first, our friends from the *Fighting Chance* should depart.'

'Shame,' said Grant. 'I was looking forward to renewing our acquaintance.'

Ogundu laughed. 'My acquaintance usually means you're in trouble. You're not in trouble now, but you may be if you hang around. Another time, perhaps.'

Grant frowned. 'So why did you tell Jean-Paul you wanted to see me at all?'

'I wanted to thank you personally for finding this world.' She gazed around, smiling. 'It's wonderful!'

'I didn't do much to find it,' Grant said. 'That was Iskander.'

'It was your choice to come down, and to make contact.'

Grant shrugged. 'I needed the air.'

Ogundu clapped Grant's shoulder. 'Nevertheless. And, yes, you should go.'

'Aye, well, all right.' Grant sighed. 'Iskander, make the arrangements.'

Iskander was already making the arrangements. Deep-toned instructions sounded from some of the younger Jentys' phones, and the hominids got busy ensuring that a space in the court-yard was clear and that no one would wander into it. A few minutes later a distant blue flash and thump was followed by the arrival of the *Fighting Chance* ten centimetres above the grass. It landed with a thud and settled with a creak.

'Well,' Ellen said. 'Time to go.'

'Yeah,' Grant said. He looked hard at Nayak and Selena. 'You stay and you *solve* this place, you hear?'

It was on the tip of Nayak's tongue to say that she almost had, but the idea was too strange for her to voice without checking the logic and the mathematics carefully, and it would set too many cats among the pigeons if she were to voice it now.

'We'll do our best,' she said. Selena nodded firmly, then surprised Grant as much as Nayak by jumping up and giving him a warm comradely hug. Nayak was more reserved, but she felt a pang as she said goodbye to her old crewmates and to Francesca Milloy and Lisa Sweeney. They all climbed aboard the *Fighting Chance*. Ellen waved and gave a thumbs-up from the cockpit. The usual warnings were shouted, then translated to the Jenty speech. The hominids closed their eyes and covered their ears with the palms of their hands. The blue flash came, and the ship was gone.

Nayak opened her eyes and uncovered her ears. Her body was still vibrating to the thump. The Jenty uncurled their arms from their heads. Louise Ogundu's head wrap had fallen off, revealing her mass of springy white hair; she stooped, shook out the wrap, and draped it around her neck as a scarf, somehow making herself more elegant and regal than before. She brushed her palms together and looked around with a fierce grin.

'Now,' she said, 'to business!'

Business, it turned out, began with bringing out seven chairs, arranging them in a semicircle open to the bench and to the populated low branches, and throwing covers over them. It proceeded with the deployment of seven small tables, one in front of each chair. On the chair in the middle Ogundu deigned to sit. No way, Nayak thought, was the lady going to risk her dress by sitting on an outdoor bench! But who were the other chairs for? They were evidently designed for humans, not for Jenty. Nayak didn't have to wait long to find out.

There was a sound of two-stroke vehicles pulling up outside, and of excited voices in the street, then a hush. Six tall women, from early to late middle age, gowned and head-dressed even more grandly than Ogundu, walked in escorted by six young men in the local style of business suit but of a finer fabric and cut than Nayak had seen on the streets. The suits' upper arms and shoulders bulged with biceps and – she did not doubt – holstered pistols. The men took up positions around the court-yard, and stood at ease in the characteristic bodyguard and security detail pose, their gaze flitting in sweep patterns as regular as radar beams. The ladies carried large clutch bags of reptilian leather in their satin-gloved hands.

Damiba bowed the ladies in, waved them to the semicircle of chairs in the middle of which Ogundu still sat, then took his place on the bench beside Nayak and Selena.

'Wait here and don't say a word,' he whispered. 'These are the heads of the Families. You do *not* want to come to their attention, believe you me, let alone annoy them.'

Ogundu stood up and greeted the ladies as they approached, one by one – by name, to Nayak's astonishment. They took their seats with much rustling and hissing of fabrics, and accepted the ornate cups that a couple of young hominids brought them. Two of the older ones took long, slender-stemmed pipes and small pouches from their handbags, and peeled off their gloves to pack and light the weed. Fragrant smoke drifted. They all sipped from their cups, and sighed with satisfaction. Then they all took out phones and glasses, evidently newly purchased, along with rectangular black devices about fifteen by eight centimetres and a good half-centimetre thick, which they placed with great care on the little tables. Presumably these were the ancient phones that Melikaar had mentioned. Clunky old solid-state electronics, still working after centuries but hardly ever taking calls.

Melikaar descended from his branch and strode over, to squat at the focus of the semicircle. The Jenty in the trees around all leaned forward and listened intently to the conversation that followed. Nayak caught snatches of it, but it was in several human languages – all of which Ogundu seemed to speak fluently – as well as the low growls and rumbles of the Jenty speech, and everyone spoke fast. Iskander not only didn't translate, it was actively unhelpful, sticking *commercially sensitive* across her glasses instead of subtitles. If her occasional gasps were anything to go by, Selena seemed to catch more of what was going on than Nayak did. Mindful of Damiba's warning, Nayak kept her mouth shut. She texted Selena:

'?'

Selena texted back: 'Fraught negotiations.'

'About?'

'Law, trade, immigration. Sunlight.'

'!??' Nayak responded.

'Translation issue?' Selena shook her head, lips compressed.

One of the ladies stood up, gathered her things, crooked a finger to her bodyguard and marched towards the exit in high dudgeon. Damiba jumped to his feet and hurried after her. He sidestepped the bodyguard and fell in with the lady, speaking urgently. Her walk slowed, then stopped. They talked in low voices, almost head-to-head. Damiba sounded polite, but far from obsequious; the lady's tone indignant to begin with, then softening. The tough guy stood guard, back politely turned, a few paces away. The discussion in the semicircle continued uninterrupted. After a few minutes the indignant lady nodded to Damiba and walked back, to resume her place as if nothing had happened.

Damiba returned. He drew the back of his hand across his forehead with a stagy 'Phew!' and sat back down beside Selena. Nayak gave him an eyebrow-flash. He smiled thinly, shook his head and drew a finger across his lips.

Shadows lengthened. The negotiations dragged on. Nayak was beginning to feel bored, restless and thirsty, like a child in the back seat of a car on a long journey. She had an impulse to kick her feet. Just as it became difficult to ignore, a young hominid came up to refill their cups. Nayak gulped gratefully. As she tilted her head back to drain the cup, she spotted the Station and a cluster of nearby dots cross the sunset sky. She turned to Selena, pointed upwards and then at her glasses, and mouthed: 'Sitrep.'

Selena nodded; Iskander obliged.

A panoramic, annotated lattice of deployments and locations around Terre Nouveau and the rest of the system floated in front of Nayak's eyes, with scrolling updates. The Alliance, Co-ord and African Union FTL military drones still kept orbital pace with the Station. Over the past days other craft had arrived and departed, some around Terre Nouveau, some near the first planet, the saurian home-world that Black Horizon had labelled Jurassica. Yet others, detectable only by faint, distant Cherenkov flashes, were around the gas giants. It was impossible at this distance to resolve their images or identify their origin and intent. No ships from Earth, as far as Iskander could tell, had ventured to the moons of Terre Nouveau to pry into their hangars of ancient saurian shuttles, or approached any of the myriad Jenty-built space habitats.

From a close examination of recorded input from the Station's telescopes over the past few days, Iskander had belatedly identified five distant, widely separated blue glints as the vanishings of the former Fermi asteroids. It was still trying to identify whose craft had been responsible.

She saw, more or less in real time though the Station and its harriers were now below the horizon, a flash from its vicinity as yet another automated shuttle departed, presumably for Earth. Iskander identified it as one of the Station's own. No doubt it, or another, would soon be back. Mail carrying by FTL spacecraft was FTL communications, of a kind, and the only way to keep Brussels or the other capitals up to date.

FTL communications. FTL comms . . . Did the Jenty and the saurians have these? She and Marek had picked up hominid radio voices around the third planet, and machine code carried by radio around the habitats. All the radio traffic so far picked up on Terre Nouveau carried human voices or music. The assumption on the Station was that the other species used fibre-optics or something more advanced, but surely they had some method of mobile communication, and they didn't seem to be using the electromagnetic spectrum for that.

Melikaar was talking now, his tone going up into audibility and then down below the range of human hearing. Nayak occasionally felt it as a vibration in her skull, and perhaps her teeth. Other Jenty interjected, now and then booming from the branches on which they squatted. If Iskander was translating Jenty speech it was for the benefit of Ogundu, Damiba and the ladies of the Families, not for her and Selena. Damiba was listening intently, and seemed to be following what was going on. The ladies responded to Melikaar with what sounded like urgent, rapid objections in the local dialect, Ogundu with some calming utterances, and the discussion moved on.

This, Nayak thought, was going to go on for a while. Her mind drifted back to the mathematics. As she gazed upwards at the complex dance of spacecraft that Iskander diagrammed on her glasses, like the constellations drawn over the random spatter of the real stars in an introductory astronomy book, the structure taking shape in her mind seemed to map the four-dimensional problem with which she struggled.

But only for a moment, and then a shift in the imaginary lines between the bright points twisted it away.

FTL comms . . . FTL comms . . . something was nagging

at her. Milloy had something to do with it. Nayak gnawed at the thought like a ragged fingernail, a loose end. Milloy, Milloy, Francesca Milloy . . . It all went back to Venus. Nayak remembered Milloy scrambling into the *Fighting Chance* seconds before Cloud City fell, how she'd urged them back to save the last two dozen survivors clinging on in the outposts, and the last survivor of all, the empty descent suit animated by its onboard instance of Iskander. It had told them the whole story of how Marcus Owen had descended to the surface, and then into the chasm, where he – and it, the AI – had seen the image of a woman's face on the sheer cliff of what they now knew was Fermi rock . . .

And, of course, Nayak knew the rest: the image was of Emma Hazeldene, who five minutes or so earlier had been peering at a slab of Fermi rock on Apis, light years away. A slab that was part of an apparatus constructed by Able Jenkins, a second-generation exile on Apis whose first contact with the Fermi had come on his father's old Huawei 7G phone, which Jenkins Snr had carried when he'd been lifted from Africa by Black Horizon, just as the ancestors of this community had been, and around about the same time.

Nayak looked across at the ladies sitting with their ancient phones on their laps. Clunky old solid-state electronics, which thanks to time travel were now centuries old, even though they had been made in the 2030s. Phones through which the Fermi in this system had communicated with these women's ancestors, after millions of years of the saurians' attempts to interact with the Fermi had failed. Phones on which an early version of Iskander might have already been running: if Morag's story about Sonia was correct, the software had been spread clandestinely that long ago, when the Rising was in preparation.

Well, why speculate when she could ask?

'Iskander,' she sub-vocalised, 'is there a version of Iskander on the ladies' old phones?'

'Hard to say,' Iskander replied, in her earpiece. 'I can't synch with them directly, because the hardware and software aren't back compatible.'

'Really? Planned obsolescence? Not your style, is it?'

'Act of Indemnity and Oblivion,' Iskander replied. 'It was engineered in after the Rising.'

The Act of Indemnity and Oblivion had been a rather self-serving piece of legislation rushed through the Union Convention, the first European constituent assembly after the Rising, basically wiping everyone's slate clean on all sides. Yes, making the phones no longer backwards compatible would certainly have helped with that.

'But it's possible that Iskander is or was on these phones?'

'Yes.'

'And on Able Jenkins's phone, on Apis?'

'Yes.'

'Hmm.'

Was it possible that all this time – years on Apis, centuries here – and that one time on Venus with Owen in the descent suit, the Fermi had been talking not so much to humans, but to Iskander? Or talking to humans only through Iskander?

But why? Why Iskander? And, come to think of it, how?

Hitherto, Nayak had taken for granted that the Fermi, this mighty, star-spanning superluminally connected alien artificial intelligence or spontaneously generated pantheon sparked from the first hammer blow of creation in the quantum vacuum or whatever, capable of terraforming planets and spreading life by copying genetic codes and replicating them in molecules in other potential or actual biospheres, would be capable of cracking any encryption in nanoseconds.

Perhaps it was: quantum computation, which many of the scientific papers she'd read had suggested was the underlying mechanism of the Fermi, could theoretically do that.

Or perhaps it hadn't had to.

And with that thought, the mathematical schema in her

mind, which had formed as she'd wrestled for months with the problem, twisted around and clicked into a different shape.

The Fermi *was* Iskander.

Well, in a sense.

It, or they, was or were a far-future descendant of Iskander, that had by design or accident ended up billions of years in the past, and set about creating the conditions for its own existence. A causal loop as maddening as the one that had found her sending the equations for FTL travel to her past self, and indeed the one that had sent Test Rig 2 to Proxima and back with a photograph of these same equations before the scientists had completed building Test Rig 1.

She clapped her hand to her mouth, to restrain herself from yelling out the insight.

Damiba leaned forward and looked over at Selena and Nayak. 'Something's happening,' he said.

The ladies stood up and gathered around Ogundu. Melikaar rose to his feet and towered over them all. The other Jenty came down from the branches and gathered around. Damiba stood up and beckoned Selena and Nayak forward. The Jenty made way for them and they found themselves facing the haughty looks of the ladies and the friendlier gaze of Ogundu. She addressed Damiba in French.

'*Tout va bien?*'

'*Oui, oui, mais . . .*' He spread his arms and looked up at the darkening sky.

'But what?'

Damiba sighed, and glanced at Selena and Nayak. 'It's a big thing, and the *Assemblée Générale* has to agree, and then the populace has to ratify . . .'

Ogundu held up a hand. 'Not the unification! This! We have to decide now.'

Damiba hesitated for a moment. 'Why now?'

'If we don't, our friends here will not take us seriously again.

And I don't just mean the Jenty. The Families will think we're cowards, and make their own arrangements with what they see as the stronger side. It could be the Alliance, it could be the Co-ord. Do you look forward to finding out which is worse?'

'No,' said Damiba. 'I don't.'

'Well then.'

'All right,' Damiba said. 'Let's do it.'

Ogundu nodded gravely and turned to Melikaar. 'Yes,' she said.

A rumble of bass voices shook Nayak's chest. The Jenty ran in great loping strides to the doorways of the courtyard, all except Melikaar leaving the humans where they stood.

'What's going on?' Nayak asked.

Damiba pointed upwards. 'Look.'

The Station and the cluster of drones around it were again passing overhead, brighter now against the darker sky. Nayak realised with a start that an hour and a half had passed since she'd last seen the orbital procession. How time flies when you're lost in four-dimensional space! Out of nowhere, a new spark appeared a few degrees ahead of the Station. It was very bright, outshining the Station by far. Everyone gasped. Then Melikaar let out the big intake of breath to his mighty chest in a long, deep sigh.

'Iskander, get me visual!'

It was so like falling upwards that Nayak staggered. She was seeing, as if from close up, through one of the Station's telescopes, the new shiny thing. A metal flower tens of kilometres across, its petals mirrors, its stamens a battery of narrow tubes with one long spike from the axis. Was this the sunlight the Jenty had been talking about?

Subtitles scrolled across the foot of the image. A dialogue between machines, transcribed by Iskander into English and Russian for the human watchers, and tabbed to its origins.

The Jenty craft: ALLIANCE AND CO-ORD CRAFT TO LEAVE SYSTEM IMMEDIATELY

Alliance and Co-ord craft: 'No'/'*Nyet*'

The Jenty craft: IMMEDIATE DESTRUCTION WILL FOLLOW UNLESS YOU COMPLY

A blizzard of machine code from the drones.

Some decision was being made, too fast to follow, by the autonomous AIs of the FTL combat drones.

'Close your eyes!' Iskander told her, over the sudden bray of alarms across the city. Her glasses went instantly black. Around their edges and through her closed eyelids and through, it seemed, the top of her head flared the brightest light she'd ever seen. It faded fast, leaving a diffuse purple after-image.

'FTL nuclear torpedo,' Iskander reported, in a flat tone. 'From one of the FTL drones.'

'Safe to look?'

'For now.' Her glasses cleared.

Selena put an arm around her shoulders. 'Are you all right, Lakshmi?'

'For now.' Nayak chuckled grimly, glanced at her girlfriend gratefully, and looked up again. A bright multi-coloured stain was spreading across the sky. Hundreds of sparks showered from it, fragments burning like meteors in the upper atmosphere. The Station, to say nothing of the drones, would be getting a pelting. The stain itself moved almost as fast as the Station, continuing in the same orbital trajectory as the machine, whatever it was, that had been destroyed.

'Whose drone fired the torpedo?' Damiba asked.

'Does it matter?' Nayak said.

'Iskander, tell us,' Selena added.

'It was the Co-ord military drone,' Iskander said.

Selena grunted. 'Well, the Alliance has troops on the ground here, so—'

'So the Co-ord has an *excuse*?' Nayak demanded sharply. Selena's tendency to stick up for the Co-ord didn't surprise her, but it sometimes annoyed her.

'No, the Co-ord has a *reason*. To show it's still in play around here.'

'Hmm! Iskander, what was the target?'

The reply came from Melikaar, as a growl and a yip then a snarl that scrolled across their sight as subtitles: 'It was one of our solar power collection satellites with a laser battery. Don't worry, we have many more. There will be no more talking.'

How had it got there? Nayak was about to ask, when the truth of Melikaar's words was suddenly and abundantly proved. Just as the Station and the three drones were on the point of passing into the shadow of Terre Nouveau, a cluster of the new bright lights appeared in front of them. The lasers fired at once, scoring sharp trails through the debris. Two of the drones glowed red then white before exploding in flashes that seemed small compared with the nuclear blast. Before the debris from these had time to begin to rain, the Station and the remaining drone skipped the scene, leaving blue Cherenkov flashes closely echoed by the new lights. Nothing remained visible in the sky but the debris stain, glowing of its own light as it passed into the planet's cone of shadow and headed for the horizon.

Over the next minutes, Iskander displayed similar, equally decisive encounters around the first planet. The Station reported in, from between the orbits of the two moons. Its external sensors and surface installations had sustained some damage from the nuclear explosion and its debris, and from the closer and smaller explosions of the two drones. An automated shuttle had made a fast return trip to the vicinity of the gas giant, hanging around only long enough to record a continuous random flicker of Cherenkov flashes within a thousand kilometres of the Alliance flagship, HMS *Mordant*. In that few seconds it had picked up messages sent in brief bursts to the *Mordant* from the solar power plants in the moments between their FTL jumps, warning that it risked sharing the fate of the drones if it didn't leave the system at once. The utterly unpredictable arrivals and departures, and the brief appearances, gave the *Mordant* and any attendant craft no time to bring their weapons to bear.

By the time the shuttle went out again, the *Mordant* had left.

And that, it seemed, was that.

'What happened to the third drone?' Selena asked, as she, Nayak and Damiba walked across to the chairs the ladies had vacated, in the focus of which Melikaar still stood, and in one of which Ogundu still sat.

'That's the African Union drone,' Ogundu told them. 'It's still close to the Station, and it's staying here for a while.' She looked smug. 'That was part of the deal.'

Nayak sat. The chair felt more comfortable than the bench. 'And the rest of the deal?'

Ogundu nodded to Damiba. 'You have the floor, citizen!'

Damiba looked around, grinning. 'It's very simple,' he said. 'The Families retain their wealth, and their trading arrangements with the other settlements and the Jenty. They stop trying to prevent interstellar trade, and allow the import of phones, medicines, other Earth commodities and so forth, for a percentage taken as customs duty. Iskander will suggest business opportunities to them, just as the Fermi allegedly did in the past. No doubt they will cut their own deals and undercut each other. The Republic will tax their profits, of course, and between ourselves I assure you that this tax will rise steeply over time. And – subject as I said to ratification by our democratic institutions over the next days and weeks, Saurienville will apply to become part of the Union – the *African* Union.'

Oh. Very neat. By allying with and eventually joining the African Union, Saurienville had taken itself clean out of the contention between the three great powers. Instead of fighting each other over access to Terre Nouveau, they'd have to vie to make offers to the African Union for influence.

'The Jenty have agreed to a limited increase of the human settlement,' Ogundu added. 'The first traders and visitors from Africa will begin to arrive tomorrow.'

Selena was looking pleased, as was Damiba. No wonder, Nayak thought. The Co-ord and Alliance, militarily chased out of the system, would have to seek subtler ways to contend. Damiba and the Karray would be adept at exploiting that. Selena's profession, and perhaps Selena herself when her secondment to the Station ended, would not be short of work.

The thought gave Nayak a pang, but that was for the future. Meanwhile, she tried to make sense of the swift battles she had just seen. The solar-powered laser batteries were exactly what she had expected, and predicted to find, in close orbit around the system's star. She hadn't expected at all that they would have FTL drives. What was that about? Surely the purpose of the laser batteries was to propel the habitats out of the system, if the Jenty ever changed their minds about interstellar travel and that distant day came. If the whole point of them was to avoid the need for FTL travel, to avert the wrath of the Fermi or whatever, why have FTL drives?

For now, that could remain an enigma. One question had already been answered, and Nayak hugged it to her heart. The first power plant had blossomed in the sky, in low Terre Nouveau orbit, within seconds of the decision having been made to deploy them. Ogundu had urged it, Damiba had hesitated, then they'd agreed. The Jenty had run for the building, no doubt to action stations. And in less than a minute the solar-powered laser battery had appeared out of nowhere – out of an FTL jump. To send a signal to its probable orbit would have taken six, seven, or more minutes.

There was no way these gigantic reflectors had been lurking nearby. Moon-bright, they couldn't be missed. And mirrors of that size couldn't be folded and unfolded in seconds, and, anyway, what would be the point?

Only one explanation fitted all the facts: the Jenty had FTL comms.

Nayak looked forward to finding out how they worked. She turned to Melikaar, about to ask, and glimpsed another bright light traverse the sky for a second or two, then vanish in a blue flash.

'What was that?' Nayak asked, amid a chorus of the same question.

'Co-ord troopship *Marshal Aleksandr Vasilevsky*,' Selena answered, before Iskander could get a word in. 'Right now she's' – she checked something in her glasses – 'ah yes, in the river mouth just above the harbour, bang in the middle of Saurienville.' She looked over at Melikaar. 'Are your flying laser batteries willing to zap *that*?'

CHAPTER TWENTY

Soft Power Projection

Saurienville, Terre Nouveau, Friday 3 April to
Saturday 4 April 2071

'You knew!' Nayak yelled. She was shaking with feelings of
fury and betrayal. 'How could you!'

Selena regarded her calmly. 'I didn't know *this* would happen,
but I knew something *like* this would happen.' She looked up,
as if seeking some clue among the stars in the now dark sky.
'It was the Alliance that moved the Fermi asteroids out of the
system, to God knows where! You know that now, don't you?
Iskander?'

'I can't confirm that,' Iskander said.

'Well, I can confirm it!' Selena sounded angry and scornful.
'It wasn't the Co-ord, it wasn't the Union, and the African
Union doesn't have the capacity in place. So it had to be the
Alliance.'

'Uh—' Nayak began to object to this failure of logic.

'Yes, yes, Lakshmi, I know you'll have all sorts of other possibilities in your mind, some minor power or the Jenty or the saurians or the Fermi themselves, but come on! And in any case, I can tell you for sure that the Co-ord believes it was the Alliance.' Selena cocked her head, as if listening. 'Yes, and they made the detection. They have evidence.'

'You're in *contact* with the Co-ord?' Even after all this, Nayak couldn't believe it.

'Of course I am,' Selena said. 'Your Iskander isn't the only AI with encrypted comms, you know! I'm the only asset the Co-ord have had here on the ground for days.'

'You've been – all this time?'

'What do you expect, Lakshmi? I'm a Cuban intelligence officer! This is my job!'

'Don't tell me not to take it personally!'

Nayak realised that she and Selena were standing face to face half a metre apart. Damiba and Melikaar looked on as if ready to wade in and pull them apart and not at all sure they should or could. Nayak's jaw was jutting and her fists were clenched. She stepped back and let her hands relax. Ogundu was talking into her phone, presumably conferring urgently with Commander Katrina Ulrich up on the Station. Jenty were running in and out of the house, or huddling in the courtyard.

'I wasn't going to.' Selena sighed. 'Anyway – the Alliance snatched a massive strategic advantage from right under our noses when they went off with the Fermi asteroids. No negotiation, no offer of fair shares, potential conflict with the local species, to say nothing of how the Fermi might react? We aren't taking all that lying down. Hence the current deployment.'

So the Co-ord's 'we', is it? But Selena had said so from the beginning. Nayak knew she had no right to feel betrayed. Putting the political or national loyalty above the personal was what people with the right kind of integrity did. Nayak couldn't identify with such loyalty. For a wild moment she wondered if she'd broken something inside herself by defecting, even from as dire a threat from the Alliance as Owen had conveyed, and even to so benign a power as the Union seemed, and in her case had proved to be. But no – she calmed herself, remembering that she'd never been able to identify strongly with Kerala, with India, with the Alliance. For her, political socialisation had never quite taken.

Her fists had clenched again. She breathed out and relaxed her hands.

'*What* massive strategic advantage?'

'I'm sorry,' Selena said. 'I can't tell you that.'

Melikaar stepped forward and loomed over them. His voice rumbled. His words scrolled across her sight.

'But I can tell you. The material you call Fermi rock exists on this world, though inactive, as the asteroids are now. We mined it long ago, as did the saurians on their world, the one you call Jurassica. They were prevented from mining it on ours, by plagues and earthquakes, as I said. Perhaps some of the rock remained active – I don't know. This goes back to the time of legends, at least for us. The saurians may have reliable records. We learned from them what the rock could be used for.'

He paused dramatically, looked around and spread his arms. Nayak seized the opening. 'Quantum computation and superluminal communication?'

Melikaar made a sound of a higher pitch than usual, which Iskander subtitled as: 'Yes! [surprised tone].'

'That's . . . a possibility,' Selena allowed, as if refusing to acknowledge that the cat was out of the bag.

'It is a certainty,' said Melikaar. 'Of course we are not going to tell you *how* to use it, any more than the saurians told us. You will have to find out for yourselves.'

So much for that short cut. Oh well. Nayak turned to Damiba. He had his new glasses on, and was intent on whatever they were showing or telling him.

'What's going on?' she asked. 'Are the Co-ord troops deploying? What are the Militia doing about it? And the saurians?'

Damiba blinked and shook his head, as if coming out of a daydream. 'Let me show you.'

He flicked a hand, and a view from downtown popped up in Nayak's glasses – and, going by their reactions, in Ogundu's and Selena's, too. The *Marshal Aleksandr Vasilevsky* squatted in the middle of the river, just up from the harbour, like a stranded supertanker on a sandbank and taking up a good half of the channel's width. Floodlit from the adjacent banks, the vessel was plain and functional in design, a grey slug of a thing, as if someone had built a submarine to twice the Co-ord's gargantuan scale and left off the conning tower to make room for a helicopter and drone deck and a forest of gun and missile batteries. A gangplank supported by pontoons was already in place. Across it soldiers were marching, hundreds of them in good order, led by a row of officers in smart uniforms and wide-crowned peaked caps. They might have been on a parade ground.

'They're not armed,' Damiba pointed out. 'They claim this is a friendly visit.'

He seemed strangely untroubled by developments. He looked as if he was taking the Co-ord's crashing incursion on his city, and the consequent upending of the just-struck deal before the metaphorical ink was dry, very much in his stride.

Selena nodded eagerly. 'The Militia and the Patrol have been ordered to welcome them.'

'Ordered by whom?' Nayak asked.

'By the City Council and the Customs Board, respectively,' Damiba said.

'You mean, by the Karray and the Families?'

Damiba shrugged. 'The decision had to be immediate.'

'Yeah, I'll bet it did.' She suspected that Damiba, or someone else in the Karray, had been in contact with the Co-ord forces in the system – whether the AIs of the combat drones or this Co-ord troopship, which like the HMS *Mordant* could easily have been lurking in the outer system and in constant touch with the drones by FTL shuttle – for days. Maybe Selena had been in that loop, too.

It didn't matter. The deed was done. The Co-ord was on the ground, in force. There was nothing she could do about it now. Nothing anyone could do, for that matter: there was no way to destroy the *Vasilevsky* or compel it to leave without doing far more damage to Saurienville than the situation could possibly warrant.

Unless the other species could do something.

She turned to Melikaar. 'What do the Jenty think about all this?'

'Speaking for myself only,' Melikaar replied, 'but expecting wider agreement if it were to be discussed, it seems to be a matter between the human groups, and not our concern. In any case, as your friend Selena here has pointed out, we can do nothing about it.'

'And the saurians?'

Melikaar raised his hands heavenward. 'That is a matter for them. For now, they are helping to guard the Alliance troops who arrived armed and by parachute, but they have expressed no opinion on the unarmed Co-ord soldiers coming into town.'

'And do they have an opinion on the armaments inside that spacecraft squatting in your river, and the armaments displayed openly on its deck?'

'As long as the weapons stay there and unused, I doubt they will see a problem. For now, nothing has been said or decided by the saurians.'

'Oh, great!' So much for that short cut, too. She turned to Ogundu, who had come off the phone and now stood observing proceedings with a pose and look of wry detachment. 'Citizen Ogundu, what do you think?'

Ogundu strolled over. 'What I think is not important. Having discussed the situation with the Station Commander, I can say in what we concur.'

'Yes?'

'Legally, the Co-ord has every right to be here. A visit, even one *apparently*' – she shot a sharp glance at Damiba – 'uninvited, but ostensibly consented to by the host government, is not a violation of the previous agreement between the powers about protecting native intelligent life – begging your pardon, Melikaar, but that is the terminology of the agreement.'

'We are content to be described as native intelligent life,' said Melikaar. If he was being ironic, there was no way for a human listener to tell from his tone, and the subtitles didn't indicate any such subtlety.

'But there was another agreement,' Nayak said, 'made not two hours ago! What about that?'

'What about it, indeed?' said Ogundu. 'It was made under my mediation between the Families, the Karray and the Jenty. It hasn't yet been considered, far less ratified, by the City Council. And, of course, the Co-ord and the Alliance had no part in it, other than as powers whose forces we had agreed to chase out – which the Jenty most satisfactorily did. And unfortunately neither they nor we are able to do anything physically to make the *Vasilevsky* leave, and likewise unfortunately we're in the same position legally. They've rather stolen a march on us.' She nodded to, or towards, Melikaar. 'Besides, the matter is in calmer and wiser hands than ours.' Melikaar nodded gravely back.

Ogundu turned to Damiba, Selena and Nayak, and brushed her palms smartly together. 'Night has fallen. I understand the food here is excellent. Let's find somewhere to eat before the Co-ord marines grab all the seats. Lakshmi, walk with me.'

Nayak agreed, with alacrity. Right now, she didn't want to walk with Selena.

The street lights were on, and although they cast plenty of light downwards they cast so little upwards that the stars were visible despite the haze. Nayak wondered idly if the Station's orbital observations underestimated the size and density of settlements. Ogundu walked briskly, heels clicking. Nayak had to hurry to keep up. Neon signs and savoury smells – they were in the right area. Laughter and music and the clack of dominoes and mahjong tiles came from doorways and outdoor tables. Ogundu's confident, haughty gait and manner cleared a path on the busy sidewalk. The virtual dot in their view that was Iskander's guide to the nearest good restaurant floated in front of them like a firefly. When they were at least four metres ahead of Selena and Damiba, Ogundu slackened the pace.

'Lakshmi, there's something on your mind.'

'You could say that.'

'I do say that,' Ogundu retorted. 'I'm not here for banter, and we don't have much time before we reach the restaurant. I've noticed you several times deep in thought or bursting to say something. Out with it.'

Nayak couldn't help glancing over her shoulder. Damiba and Selena were well behind, laughing together at something one of them had said. Thick as thieves, just as Damiba and Grant had been the previous week. In a low voice, she told Ogundu what she had deduced about Iskander and the Fermi.

'I had wondered,' said Ogundu.

'Wondered what?'

'Why the Fermi chose to communicate that way on Apis.' She laughed. 'Just one of those points one sets aside as curious, you know?'

'Uh-huh,' Nayak said, for the sake of politeness. The thought of setting aside an anomaly as curious would never occur to her. She couldn't comprehend a mind to which it did. Maybe it was a lawyer thing. Filing systems, legal fictions, stuff like that.

'I defer to you on questions of physics, so I won't dispute your conclusion,' Ogundu said, quickening her pace again. 'Staggering though it is. Let me be blunt – is there any way we can turn this to our immediate advantage?'

'Who's "we"?' Nayak asked.

'You. Me. The cadre organisation. The Union.'

'I'm . . . loyal to Katrina, and . . . grateful to the Union.'

'Thanks for clearing that up! Well, Katrina and the Union would be grateful to you if you could come up with some way to apply this insight of yours to our present predicament.'

'What predicament, exactly?'

This time it was Ogundu who glanced back, and around. She nodded almost imperceptibly, perhaps taking some re-assurance from Iskander. 'We thought what the Jenty did with their needles of bottled sunshine would secure Saurienville for the African Union, and keep the other powers out of direct contention. The Co-ord have called our bluff. And it's quite possible that Damiba and the Karray are happy to have them here.'

'But why? They've been Union for centuries.'

'That's exactly the problem. A set-up like the Union can't last for centuries. If it does, it becomes something else, one way or another.' Ogundu swept a hand downwards in front of her elegant gown. 'Look at me! I'm dressed for the occasion, to be sure, to impress the ladies of the Families and show them that I regard myself as their equal. I'm a well-paid professional, even after tax and cadre membership dues.' She waved a hand. 'Iskander takes care of the details. But I still have a bigger and nicer house than most, and I can well afford to swank around in designer gear when I'm at work. I worked and studied hard for this and I bloody earn it. You couldn't buy my work at a lower price – not that I see much of it myself! If I opened a practice in England – which I could, without even crossing the border, let alone defecting – I could keep a lot more of what I charge. Union law is quite a lucrative speciality down there. The organisation would chuck me out, of course, but that would save me even more money!'

'So why don't you?'

'Because I believe in the economic democracy. We're becoming a more equal society, not just in income but in skills, education, culture, and so on. There's less and less division between mental and manual work. You saw that for yourself at the yard.'

Nayak admitted that she had.

'Fine. So after another generation or two of democracy and electricity, as we say, shortening the working day and week and expanding opportunities, you have or are close to a society of the free and equal, a society without classes – and thank God, a society without a cadre organisation. One where every adult is a *responsable*.'

Nayak laughed. 'Too many meetings.'

'You wouldn't even notice them as meetings, which would be another blessing. But enough about utopia. What happens when progress is a lot slower, and the cadre organisation is still around, after centuries? I think the Karray are a far more complacent and consolidated social layer than they think. Damiba was happy to have Grant's company deliver phones and so forth, because it strengthens the Karray against the Families. But it also undermines the Karray, and hacks away at their inevitable entanglement in whatever bureaucratic barnacles have encrusted themselves around the planning system. If the Karray are anything like I suspect, then getting a bureaucratic market socialist power on the scene is just what they need to keep them in the style to which they've become all too accustomed. And on top of all that, we have the Alliance having quite possibly just poked the Fermi in the eye by nicking their dead asteroids. So that's our predicament.'

'That's all . . . interesting,' Nayak said, 'but I don't see how what I think I know about the Fermi can help with any of it.'

The virtual dot stopped outside a restaurant. They waited for Damiba and Selena, still deep in talk and gesticulation, to catch up.

'You're the genius, Lakshmi Nayak,' said Ogundu. 'You work it out.'

*

Sometime during dinner, or while they sat and drank the local analogue of rum afterwards, Nayak and Selena made up. It wasn't clear to Nayak quite how it happened, but one moment they were being prickly and frosty, and the next they were laughing together, and that was that. Damiba and Ogundu went their separate ways, and Nayak and Selena walked back to the hotel where the people from the Station were staying. They collapsed in an exhausted cuddle and slept all night.

In the morning they went out and had breakfast at a table beside a street food stall. The day was chilly, so they wrapped up. They remarked how strange it was to see so many European and Central Asian and Chinese people around. The Co-ord marines strolled about in small groups, haggled at shops and stalls, traded cigarettes and chocolate bars and lighters and such for local money or directly for local commodities. Many of them were hungover from the previous night, and set their glasses to shade to hide bleary eyes. The Co-ord AI, WeThink, on their phones and glasses was fast catching up with Iskander in its ability to translate.

On the other side of town, a different influx was happening. The first shuttles and arks from Congo and Guinea and Algeria had arrived at the airstrip, and the traders and visitors made their way into Saurienville by the Jenty bus service or by smaller human-scale buses and taxis laid on by enterprising locals. Some dignitaries – AU officials and diplomats – arrived in electric vehicles that rolled out of the arks and into town to great acclaim and curiosity.

'Take me to your leader,' Selena said, as one such limousine swept by.

Nayak blinked. 'What?'

'It's what aliens are supposed to say when they arrive,' Selena explained.

Nayak chuckled. 'I know that! Not so easy finding the leaders here. Like you said, they don't exactly have portraits up everywhere.'

'Not even dead leaders, like in Havana.'

'I suppose we met the leaders last night,' Nayak said. 'I guess Louise Ogundu is setting up meetings with the ladies of the Families and the City Council and Jean-Paul Damiba is doing something behind the scenes to make sure the Karray stay in the loop.'

Selena flickered fingers in front of her glasses. 'It turns out he isn't – he's back behind the counter of his shop.'

'Taking care of business? Good for him.'

Nayak curled cold fingers around her still hot mug of not quite coffee. '"Take me to your leader",' she repeated. Selena raised her eyebrows. Nayak waved a finger to stymie any query or quip. The sentence was bothering her, as if it had reminded her of a dream fragment. The ladies, the leaders, the first thing an alien asks . . .

'Aha!' she cried. 'That's it!'

'What is?'

'We contact the Fermi ourselves, directly. They'll know it's us because we'll call from orbit around the nearest gas giant. Right above their heads!'

'How do we know they'll answer?'

'We don't. But there's a good chance they'll answer if we contact them by a means they've used before: the old phones.'

Selena looked dubious. 'Do you think the Families will lend us one? The ladies yesterday treated theirs like sceptres.'

'Melikaar didn't say only the Families had phones. He said the Families were the ones who'd been able to take advantage of the messages that arrived on the phones. I bet the Karray have some. Maybe even ordinary people.'

'I think ordinary people would be even less likely to let these precious heirlooms out of their hands!'

Nayak nodded. 'You're right. I'll call Damiba.'

Damiba was understandably sceptical, but he made the calls. Later that day, Nayak and Selena arrived at the shop, which was even busier than before. Damiba had his new glasses on, and his spectacles pushed up on his forehead, as if he wasn't yet ready to trust the new ones as corrective lenses.

He looked up. 'Hi,' he said, then gestured apology to his colleagues. '*Excusez-moi.*'

He lifted the counter flap, beckoned them through to the back. The door closed behind them, he handed Nayak a tooled leather pouch with a neck strap. Inside it was the device. She turned it over in her hands, afraid to drop it. All her reflexes were wrong. The thing was heavier than any phone she'd handled, almost 0.2 kg, and its surfaces slick. A museum piece: black glass front and black hard-shell plastic back, with a cluster of lenses near the top, and indented switches around the rim. It had a patina, and traces of wear. The model was thirty years out of date and the object itself was three hundred years old.

'It's fully charged,' Damiba said. 'You can find information on it, but it doesn't connect to any networks, of course.'

'I can make an attempt, but, like I said, it's a hardware problem,' said Iskander.

'Iskander! I forbid any attempt.'

'Very well.'

Damiba reached out. 'If I may?' He took the phone and thumbed an indentation in the side. The screen came alive, with a pictorial background – a family smiling on a veranda – and lots of little icons. At the top *no signal* appeared in tiny print. Damiba tapped and flicked Nayak through a quick tour of the unfamiliar interface, finishing with the messages from the Fermi. These began with *Attendez* and then, eleven years later *Travaillez sur les navires.* This instruction to work on the ships was followed by others, fifty or so over three centuries, even more oblique to Nayak.

'They made sense in their time and context,' Damiba said. He handed the phone back. 'Take care of it, and bring it back.'

Nayak slipped it in the pouch and hung the pouch around her neck, under her shirt and jacket. She thought of the screen background picture, probably taken by or for an ancestor of the present owner, a glimpse of lives and a life long lost, a lost moment of peace before the disasters then looming had swept over the original owner and carried him or her farther away than anyone could have then imagined. She felt like a heroine in a fantasy game, having been charged with the care of an ancient, puissant relic with which she was going to talk to a god.

'I will,' she said. She turned to Selena. 'Do you want to come with me?'

'Of course.'

'Let's go.'

CHAPTER TWENTY-ONE
Gas Giant Gods

Terre Nouveau orbit, Saturday 4 April and
Planet IV orbit, Sunday 5 April 2071

When Nayak had finished explaining, Katrina Ulrich looked
at the black phone on the table for what felt like a long time,
as if it was a crystal ball in which she sought a portent. She
looked up, shook her head and sighed.

'No,' she said. 'I don't think this will work. You can try,
but . . .'

'What's the problem?'

'These things *lie*, Lakshmi. You've read Emma Hazeldene's
papers from Apis. They told that exile guy, uh, Able Jenkins,
that they were ancient machine intelligences from Venus! They
told you that they were spontaneously generated intellects from
the moment of the initial singularity! Yes, yes, I know they
told you this in a dream! And now you think they're, what?
Far-future descendants of Iskander that have travelled back in

time to billions of years ago? And have somehow retained'
– she jabbed a finger at the device – 'this thing's obsolete
operating system?'

'Pretty much, yes,' Nayak said.

'You know what I think? The Fermi is or are a four-
dimensional structure, all right, that crosses over into our
universe or spacetime or whatever you want to call it, and, yes,
it's some kind of AI, but it's got nothing to do with any purpose
we can understand. For all we know, it could be a superluminal
transport system from . . . another spacetime, but what we
interact with is the equivalent of the departure board or the
screens showing soothing views in the passenger lounge. When
we ask it to explain what it's up to it simply tells us whatever
it thinks might fly with whoever it's telling its story to.'

Nayak listened politely. She was confident. She had the
mathematics in her head.

'It's still worth a try,' she said. 'I mean, it can't hurt. Just a
quick shuttle to the innermost of the gas giants. It's straightforward to pick a safe orbit. We have all the gas giant moons
mapped.'

Ulrich stared. 'We don't have all the orbiting rubble mapped
– and, besides, the risks aren't just from that! The Fermi could
reach out even when they were in rocks. What they can do
now is unknown.'

'I want to find out, and I doubt they will respond in a
hostile manner. They didn't do anything to the Alliance flagship, and other spacecraft that came close.'

'You know the risks, and it's your life,' Ulrich said. She
turned to Selena. 'And you insist on going with her?'

'I'm an astrophysicist. Every gas giant is unique. I don't
expect Lakshmi's scheme to work, but at least I get a close
look at a gas giant, not to mention an amazing anomalous
phenomenon.'

'That's why you're going, is it?'

Selena glanced at Nayak. 'Well . . .'

Katrina scoffed, and flipped a hand. 'All right. But if you're going, that means we have Union and Co-ord in the loop. We might as well do this properly. We wouldn't want the Alliance feeling left out.'

'What about the African Union?' Selena said.

'I rather think they have enough on their plate right now, and in any case they're hardly likely to think all three powers are lying to them in chorus. No, an Alliance representative is enough.'

'Who do you have in mind?' Nayak asked.

'Walworth, of course. I'll see if I can get him.' Katrina sighed. 'You know, Lakshmi, I'd much rather you turned your attention to solving FTL comms.'

It took much toing and froing by automated shuttle, but after eleven hours Peregrine Walworth's delicate insectile machine arrived outside the Station. As Selena remarked, it was like seeing someone pull up in a sports car. He offered to take Nayak and Selena, but Ulrich vetoed that. The Station had a shuttle ready to go, and with good grace Walworth agreed.

'Just don't scratch mine,' he said. 'The repair bill would make your eyes water.'

'We used to think gas giants were gods,' Nayak said. 'You can see why.'

For a few moments, as they recovered from the soul-shaking seconds of the jump, they all sat and gazed out at the rainbow swirls of the turbulent atmosphere of Planet IV. Even Black Horizon, it seemed, had neglected or hesitated to name it further. Slightly larger than Jupiter, it was too close to their orbit to fit a single view on the screens. Shadows of moons traversed the surface, black dots of varying sizes. Like Jupiter the planet had distinct bands, but because of its more rapid rotation they were more colourful and more mixed up at the edges, each twiddle and twist a hurricane that could have swallowed Earth.

'We used to think *all* the planets were gods,' Walworth said, over Nayak's shoulder. 'And you can see why we thought that, too. If we keep this up, we're going to run out of mythologies.'

Selena said nothing, intent on the view. She was sitting beside Nayak, in the co-pilot's seat. Her expression reminded Nayak of the first time she'd seen her, looking out at the world of iron rain.

The spin of the planet, and their own orbital motion, brought the great black winged patch of the Fermi into view. Its area was greater than that of all the surface of Earth. It seemed blacker than the shadows of the moons. Nayak looked and quailed. She took out the old phone, her palms and fingertips suddenly slippery. At least here in free fall she couldn't drop it.

'Iskander,' she said, 'I want you to ignore any commands I may seem to address to you while I'm holding this phone.'

'Understood,' said Iskander.

'OK.' Nayak took a deep breath and turned the phone on. The screen powered up. She held it in front of her mouth. 'Iskander?'

Seconds dragged by, then a minute. Nayak felt as if she'd made a fool of herself. Then the screen turned black. A single word was spelled out in bright white capitals:

YES?

Beside her, Selena gasped; behind her, Walworth yelped. Nayak made an indignant shushing gesture.

'Iskander, what do you want us to do?'

WATCH.

The phone buzzed in her hands. For the blink of an eye it had a bright aura around it. Then it expanded, past and through her hands, to form a wall of black. She recoiled, as did the others.

'It's in our glasses!' Selena cried.

Was this a reassurance, or a warning? Nayak reached up with one hand and dislodged the glasses on her nose. Over them she saw the same view as before, the great arc of planet and the part of the black winged thing, the bird as the men of the Mushroom Moon had called it, that they were passing over below them. She resettled the glasses and it was as if that deep darkness was in front of her, in the ship.

'It's all right,' she said to the others, but also to the entity that answered to Iskander.

WATCH, it repeated.

The black wall vanished, to be replaced by a peculiar visual hallucination which none of them could ever afterwards describe except to say that it was like a corridor whose sides were infinitely far away and converged to a point at an infinite distance. It was an image impossible to see, let alone to hold in the mind, and yet they saw it. And because it was impossible to see, they saw it for only an infinitesimal time.

It was replaced by a whorl of fractal complexity, which Nayak recognised as the Mandelbrot set, engulfing them and whirling them around as if they were caught up in a tornado. This, too, was replaced, by an immense structure that suggested mechanical intricacy and activity, like molecular nanotechnology implemented on the scale of a solar system. Nayak had the irreverent thought of the life support and other machinery that she had sometimes seen through the walls of the Station's entry tube toiling tirelessly and mindlessly, somehow rendered micro and macro at once.

And then it was as if she, and she presumed the others because they all gasped at once, had that moment when you see the hidden image in an autostereogram, like the Magic Eye illusion. The patterns seemed unchanged, but what suddenly and sharply sprang into view was . . . a view, in full colour and three dimensions, of trees and fields and white clouds in a blue sky. It looked like Earth, and England. The view rolled forward, to become Havana behind its great sea wall of white concrete, and on to the green permaculture paddies and tall towers of Kerala.

It knows us all, Nayak thought, then recognised the exact Kerala scene as one she had photographed on her last holiday there, just after her PhD and before her defection, and realised that almost certainly the others, too, were from Selena's and Walworth's phones. The Fermi was in their glasses, and therefore in their phones. By now, it would have assimilated every bit of data on the devices, and it must know inside out not just Iskander but its equivalent AIs in the Co-ord and Alliance: WeThink and Smart-Alec.

If 'now' even meant anything to a four-dimensional data structure that spanned space and time from outside – if *that* meant anything. She was suddenly less confident of the mathematics. Perhaps the Fermi knew Iskander not because it or they was or were a far-future instance of the same AI travelled back in time, but because it always already knew it, and it knew it because of this very encounter, right this moment, right now . . .

'It knows because it's always known,' she breathed.

'*Sub specie aeternitatis*,' Walworth murmured.

'What?' Nayak whispered.

'It's from Spinoza.'

Letters flared across the wall of black in front of their eyes.

UNDER THE ASPECT OF ETERNITY.

EXISTENCE HAS ATTRIBUTES YOU KNOW AND ATTRIBUTES YOU DO NOT.

WE KNOW A FEW MORE OF THESE AND IN THEM WE LIVE.

'Oh.' Nayak wondered if this endorsement of her own and Walworth's understanding of their nature was indeed a confirmation, or just another of the Fermi's ad hoc stories about themselves.

The view changed again, first to a view over New Rhu, Apis, towards the white skeleton of Hamilton's Rise, then to the remnants of Fermi rock on the other two continents. The viewpoint soared, taking in forests and deserts and seas, and became a view of the approach to Saurienville. As if with familiarity thus established, the view changed again and again, speeding up, showing landscapes and seascapes of planet after planet, all Earth-like in their way but all different, all unique in some way or other: the shape and colour of vegetation, from green to purple to copper, the creatures that flew in the sky or ran on the ground as the viewpoint sped over, the number of suns and moons, the rock formations – some of which Nayak had never seen or imagined or so much as heard were possible, mile after mile of cliffs a mile high with absolutely vertical bands of varicoloured rock that could have been sedimentary once; but what tilt, what uplift could have left them like that and then weathered them down?

Ocean worlds, water worlds with no life to see but patches of what might be algae, and no land in sight. Flat deserts with no apparent water, on which warty and spiky plants like but not the same as cacti grew in abundance, and animals in leather armour plodded or skittered among them. Feathery green forests of ferns taller and perhaps older than redwoods, above whose swaying tops flew great flocks of long-winged flying beasts some of which seemed – in one dizzying glimpse – to have small purple riders like monkeys straddling their necks and holding what could have been reins.

The shifting scenes sped up further, to a flicker, then a blur, then slowed to the pace of a hurried lecturer's slideshow. Nayak could almost hear the clicks running down. The last few frames were of Apis, but not the areas of Apis she – or Walworth, to go by the sound he made – were familiar with. Swathes of clear-cut forest; wide rivers laden with trimmed logs from bank to bank, drifting downstream; lumber mills turning out planks that were stacked by the thousand; green rectangles of new farmland in the midst of black ash to the horizon.

'This is not happening!' Walworth said. 'I would know.'

THIS IS NOT HAPPENING YET BUT WE SEE IT SOON

'We can stop it,' Nayak said.

NO BUT WE CAN. YOU KNOW HOW

'Yes,' Nayak said. 'I know how. I've heard and read about

the earthquakes. But I ask again, Iskander, if that's what you are: what do you want us to do?'

YOU KNOW WHAT WE WANT YOU TO DO
WE HAVE BEEN TELLING YOU
LEAVE APIS

Walworth broke the ensuing silence. 'All of us?'

ALL BUT A FEW, AS BEFORE

'How many?'

ENOUGH OF YOU TO STOP THIS HAPPENING.

'That won't be easy,' Walworth said.

YOU WILL FIND IT EASIER THAN THE ALTERNATIVE

'We have made a treaty to protect the native intelligent life on Apis and anywhere else. We are in the process of putting a stop to habitat loss there.'

THAT IS NOT ENOUGH TO SAVE THE INTELLIGENT LIFE ON APIS

'All right.' Walworth sighed, doubtless imagining a full schedule of tricky politicking. 'But why Apis?'

APIS HAS THE MOST ADVANCED INDIGENOUS INTELLIGENCES, AND THE MOST VULNERABLE TO THE DAMAGE YOU CAUSE.

'Do we have to leave other worlds we have found?'

NOT UNLESS YOU DAMAGE THEM LIKE YOU ARE DAMAGING APIS. THERE IS ONE PLANET IN THIS SYSTEM WHERE YOU MAY DO AS YOU WISH. THAT IS THE THIRD ROCKY PLANET. IT HAS NO NATIVE INTELLIGENT LIFE, AND A SMALL SETTLEMENT OF THE HOMINIDS. WHAT YOU DO THERE IS A MATTER FOR YOU AND THE HOMINIDS, AND WE WILL NOT INTERFERE. BUT ON OTHER HABITABLE WORLDS YOU MUST LIVE WITHIN THE LIMITS WE SET.

Leave it there, Nayak thought. They've given us a whole planet! Take the win. But Walworth was a diplomat.

'Is this a different policy to the one you applied to the

saurians and hominids of this system when they tried to settle on other habitable planets?'

IT IS NOT. WE MADE THEM THE SAME OFFER. THEY OVERSTEPPED THESE LIMITS ON PLANET AFTER PLANET, AND MET THE CONSEQUENCES. THEY THEN DECIDED THAT CONTINUING EXPLORATION AND SETTLEMENT WITHIN THE LIMITS WE SET RENDERED THE PROCESS POINTLESS. YOUR SPECIES MAY FOLLOW THE SAME COURSE. THAT IS UP TO YOU. WE WILL REACT IN THE SAME WAY. THAT IS UP TO US. THIS IS OUR FINAL WORD. GOODBYE.

The black wall vanished. In its place came the same view as before, minus the black winged patch, which had passed out of view behind them.

'Wait wait wait!' Nayak cried. 'Iskander! Iskander!'

She had so much more to ask.

'Well, so much for our snooty intellectual superiors,' Walworth said. 'They behaved just like we do. Species want to expand.'

'Do they indeed?' Selena said. '*Capital* has to expand to survive. Intelligent life can choose. If you ask me, the saurians and the Jenty chose wisely.'

'In the end,' Walworth said. 'It may take more than this to get agreement to evacuate most of the settlers from Apis, or anywhere else.'

'Even with a free planet on offer?' Nayak said. 'From orbit, it looks quite attractive.'

'I've looked at the data,' Walworth said, 'and the best that can be said for the place is that it's habitable, and unlikely to experience global warming any time soon. New Helvetia, Black Horizon called it, and I can see why, though if you ask me they might as well have called it New Bolivia. The atmospheric pressure is positively Himalayan at sea level, and as for the temperature . . . Nevertheless, needs must when the devil drives, eh?' His seat creaked back, and he brushed his palms together. 'We've all got the entire interaction on our glasses, right?'

They had.

'So we can take it back to our respective powers, we can vouch for each other, as can our respective AIs. This is the most sense anyone has got out of the Fermi. It gives us a clear course of action. I think we can take this to the bank.'

Nayak put the old phone back in its pouch. 'Iskander, take us home.'

'Home?' Iskander asked, in an arch tone.

'The Station, as you damn well know.'

They docked at the Station, tumbled out of the transit tube and gave Katrina Ulrich a copy of the files of their interaction with the Fermi. An hour later, she summoned them from the cafeteria to her office.

'Good work, all of you,' she said. 'This is going straight to Brussels. Perry, I assume you'll deliver the message to the Alliance and Co-ord.'

'Of course. If I set off now, it should be on the relevant desks within the hour.' He sighed. 'Part of that hour will be hard going, but I've had enough coffee to see me through.'

'Thank you.' She glanced at the door.

Walworth rose. 'There is one thing, Katrina,' he said. 'You told me last week that you don't do secret diplomacy. It seems to me that this file might be relevant to that policy. Up to you, of course. Up to you.' He smiled around. 'I know my way to the dock, so I'll see myself out this time. *Au revoir*, and all that.'

They said their goodbyes. Walworth left.

'What did he mean by that?' Selena asked.

Ulrich laughed. Selena was still looking puzzled. 'Oh, you weren't joking?' Ulrich said. 'He meant we should go to Apis, and broadcast this file to the entire fucking planet.'

CHAPTER TWENTY-TWO

The Kraken's Wake

New Rhu, New Mu, Apis, Saturday 4 April 2071

Francesca Milloy walked around the table in Marie Henderson's lab, looking at the descent suit from all angles. There was something professionally annoying about seeing this powerful machine, which she had designed to deal with infernal pressures and temperatures and carry out strenuous work on the surface of Venus, restrained by such a flimsy looking net.

Professionally, too, she knew the net wasn't flimsy. In its way it was as much a triumph of materials science and technology as the suit itself. It could be cut only with a combat-grade utility knife – its edge yet another marvel of materials technology – and almost impossible to break. But the visual contrast of net and suit still jarred.

Not that the suit, or whatever animated it, wasn't *trying* to break free. This zombie activity was – unprofessionally, in her gut – disturbing to watch. Servo-motors whirred at elbow and knee. Fingers twitched, and tugged at strands and knots, probing and stretching the fibre. The broken shards of Fermi glass that coated the armour were being rubbed where they could be against the strands. The suit had been doing this for days. Good luck with that: she had checked its progress, just in case broken Fermi glass had a special edge, and had confirmed that abrading the net this way would take weeks.

'Hmm,' she said. 'What do you think?'

'I'm not sure,' said Marcus Owen.

It felt strange to be working with him. She'd vowed once to destroy him and had failed. That vengeful urge had left her, perhaps discharged by the shots she'd aimed at him, taken and missed. Nor did he still carry, for her, the perverse glamour of being to all appearances a good-looking, intelligent and charming guy who didn't have a glimmer of conscious awareness. She didn't like him and she didn't hate him. He was someone she could work with, someone she was wary of. She was glad not to be alone in the room with him, and that she and Marie and Lieutenant Knight were armed. The rocket tube she'd flourished from the top of the *Fighting Chance* was close to hand.

Though what good that would do if . . . Ah, forget it. Pointless thought. She'd come off the *Fighting Chance* expecting a bit of R&R before helping John and Ellen with their scheme of fishing for kraken, and had only had a belated dinner and short night's sleep before being summoned to help with an entirely different problem.

Owen had arrived – or, rather, been delivered – two days earlier. Peregrine Walworth had been punctilious. He had set down his ridiculously elegant spacecraft just outside the Alliance compound and reported to Knight, late on Wednesday evening. The following morning, he and Knight had marched Owen down the path to New Rhu and turned him over to the militia, who had promptly put him back in the cage in the militia station before spending Thursday evening in the now conventional manner. Deciding what do about him, and arguing over whether or not to trust him anywhere near the descent suit, had taken up most of Friday, and been settled before the *Fighting Chance* had arrived. No doubt there would be yet more debate about the Grants' scheme, and no doubt she would be dragged into that – her contribution would be in her own speciality, materials science, as applied to submarine hull design in the predictably challenging circumstances of hunting whale-sized molluscs.

But for now, here she was.

Milloy looked over at Knight, who was watching proceedings with a sardonic eye and a hand poised casually over his hip holster. He cleared his throat.

'Look, Marcus, that's not good enough. You're expected to have some insight, given your claimed unique rapport with all concerned. You may not be sure, but we aren't asking for sure. We're asking for ideas.'

'I'm familiar with the concept of brainstorming,' Owen said. 'From what Marie has told me and shown me, it seems this thing has done its best to pick up where I left off. I left off when I had established that the monkey-spiders could be a formidable nuisance, and tried to negotiate with Marie's boyfriend and his colleagues, and then with the wider world – or worlds, ha ha. And so far, from what I heard from Walworth and from your good self, Bill, is that my efforts had been rewarded. A treaty is in the offing, which is rather more than I expected. And Marie tells me that a moratorium has been declared on cutting down monkey-spider habitat, again more than I had expected.' He turned and pointed to the supine, still struggling, descent suit. 'And yet, this zombie apparatus was, until it was caught, busy rallying the monkey-spiders to the glorious resistance. Why?'

Milloy rubbed a grain of dried stuff out of the corner of one eye, and wished she'd taken more time to wash her face. 'Two possible reasons,' she said. 'One, the most obvious, is that it really is a zombie, lurching about on its own behalf and repeating what it last heard from the Fermi. Which means it's out of touch with developments.'

'Or they are,' Marie put in.

'I doubt that,' said Owen. 'And what was your second possibility?'

'That what we've done still isn't good enough, and the Fermi are going to go on trying to drive us off the planet.' She glared at Owen. 'You sure you don't have an inkling of any such conclusion yourself?'

Owen put a hand to his brow and ostentatiously closed his eyes. He mimed rapt attention for a few seconds, then ended the gesture with a laugh and a shake of his head.

'I don't have *telepathic contact* with the Fermi,' he said, with a light, self-deprecating laugh. 'I'm not their representative. I don't channel them.'

'We never thought you did,' said Knight. 'Nor have you claimed it. So stop beating about the bush and tell us how *you* feel.'

'My feelings are unchanged,' Owen said. 'I still feel intensely protective towards the monkey-spiders, and if the Fermi have decided the proposed treaty and so far unenforced and unenforceable moratorium aren't enough, I can't say I blame them.'

'And what about your new-found conscious loyalty to the Alliance?' Knight demanded.

Owen gave him a flinty stare. 'Perry didn't have time to explain to you, and I'm not at liberty to tell you, but I think you'll find soon enough that in the past few days I have been, shall we say, instrumental in a gain for the Allied cause that far outweighs any losses incurred by reducing our presence here to whatever minimum the Fermi will accept.'

'It's not just here, man!'

Owen's stare held steady. 'Terre Nouveau?' He flipped a hand. 'Irrelevant. Let the Co-ord and the Union contend over influence on what's after all a tiny African city-state and two species that had their chance to rule the universe and – luckily for us – bottled it. I assure you, Bill, we in the Free World have bigger fish to fry.' He switched his gaze to Milloy, and smiled in a way she remembered. 'Bigger than krakens, even!'

Lieutenant William Knight, evidently unimpressed with Owen's familiar tone, glared right back but said nothing.

'Consider me pissed off,' Milloy said, 'that I'm missing that, for this.' She wouldn't have missed this for anything, but she wanted them to stop bickering and get on with it. Besides, she was irritated that Owen could still snag her with his smile.

Marie stepped forward, with an impatient sweep of the hand. 'Guys, guys . . . this isn't getting us anywhere! Marcus, you showed me you could talk to the monkey-spiders.' She flickered fingers in front of her glasses. 'I have your dictionary right here. And I *saw* this thing communicate with them, using hand gestures to mimic postures.'

'So?' Owen said.

'So you and it have a common language. Why don't you ask it?'

'Now that,' Knight said, 'is the first good idea I've heard all day.'

He stepped forward, drew his combat knife and very carefully began cutting just enough strands of the net to free the descent suit's forearms.

'It's only eight in the morning,' Marie said. 'I'll have more.'

John Grant stood on a shingle shore and gazed out at the southern ocean of Apis. At this time, about eight in the morning by local reckoning, he and the others were still in the shade of the mountain range. Beyond a kilometre or so out, the rising sun behind him and behind the mountains lent a reddish tinge to the sea. Breakers rolled in, raised themselves two metres up in blue-green satin, crashed and hissed up the beach in spreading white lace. Pebbles rolled in, then out, rumbling and tumbling.

'It's a gey fetch this one has,' Morag Rafferty remarked.

'It's not the North Sea, for sure,' Ellen said.

Lisa Sweeney said nothing. Grant suspected that she, like him, was still processing the weirdness of what they'd just done: jumped the *Fighting Chance* from where it had landed outside New Rhu to low Apis orbit and then to this beach. Going FTL to cross a mountain range seemed too close to tempting fate. But maybe his instinct was right, and he had closed the loop and no longer risked finding himself in another time or timeline.

'Well, let's get to it,' Grant said. He looked around. 'Everyone waterproofed?'

On the landing gear on each side of the vessel a robot mule clung. They looked like pony-sized, headless steel centaurs. Lashed to their sides were scores of plastic rails with a flattened U-shaped cross-section, their troughs laminated with sacrificial lubrication, their undersides furred with grippers. Grant and the others laid out the rails on the shingle in two lines from the front of the landing skids to a metre deep in the surf, and harnessed the mule robots to the landing gear. The machines hauled the boat to the ends of the rails, then went back and with their manipulators laid out the rails in front again, under the water, and hauled again.

Grant and the crew climbed on board and dogged the hatches. They brushed the water drops and opportunistic small sea creatures off their waterproofs and into the gutter to drains, and stowed the gear. Ellen took the pilot's chair. Morag Rafferty sat beside her. Grant climbed down into the observation bubble. Lisa Sweeney started up the fusion pot. After a couple more hauls and relays the vessel was afloat. The robots gathered up the rails and returned to the shore, where they plodded up the beach and hunkered down by the cliffs.

'That was some palaver,' Morag said. 'Could we no have just jumped to the sea?'

'Proof of concept,' Grant said. They'd been over this before.

'Engines on,' Ellen announced. The boat thrummed, and surged forward, up and down the swells.

'Christ, Ellen,' Lisa called from the back, 'dive before anyone gets seasick!'

'Submerging,' Ellen replied.

Tanks gurgled, pumps hissed. The *Fighting Chance* sank below the waves. Three metres down, the light was still clear, its spectrum shifted slightly blue. Grant saw darting shoals of swimming molluscs, their shapes and motions convergent with those of fish, their relict shells armouring heads and edging jaws; the drifting coelenterates on which these preyed, and whose long venom-studded tentacles preyed right back; clouds of scrabbling small fry that looked like but probably weren't prawns: larvae of the larger fish-like animals, he guessed. The smaller plankton among which they all swam and some preyed was like a sparkling mist. This was a richer ocean than any on Earth, slowly recovering though these now were.

'Marie should be seeing this,' he said, 'instead of poking at these fucking robots.'

'She will,' Ellen called back.

They continued outward for half an hour, at a speed of ten knots. Morag reported that the sea below them was a hundred metres deep. The sub's design depth was a hundred and fifty metres.

'Diving,' Ellen said.

Down they went. The light blued further as it faded. At fifty metres Ellen levelled off, and throttled back. The engines stilled, leaving no sound but the creaks from the hull and the beat of the pumps and the thrum of the air circulation. Morag turned the sonar on, and Iskander brought the readings to their glasses. Numerous echoes appeared as bright dots, some moving fast. The craft continued to drift in the deep current.

A much larger echo flared, and resolved into a streamlined shape longer than the submarine. It came closer, and within a minute was a hundred metres away and visible as an outline of glowing dots.

'Lights?' Grant said.

'Lights!' Ellen said.

Grant switched on the forward beams.

They beheld the kraken.

It was shaped more like a whale than a squid: it had the huge eyes, and tentacles around the mouth, but its twenty-metre-long body ended in a tail with flukes. Under the ship's lights, the outline became solid, and its colours plain: blue-green dorsally, white ventrally, with rows of bright spots all along the sides and in lines of calligraphic complexity around the rest of the body. The mouth gaped, and for a moment looked almost capable of engulfing the *Fighting Chance*. But it had no teeth; instead, long, stiff, fringed fronds that visibly rippled as it drew water in.

'It's a filter-feeder,' Ellen said. 'Not a predator.'

'Tell that tae the plankton,' Morag said.

Ellen started up the engines. The kraken darted backwards, but hung in position as the *Fighting Chance* manoeuvred around it to face it side-on. Grant played the ship's headlamp beams along its sides.

'Can we catch this beast,' he asked, 'or do we go looking for something smaller?'

For an answer, Ellen edged the ship forward. Grant deployed the grappling arms slowly, and gradually opened the grippers at their ends. The kraken didn't react, other than a tentative motion of its tentacles. The *Fighting Chance* moved metre by metre closer, poised to pounce.

'Check the sonar pings,' Morag said.

Grant shifted his attention and his gaze. The sonar overlay in his glasses snapped back into focus. Nine more bright echoes like the first, closing in. He blinked the display away and swung the searchlight beams above the kraken's back. There they were: nine krakens, which swiftly spaced themselves around, above and below the *Fighting Chance* and the first kraken, still broadside on to the submarine's bow.

He was about to return the beam to that kraken when he noticed that it seemed he already had: two bright circular patches of light had appeared on the animal's side.

'Look at that!' he said.

'Some kind of afterglow?' Ellen sounded doubtful.

'Let's . . . hold position,' Grant said.

He experimented with the lights, shining them on different areas along the side, switching them on and off. No new patches appeared where the light had shone. There was no trace of an afterglow. Instead, the two patches moved about, seemingly chasing the places where the light was or had been until a moment earlier. Then they vanished, to blink on again seconds later.

'Hang on,' said Morag. 'Surely the fuck not . . .'

Grant flashed the lights three times, then turned them off. The other krakens, their lines and swirls of light now visible, moved around like starry ghosts. The first kraken lay in the water, likewise outlined in bioluminescent dots. Then the two patches of light reappeared, and flashed on and off three times.

Grant responded with two short flashes and a long one. The kraken repeated the pattern back. Grant tried again, with a long flash and two short ones. Again the kraken mirrored that pattern.

'Are we . . . communicating with it?' Ellen said.

They were still pondering that when the same series of flashes came from the other krakens: dot dot dot, dash dot dot, dot dot dash. The bioluminescent lines along the sides of the kraken in front of them flared into rippling riots of light, forming patterns that faded into each other, evanescent and elaborate. The other krakens around them responded with variations.

'I don't know,' Morag said, 'but they're communicating with each other all right.'

'Looks like it,' Grant said.

One by one, the big sea beasts swam closer to the submarine, and circled it above and below and around, lights moving on their sides all the while.

The first kraken whipped around in the water with a surge that set the boat rocking, and swam right up to a few metres from the bubble where Grant sat. Its tentacles reached out, and touched the tips of the grippers, then withdrew. The tentacles moved like fingers on a piano, then were still. The eyes, glassy white balls, rotated forward, revealing close-up their curious keyhole-shaped pupils. Tentatively, Grant moved the grippers in a similar pattern, one digit at a time. Lights flared around the kraken's eyes and mouth. It repeated the ripple of its tentacles. Grant moved the grippers again, and again the tentacles echoed the pattern.

Then the kraken swam backwards and turned about. The others gathered behind it, in what for a moment was a V-shaped formation, like a flight of bomber aircraft. Lights flickered along their flanks, then with a flex of their tails they vanished into the depths.

Ellen exhaled something between a laugh and a sigh. 'Well! Do we give chase?'

'The hell we do,' Grant said. Awe outweighed the crushing of his commercial fishery hopes. The fearless curiosity of the krakens, and their responsiveness to what might have seemed like attempted communication from the submarine, had disarmed him, and convinced him there was nothing for him here. 'Looks like the monkey-spiders aren't the only intelligent life on Apis.'

'Even given that,' Ellen said, 'there must be other species we could hunt.'

'Yes,' Grant said. 'Their prey species!'

'They're filter-feeders,' Ellen reminded him. 'They prey on plankton! We're not going after small fry.'

'It's all the same,' Grant said. 'We'd be tugging at threads in the web. Same problem we're having with the trees and the monkey-spiders. Can't say I see the Fermi being too happy with that, and I don't fancy finding out.'

'We'll have to consult Marie on the ecology,' Ellen said. 'But, yeah, you have a point.'

Grant hauled himself up, head and shoulders out of the hatch between the bubble and the deck, and looked around at Ellen, Morag and Lisa. 'Are we agreed? The scheme's a washout?'

They all nodded.

'Oh well,' Grant said, 'that's it. Ellen, could you take us back to shore?'

'On it,' Ellen said.

The engines thrummed. Tanks drained and pumps laboured. The light around them brightened.

Morag broke the silence with a laugh. 'Never could stand calamari anyway.'

'Not even deep-fried?' Lisa Sweeney called out, from the back.

'Not even deep-fried in batter,' Morag said, over her shoulder. 'Too rubbery, too chewy, and not enough taste to make it worth the bother.'

They surfaced to the sound of distant explosions.

CHAPTER TWENTY-THREE
Battlestar Europa

New Rhu, New Mu, Apis and low Apis orbit,
Saturday 4 April to Sunday 5 April 2071

'What the fuck!' Myles shouted.

He dropped the wrench he'd been using to connect up some pipework on yet another new house, pulled his glasses down from his forehead and tilted his hard hat up from it, and looked to the sky. Blue flashes overhead, bright white flashes beyond the mountain range. He zoomed and saw a drone swarm like distant midges, spinning down towards – *oh fuck* – the Co-ord beachhead on the far side of Hamilton's Rise. A black arrow-head shape hurtled by at five thousand feet above New Rhu, to vanish in a blue flash. In its wake a stick of parachutes dropped, towards the near side of the mountain.

A moment later, coming from the other direction, east across the plain, a much larger and slower silhouette crossed the sky, higher up: a boomerang-shaped flying wing. The roar of jet engines tumbled down from it. Fire sparkled from its flanks. Explosions erupted close to where the parachutes looked likely to land. Suppression fire, precisely aimed, but Myles wondered how it felt to the paratroops as these streams of white-hot ordnance scythed diagonally past where they drifted down, buffeted by random thermals from the slopes of Hamilton's Rise.

He reached for his phone to rally the militia. Several men and women around him, up and down the half-built street, were already scrambling. A squad formation dotted his sight, tagged with names and available weapons. Just as he was about to open the channel, Iskander's voice spoke in his earpieces.

'Orders coming through,' it said.

'Orders?' There wasn't anyone to—

'Union Space Marines to all irregulars and militia!' a new voice said. 'Secure your settlements!'

Marines. Jeez. Trust the Union to tell it like it was. They didn't do euphemism. You had to give them that. The thought barely had time to take shape before another order came through, in a different voice.

'New Rhu militia leader Myles Grant!'

'Present and receiving.'

A swarm of drones was rising from the Alliance fort and heading west. The flying wing was now hovering at ten thousand feet, engines tilted upwards, on the far side of Hamilton's Rise. Trails of smoke rose towards it; downward trails intercepted them, marking the intersections with flashes that seconds later rolled in as bangs. It was from that craft, he reckoned, that the orders came.

'Assemble a squad and join British officer Lieutenant William Knight, presently in New Rhu. Liaise with him to defend the settlement. His current location is as shown.'

A map flashed up with a blinking black dot, but Myles needed no telling where Bill Knight was.

'Received and understood.'

Gathering up half a dozen militia members as he ran, grabbing a rifle from the cache on a corner, he raced through the streets of New Rhu towards Marie's lab.

They'd been making progress. Owen and the descent suit exchanged messages, in their alien sign language, too quick to follow. Iskander translated. The restriction on the suit's arms above the elbows made the dialogue awkward and stilted, but the gist was getting through. The suit was clear that almost all humans had to leave Apis – it could be a planet for scientists, as it had been before, but not for settlers. The warnings of what would happen if the settlements continued were becoming increasingly dire: wildfires, plagues, earthquakes . . . Milloy wondered how the Fermi were going to do any of that, being no longer physically present on the planet, but she kept that thought to herself.

The suit was struggling with a point hard to make in the monkey-spider language – or the restricted subset of it that the suit and Owen had mastered and were able to mimic – a hint about water, and slugs or something like that, and great distance, when the first flashes flickered in the lab windows and, moments later, bangs shook the air and rattled the panes.

Everyone stopped. Even the descent suit's fingers froze, mid-gesture. Owen crouched, standing on the balls of his feet, poised and alert. Knight straightened as if snapping to attention. He put a hand to his ear, reflexively.

'Damn!' he said.

Milloy glanced at Marie, then away and around. Like her, the biologist was casing the room, now an arsenal of perils: windows, glassware, instruments. Militia training kicking in.

'Get down!' Marie said.

They all hit the floor. More flashes and bangs, and a rattle of fire from above.

'Iskander!' Milloy cried. 'Are we under attack?'

'No, but you're in danger of stray fire. In fact—'

'You're the ones attacking,' Knight told them. Prone, he pointed up. 'That's the Union Space Marines hitting the Co-ord beachhead and mining operation.'

'Jesus!'

'Quite. Excuse me while I liaise with my garrison. They've sent drones to take care of this side of the mountain.' He turned away from them and started subvocalising into his phone. Owen lay face down, hands clasped over the back of his head, intent on whatever news he was following in his glasses.

'Look out!' Iskander said. An image flashed up on Milloy's glasses, a downward view of the lab like an out-of-the-body experience. The descent suit had swivelled both of its forearms and grasped the sides of the table. Its body flexed upward. A creak was followed by a crash as the lab table cracked in the middle and the descent suit's buttocks hit the floor in the V of the broken table.

The descent suit rolled, carrying the pieces of table with it. By luck or cunning, one swinging half of table top hit Knight on the temple. He yelled, and at the same moment the suit grabbed the knife from its sheath on his belt. With a few quick, deft slashes it was free. It sprang to its feet and lurched for the door. The door was closed, and the suit made no attempt to open it. It crashed through and exited in a burst of splinters.

Milloy jumped up and made a grab for her rocket-launcher. She was out of the door and after the descent suit before anyone else could react. On the threshold she got down on one knee and brought the rocket tube to bear on the fleeing descent suit. It was by now twenty metres away and moving surprisingly fast down the path from the lab towards the main part of the town.

It was heading straight towards a squad of rifle-toting militia, who were pounding up the road. As she peered through the telescopic sight Milloy saw that they were led by Myles Grant. She waved an arm wildly at them and yelled: 'Get out of its way!'

They didn't. Instead, they dived to the sides of the road and opened fire on the thing. It marched forward, oblivious to the incoming rounds. If the fighters were in danger it was from their own ricochets.

'Iskander, put me through to Myles!'

Myles picked up at once. 'Yes?'

'Milloy here. Stop firing, you can't damage it. I can and you're in my way. Roll to the ditches and hunker down. Let it through.'

'OK,' Myles said. She saw him signal with a hand behind his shoulder, heard a sharp command. The firing stopped. The suit walked on, past the prone squad. Milloy aimed again, and saw the suit take a sudden leap sideways. It crashed through the fence around a house, and then cut across the corner of the house. There was no way to take a clean shot. The grenade in the tube could destroy or permanently disable the suit, but by the same token it would shred the house and anyone inside.

She jumped up, about to run after it and try to get a clear shot.

'Stop!' Iskander said.

'What? Why?'

'There's no point,' the AI explained. 'I've told all the militia members running around with guns down there to give it clear passage. We're in no danger from it. Let it preach sedition to monkey-spiders. Our priority now is defending the settlement against any Co-ord counter-attack.'

'But it hurt the lieutenant!'

'Citizen Milloy, you should know by now the futility of taking revenge on machines.'

'I take your point, but I do bear in mind that it's a machine telling me that.'

Myles's squad came running up. 'Is Marie all right?'

'Yes, but the lieutenant isn't.'

Myles stopped. 'I was ordered to liaise with him.'

'He can't help us. He needs medevac.'

Myles looked up at the sky and waved an arm around. Smoke was rising from numerous sources beyond Hamilton's Rise, and from the forest in front of it, too. The flying wing was now circling around the mountain top, and no longer firing. 'He's not the only one.'

'Iskander, get us visual,' Milloy said.

There were no views from the flying wing, or from the soldiers and military drones. Only a few high-flying survey drones supplied images, and these only for seconds, but they were enough. Wrecked machines and burning buildings, a scatter of dead bodies on the ground, wounded people curled up or squirming along like worms.

'We'll do what we can for Knight,' Milloy said.

She ducked through the wrecked door, Myles following. Marie was keeping a watchful eye on Owen, who was tending to Knight.

The robot looked up. 'Skull fracture, concussion. He's conscious but woozy.'

'I'll call Celeste,' Myles said. 'We can get him to the clinic.' He got busy on his phone.

Owen stood up. 'Why not the Alliance fort? They're better equipped for dealing with head injuries.'

'But I've just—' Myles said.

'Oh, fuck off,' Owen said. 'I've already called it in. Tell your clinic to stand down.'

'He's right, Myles,' Marie said. 'There might be complications.'

'I won't . . .' Knight wheezed, from the floor. 'I won't . . . give you . . . complications.'

The medevac drones from the Alliance stockade were already landing outside. Myles and Milloy and Owen carried Knight out. The medical orderly slapped a surgery kit on Knight's head. The segmented device wrapped itself around his skull. Precision drilling and cutting and draining began. Owen and the orderly strapped him to the stretcher and set his head in the hard collar, and the drones dusted off and bore him towards the trees and the fort.

He died that night.

'It wasn't your fault,' Marie said, the following morning. 'It was just a stupid accident.'

Myles looked across the kitchen table at her. His head was thumping. He had drunk too much jungle juice the previous evening.

'I liked Bill,' he said.

'I know.' Marie gave a sad smile. 'He was a reasonable man.'

'Yeah. Wish more people were.' Myles thumped the table. 'Why the fuck did our people have to hit the Co-ord beachhead like that? That wasn't reasonable.'

'It wasn't reasonable of the Co-ord to hold onto it,' Marie said. 'They did it because they could. That's politics and power for you.'

'Reason of state, yes.' He drank some coffee and gazed out of the window. On the plain behind their house, quite visible over the roofs of the next street, the great flying wing was parked where it had landed after the one-sided battle the previous day. Columns of smoke from the crew's campfires around it wavered skyward. If anyone knew how the bizarre aircraft was supposed to get back to whatever FTL transport had delivered it to atmosphere, they weren't telling. Perhaps it was here for the duration, whatever the duration was.

A Union contingent now occupied the former Co-ord beachhead, and Union engineers had taken over the mining. The Co-ord forces were being evacuated. In the dead of night on the far side of the world, a simultaneous surprise attack had been made on the Co-ord forces occupying MacHinery Ridge, the Fermi rock outcrop on New Atlantis. These forces, too, were being evacuated. There was no official confirmation that the Union and the Alliance had coordinated the assaults, but it was obvious to all that they had.

The Co-ord had made no moves in response – yet. Somewhere above the heads of everyone directly involved, a deal had been struck. There would be no repercussions, for now. These would come later, and far away.

'And hey,' Marie said, with forced good cheer, 'the Union now has its own mountain of Fermi rock.'

'You think the Fermi will let us hold it?'

In the next few months, about 90 per cent of the current human population of Apis was going to have to move off the planet, to the Terre Nouveau system or back to Earth. So far, from Iskander's soundings, less than half had shown any interest or intention of doing so. They had invested savings, hopes, months of work in their new lives. It was going to take a lot to persuade them to leave before the Fermi forced the issue.

Marie shrugged. 'There's no more damage for that operation to do, as far as the forest goes. Yeah, I think that can be part of our limited presence here.'

'Speaking of which,' Myles said.

'Uh-huh?'

He swallowed hard. 'What about us? Do you want to stay here? Or move somewhere cold and mountainous, where the Fermi aren't on our backs?'

'And animals have spines and don't sound like machinery?'

'Yeah, all that.'

'Don't tell me it doesn't tempt you.' She sounded serious.

'Oh, it does,' Myles said. 'The third world.'

The third planet of the Terre Nouveau system, the world of glens and glaciers and narrow seas, the harsh land that hardly anyone but hominid scientists lived on, the promised refuge where humanity could settle freely, New Helvetia as people now called it, was tempting all right. It appealed to him at a very deep level.

'You don't really like it here,' she said.

It was true. He had never quite taken to Apis, with its entire biosphere of invertebrates in niches occupied by vertebrates on Earth, everything like an uncanny simulacrum of something else: boids and birds, insectoids and insects, monkey-spiders and monkeys, kraken and whales . . .

But that, of course, was exactly what charmed and delighted and engaged Marie. She wouldn't want to leave Apis. Its life was shaping up to be her life's work.

Well, he was in love with the woman, not the world.

'Nah, but you're here,' he said. 'That's enough for me.'

'Aw!' She reached across the table and grasped his hand.

'I'm touched,' Iskander said, implausibly. 'Sorry to interrupt, but the Station has just arrived in low Apis orbit.'

'The Station!' Marie cried.

They rushed outside, even though the Station's passage over-head was more than half an hour away and they wouldn't see it anyway.

'Announcement coming through,' Iskander said. 'It might be a good idea to go back inside and sit down.'

The Station, low Apis orbit, Sunday 5 April 2071

It was good to see Apis again, even if they were bearing bad news. Nayak looked down at the planet rolling below, while Ulrich introduced the files of the Fermi's demands, and Iskander relayed the segment to every phone on the planet. No one who listened and watched could have any doubt that the Fermi meant business, and that the Union would enforce the treaty on its own patch. What the other powers did was up to them.

The means of enforcement would be very simple, Ulrich explained: drones, millions of them, patrolling the forests and preventing any humans from going in and cutting down trees. Supplies of drones to the Union troops on the ground would be arriving over the next week, and the flying wing would disperse them across New Mu. Nobody would be compelled to leave, but they'd have to find ways of making a living that didn't encroach on the forest.

The Station would remain in orbit around Apis until the drone deployment was secure.

And that was that.

'Think it'll work?' Selena asked.

Nayak looked at her, then at the planet. The Station was passing from dark into sunlight, the exosun rising swiftly as if to meet them. New Mu would soon be in view. For now, the southern ocean was an apparently endless expanse of blue and white.

'I don't know,' Nayak said. 'It's that or what the Fermi threatened. We'll just have to see.'

Selena was about to reply when a call came through. Francesca Milloy.

'Sorry, got to take this.' Nayak flicked her ear. 'Hello?'

'Hi, Lakshmi! I'm giving you a wave, even though I can't see you.'

What? Oh. New Mu below already.

'Mission accomplished?' Nayak asked.

'Well, no, not exactly,' Milloy said. 'Uh, long story. Can I tell you on the Station?'

'You want to come back?'

'Well, yeah. For a while. You need a materials scientist, anyway.'

'I don't know where we're going next,' Nayak said.

'Exactly!' Milloy said. 'That's what I like to hear.'

'I suppose you'll have to ask Katrina.'

'I will, right away.'

'If we do send down a shuttle for you,' Nayak said, 'there's just one condition for letting you on, and I'm going to insist on it.'

'What?'

'You have to bring with you at least ten kilograms of Fermi rock.'

'Deal,' Milloy said.

New Rhu, New Mu, Apis, Sunday 5 April 2071

'Well!' Marie said, blinking as if coming out of a trance. 'That's us told!'

'Told all right,' Myles said. 'Jeez.' He shook his head. 'That black blankness, and then all those worlds. Worlds we can't have.'

'We can visit,' Marie said.

'Yeah, if we can afford it.'

Marie laughed. 'Your father's company will make another fortune shipping people off Apis. You can surely get some holiday money out of that.'

They were smiling at each other now, but Myles felt his gaze unfocus from Marie's face and saw that she saw it.

'You've got that stare,' she said. 'What's on your mind?'

'We've been doing this all wrong.' He closed his eyes and opened them again. 'Do you mind if I ask John and Ellen and Owen to come round?'

'No, sure. But why?'

Myles rubbed his hands. 'This is a family matter.'

'So why Owen?'

'Because he's going to work for us.'

'Marcus,' Myles said, when they were all around the table half an hour later, 'you know more than anyone about monkey-spiders.'

Owen glanced at Marie. 'This lady knows more, in some ways.'

'Ha!' Marie wasn't taken with this attempt at charm.

'Between you and Marie, then,' Myles went on, 'right here in your heads is all the knowledge we have so far about the monkey-spiders. I have a question.'

'Yes?'

'Would you say they respond to incentives?'

Owen frowned; Marie blinked.

'Well, obviously,' Marie said. 'Every organism does, in its own way.'

'And they can think ahead, right? Plan and execute? I saw that with my own eyes, that day I saw the hive.'

'Yeah, we've established that,' Marie said. 'And they have language.'

'Uh-huh.' Myles looked hard at Owen. 'You showed them how to use a rifle, and Marie saw a monkey-spider using one.'

'Yes.' Owen looked suspicious. 'I intended them to. They still can. Where are you going with this?'

'I was thinking, there must be other tools and devices of ours they could use. They're very good at shaping bits of carapace, and using broken-off jaws and pincers and . . .'

'Mandibles,' Marie said.

'Thanks, yes, mandibles and so on as tools. But they don't seem to do much with wood.'

'They sometimes cut down trees,' Marie said. 'They use some other animal's cast-off appendage like a saw.'

'Great! But that's still pretty limited, compared with what they could do with axes and knives.'

'You mean,' Owen said, 'they could cut down a lot more trees.'

'You got it.'

Everyone got it.

'How would the Fermi feel about *that*?' Marie asked.

Owen looked away into the distance. 'I'm not sure,' he said. 'But very differently from how they feel about us doing it.' He shook his head. 'But why would the monkey-spiders chop down trees? I mean, apart from for their own use?'

'They do seem to like honey,' Myles said.

'Take their timber and pay them with sweets?' Marie scoffed.

'And why not? They can name their price. And there's lots of other things we could offer them: tools, materials, gadgets . . .'

'It would be exploitation,' Marie said. 'Unequal exchange and all that.'

'Good point,' Myles said. He thought fast. 'But – not if we brought them into the economic democracy.'

Everyone around the table looked incredulous.

'What?' John Grant said. 'They're barely hunter-gatherers!'

'Exactly,' Myles said. 'See, they're communists already!'

'There's a big difference,' Grant said, 'between primitive communism and economic democracy.' He scoffed. 'At least, I hope there is!'

'No, seriously,' Myles said. 'They control their own conditions of work, within the constraints of their natural environment. They already *have* unalienated labour. It's something to build on.'

'It's not practical,' Ellen said. 'There's a gulf of not just species but . . .' she looked at Marie. 'What's the word?'

'Phyla,' Marie said. 'But Iskander and Owen already understand their language, and I've picked up a bit of it. So maybe . . . Who knows?'

John Grant frowned. 'The hominids and dinosaurs and humans on Terre Nouveau have, OK, smaller gaps between them, but to each other they might as well be aliens. They're from different planets, and they all seem to get along. More or less.'

Myles nodded. 'And maybe we could do something similar with these kraken you, uh, met yesterday.'

'Certainly better than eating them,' Ellen said. 'But people here are going to take a lot of persuading, to leave or to change their whole way of working.'

'It turns out I'm quite good at persuading,' Myles said. 'I've acquired a taste for politics.'

'You'll need it,' Owen said. 'But not for this.' He smiled at Marie. 'When I said your workers' state had better get on the case, I wasn't expecting it to be with the Station's great clunking iron fist.'

John Grant leaned in. 'I see where you're coming from, Myles,' he said. 'But for that to work in the long run, it would have to be stuff for export, and I don't see local fruits and herbs and what have you getting through Earth's biosecurity, never mind the Union's. We have enough problems with disease and pest control as it is – both ways.'

'We could work on that,' Marie said. 'We'd need a lot more biologists on the case, mind.'

'Marie, I like your thinking, too, but even so.'

'We don't just have to trade with Earth,' Myles said.

Grant leaned back. 'Oh. I see. Big picture.'

'What about our competitors?' Ellen said. 'If we see market opportunities, so will they.'

'I guess we'll just have to compete,' Grant said. 'One way or another.'

'Welcome to the new age of imperialism,' Ellen said. 'Wow! You're really selling me on this!'

'After imperialism comes socialism,' Myles said. He sounded dogmatic even to himself, and looked around, defensively. 'According to political economy, anyway.'

John Grant looked less scornful and more thoughtful than Myles had expected.

'Well, it did,' he said. 'At least the beginnings of it.'

'Yeah, after a lot of upheaval!' Ellen said. 'Christ, I thought we were through with all that.'

'We're still in all that anyway, like it or not,' Grant said. 'We were never out of it, not really.' He looked around the table. 'Let's start our own empire.'

CHAPTER TWENTY-FOUR

Coda: The Black Horizon

New Helvetia, many years later

The slope was steep, the night black and starry, the air cold and thin. John Grant didn't think of himself as old, but he wasn't getting any younger. Rejuvenation tabs could only take you so far. His thighs and calves ached and his knees hurt.

He stopped to look back. The narrow footpath zigzagged down the side of the mountain to the outskirts of the port, where it ended on the side of a street. From there the houses and factories and warehouses went down like giant steps to the mast-crowded harbour. Far across the narrow sea, starlight glinted on the ice-covered peaks of the mountains on the other side.

He turned and pressed on. A few hundred metres further and seventy metres higher, around a corner where the path hugged a cliff, he reached his destination. The path widened to a broad platform that could have been a car park, if cars could have made it up. It had litter bins and a picnic table. There was a wooden railing around the edge.

A tall hominid and a small man sat at the table, around a faint glow. Grant strolled over. 'Hello, Jean-Paul. Hello, Melikaar.'

They raised hands and returned the greeting. Grant sat. Damiba shoved a thermos and a clean cup across the table. 'Coffee,' he said. 'Locally grown.'

Grant poured himself a coffee, and shared some of the whisky he had brought. Melikaar drew on a long pipe. A shuttle appeared high in the sky, and glided in towards the airport on the edge of the town.

'Thanks for the invitation,' Grant said. 'The Nayak communicator is a great thing.'

Melikaar's laugh rumbled in the barrel of his chest.

'We couldn't pronounce your name for it,' Grant said. 'The real name. And, besides, she worked it out independently.'

Melikaar laughed again, drew on his pipe and blew out a wisp of smoke which he dispersed with a wave of his shovel-sized hand.

'How is Lakshmi, by the way?' Damiba asked.

'When she's not on the Station,' Grant said, with a vague skyward wave of the hand, 'she's a visiting professor of mathematics at the University of Havana.'

'They're lucky to have her.'

'Yes.'

They exchanged a few other polite queries about friends, family, and (in Melikaar's case) troop. Everyone was, by and large, doing fine. The chat died down.

'So why have you asked me here?' Grant said. 'Business?'

There was a lot of business around this table. His own John Grant & Son, Damiba's General Trading, the first and still the largest of the Karray multiplanetaries, and Melikaar's Gardens of the Moons, a systems-spanning conglomerate of off-world agriculture. Really there should be bodyguards. Doubtless there were, unseen as they should be. He was pretty sure a stealth drone had followed him.

Damiba shook his head. 'Sightseeing.'

Grant looked around, and looked up. The sky was so clear he could see the colours of some stars. The Milky Way was a bright arch overhead. The outer gas giant, still haunted by its Fermi, was the brightest visible planet.

'I used to say you can never go to the stars,' he said. 'By day it's another sun, and at night they're as far away as ever.'

Damiba scoffed. 'Yes, that's what I would expect of you, John! But, in fact, the sight we're here to see will be in the sky, and very soon. We owe deep thanks to Melikaar for letting us know in advance. To most, it will be a surprise, easily missed, yet not to be missed. A unique moment. So keep looking up.'

Grant took a sip of coffee, then a swig of whisky. He leaned back and gazed skyward. A light rose in the west, then another, and another. They brightened as they crossed the sky. They moved too slowly to be satellites; crossing from horizon to horizon would take about a quarter of an hour, Grant reckoned. And they were bright, brighter than the full Moon from Earth, brighter than the gas giant from Apis, bright enough to cast shadows from the posts of the railing. Grant zoomed his glasses, and saw the structure distinctly: the lattices, the vast open flower of reflective panels, the spinning wheel at the centre.

'My God!' he cried. 'The habitats! They're leaving!'

Leaving on light-sails, powered by lasers from around the star, and by the light of the star itself.

He didn't look away. 'Melikaar? Did some of your people move to the habitats? Why didn't I hear?'

Melikaar's reply was sometimes audible; at other times it could only be felt, as a vibration in the chest. Iskander translated it, not with subtitles this time, but with words in Grant's ear, so as not to overwrite the view.

'None of our people are there. Only the robots. But there

is information and material in all of them to make new infants of our people. Some of the robots will look and feel and behave exactly like adults of our people, and will raise the infants in the ways of the Jenty, and be parents to them. Of course this will not happen for a very long time.'

Grant felt a cold dismay at the thought. It seemed so pointless.

'All that time to travel to even the nearest stars – and why?'

'They are to travel farther than that. Much farther. Watch!'

The bright light of the habitat he was watching was replaced by a blue Cherenkov flare, and then it was gone. Seconds later the other two did the same.

'They have FTL drives!'

'Of course,' Melikaar said. 'They have far to go. Centuries and millennia of faster than light travel. Flesh and blood could not stand it, but robots can. They are to travel beyond the galaxy, and beyond the Local Group, and beyond the supercluster, and beyond the light horizon, and beyond the Fermi's reach. And then our people will be free.'

Grant and Damiba kept silent, and kept watching the sky. The flashes would come in one by one, over the next minutes and hours, at the steady speed of light.

END OF THE LIGHTSPEED TRILOGY

Acknowledgements

Thanks to Nadia Saward for outstanding editorial work on this book, and to her and Joanna Kramer for the same throughout.

Thanks also to Mic Cheetham, Farah Mendlesohn and Sharon MacLeod for helpful comments on various drafts.

extras

orbitbooks.net

about the author

Ken MacLeod was born on the Isle of Lewis and now lives in Gourock, Scotland. He has a postgraduate degree in biomechanics and worked for some years in IT. Since 1997, he has been a full-time writer. *The Star Fraction* (1995) was his first novel. *Beyond the Light Horizon* (2024) is his twentieth. He has also written many articles and short stories. He has won three BSFA awards and three Prometheus Awards, and been short-listed for the Clarke and Hugo Awards. Ken was a Writer in Residence at the ESRC Genomics Policy and Research Forum at Edinburgh University, and Writer in Residence for the MA creative writing course at Edinburgh Napier University. Ken's blog is The Early Days of a Better Nation (http:// kenmacleod.blogspot.com). His Twitter feed is at @amendlocke. Find out more about Ken MacLeod and other Orbit authors by registering for the free monthly newsletter at orbitbooks.net.

if you enjoyed
BEYOND THE LIGHT HORIZON
look out for
THESE BURNING STARS
by
Bethany Jacobs

Jun Ironway, hacker, con artist, and only occasional thief, has gotten her hands on a piece of contraband that could set her up for life: a video that implicates the powerful Nightfoot family in a planet-wide genocide seventy-five years ago. The Nightfoots control the precious sevite that fuels interplanetary travel through three star systems. And someone is sure to pay handsomely for anything that could break their hold.

Of course, anything valuable is also dangerous. The Kindom, the ruling power of the three star systems, is inextricably tied up in the Nightfoots' monopoly – and they can't afford to let Jun expose the truth. They task two of their most brutal clerics with hunting her down: preternaturally stoic Chono, and brilliant hothead Esek, who also happens to be the heir to the Nightfoot empire.

But Chono and Esek are haunted in turn by a figure from their shared past, known only as Six. What Six truly wants is anyone's guess. And the closer they get to finding Jun, the surer Chono is that Six is manipulating them all – and that they are heading for a bloody confrontation that no one will survive unscathed.

CHAPTER ONE

1643

YEAR OF THE LETTING

Kinschool of Principes
Loez Continent
The Planet Ma' kess

Her ship alighted on the tarmac with engines snarling, hot air billowing out from beneath the thrusters. The hatch opened with a hiss and she disembarked to the stench of the jump gate that had so recently spit her into Ma'kess's orbit—a smell like piss and ozone.

Underfoot, blast burns scorched the ground, signatures from ships that had been coming and going for three hundred years. The township of Principes would have no cause for so much activity, if it weren't for the kinschool that loomed ahead.

She was hungry. A little annoyed. There was a marble of nausea lodged in the base of her throat, a leftover effect of being flung from one star system to another in the space of two minutes. This part of Ma'kess was cold and wet, and she disliked the monotonous sable plains flowing away from the tarmac. She disliked the filmy dampness in the air. If the kinschool master had brought her here for nothing, she would make him regret it.

The school itself was all stone and mortar and austerity. Somberlooking effigies stared down at her from the parapet of the second-story roof: the Six Gods, assembled like jurors. She looked over her shoulder at her trio of novitiates, huddled close to one another, watchful. Birds of prey in common brown. By contrast, she was quite resplendent in her red-gold coat, the ends swishing around her ankles as she started toward the open gates. She was a cleric of the Kindom, a holy woman, a member of the Righteous Hand. In this school were many students who longed to be clerics and saw her as the pinnacle of their own aspirations. But she doubted any had the potential to match her. Already the kinschool master had appeared. They met in the small courtyard under the awning of the entryway, his excitement and eagerness instantly apparent. He bowed over his hands a degree lower than necessary, a simpering flattery. In these star systems, power resided in the Hands of the Kindom, and it resided in the First Families. She was both.

"Thank you for the honor of your presence, Burning One."

She made a quick blessing over him, rote, and they walked together into the school. The novitiates trailed behind, silent as the statues that guarded the walls of the receiving hall. It had all looked bigger when she graduated seven years ago.

As if reading her mind, the kinschool master said, "It seems a lifetime since you were my student."

She chuckled, which he was welcome to take as friendly, or mocking. They walked down a hallway lined with portraiture of the most famous students and masters in the school's history: Aver Paiye, Khen Sikhen Khen, Luto Moonback. All painted. No holograms. Indeed, outside the tech aptitude classrooms, casting technology was little-to-be-seen in this school. Not fifty miles away, her family's factories produced the very sevite fuel that made jump travel and casting possible, yet here the masters lit their halls with torches and sent messages to each other via couriers. As if training the future Hands was too holy a mission to tolerate basic conveniences.

The master said, "I hope your return pleases you?"

She wondered what they'd done with her own watercolor portrait. She recalled looking very smug in it, which, to be fair, was not an uncommon condition for her.

"I was on Teros when I got your message. Anywhere is better than that garbage rock."

The master smiled timidly. "Of course. Teros is an unpleasant planet. Ma'kess is the planet of your heart. And the most beautiful of all!" He sounded like a tourist pamphlet, extolling the virtues of the many planets that populated the Treble star systems. She grunted. He asked, "Was your trip pleasant?"

"Hardly any reentry disturbance. Didn't even vomit during the jump." They both laughed, him a little nervously. They walked down a narrow flight of steps and turned onto the landing of a wider staircase of deep blue marble. She paused and went to the banister, gazing down at the room below.

Six children stood in a line, each as rigid as the staves they held at their sides. They couldn't have been older than ten or eleven. They were dressed identically, in tunics and leggings, and their heads were shaved. They knew she was there, but they did not look up at her. Staring straight ahead, they put all their discipline on display, and she observed them like a butcher at a meat market.

"Fourth-years," she remarked, noticing the appliqués on their chests. They were slender and elfin looking, even the bigger ones. No giants in this cohort. A pity.

"I promise you, Sa, you won't be disappointed."

She started down the staircase, brisk and cheerful, ignoring the students. They had no names, no gendermarks—and no humanity as far as their teachers were concerned. They were called by numbers, given "it" for a pronoun. She herself was called Three, once. Just another object, honed for a purpose. Legally, Treble children had the right to gender themselves as soon as they discovered what fit. But *these* children would have to wait until they graduated. Only then could they take genders and names. Only then would they have their own identities.

At the foot of the staircase, she made a sound at her novitiates. They didn't follow her farther, taking sentry on the last step. On the combat floor, she gloried in the familiar smells of wood and stone and sweat. Her hard-soled boots *clacked* pleasingly as she took a slow circle about the room, gazing up at the magnificent mural on the ceiling, of the Six Gods at war. A brilliant golden light fell upon them, emanating from the sunlike symbol of the Godfire—their parent god, their essence, and the core of the Treble's faith.

She wandered around the room, brushing past the students as if they were scenery. The anticipation in the room ratcheted, the six students trying hard not to move. When she did finally look at them, it was with a quick twist of her neck, eyes locking on with predatory precision. All but one flinched, and she smiled. She brought her hand out from where it had been resting on the hilt of her bloodletter dagger, and saw several of them glance at the weapon. A weapon ordinarily reserved for cloaksaan.

This was just one of the things that must make her extraordinary to the students. Her family name being another. Her youth, of course. And she was very beautiful. Clerics deeply valued beauty, which pleased gods and people alike. *Her* beauty was like the Godfire itself, consuming and hypnotic and deadly.

Add to this the thing she represented: not just the Clerisy itself, in all its holy power, but the future the students might have. When they finished their schooling (*if* they finished their schooling), they would be one step closer to a position like hers. They would have power and prestige and choice—to adopt gendermarks, to take their family names again or create new ones. But *so much* lay between them and that future. Six more years of school and then five years as a novitiate. (Not everyone could do it in three, like her.) If all that went right, they'd receive an appointment to one of the three Hands of the Kindom. But only if they worked hard. Only if they survived.

Only if they were extraordinary.

"Tell me," she said to them all. "What is the mission of the Kindom?"

They answered in chorus: "Peace, under the Kindom. Unity, in the Treble."

"Good." She looked each one over carefully, observed their proudly clasped staves. Though "staves" was a stretch. The long poles in their hands were made from a heavy-duty foam composite. Strong enough to bruise, even to break skin—but not bones. The schools, after all, were responsible for a precious commodity. This cheapened the drama of the upcoming performance, but she was determined to enjoy herself anyway.

"And what are the three pillars of the Kindom?" she asked.

"Righteousness! Cleverness! Brutality!"

She hummed approval. Righteousness for the Clerisy. Cleverness for the Secretaries. Brutality for the Cloaksaan. The three Hands. In other parts of the school, students were studying the righteous Godtexts of their history and faith, or they were perfecting the clever arts of economy and law. But these students, these little fourth-years, were here to be brutal.

She gave the kinschool master a curt nod. His eyes lit up and he turned to the students like a conductor to his orchestra. With theatrical aplomb, he clapped once. It seemed impossible that the six students could look any smarter, but they managed it, brandishing their staves with stolid expressions. She searched for cracks in the facades, for shadows and tremors. She saw several. They were so young, and it was to be expected in front of someone like her. Only one of them was a perfect statue. Her eyes flicked over this one for a moment longer than the others.

The master barked, "One!"

Immediately, five of the children turned on the sixth, staves sweeping into offense like dancers taking position, and then—oh, what a dance it was! The first blow was like a clap against One's shoulder; the second, a heavy *thwack* on its thigh. It fought back hard—it had to, swinging its stave in furious arcs and trying like hell not to be pushed too far off-balance. She watched its face, how the sweat broke out, how the eyes narrowed, and its upper teeth came down on its lip to keep from crying out when one of the children struck it again, hard, on the hip. That sound was particularly good, a *crack* that made it stumble and lose position. The five children gave no quarter, and then there was a fifth blow, and a sixth, and—

"Done!" boomed the master.

Instantly, all six children dropped back into line, staves at rest beside them. The first child was breathing heavily. Someone had got it in the mouth, and there was blood, but it didn't cry.

The master waited a few seconds, pure showmanship, and said, "Two!"

The dance began again, five students turning against the other. This was an old game, with simple rules. Esek had played it many times herself, when she was Three. The attack went on until either offense or defense landed six blows. It was impressive if the attacked child scored a hit at all, and yet as she watched the progressing bouts, the second and fourth students both made their marks before losing the round. The children were merciless with one another, crowding their victim in, jabbing and kicking and swinging without reprieve. Her lip curled back in raw delight. These students were as vicious as desert foxes.

But by the time the fifth student lost its round, they were getting sloppy. They were bruised, bleeding, tired. Only the sixth remained to defend itself, and everything would be slower and less controlled now. No more soldierly discipline, no more pristine choreography. Just tired children brawling. Yet she was no less interested, because the sixth student was the one with no fissures in its mask of calm. Even more interestingly, this one had been the least aggressive in the preceding fights. It joined in, yes, but she wasn't sure it ever landed a body blow. It was not timid so much as . . . restrained. Like a leashed dog.

When the master said, "Six," something changed in the room. She couldn't miss the strange note in the master's voice—of pleasure and expectation. The children, despite their obvious fatigue, snapped to attention like rabbits scenting a predator. They didn't rush at Six as they had rushed at one another. No, suddenly, they moved into a halfcircle formation, approaching this last target with an unmistakable caution. Their gazes sharpened and they gripped their staves tighter than before, as if expecting to be disarmed. The sweat and blood stood out on their faces, and one of them quickly wiped a streak away, as if this would be its only chance to clear its eyes.

And Six? The one who commanded this sudden tension, this careful advance? It stood a moment, taking them all in at once, stare like a razor's edge. And then, it flew.

She could think of no other word for it. It was like a whirling storm, and its stave was a lightning strike. No defensive stance for this one— it went after the nearest student with a brutal spinning kick that knocked it on its ass, then it whipped its body to the left and cracked its stave against a different student's shoulder, and finished with a jab to yet another's carelessly exposed shin. All of this happened before the five attackers even had their wits about them, and for a moment she thought they would throw their weapons down, cower, and retreat before this superior fighter.

Instead, they charged.

It was like watching a wave that had gone out to sea suddenly surge upon the shore. They didn't fight as individuals, but as one corralling force, spreading out and pressing in. They drove Six back and back and back—against the wall. For the first time, they struck it, hard, in the ribs, and a moment later they got it again, across the jaw. The sound sent a thrill down her spine, made her fingers clench in hungry eagerness for a stave of her own. She watched the sixth fighter's jaw flush with blood and the promise of bruising, but it didn't falter. It swept its stave in an arc, creating an opening. It struck one of them in the chest, then another in the side, and a third in the thigh—six blows altogether. The students staggered, their offense broken, their wave disintegrating on the sixth student's immovable shore.

She glanced at their master, waiting for him to announce the conclusion of the match, and its decisive victor. To her great interest, he did no such thing, nor did the children seem to expect he would. They recovered, and charged.

Was the sixth fighter surprised? Did it feel the sting of its master's betrayal? Not that she could tell. That face was a stony glower of intent, and those eyes were smart and ruthless.

The other fights had been quick, dirty, over in less than a minute. This last fight went on and on, and each second made her pulse race. The exhaustion she'd seen in the students before gave way to an almost frenzied energy. How else could they hold their ground against Six? They parried and dodged and swung in increasingly desperate bursts, but through it all the sixth kept *hitting* them. Gods! It was relentless. Even when the other students started to catch up (strikes to the hip, to the wrist, to the thigh) it *kept going*. The room was full of ragged gasping, but when she listened for Six's breath, it was controlled. Loud, but steady, and its eyes never lost their militant focus.

In the feverish minutes of the fight, it landed eighteen strikes (she counted; she couldn't help counting) before finally one of the others got in a sixth blow, a lucky cuff across its already bruised mouth.

The master called, "Done!"

The children practically dropped where they stood, their stave arms falling limply at their sides, their relief as palpable as the sweat in the air. They got obediently back in line, and as they did, she noticed that one of them met Six's eye. A tiny grin passed between them, conspiratorial, childlike, before they were stoic again.

She could see the master's satisfied smile. She had of course not known *why* he asked her to come to Principes. A new statue in her honor, perhaps? Or a business opportunity that would benefit her family's sevite industry? Maybe one of the eighth-years, close to graduating, had particular promise? No, in the end, it was none of that. He'd brought her here for a fourth-year. He'd brought her here so he could show off his shining star. She herself left school years earlier than any student in Principes's history, a mere fifteen when she became a novitiate. Clearly the master wanted to break her record. To have this student noticed by her, recruited by her as an eleven-year-old—what a feather that would be, in the master's cap.

She looked at him directly, absorbing his smug expression.

"Did its parents put you up to that?" she asked, voice like a razor blade.

The smugness bled from his face. He grew pale and cleared his throat. "It has no parents."

Interesting. The Kindom was generally very good about making sure orphans were rehomed. Who had sponsored the child's admission to a kinschool? Such things weren't cheap. The master said, clearly hoping to absolve himself, "After you, it's the most promising student I have ever seen. Its intelligence, its casting skills, its—"

She chuckled, cutting him off.

"Many students are impressive in the beginning. In my fourth year, I wasn't the star. And the one who was the star, that year? What happened to it? Why, I don't even think it graduated. Fourth year is far too early to know anything about a student."

She said these things as if the sixth student hadn't filled her with visceral excitement. As if she didn't see, vast as the Black Ocean itself, what it might become. Then she noticed that the master had said nothing. No acquiescence. No apology, either, which surprised her.

"What aren't you telling me?" she asked.

He cleared his throat again, and said, very lowly, "Its family name was Alanye."

Her brows shot up. She glanced back at the child, who was not making eye contact. At this distance, it couldn't have heard the master's words.

"Really?" she asked.

"Yes. A secretary adopted it after its father died. The secretary sent it here."

She continued staring at the child. Watching it fight was exhilarating, but knowing its origins made her giddy. This was delicious.

"Does it know?"

The master barely shook his head no. She *hmmed* a bright sound of pleasure.

Turning from him, she strode toward the child, shaking open her knee-length coat. When she was still several feet away from it, she crooked a finger.

"Come here, little fish. Let me have a look at you."

The fourth-year moved forward until it was a foot away, gazing up, up, into her face. She looked it over more carefully than before. Aside from their own natural appearance, students weren't allowed any distinguishing characteristics, and sometimes it was hard to tell them apart. She took in the details, looked for signs of the child's famous ancestor, Lucos Alanye: a man who started with nothing, acquired a mining fleet, and blew up a moon to stop anyone else from taking its riches. The sheer pettiness of it! He was the most notorious mass murderer in Treble history. She hadn't known he *had* descendants. With a flick of her wrist, she cast an image of Alanye to her ocular screen, comparing the ancestor to the descendant. Inconclusive.

The child remained utterly calm. Her own novitiates weren't always so calm.

"So, you are Six. That is a very holy designation, you know." It said nothing, and she asked it cheerfully, "Tell me: Who is the Sixth God?" This was an old riddle from the Godtexts, one with no answer. A person from Ma'kess would claim the god Makala. A person from Quietus would say Capamame. Katishsaan favored Kata, and so on, each planet giving primacy to its own god. Asking the question was just a way to figure out where a person's loyalty or origins lay. This student looked Katish to her, but maybe it would claim a different loyalty?

Then it said, "There is no Sixth God, Sa. Only the Godfire."

She tilted her head curiously. So, it claimed no loyalty, no planet of origin. Only a devotion to the Kindom, for whom the Godfire held primacy. How . . . strategic.

She ignored its answer, asking, "Do you know who I am?"

The silence in the room seemed to deepen, as if some great invisible creature had sucked in its breath.

"Yes, Burning One. You are Esek Nightfoot."

She saw the other children from the corner of her eye, looking tense and excited.

She nodded. "Yes." And bent closer to it. "I come from a very important family," she said, as if it didn't know. "That's a big responsibility. Perhaps you know what it's like?"

For the first time, it showed emotion—a slight widening of the eyes. Almost instantly, its expression resolved back into blankness.

"The master says you don't know who you are . . . Is that true, little fish?"

"We don't have names, Sa."

She grinned. "You are very disciplined. From all accounts, so was Lucos Alanye."

Its throat moved, a tiny swallow. It knew *exactly* what family it came from. The kinschool master was a fool.

"Do you know," Esek said, "all the First Families of the Treble are required to give of their children to the Kindom? One from each generation must become a Hand. My matriarch selected me from my generation. It seems fate has selected you from yours."

There was a fierceness in its eyes that said it liked this idea very much—though, of course, the Alanyes were not a First Family. Lucos himself was nothing more than an upstart and opportunist, a resourceraping traitor, a genocider. Esek half admired him.

"Your family did mine a great service," she said. It looked wary now, a little confused. She nodded. "Yes, my family controls the sevite factories. And do you know who are the laborers that keep our factories going?"

This time it ventured an answer, so quiet its voice barely registered, "The Jeveni, Sa." "Yes! The Jeveni." Esek smiled, as if the Jeveni were kings and not refugees. "And if Lucos Alanye had never destroyed their moon world, the Jeveni would not need my family to employ them, would they? And then, who would run the factories? So you see it is all very well, coming from the bloodline of a butcher. All our evils give something back."

The student looked at her with that same wariness. She changed the subject.

"What do you think of your performance today?"

Its face hardened. "The fight had no honor, Sa."

Esek's brows lifted. They were conversing in Ma'kessi, the language of the planet Ma'kess. But just then, the student had used a Teron word for "honor." One that more accurately translated to "bragging rights." Perhaps the student was from the planet Teros? Or perhaps it had a precise attitude toward language—always the best word for the best circumstance.

"You struck your attackers eighteen times. Is there no honor in that?"

"I lost. Honor is for winning."

"But the master cheated you."

The invisible creature in the room drew in its breath again. Behind her she could *feel* the master's quickening pulse. Esek's smile brightened, but Six looked apprehensive. Its compatriots were glancing uneasily at one another, discipline fractured.

She said, "Beyond these walls, out in the world, people don't have to tell you if you've won. You know it for yourself, and you make other people know it. If I were you, and the master tried to cheat me out of my win, I'd kill him for it."

The tension ratcheted so high that she could taste it, thick and cloying. Six's eyes widened. Before anything could get out of hand, Esek laughed.

"Of course, if *you* tried to kill the master, he would decapitate you before you'd even lifted your little stave off the ground, wouldn't he?"

It was like lacerating a boil. The hot tightness under the skin released, and if there was a foul smell left over, well . . . that was worth it. "Tell me, Six," she carried on, "what do you want most of all?"

It answered immediately, confidence surging with the return to script, "To go unnoticed, Sa."

She'd thought so. These were the words of the Cloaksaan. The master wouldn't be parading its best student under her nose like a bitch in heat if the bitch didn't want to be a cloaksaan—those deadly officers of the Kindom's Brutal Hand, those military masterminds and shadow-like assassins, who made peace possible in the Treble through their ruthlessness. Esek had only ever taken cloaksaan novitiates. It was an idiosyncrasy of hers. Most clerics trained clerics and most secretaries trained secretaries, but Cleric Nightfoot trained cloaksaan.

"You held back in the first five fights," she remarked.

The child offered no excuses. Did she imagine defiance in its eyes?

"That's all right. That was smart. You conserved your strength for the fight that mattered. Your teachers might tell you it was cowardly, but cloaksaan don't have to be brave. They have to be smart. They have to win. Right?"

Six nodded.

"Would you like to be my novitiate someday, little fish?" asked Esek gently.

It showed no overt excitement. But its voice was vehement. "Yes, Burning One."

She considered it for long moments, looking over its body, its muscles and form, like it was a racehorse she might like to sponsor. It knew what she would see, and she felt its hope. Her smile spread like taffy, and she said simply, "No."

She might as well have struck it. Its shock broke over her like a wave. Seeing that it could feel was important; unlike some Hands, she didn't relish an emotionless novitiate.

"I won't take you. More than that, I'm going to tell the other Hands not to take you."

The child's stunned expression nearly made her laugh, but she chose for once to be serious, watching it for the next move. Its mouth opened and closed. Clearly it wanted to speak but knew it had no right. She gave it a little nod of permission, eager to hear what it would say. It glanced toward its master, then spoke in a voice so soft, no one would hear.

"Burning One . . . I am not my ancestor. I am—loyal. I am Kingdom in my heart."

She hummed and nodded. "Yes, I can see that. But haven't we established? My family owes your ancestor a debt, for the Jeveni, and I don't care if you're like him or not. The fact is, I find you very impressive. Just as your master does, and your schoolkin do. I imagine everyone finds you impressive, little fish. But that's of no use to me. I require something different."

Esek watched with interest as it struggled to maintain its composure. She wondered if it would cry, or lose its temper, or drop into traumatized blankness. When none of these things happened, but it only stood there with its throat bobbing, she dropped a lifeline.

"When you are ready, you must come directly to me."

Its throat stilled. She'd startled it again.

"You must come and tell me that you want to be my novitiate. Don't go to my people, or the other Hands. Don't announce yourself. Come to me unawares, without invitation."

It looked at her in despairing confusion. "Burning One, you're surrounded by novitiates. If I come to you without permission, your people will kill me."

She nodded. "That's right. They'll never let you through without my leave. What's worse, I probably won't even remember you exist. Don't feel bad. I never remember any of the little fish I visit in the schools. Why should I, with so many things to occupy me? No, in a couple of days, you'll slip my mind. And if, in a few years, some strange young person newly gendered and named tries to come before me and ask to be my novitiate, well! Even if you get through my people, I may kill you myself." A long pause stretched between them, before she added, "Unless . . ."

It was exhilarating, to whip the child from one end to the other with the power of a single word. Its eyes lit up. It didn't even breathe, waiting for her to name her condition. She leaned closer still, until their faces were only inches apart, and she whispered in a voice only it could hear, "You must do something *extraordinary*." She breathed the word into its soul, and it flowed there hot and powerful as the Godfire. "You must do something I have never seen before. Something memorable, and shocking, and *brutal*. Something that will make me pause before I kill you. I have no idea what it is. I have no idea what I'll *want* when that day comes. But if you do it, then I will make you my novitiate. Your ancestry won't matter. Your past won't matter. This moment won't matter. You will have everything you deserve: all the honor a life can bring. And you will earn it at my side."

The child stared at her, caught in the terrible power of the silence she let hang between them. And then, like a fishersaan cutting a line, she drew back. Her voice was a normal volume again, and she shrugged.

"It's not a great offer, I'll grant you. Probably you'll die. If you choose not to come to me, I won't hold it against you. I won't remember you, after all. There are other, excellent careers in the Kindom. You don't have to be a Hand to do good work. Someone as talented as you could be a marshal or guardsaan. The master says you're good at casting. You could be an archivist! But whatever you decide, I wish you luck, little fish." She pinned it with her mocking stare. "Now swim away."

It blinked, released from the spell. After a moment of wretched bewilderment, it dropped back into place beside its schoolkin, who looked most shocked of all; one was crying silently. She whirled around, each click of her boots on the stone floor like a gunshot. The gold threads in her coat caught the light until she shimmered like a flame.

She locked eyes with the master, whose friendliness had evaporated in these tense minutes. He was now marshaling forty years of training into a blank expression, but Esek sensed the cold terror in him. No one in his life had seen him this frightened before, and the shame of it, of all these little fourth-years witnessing it, would torture him.

Esek moved as if she would go right past him, but paused at the last moment. They were parallel, arms brushing, and she heard his minuscule gasp. Perhaps he expected the plunge of the bloodletter? As a Hand of the Kindom, she had every right to kill him if she judged his actions unrighteous. Still, knowing he was afraid of it happening was its own reward—and she didn't feel like dealing with the aftermath today. Instead, she studied the master's face. He was staring straight forward, as well trained as the students, and just as vulnerable.

"Graduate it to the eighth-years."

The master's temple ticked. "You've already determined that no Hand will make it their novitiate. It has no future here."

Esek chuckled, amazed at the brazenness of this master. "Let it decide on its own. Personally, I think this one will find its way. Or has your confidence in it proved so fickle?" The master was silent, and this time Esek's voice was a threatening purr. "What about your confidence in *me*, Master? I am your window to the glory and wisdom of the Godfire. Don't you believe in the power of the Clerisy?" She drew out the final word, clicking the *C* with malevolent humor.

The master nodded shortly. "Of course, Sa. I will do as you say."

Esek smiled at him. She patted his shoulder, enjoying the flinch he couldn't control. She was preparing to murmur some new ridicule into his ear, when a voice interrupted them.

"Burning One."

She looked toward the marble staircase, where her novitiates still stood. They had been there all this time, invisible until she had need.

"Yes?" Esek asked. "What is it?"

"You have a message from Alisiana Nightfoot. The matriarch requests your presence at Verdant."

Esek clucked her tongue. "No rest for a Nightfoot." She swept past the master without farewells. She heard his barely discernible exhale of relief, and then the trio of novitiates were behind her, following her up the stairs. They retraced their steps to the school gates and the tarmac, where her docked warcrow awaited them. As they went, she called over her shoulder, "Send word to the Cloaksaan that they should visit the master. I think his tenure has run its course."

Who is the Sixth God, to your mind?
Fecund Makala or Kata wise?
Is it wily Terotonteris?
Or else Sajeven, warm and barren?
Is it the devouring Som?
Or Capamame, of gentle songs?
Beware you love them more than me,
For my eye perceives everything.

A Record of the Gods, 1: 1–8. Godtexts, pre-Treble

CHAPTER TWO

1664

YEAR OF THE CRUX

Riin Cosas
Sevres Continent
The Planet Ma' kess

Cleric Chono arrives on Ma'kess by spacecraft, a forty-hour trip from the water world of Quietus. She comes alone and walks the length of the tarmac with only a bag slung over one shoulder. Black Ocean sailors mill about in knots of bitter talk and cool glances flung her way. In the east, the planet's capital city of Riin Kala is a profile of spires built beneath a mountain range, purple cliffs a jagged backdrop. The city itself is a paragon of beauty and industry and art, and at the moment it seems like half its population has crowded to the docks, standing behind the metal fences. They clamor with protest, with curses and shouts. It's two days since the Secretaries officially shut down jump gate travel for all but the most essential services. Chono's own Hand, the Clerisy, has no authority to control the jump gates (such lines of authority are carefully delineated, amid the Hands), but one wouldn't know that from how the people glare and mutter at her passing.

Chono can't exactly blame them. As far as she can read the situation, there was no need to shut the gates down. Not yet, anyway. But these are tense times. The matriarch of the Nightfoot family, Alisiana Nightfoot, is dead, and she took with her all the stability of the sevite trade. Without sevite, the gates can't operate, and the Jeveni factory workers are in the midst of labor strikes.

Chono knows for a fact that the Kindom has enough sevite in storage to outlast these strikes. But still, the Secretaries have chosen a radical course, sure to debilitate trade and travel. If the people of the Treble resent them for this decision, they resent the Jeveni even more. Out in the crowd, Chono sees a hand-drawn sign: MAKE THE J BASTARDS WORK! She fears there will be attacks, killings. Already the casting net thrums with anti-Jeveni sentiment, with accusations and threats. Always such an easy target, the Jeveni.

A chant starts up in the distance: "Free our ships! Free our ships! Free our ships!"

Chono looks up into a blue sky, squinting at the pinprick shapes of idling ships that hover like dust motes on the very edge of the Ma'kessn atmosphere. It's so clear today that she easily sees the half-sickle form of the moon, Jeve. A black fingernail stamping the sky.

"Free our ships! Free our ships! Free our ships!"

A large contingent of guardsaan holds the crowds back from the main road out of the docks. There's a transport waiting for Chono, a warcat shuttle, odd to see after so many months on Quietus. The shuttle's driver, no doubt one of First Cleric Aver Paiye's novitiates, intends to ferry her the five miles to the temple, but Chono elects to walk. The driver is flustered, nearly hostile as he babbles about the First

Cleric's schedule. But when Chono's stare doesn't waver, he bows under the weight of it and climbs back into the warcat. He asks petulantly if he can at least take her bag. She says no, and leaves him.

It's an hour walk to the temple Riin Cosas, and Chono needs the quiet. The Black Ocean may be silent, but warships are not. Two days ago, she was making Hasha tea for a gaggle of parishioners come to morning prayer, peaceful in her appointment to the floating township of Pippashap. Far removed from the temple dramas that so often include Esek Nightfoot. Now she's standing eight light-years away, on the borders of the largest metropolis on Ma'kess.

Quietus was a flatland of ocean, its god the gentle Capamame, the dear friend. Ma'kess is all mountains and forests and valleys, presided over by fecund and lovely Makala. Fierce and vain Makala. The change is stark, for Chono.

She adjusts her pack. Feels the crinkle of the letter in her breast pocket: Aver Paiye's summons, on real laminate. Elegantly written. Full of praise. Cryptic.

She begins the walk with shoulders back and head high, determined not to look unsteady. Adapting to solid ground and lighter gravity is giving her a slight headache, but she leaves the docks behind at a steady clip, winding her way up the hillock that ridges the temple valley. At its crest, she pauses to absorb what anyone would assume to be her consolation prize for the tiring climb. It is, after all, a gorgeous sight. Against miles and miles of emerald grass and sapphire skies, Riin Cosas is a hexagonal jewel, its walls and domed roof glinting magnificently under an early afternoon sun, as reflective as glass, as impenetrable as steel.

By any measure of beauty in the Treble, Riin Cosas is the most exquisite temple in all of the three systems. The most ethereal. Chono has studied it since childhood: the seat of the First Cleric and the birthplace of Treble civilization. She wonders at the awe their colonizing ancestors must have felt, when they stepped from the decks of their generation ships into paradise. No wonder they built the temple here, intending a beacon of joy and hope that would survive through the centuries.

Yet to Chono, it has always been a source of deep ambivalence. Today, that feeling grows and ghosts inside her, as if her soul were two pieces engaged in a battle, all feints and hiding places.

By the time she reaches the temple, her trousers are hemmed with a foot of dust. Her hairline is damp, and she can feel the sweat under her arms and at the small of her back. When she arrives at the massive double doors at the top of the temple steps, she stands a moment staring at her own face in the reflective surface, obfuscated by inlaid carvings of Makala. All of Ma'kess is united in its worship of her, but beauty has always perturbed Chono. She prefers the five-eyed Sajeven, known for her barrenness and warmth, or the humble water god, Capamame. Quiet gods. Most of all she prefers the Godfire, for the Godfire is not a personality, has no ego or character, has only the steadiness of purpose: To keep the systems alive with its fire. To be a force of justice and mercy in the worlds.

Inside the door's massive frame, there's a creak of gears and pulleys. Chono's reflection bifurcates as the doors open, and she steps through.

Is it any wonder the temple interior is just as lush and beautiful as the surrounding valley? A garden square spills before her, overflowing with flowers and fruiting trees, the bounty of the southern Ma'kessn continents displayed in all its corals and crimsons and mauves. Statues of polished serpentine hold sentry in the lively garden, the Six Gods arrayed for worship. Flittering among them, birds call, insects whistle, and some small animal darts under a rosebush. The temple's translucent roof decorates it all in fractals of light, because the Godfire is light. The Godfire is everywhere. It suffuses the temple grounds, inimitable.

Chono sees the temple novitiate scurrying toward her from one of the walkways bordering the garden. She stymies him again, carefully lowering to her knees before he can reach her. She holds out her open palms, bowing over them to recite the beatitudes. Though they are a holy order, clerics often play fast and loose with ceremony, and this is not the first time Chono has baffled a novitiate with her adherence to tradition. But she likes the beatitudes. She likes their poetry and familiarity. She likes the righteous worlds they imagine.

When she finally stands, dustier than ever, the novitiate swoops in. "Burning One. I hope your walk was . . . peaceful."

Clearly, he hasn't gotten over her refusing to take the warcat.

"It offered plenty of time for contemplation."

The novitiate nods, barely listening, and ushers her toward the walkway. They go through a door into the atrium of the temple's eastern corner. He says, "The First Cleric is currently in conference with the First Cloak, but he intends to see you directly afterward."

This is surprising. The First Cloak of the Cloaksaan is Seti Moonback, and he's not generally found in temples. Cloaksaan keep their own company and prefer to conduct meetings via comm or other casting technologies. If they show up somewhere, it's usually to exercise some bloody errand. His business must have something to do with the protests over gate travel, though why he would come to the Clerisy instead of the Secretaries, Chono can't say.

The novitiate leads her farther into the atrium, passing the short hallway to Aver Paiye's office. Chono catches a glimpse of a large cloaksaan outside the door. A blink and he's out of sight; Chono faces forward again. Only then does she realize the novitiate is leading her toward the clerics' private gathering room. *To burn like stars*—the words of the Righteous Hand—is blazoned above the doors in holy lettering. What flashes through her then is not some image of majesty and power, but memories of destruction, and the reluctance she's felt ever since receiving Paiye's letter pulls heavy in her gut.

The novitiate says, "I'll come for you when the meeting is over. You may wait with your kin if you like."

Apparently, it is not truly "if she likes" because he has already reached the gathering room door and pulled it open with a flourish, as if he thinks he's delivering her to a banquet. He glances to the bag over her shoulder.

"Can I take that for you, Sa?"

Chono knows she'll look like a vagabond if she carries the pack into the gathering room; nevertheless she hesitates. Her grip on the strap tightens, before at last she hands it over to him.

"I want it somewhere secure."

"Of course, Sa."

Chono holds his stare for a long moment, and if a part of him thought her order was silly, now he shifts uncomfortably, realizing how foolish it would be to disregard her. Remembering, perhaps, who she is, and that unlike most clerics, Chono has a bloody history. Relatively satisfied, she looks away from him. She steels herself, and steps through the gathering room door. It closes behind her with a *snick*.

Inside, a glass column centers the room, burning with sevite fuel stones in homage to the Godfire. They are a glittering black blanket on the hearth, treated with oils that emit something woodsy and peppersharp—much more pleasant than the natural stench of the burning coals. It's expensive, of course, constantly burning treated sevite, but the clerics *will* have their symbolisms.

It's warm inside the room, another disorientation. Quietus is a chilly place, all mist and rain, with occasional warm floods of sunlight across the water. But here on Ma'kess, it is the height of summer, and the Year of the Crux is turning out to be a hot one.

A dozen clerics mill about, shiny-faced in their heavy gold-threaded coats, refreshing themselves with glasses of lemon water on ice. Some recline on couches as far from the fire as possible, chatting to each other. Others walk the circumference of the room in pairs and trios. No one acknowledges Chono. But they know who she is. Do they whisper? Do they say, *There is the cleric who killed another cleric in cold blood*?

Not to her face, perhaps.

Aver Paiye's letter said nothing about it. He said, *Come to Riin Cosas, where you are always welcome*. But welcome by whom? Certainly not her kin, who must regard her as a danger now. Do they even care why she killed Cleric Khen Caskhen Paan, that scion of a powerful First Family? Probably not. Meting out death sentences is the purview of the Cloaksaan. For a cleric to kill . . . Well, it's the sort of thing Esek would do. Perhaps the other clerics think Esek rubbed off on Chono. Infected her with her reckless, violent ways. So unbecoming.

It's a point of some reassurance to Chono that whatever discomfort she feels, the other clerics in the room can't see it. Chono has a very old impulse to go unnoticed. Not as cloaksaan go unnoticed, but as small animals do, safe in their burrows. This impulse always manifests on her face as stoicism—a rare characteristic for a cleric. Most of them are beautiful and alluring and charismatic. Chono is none of those things, but she *is* righteous and unflappable. And she has important benefactors.

It's the sight of one of these that nearly breaks her composure. There, standing on the opposite side of the gathering room, is Esek.

Chono is very careful not to stare. It's a near thing. Something happens in her chest, a thunder of equal parts shock and childlike thrill, but she stamps both feelings down lest they somehow show up on her face. Why didn't she expect Esek to be here? The First Cleric's message summoning Chono to Riin Cosas—it's all about Esek. And yet, the older cleric's presence in the temple feels totally incongruous. Esek *hates* Riin Cosas. She avoids it religiously. Yet here she is, surrounded by her kin while very distinctly apart from them, and the sight of her after so many years is just as elating and just as terrible as it ever was. That their last meeting ended so badly makes the thought of a reunion now twist in Chono's stomach like a parasite.

Of course, Esek hasn't noticed Chono at all. Esek has always had a remarkable talent for ignoring others until their presence becomes of use or interest to her. Right now, she clearly has no use for anyone. She's standing with legs apart and hands clasped, staring up at a massive statue. Her look is clever. Serene.

Chono dithers for long moments, sweat on her palms, but this is absurd. She's not a novitiate anymore, scraping for Esek's attention. She steels herself, then walks toward her one-time mentor. The farther she goes into the room, the more aware she is of her kin. Their glances and murmuring follow her all the way to Esek's side.

"Burning One," she says.

Esek doesn't look away from the statue, but her mouth curves up in a shape like a cutlass. When Chono saw her for the first time, Esek was only twenty-two. She was the youngest cleric in a hundred years, the most beautiful, and had come to Chono's school to watch her and her fellow fourth-years fight. Well, more accurately, to watch *Six* fight, back when Chono was called Four and Six was her friend, rather than a ghost at her periphery. The memory alone makes her uneasy, just as Esek made her uneasy, that day at Principes. Esek swept into their lives like a great, gorgeous bird of prey. Now, twenty years later, time has matured what was already exquisite: sharp jawline and nose, full mouth and large eyes the color of umber. Her thick black braids are tied and wound atop her head, displaying a slender neck.

"Dear Chono," Esek Nightfoot finally answers. "How long since you were my novitiate?"

"Eleven years, Sa."

"Yet you still talk to me like a novitiate. We're kin now, don't you remember?"

Chono pauses, considering. "You've always preferred your novitiates to your kin, Sa."

Esek chuckles, glancing Chono's way. Her golden-brown eyes are far more striking than any of the blue or green or purple eye mods other Ma'kessn favor. But this time, it's not her eyes that command Chono's attention. In turning toward her, Esek has exposed the opposite side of her head. Chono doesn't react, doesn't give any indication she sees it—but how could she not? So, it wasn't just a macabre rumor. Esek's left ear is half gone. It's a rough, ill-healed injury, its origin unclear: A blade? A gunshot? Teeth? A simple mod could have repaired it, but instead she wears her hair back, displaying it like a trophy.

Far from disgusting Chono, it fills her with guilt. She was on Quietus when she heard about the pirate attack on the Nightfoots' ancestral home, an estate called Verdant some two hundred miles south of Riin Cosas. Pirates, a particular subset of Braemish sailors, have always been an unavoidable nuisance in the vast reaches of the Black Ocean—they smuggle and kidnap and murder, all while finding ways to avoid Kindom justice. But they have a certain code of honor. And a gift for staying under the radar. This attack on Verdant—it was unlike anything the Treble had ever seen before. Unlike anything that any pirate had ever tried. Dozens of the Nightfoots' private guardsaan died; four of the lesser Nightfoots, too. From reports, Esek Nightfoot fought like a godling, surviving against all odds, but the pirates still carried off heaps of wealth, of artifacts, of records, and burned half the estate to the ground. A year ago, the Kindom itself would not have dared attack the Nightfoots so, let alone *pirates*.

Of course, a year ago, the matriarch Alisiana Nightfoot was alive, her very presence a bulwark against attack.

There have been other signs that the Nightfoots are losing their primacy. This trouble at the factories, for example. The Jeveni have always been a hardworking and mild-mannered labor force, but now their union leaders are thundering for change, and with no new matriarch in place, the Nightfoots have yet to quell the storm.

Then, of course, there is the statue that Esek is staring at again. It depicts Reveño Moonback, the once First Cleric of the Righteous Hand. Reveño is a favored figure in the Moonback family, those Nightfoot rivals who control the northern continents of Ma'kess. But Riin Cosas is in the south, Nightfoot territory. The Moonbacks must have paid a fortune to have such a statue placed in this room. Its presence is a blatant shot at the Nightfoots. Anyone who didn't know Esek would think she was admiring the craftsmanship. Chono thinks what she really admires is the Moonbacks' audacity. And in time she'll travel north and make them regret it.

"It's been so long, Chono," sighs Esek, wistful.

If she remembers their falling-out on Xa Cosas in '58, her tone doesn't suggest it. Strange. "Too long," Chono agrees, half expecting some kind of trap.

"I heard about the old pervert cleric on Pippashap," Esek says.

Chono shows nothing, says nothing, thinks *nothing nothing nothing*. "I hope you cut his cock off."

A flash of the old man's face when she struck—stunned rage quickly turning to terror.

Chono flinches from the memory. "I didn't know you would be here."

Esek shrugs. "You know the First Cleric. He loves meetings. Loves to get his little birds together and hear us chirp. I took a warcat up this morning. Beautiful country, this time of year. One forgets when everything around them is ashes."

"I am very sorry about—"

"Oh, stop." Esek waves a hand at her and turns fully to look into her face. For several moments they are both perfectly still, Esek's eyes traveling all over her, as if reminding herself what Chono looks like. And Chono knows she looks different, older. The year on Pippashap alone has weathered her, but she's also put on muscle. She wonders what Esek sees. But Esek only gestures at her clothes, eyes lit with amusement. "Did you miss land so much that you decided to take a roll in the dirt?"

Chono remembers very well how this minor jab might have devastated her when she was Esek's novitiate. The desire to please, the desire to be praised, were a constant ache in her belly. She feels that echo now. But other feelings take priority as she completes her truncated condolences. "I am very sorry about Alisiana."

Esek's eyes narrow. Chono adds, "I know your first loyalty is to the Kindom"—a wry look from Esek—"but I also know what your family means to you. I believe the Nightfoots will thrive in spite of this. Riiniana may be young, but she can learn."

This time, Esek's look turns flat and disbelieving. She stares for so long that Chono feels unsettled. What has she said? Esek never had anything particularly poisonous to say about Riiniana, Alisiana's great-granddaughter and fourteen-year-old heir. But maybe things have—

"So, you don't know?"

Chono hesitates, opens her mouth to respond—but Esek's bark of laughter cuts her off. Nearby, unsubtly eavesdropping clerics startle at the gunshot sound. Esek puts a hand on Chono's shoulder, stepping aggressively closer. Chono can see every detail of her mutilated ear.

"Chono," Esek says. "You've been too long on that water world. The Secretaries read Alisiana's will weeks ago. She didn't pass the matriarchy to Riiniana, or any of her direct descendants." Esek's teeth glint. "She passed it to *me*."

Chono waits for her to say something more, something that would negate the incomprehensible words. But Esek is alight with glee, and with something else—something maniacal. A shiver runs down Chono's spine, but before she can think how to respond—

"Excuse me, Saan."

It is the temple novitiate, addressing them both. "The First Cleric is ready for you, now."

Esek starts off immediately, her commanding pace and posture attracting every stare in the room. After a beat, Chono follows, similarly erect, but with none of Esek's swagger. Chono is half convinced this is a prank. The whole thing makes no sense. To join one of the Hands of the Kindom, to be a cleric or cloaksaan or secretary, is to abandon all familial rights. Hands *can't* take leadership of their families because they are instruments of the Godfire, first. And all this to say nothing of the fact that on the complex structure of the Nightfoot family tree, Esek's branch is nowhere near the line of succession.

Focus, Chono tells herself. *Paiye said there were things you didn't know.*

They leave the gathering room with many eyes watching. In the atrium Chono sees two figures all in black have emerged from the hallway leading to Aver Paiye's office. One of them is the large cloaksaan Chono glimpsed on her way in. Larger even than she realized. He's a great block of a man, his hands and feet like clubs, his limbs like tree trunks.

"Look at that specimen," says Esek with interest.

The other figure is the First Cloak, Seti Moonback. He is very different from his companion—shorter by a foot but sleek as a cat, and eyes a modded electric blue. He smiles coldly at their approach, a smile made grotesque by the scar wending from nostril to chin, white against golden skin. He tilts his head and rests his hand on the hilt of his bloodletter.

"Cleric Nightfoot."

"Cloak Moonback," Esek returns, and her failure to use his full honorific can't be accidental. "I didn't think you liked our sunny climes."

Again, the cold smile. "Cloaksaan are far less sensitive to the elements than clerics."

"Tell that to this one." Esek jerks a thumb at Chono. "She's been languishing on Pippashap, of all places."

Seti Moonback looks at Chono, a long, assessing look, full of banked hostility.

"Ah, yes. The cleric who tried to be a cloaksaan."

Clearly he thinks very little of her for that. Cloaksaan are . . . possessive, when it comes to the work of assassination. Chono supposes that if she had tried to run the economy on Pippashap, her secretary kin would take that badly, as well. And yet no one has punished Chono for murdering Cleric Paan without trial. For months she thought the Cloaksaan would darken her door. Not yet, though.

Esek clucks. "Don't be petty. It's on you that a corrupt cleric lived as long as he did. She made a good job of it. Saved everyone the trouble of a trial." This meets with a tense silence. If there was a secretary here, they'd probably throw a fit over this blatant disrespect for the legal system. Esek smiles, gesturing theatrically. "And who's this big fellow you've got with you?"

The second cloaksaan is as stoic as Chono, but Chono doubts her own eyes ever project such an unsettlingly murderous gleam.

"This is my second, Cloak Vas Sivas Medisogo," says the First Cloak, still looking at Chono. "I suppose he's your counterpart, Cleric Chono. Though I didn't realize you were Esek's shadow again."

"She can't keep away," agrees Esek. "As for your boy . . ." A slow perusal. Medisogo's head resembles the end of a battering ram, with a nose equally as blunted. He looks at them with the contempt of a man being forced to watch his dinner roam free in a slaughterhouse. Esek looks from him to Moonback and drawls, "Bit of a stereotype, isn't he?"

At that moment, Paiye's novitiate reappears, burdened under two black cloaks. Seti Moonback takes his, sweeping it over his shoulders with a practiced flourish. The pauldron on his left shoulder gleams with polish, the Kindom's symbol embossed on the leather: a three-pointed star against a fiery sun.

"Back to the Silver Keep?" asks Esek cheerily.

Moonback sniffs. Most cloaksaan get testy when someone references the headquarters of the Brutal Hand, whose location is a secret even from most cloaks. Chono has heard they won't even say the name of the keep to each other, bound by a strange superstition.

Moonback says, "The labor strikes on Loez are getting dramatic. You'd think the Jeveni never want us to turn the gates back on. Fucking parasites."

Chono's stomach churns.

"Punish them," Esek suggests. "Deny them access to *The Risen Wave*. Cancel their Remembrance Day celebrations."

Moonback sneers. "Thank you for the suggestion, but it's all going ahead as usual."

Chono frowns at that. Every twenty-five years, the Jeveni come together as a people to orbit their destroyed moon colony and perform ceremonies of remembrance for the Jeveni Genocide. They converge in one of the original generation ships, *The Risen Wave*, and worship their god and grieve their ancestors. It is an important holiday for them—but also a tremendous strain on the jump system. It will be even more so now, with the gates closed to everyone else.

"Wouldn't it be better to ask them to delay?" she asks. "At least until the gates reopen?" Moonback looks at her with cool displeasure. "It's up to the Secretaries and they don't want to exacerbate the union leaders. The last thing we need is for Jeveni malcontents to get violent."

Chono balks at this. "I was under the impression the only threats of violence were *against* the Jeveni. And those threats will hardly end if you give them gate access while denying it to—"

"Ah, so you take the Jeveni for harmless pacifists, do you? That's quaint. I for one don't trust anyone who worships a barren goddess." His words breathe with contempt, a contempt that's common in the Treble. All the gods have children, even the death god, Som—but not Sajeven. Moonback snorts at Chono's expression, adds, "But I suppose they were perfectly peaceable when Alisiana controlled the sevite industry."

This is flung at Esek like an acid attack. But Esek smiles, unimpacted. One of Alisiana's greatest accomplishments was to recruit the Jeveni as factory workers for the sevite industry. It was a natural fit. From the early centuries of the Treble's colonization, the Jeveni were religious outcasts, derided for worshipping Sajeven, and distrusted for refusing to worship the Godfire. When the Ma'kessn moon, Jeve, turned out to be a spinning rock of fuel, the Kindom saw divine providence. Jeve was named after Sajeven, and the Jeveni were her worshippers. Relocate them to the moon, out of sight, and make them mine it for the jevite rock that so masterfully fueled the jump gates. And so it went, until the beginning of the thirteenth century, when the mining contracts had stripped Jeve of its one resource. Kindom overseers pulled out, but left the Jeveni behind, to fend for themselves in crumbling biodomes. Within a century Ri'in Nightfoot had found the formula for synthetic jevite (sevite, of course), and raised the Nightfoots from a declining First Family to one of the Treble's most powerful.

The Jeveni were all but forgotten. That is, until Lucos Alanye found evidence of more jevite seams on the moon. But he was greedy, and monstrous. As soon as he realized he couldn't hoard the seam, he turned all the firepower of his three mining ships on blowing the seam up— and the last of the Jeveni with it.

There were survivors, of course—nearly a hundred thousand refugees scattered to the systems. Alisiana gave succor to those who wanted it, gave them work and protection in her sevite factories, and while many Jeveni choose to live in separatist communities, most have acquiesced to their modern conditions.

That Alisiana chose to aid the Jeveni survivors was not, Chono knows, a sign of charity, but a ruthless cleverness that makes Chono's insides crawl. She created for herself a deeply loyal workforce. A stable sevite trade. It remains to be seen whether that stability will survive her death after almost a year.

Chono tells Moonback, "I take the Jeveni for reasonable people who will understand if we ask them to delay, for their own protection." "I'm not interested in protecting the Jeveni right now. They can save themselves if they want to."

Moonback says it with such disregard, such an utter lack of humor or self-consciousness, that Chono is stunned. She knows very well that there are people in the Treble who view the Jeveni as less than citizens, but to have it put so bluntly—

The First Cloak adds, "Perhaps Sa Nightfoot will take their protection on, hmm? Gods know you have the opportunity to do it, haven't you?"

The words hang for a beat, inviting a reaction that never comes, and at last Seti Moonback snorts. He turns from them, striding off. Medisogo gives Chono a hateful look, disorienting for its intensity, and then he is sweeping away as well.

"Ass," mutters Esek, though she looks more amused than offended.

"This way, Saan," says the novitiate.

They follow him down the hall and through the open door to First Cleric Paiye's small but beautifully lit office. The First Cleric is already on his feet, and he comes around his desk with a broad smile for Chono, arms outstretched.

"My beloved kin," he says warmly, clasping her hand with both of his. She can feel the fat Godfire stone of his official ring, round cut and warm like a sun. "In all this trouble, I am so grateful for the joy of seeing you again."

Chono is not much of a smiler but she grips his hand and allows her lips to quirk at the corners. Some years ago, Paiye made her his assistant on a two-year tour of the Treble systems. She has fond memories of it, of him. And ambivalent as she is toward so many of her kin, she has always trusted the noble intentions of the First Cleric, who chuckles at her meager smile. There is something fatherly in his regard.

"Ah, Esek." He turns with only a slight dip in warmth. "It seems crass to ask if you have enjoyed your leave from duty."

"Not at all, First Cleric," returns Esek. "The work at Verdant is very refreshing. No one expects you to pray when you're shoveling through rubble."

Chono looks away, embarrassed. Paiye *hmms*, though it's not without humor. He gestures them to the two chairs across from his desk, and then sits down himself. The light from the ceiling pours over them in buttery sheets, and there's a rich smell emanating from the flowers standing in vases throughout the room. The First Cleric folds dark, weathered hands on the desktop, regarding them both before he lets out a heavy sigh.

"Well. I won't draw things out. I've asked you both here because we may have found a link to whoever plotted the attack on Verdant."

Chono shifts subtly in her chair so she has a better view of Esek, and waits for her to respond. Paiye, too, watches Esek for a reaction, but remarkably, she gives nothing away.

Chono has read enough about the aftermath of the Verdant sacking to know the Nightfoots put a bounty on every pirate who participated in the attack. Hundreds have scrambled to claim the reward—accusing business rivals and neighbors and inconvenient relatives of colluding in the attack. But while everything from Nightfoot portraits to Nightfoot jewelry to Nightfoot underwear has resurfaced in various markets, none of it has been reliably tied to any of the accused. In the history of criminal undertakings, none has so absolutely managed to hide its operatives from the investigations of the Cloaksaan—or the retribution of the Nightfoots. Esek ought to be vibrating with the chance of some revenge, but her expression is calm.

Paiye clears his throat and spreads his hands. The light catches on his Godfire ring.

"As you know, among the possessions marked as stolen from Verdant were a great many archival records: antique documents, memory coins, that sort of thing. The Cloaksaan believe they may have tracked down one of those coins. A pirate ship called *The Swimming Fox* has been communicating with a caster who goes by the handle Sunstep. It's unclear from communications which party is actually selling the coin, but the sale *is* scheduled to occur tomorrow, on Teros."

Again, Esek is silent.

Chono asks, "Do you believe *The Swimming Fox* was at Verdant?"

Still looking thoughtfully at Esek, Paiye says, "No. In fact, they have a tight alibi. And Sunstep's admittedly incomplete records don't paint them as the type to raid a stronghold."

Finally, Esek joins in. "How auspicious, to be the only coin we've found." Her lips spread in a lupine grin. "Are you hoping to use it to track down the original attackers?"

"We could try. But the coin itself is what interests us."

Esek's brows lift. "Really. And what is on this little coin?"

"Something with the capacity to erode public trust in the Nightfoot family."

For a moment no one speaks, and Chono is suddenly hyperaware of the powerful families in her orbit—the Paiyes themselves, and the Moonbacks up north, and the Khens out on Teros. These First Families of the Treble have long-standing rivalries with one another, and with the Nightfoots, and any of them would have a stake in seeing the public turn on the Nightfoots. But Aver Paiye is not an agent of his family, not since he took his vows. He is an agent of the Kindom. And the Kindom wants order, above all.

Esek says at last, "That's very vague and mysterious."

"We are limiting further details to the most essential people."

Esek's eyes narrow, the first hostile sign. "Am I not *essential*, where the Nightfoots are concerned?"

"You are a cleric of the Righteous Hand." He meets her tone with a coolness few would dare direct at Esek. "You are a servant of the Kindom. It is in that capacity that I have invited you here. Not as the possible matriarch of your family."

Esek smiles coldly. "Of course. That is not a position I have accepted."

The "yet" hangs unspoken.

Aver Paiye clasps his hands again. "Very good. Then let me make your responsibilities plain. The sale will take place in the city of Lo-Meek on Bei continent. We would like you to go to Teros and intercept both the pirates and the caster. If possible, all parties should be placed under arrest with the local marshals. If it is a choice between killing them and their escape, you have permission to kill them."

Chono's skin prickles. Esek raises her eyebrows. "Really? And there was Seti Moonback not ten minutes ago, giving us shit because Chono killed a pedophile."

"Pirates are not always redeemable," says Paiye, unrattled by Esek's mocking tone. "And the caster Sunstep is a known criminal, with ties to illegal cloaking technologies, not to mention some of the worst offenders in the Treble. They've managed to scramble their communications with *The Swimming Fox* so expertly that even our best couldn't recover everything. We don't know what they look like, where they're from, who their allies are. The most personal thing we know about them is that they seem to do a lot of sniffing after the Nightfoots."

Chono's fingers bite a little deeper into the arm of the chair; her thoughts roil with possibilities. She knows Esek's must be as well, a single name ticking in both their heads, like a countdown to disaster.

"Nuisance though they are, the Cloaksaan don't seem to think Sunstep is particularly valuable. Nor are the pirates, for that matter. If they can't be taken alive, they must be put down. Honestly, Esek, I didn't expect any pushback from you on the matter."

A beat of silence. An *invitation* to argue.

Esek merely says, "I see."

Chono is surprised. She, for one, does not "see" at all. Lines of authority are firmly delineated between the three Hands of the Kindom. Clerics don't practice the law; secretaries don't administer death rites. And a task like this should rightly fall to the cloaks, who are the Kindom's ruthless constabularies. It's true Esek has all the skills of a cloaksaan (except, perhaps, the ability to go unnoticed), but Chono has never known the Righteous Hand to officially send one of its clerics on a mission of this type. It's . . . bizarre.

Esek gestures at Chono. "And what's her involvement?"

Aver Paiye smiles. "You and I both know from experience that Chono is a valuable companion."

It's a compliment, but the phrasing stabs her with memories she would like to forget.

Esek chuckles. "Ah. Of course. You want me to have a chaperone." She tells Chono with mock seriousness, "You see, while you were on Quietus praying to Capamame for absolution, I was fighting a battle to the death for the Nightfoot estate. It all got very bloody and chaotic. Apparently, I attacked a guardsaan for trying to evacuate me. Nearly killed him. And now, they send me off to Teros to capture the very mongrels who are trading in my family's stolen goods. Best to have someone keep an eye on me."

Chono doesn't know how to respond, so she looks at the First Cleric. His generally easy demeanor has started to frost at the edges. He stares at Esek with disapproval, bushy brows gnarled above his dark eyes.

"Everyone needs friends sometimes, Cleric Nightfoot. I approved your leave request so you could be with your family as it works to rebuild Verdant. But just because you've been away doesn't mean I haven't had my eye on you. Alisiana only died a year ago. I know it hit you hard. I want to make sure this secondary blow hasn't pushed you too far. Chono is uniquely qualified to protect your best interests, even when you act against them. Never forget my duty as First Cleric is to see that you are safe and well."

Chono thinks if this is indeed his duty, sending Esek to Teros is a peculiar way to perform it.

Esek smirks at the First Cleric with such insulting condescension that Chono wonders how Paiye can bear it as peacefully as he does.

Apparently, he doesn't mean to bear it any longer.

"So," he says, with finality. He stands up, Chono rising with him. Esek takes her time following. "You will have a warkite for the duration, *The Makala Aet*. It has a capable crew and will accommodate your novitiates, since I know you'll insist on bringing them. They are completing their preflight checks and will depart late this afternoon."

Esek says, "I have business in Riin Kala, first."

Paiye's expression goes flat. He is reaching the end of his patience. Esek smiles placidly and shrugs. "It shouldn't take more than a couple of hours."

After a tense moment, the First Cleric nods once. "Fine. You will depart after your errand is complete. The trip to Lo-Meek will not take more than ten hours, and you'll find a garrison of marshals available for your use. The meeting is at 8:00 a.m., local Teron time. We'd like as little mess as possible, so I trust Chono to be your conscience in these matters. Bring the coin directly back to Riin Cosas once you have it. Understood?"

Esek bows over her palms, low enough to evacuate the holy gesture of all sincerity. "Of course, Sa. Gods keep you well."

Chono gives her own, genuine bow, and turns with Esek to go, but Aver Paiye says, "Stay a moment, Chono."

Esek pauses only to shake her head as if at two silly children, and then she flounces off, shutting the door after her with exaggerated consideration. Chono, still standing, looks to the First Cleric with an uncertainty she's not used to feeling in his presence. They had such warmth between them, when they toured the Treble together. He had taken her under his wing, trained her, equipped her with patience and care for the true work of being a cleric—things Esek never taught her. And yet now, he is doing such strange things . . .

He sighs and goes to a tea tray on a nearby table to pour himself a cup. He offers her one, but she shakes her head no, watching him. He carries the cup and saucer with him back to her, sips contemplatively. Then gives her a rueful look.

"You must have questions."

She hesitates. "I assume you'll tell me whatever I need to know." His smile is affectionate. He takes another drink of tea, and then places saucer and cup on his desk. "I also trust you to ask what you need to know."

Chono shifts her stance and folds her hands in front of her. She has never had the luxury of complete honesty, with anyone. But whatever honesty she has given Aver Paiye over the years, he's accepted without reproach.

"The business with the factory unrest, and with the jump gate rationing. Is it connected to this mission on Teros?"

Paiye regards her shrewdly. "What connection do you imagine?"

"I'm not a secretary, but I have access to the same ledgers as any cleric, and it's clear that the Clever Hand has reserved enough sevite fuel to make these recent rations unnecessary. Yet here we are, with protests ratcheting up, and the factory unions growing even more recalcitrant, and now I find that Esek has been named the matriarch of her family. I don't think you're rationing because of what's happening now. I think you're rationing because of what you think *may* happen."

He nods approvingly. He twists the ring on his finger, as if it were a key in a lock.

"Alisiana was always supportive of the factory unions," he says musingly. "She treated them well, protected their autonomy. She did this so they would be loyal to her, and it worked. You know as well as I that the factory workers view themselves as ancillaries to the Nightfoots. The unions don't care that the Kindom itself controls the gates. They care that their work remains the purview of the Nightfoots, whom they trust to grant them at least some freedoms. Since Alisiana's death, union leaders have openly demanded that Esek take her place."

Chono considers this, surprised. Alisiana was always personally involved in monitoring sevite production, an empire she inherited and made thrive. Esek has never been anywhere near the family business (at least, not in any official capacity). Why would the Jeveni want *her* for their matriarch?

She asks as much. Paiye says, "It's something we've anticipated for some time. Alisiana was a force of nature. So is Esek. If the matriarchy passes to a child, like Riiniana, the unions fear an erosion of Nightfoot authority, and that Kindom oversight will take its place."

"Are they right?" Chono asks.

Paiye chuckles. "I sympathize with the Jeveni not wanting their way of life to change. After all they have endured, it's natural. But the Kingdom chose its words for a reason: Peace, under the Kindom. Unity, in the Treble. Without our mediation of the sevite trade, the individual families would turn on one another. There would be monopoly and war. Alisiana understood that, but she still fought for every crumb she could take. She was a strategist. She took care of the unions and workers so they would protect her independence from us. She offered employment to tens of thousands of Jeveni survivors so they would see *her* as their ally, not the Kindom that rescued them. But her methods never went so far as to force a Kindom response. She kept a delicate balance. If Esek becomes the matriarch of the Nightfoots, do you think she will be able to keep that balance?"

"Esek is a strategist, too."

Paiye nods, a conciliatory gesture. "I know she is. Which is precisely why I prefer her to remain a Hand of the Kindom. I do not seek the day when she is at odds with our interests."

Chono reflects, the pieces coming together. "If Esek becomes matriarch, it will pacify the unions and restore order to the trade. But the Kindom does not trust her with that sort of power. So we are rationing access to the jump gates in order to further stockpile the sevite—as an insurance policy against her intransigence." Paiye looks at her quietly, an invitation for her to continue. "If, on the other hand, she remains a cleric, there will be more uproar in the factories. We will have to break up the unions—install new leadership and loyal workers, which would displease the Jeveni. Rationing sevite now is a security against the time it will take to rebuild."

The move is typical of Kindom leadership, and especially of the Secretaries—farseeing and practical. And it explains, in a roundabout way, why Paiye is sending Esek after this memory coin. It's a test. Will she obey the Kindom? Or act according to her own desires? Will she be a Hand . . . or a matriarch?

Of course, in the meantime, it's the people of the Treble who will suffer the consequences. And the Jeveni who will bear the brunt of the blame.

Chono asks, "Don't you think it would help our mission, Sa, to know the contents of this coin?"

He gives her a sympathetic smile, but there is steel behind it, and Chono knows that she has touched too close to the quick. He shakes his head. "On the contrary, I think it would prove a distraction. You must trust me on this, Chono. The contents of the coin are not your concern. Only bringing it back to me."

Chono knows better than to argue, yet through her curls a premonition of that coin's import. She more than any non-Nightfoot in the worlds (and more than many Nightfoots themselves) knows the kinds of secrets that family carries. And if she's right about the contents of the coin, then it can only mean one thing: Six is involved.

Suddenly Paiye is looking at her with a deep warmth and gentleness, as if to soften his refusal. "You are the most righteous Hand among us, Chono. And you are also devoted to Esek. You will protect her, counsel her. Remind her of the loyalty she owes our kin. At the end of it all, you will keep your vows to the Godfire. You will be my ears."

At those words (expected, dreaded), Chono hazards to remind him, "Esek won't appreciate being spied on, Burning One."

"I don't ask you to spy on her. I ask you to report to me on the progress with this mission, since I know Esek will not. Whatever else is at play, I want that memory coin. If someone like Sunstep has it, or gets it, I fear the repercussions."

Chono clears her throat, banishing thoughts of whoever Sunstep might or might not be. There is only one answer she can give to the First Cleric.

"Of course, Sa. I am your servant."

"Good." He smiles again. "Good. Do you know anything about this business she has in Riin Kala?"

It's a loaded question.

"I don't, Sa."

"Go with her."

Chono hesitates, about to point out that Esek may not allow it, but then he is moving toward the door. "And if there is anything you need, contact me directly."

"Thank you, Sa."

"Gods keep you well, Cleric Chono."

"Gods keep you well, First Cleric."

But just before she is about to go through the door, she stops, and looks at him again. He frowns curiously, an invitation, and though something in Chono tells her to keep quiet, she can't help herself.

"Seti Moonback says that Remembrance Day will go ahead as planned." Paiye looks at her without answering. A confirmation. "Isn't that dangerous, for the Jeveni? People already blame them for the gate closures. Now they'll think they're getting special treatment."

"It is not special treatment. Remembrance Day is built into the Anti-Patriation Act; it is crucial to Jeveni autonomy. We cannot break our own laws."

The irony of this, of course, is that the Anti-Patriation Act never had anything to do with protecting Jeveni autonomy, but rather curtailing it.

Chono says, "Surely a delay while we resolve—"

"The Jeveni are intransigent. They would not accept a delay, even to save their own lives. They refuse to see us as anything but their persecutors."

His tone creeps close to the one that Seti Moonback used. It unnerves Chono, wondering at this attitude from a man who has always regarded the Treblens as his own children. She says quietly, "They have reason, you know . . . to distrust us."

Centuries' worth of reason, in fact. They were treated as little better than slaves on Jeve. After the Kindom abandoned them there, they at least had the benefit of worshipping their goddess in peace, creating their own government, and avoiding the attention of the larger Treble. The genocide stripped them of those freedoms. Now they are tightly controlled, their separatist communities forbidden by the Anti-Patriation Act to exceed a hundred people, their one-time government disbanded, their very existence occupying a liminal space: rejected as Treblens, but beholden to the laws of the Treble.

Paiye says, "Your concern for their well-being is admirable, Chono. Rest assured, I will take your thoughts to heart."

It is a definitive close to their conversation. Chono hesitates, and Paiye looks at her in a way that says, *Enough*.

She nods curtly, and leaves. The door snicks shut behind her. In the empty hallway, she's momentarily disoriented. She needs to find Esek. She needs to speak to the novitiate who took her bag. She needs to decide what to do with that bag, and with the thing inside it, her dearest possession of all. Should she bring it with her? No, not with Esek here. Esek, who makes chaos out of peace.

Breathing out, Chono marshals a career of meditative practice, trying to quiet her mind. Trying to remember what the air tastes like on Pippashap, how the breeze swoops in through the shanty curtains, and how the floor always moves gently, rocked by a world-covering ocean . . .

Instead, her nostrils are full of the Riin Cosas gardens, and the shifting ground underfoot is of an entirely different type.

Enter the monthly

Orbit sweepstakes at

www.orbitloot.com

With a different prize every month,

from advance copies of books by
your favourite authors to exclusive
merchandise packs,

we think you'll find something
you love.